KISSING THE BEAST

"I don't want to fix you," she said, noticing how her voice had gone breathy.

His eyebrow rose. "No?"

She shook her head. "I want to know you—to understand you."

"What I am is what you see." Roderick held his arms away from his sides and they seemed to stretch from one wall of the room to the other as he loomed before her. "A beast. The new Cherbon Devil. Broken, scarred. Rather unpleasant."

Michaela shook her head again, but the movement was slight, so mesmerized was she by his very presence, the energy rolling off of him. She stepped closer to him, as if drawn.

"Are you going to kiss me again?" He gave her a dangerous grin, the scar on his cheek going white by his eye like a warning.

But she could not heed it. "I think I shall." She licked her lips. "Do you mind?"

For one who was so deliberate in his movements, Roderick had taken her into his arms within the span of a blink, and this time, it was he who kissed her. . . .

Books by Heather Grothaus

THE WARRIOR

THE CHAMPION

THE HIGHLANDER

TAMING THE BEAST

Published by Kensington Publishing Corporation

TAMING *The* BEAST

Heather Grothaus

ZEBRA BOOKS
Kensington Publishing Corp.
http://www.kensingtonbooks.com

ZEBRA BOOKS are published by

Kensington Publishing Corp.
119 West 40th Street
New York, NY 10018

All Kensington titles, imprints, and distributed lines are available at special quantity discounts for bulk purchases for sales
promotion, premiums, fund-raising, educational, or institu-
tional use.

Special book excerpts or customized printings can also be
created to fit specific needs. For details, write or phone the
office of the Kensington Special Sales Manager: Attn. Special
Sales Department. Kensington Publishing Corp., 119 West
40th Street, New York, NY 10018. Phone: 1-800-221-2647.

Zebra and the Z logo Reg. U.S. Pat. & TM Off.

ISBN-13: 978-1-4201-0243-7
ISBN-10: 1-4201-0243-5

First Printing: November 2009

10 9 8 7 6 5 4 3 2 1

Printed in the United States of America

For Two
I love you, whoever you are.

For Jack Belcher
Who wrote his own success story.

And for friends who have become my readers,
and readers who have become my friends.

I could not do this without you.

Prologue

The damned incense hung eternal, like death, cleaved only by the baneful dirge of screams and curses. Each clang and ring of metal—tool on tool, tools falling into bowls and against remnants of armor and ruined weaponry—was piercing. Sonorous Latin droned from the colorless lips of the robed men who mindlessly haloed the long, plastered room as if puppeted by the enormous crucifix hung at the far end. Bodies thrashed on pallets, fighting to free themselves from the hands of the surgeons who sweated and strained and worked like the dogs their patients swore them to be.

Surely this could be no faithful hospital.

For Roderick, it was Hell's antechamber.

Sobs roiled within the fiery incense as well, as if attempting to dampen the cloying stench of rot and disease merely by the weighty emotion of upward of 150 men. Men like himself, laid like so much half-butchered meat in a smokehouse. The choking smoke *was* death, in Roderick's swollen and bruised mind. He could feel its close, burning char against his already-fevered skin, licking away at his sanity, slurping up his very life.

He waited his turn with the surgeon, who would come soon, Hugh promised. Very soon.

Roderick would have added his own screams to the miserable din—he certainly had pain enough to warrant them—but after three weeks of worsening agony, he had no strength left to utter the feeblest whimper. From the ill-fated battle at Heraclea, Hugh had brought him, returning them both to that grand city of Constantinople—and ultimately its hospital—against Roderick's protests.

"In Constantinople you will be cured," Hugh had promised repeatedly. "You must only persevere until Constantinople. You must, Rick, you must!"

And Roderick had, although how, he knew not. He *wanted* to die. To escape the pain of his injuries. To avoid returning to his father in England a failure.

Yes, that was the worst of all, the thought that made Roderick's functioning eye well with thin tears—Magnus Cherbon, awaiting his son's return with hopes of the same treasure and holy favor that Magnus himself had received on his own pilgrimage. Roderick could hear his father's condemnation already: *Worthless failure! Weak, weak, weak! From your mother's damned womb you were like her. Weak! No son of mine. A disgrace.* Roderick had heard the words so many times, they were verse in his memory.

A tear at last escaped Roderick's left eye and rolled dumbly down his cheek to leap from his face onto the rough blanket beneath his head. The tear left behind a wet path as cold as the hatred it represented.

"He comes, Rick! Look!" Hugh grasped Roderick's left shoulder and squeezed, his voice sounding as if he was putting on an air of excitement for a very young child. Roderick's left shoulder and arm were the only places where his friend could touch him without causing further agony, having been saved by the stout English shield strapped to Roderick's forearm.

Roderick let his head fall to the left, thankful that the surgeon did not approach from the other side of the room, lest Roderick's injured face—bloated and stitched up like saddle leather by a young Saracen boy—prevent him from anticipating the man's approach. Roderick felt the crude courses of thick gut pull in his swollen flesh all the same—from the bridge of his nose, over his cheekbone, across and beyond his right temple. His view of the long hospital chamber was reduced to a horizontal sliver through his left eye, and he could see nothing at all through his right. Perhaps it was no longer even in its socket; Roderick could not bring himself to ask Hugh. His nose was broken badly, his cheekbone likely fractured as well. Since he'd been dragged from his mount during that bloody slaughter, the only sound in his right ear had been a dull roar, like an ocean tempest beyond the cliffs of his old home, Cherbon.

His head injuries were serious, Roderick knew. But his arm was so much worse—his right arm, his sword arm. And his left leg . . .

The surgeon neared Roderick's pallet, his long leather apron and tunic beneath stained a terrible and ghastly black. Two pale, thin lads bobbed along in the surgeon's wake, carrying his instruments in flat, shallow baskets. The man's white hair was long and thick to his shoulders, some strands escaping the tight knot of leather at his nape, and the ends looked as if they'd been dipped in blood. His eyes were deep set and wintry, his mouth hard and nearly invisible. He walked quickly, the hands swinging at his side

looking as though they had been stolen from a Saracen—
stained a deep, deep brown, his fingernails in black relief.

A squealing fear raced up Roderick's spine at the surgeon's approach, and he prayed with everything left of
his soul that he would die before the learned old man
reached him. He'd never imagined fear like this, and it
caused Roderick to scream and thrash and beg for reprieve
inside his broken shell of a body.

But outside, that shell did not so much as twitch.

"What is it?" the surgeon asked of Hugh, reaching out his
nightmarish hands and speaking even before coming at once
over the pallet. Hard fingers probed either side of Roderick's
forehead, roughly turning the splintered skull in a starburst
of fresh agony. "Head wound, yes?" Hands with the strength
of Goliath pressed his shattered right arm. "And arm, I see.
Both stitched as well as can be. Fever, yes?"

Hugh seemed to at last regain his voice at the brusque
questions and statements, given with little apparent sympathy. "Yes, yes, maestro. Fever, yes. The stitches seem to
be holding well, but his fever has steadily worsened since
Heraclea. I think perhaps it is his leg—"

Before Hugh could finish, the old man swept down
upon Roderick's left leg and jerked up the stained covering. Roderick fancied he could smell his own wound on
the breeze the surgeon created, although his nose had been
too swollen to take air in more than a fortnight.

Hugh stepped toward Roderick's feet and continued. "Perhaps the lance which pierced him was tainted with p—"

"Poison, yes," the surgeon interrupted. "And through the
thickness of his calf, no less. I've seen it often enough. Nasty
trick." The surgeon dropped the blanket back over Roderick's
leg and flicked his fingertips to the lads hovering behind

him, indicating the boys should move on. They trudged past Roderick's pallet without a glance.

The old man looked at Hugh. "He'll die." Then the surgeon stepped directly into Roderick's line of sight, putting angular cheekbones before his face. "Awake, yes? Good. You're going to die, my man," he nearly shouted, as if he knew Roderick's hearing was not in its finest capacity. "Do you understand?"

Roderick wanted to nod and thought his chin may have twitched downward. He was so thankful that the man would not be touching him with those black fingers. He let his eye close.

"No!" Hugh shouted. Roderick didn't want to open his eye again, but the sounds of a scuffle prompted a distant concern for his friend. Hugh appeared again in the narrow slit of Roderick's vision, having seized the surgeon by one arm. "No, he can not die. There must be something you can do."

The old man pulled his arm free with a cold look of warning. "The poison's been in him too long. Had I been at his side when he fell, perhaps. But now, any potion would be wasted on him—like pouring it upon the ground, and we have not enough as it is. He'll be cold by the morrow's light. I *am* sorry. Good day."

"No!" Hugh shouted again, and this time nearly pulled the surgeon off his feet. "You must try to understand—he saved my life. Anything you can do—"

"Good sir, you see the men lying about this chamber, yes?" the surgeon demanded. "Think you their lives are worth less than this man's?"

"Yes," Hugh answered immediately. "Yes, I do."

"Well, I do not," the surgeon shouted, and Roderick silently agreed with him. The surgeon turned to go, but

Hugh grabbed at the man's hand once more, this time falling to his knees behind him.

"Please, maestro, *please!* I beg of you." At the reedy catch in Hugh Gilbert's voice and the sight of him pressing his lips to the surgeon's bloodstained hand, Roderick let his eye close once more. He could not bear to see the man plead for a cause so hopeless and unworthy.

"Do you not think I would save him if I could?" Roderick heard the surgeon say in a quieter, slightly gentler voice.

"Please," was Hugh's only reply.

Roderick heard a curt sigh, and then, "Boy!" After the pattering of quick footsteps and a rustle-clink: "This will ease his pain. It's all I can spare, I'm afraid. Small dose at first, yes? Only from the fingertip, lest you wish to show him mercy and kill him outright. He may stay until he's dead, and then he must be moved. I need the pallet."

The surgeon's steps fled impatiently from Hugh's "God bless you, maestro. Thank you, thank you!"

In the next moment, Hugh's breath huffed a cool, hammering breeze on Roderick's fevered and throbbing face, and Roderick heard the *pip* of a small cork. "Here we are, Rick—what I had hoped for. Open up now." He felt Hugh's rough finger push inside his lips to scrub at his gums. A tingling warmth filled his mouth and then Hugh's finger returned. And again.

Was his friend *trying* to kill him? Roderick opened his eye as best he could while his head started a slow, buzzing spin.

Hugh's face swam before him, milky and pebbled with sweat, as he tried to fit the stopper back in the small, colored glass bottle with fumbling fingers. "Come on, come on, for fuck's sake!" The cork at last slid home and Hugh slipped the vial away inside his tunic.

"Hugh?" Roderick tried to whisper, but he heard only a gurgling "oo" blurt from his lips. It was enough to get his friend's attention.

"It's a lot, I know," Hugh rushed as he reached over Roderick, gathering together into a rough sack their few belongings scattered on either side of Roderick's pallet. "But you need it—we're getting out of here, Rick. I'm taking you to—"

"Oh," Roderick choked.

"Yes." Hugh stood and disappeared from Roderick's line of sight, but his words were still painfully clear as Roderick felt the rough blanket he rested on lift his head and shoulders. "Try to sleep," Hugh said with a whoosh of effort. "It will—"

But the rest of his friend's statement was lost to Roderick as Hugh jerked on the blanket and began pulling it like a makeshift gurney. Roderick's body started, and the white pain that exploded from the rough movement, combined with the sizzling, dazzling substance Hugh had slipped into Roderick's mouth ensured that he did, indeed, sleep.

Roderick didn't know how long he'd been unconscious, or how far Hugh had dragged him, but he didn't think it had been very long or very far, for the acrid taste of the hospital's incense was still thick and gritty in his mouth. He heard the voices before he could try to open his remaining functioning eye, which refused to cooperate at that moment, any matter. As it was, whatever drug Hugh had given to Roderick was affecting his already-disadvantaged hearing, distorting the voices and, in spots, blanking them out altogether.

He felt no pain—indeed, he was largely numb, save for

the uncontrollable trembling which had seized him. Perhaps he was cold. Or fevered. Roderick could not tell.

A quieter voice beyond the black curtain of Roderick's awareness now deteriorated into a sob, and then Roderick heard Hugh.

"I wanted to come to you first, but I didn't know—"

"No, no," a woman said. "I understand. I am glad you've brought him, although I doubt I can help him."

The voice, low and sweet and lilted, filtered through Roderick's brain in a familiar pattern. He knew this speaker. Who? Who . . . ? Aster? Ophelia? No . . .

"You gave him too much, Hugh." The woman spoke again, closer to Roderick this time. He could feel her warmth near his left side. "He may not wake." A brief image of dark, sloe-eyed beauty draped in purple silk flashed through Roderick's memory, but was gone before he could grab it properly.

Ardis? No, that wasn't it either. . . .

"Oh, God!" Hugh cried, and Roderick could hear the very depths of his friend's misery. He felt a distant sympathy for the man, obviously in a pain which Roderick could blessedly no longer feel. "I knew not what else to do! He was in such agony—I thought moving him with any less would kill him." A shuffling of feet and then Hugh's voice sounded closer, hushed though, as if speaking a quiet blasphemy. "I think he *wants* to die."

"Then he likely will," the woman said. "Without the will to live, there would be little I could do were his injuries even half."

Those sloe eyes again, and music. Dancing . . .

"You are his last hope, Aurelia," Hugh said, his words nearly a gasp. "*Our* last hope."

Aurelia.

And then the half picture of the woman's identity blossomed in Roderick's mind—Hugh had brought him to Aurelia, to the owner of the most exclusive brothel in Constantinople. Lovely, lovely Aurelia, whom he had not seen since he and his company had arrived in the city so many months ago. . . .

"I will do what I can, of course," Aurelia said. "But first we must see if he can be awakened. I have word from his family in England, left for him by a messenger only last week. Perhaps the news might rouse him."

A fuzzy rage tried to fight to the surface of Roderick's fevered brain. His only family in England was his father, and a distant cousin. Roderick wanted to hear no message from his hateful sire, and he certainly didn't want to return to Cherbon. But the anger stole too much energy from him, and so he let it go when he felt Aurelia's soft, small hand on his left arm.

"Roderick," she called softly into his ear, and the song of her voice was like a deep pool of warm water. "Roderick, can you hear me?"

He could hear her, but could command no movement from his body to indicate such. He could also hear the misplaced sound of a babe crying somewhere else in the room.

The hand on his arm squeezed. "Roderick, open your eyes and look at me, my lord."

Leave me be, Roderick said in his head, willing the woman—and Hugh—to let him slip away while the pain was still absent. The crying sound intensified.

He heard Aurelia sigh. "I must tend to Leo soon." Her words grew louder in his head, but she had not raised her voice, perhaps only drawing closer to him—yes, he could feel her breath now on his neck.

"Roderick, hear me, my lord: A messenger brings word from England. Your father is dead."

Your father is dead.

Your father is dead.

The last word—the most important word—seemed to echo in the vast cavern of Roderick's mind. And for a span of time—a second, an hour—Roderick let it swoop and circle there, as if testing its sincerity.

Magnus Cherbon was dead?

The pain was trickling back into his body now, in stomps and crashes and screams. Roderick could feel his muscles cramping and seizing. He struggled for clarity, for just one moment of lucidness before the torrent of white-hot misery dragged him under and drowned him. His eyelid seemed to weigh a thousand pounds.

Aurelia's dark hair and doelike brown eyes flickered into focus before him. She looked older, thinner, more tired from when he'd seen her last. Then, she had worn rouge and kohl, and tiny golden bells in her hair. Now, she was dim, wrapped in a shawl, her eyes shadowed naturally, and sunken.

"Roderick?" she asked, hope and surprise in her whisper. Over her shoulder Hugh Gilbert's face also appeared, and elsewhere in the room the infant wailed insistently.

"'Ome," Roderick heard himself rasp. "'El me, 'Eel-ya. Go . . . 'ome."

Roderick suddenly wanted to live.

Chapter One

May 1103
Tornfield Manor, England

It was a lovely feast, save for the pointing and whispering. And the way she was repeatedly jostled out of line when she tried to join in a dance. Or that wretched woman who had stuck out a slippered foot and caused her to fall into a serving maid, spilling half the puddings and breaking most of Lord Tornfield's beautiful little painted bowls.

As if she needed assistance making a fool of herself.

So now, Michaela Fortune hid herself away near the musicians, where she could be close to the music that would drown out the hateful things being said about her. And, seated on the stool, she could hide the glommy white stains of pudding spilled down the skirt of her only good gown. Here, she could become lost in the melody and hum along if she wished, and she could convince herself it was *truly* a lovely feast, when what she wanted to do was find that miserable woman with the spastic foot and snatch at her hair.

Turn the other cheek, Michaela reminded herself, as if

her mother had whispered in her ear. *The meek shall inherit all the earth.*

As if to drive home her mother's tireless lessons on gentleness of spirit, Michaela caught a glimpse of her parents across the hall. Lord Walter and Agatha Fortune stood against the opposite perimeter of the chamber, closely linked together as usual. Michaela's father's kindly face was turned to look down upon his wife, as if only waiting for her to express any wish he might fulfill. It was satisfying to see them enjoying themselves—they so rarely left their small holding.

Like Michaela, Agatha Fortune was often the brunt of whispered gossip, although the mother was spared the indignity of the self-conscious clumsiness that plagued her daughter. The older Lady Fortune was dismissed as ineffective and a bit loose in the brains, while the younger was treated with scorn and avoidance.

Devil's Daughter.

Hell's Handmaid.

Sister of Satan.

Or, the very worst of all, Mistress Fortune.

Miss Fortune. A clever play on words, Michaela had to admit, and of all the hated nicknames she had been cursed with, likely the most accurate. Misfortune, oh my, yes.

Her fingers pressed the warped link of metal on the fine chain resting under the bodice of her dress out of habit. For such a tiny object, its burden around her neck was as immense as any oaken yoke.

"Song!" a man's voice rang out, interrupting Michaela's self-pity. Alan Tornfield, the Fortune family's overlord and host of the feast, raised his chalice toward the trio of musicians near Michaela's hiding place. He was a handsome, mustachioed blond man of one score, ten and five, his wife's death last year leaving him and their young daughter alone in the modest manor. Michaela had never met the now-motherless Elizabeth—indeed, she'd never so much as spoken directly to Lord Tornfield. This feast was only the second time Michaela had visited the overlord's home in the whole of her score of years, although she couldn't recall the first instance, as she had been but a young child herself.

"I must have a song immediately! Who is sporting enough to lend their voice to yon strings?"

The crowd "hear-hear"-ed with enthusiastic agreement, and Michaela cringed as she spotted her own mother leaning this way and that, trying to pick out Michaela in the crowded hall. Michaela closed her eyes, as if it might make her invisible.

She was saved when Lord Tornfield announced his chosen candidate, and Michaela opened her eyes with a relieved sigh.

"Lady Juliette of Osprey, won't you indulge us?" he fairly shouted, and in a moment a tall, striking brunette dressed in rich green stepped from the crowd, a humble smile on her lovely face.

It was the woman who'd tripped her. Michaela slid her stool more fully behind the curtained backdrop.

"Do you know 'My Love Calls the Sea'?" Lady Juliette sweetly queried the trio, and the man out in front of the group bowed. In a moment, the song started.

When the woman's voice came forth, sharp and warbling, Michaela cringed again. By the time the refrain and second verse were through, she checked to see if her nose might be bleeding. She saw several of the guests wince as notes were overshot toward heaven, Lady Juliette nearly screaming to reach such heights. Michaela opened her mouth and forced her ears to pop.

"Oh, make it stop," she said loudly. No one could hear

her any matter over that terrible shrieking. At any moment, she expected Lord Tornfield's hounds to add their voices to the noise. It would have improved the tone immensely.

At last the torture was over, and Michaela could almost hear the relieved sigh of the guests before they broke out in ridiculously exaggerated applause for the obscenely wealthy Lady of Osprey.

"My God, they must be deaf," Michaela muttered. Then she gasped as she felt a tug on the back of her hair. Michaela spun around on her stool.

Shadowed by the curtain Michaela also hid behind stood a beautiful girl, perhaps ten years old, with long, shiny blond hair pulled away from her forehead and cascading down her back. Big, wise brown eyes gave her the look of a gentle woodland doe, and her impish smile brightened her otherwise pale face. She was nodding enthusiastically.

"Oh, hello," Michaela said.

The girl's smile grew a bit wider. She pointed at the curtain, indicating the guests gathered beyond, then tugged at her ear.

Michaela couldn't help but laugh. "Well, if they weren't deaf before, I daresay they are now."

The girl covered her mouth with both of her hands, and her eyes crinkled merrily.

"I am Michaela Fortune." She held out her hand and the young girl immediately took it, sinking into a curtsey. "Who are you, pretty one?"

The girl smiled at the compliment then pointed at the crowd again. She drew her pointer fingers away from each other on her upper lip, then placed a hand on her flat chest.

Michaela thought she understood. "Lord Tornfield is your father?" The girl nodded, obviously happy that her pantomime had been successful. "Well, how do you do, Lady Elizabeth?"

The girl curtsied prettily again, and Michaela wondered at her lack of speech. She had heard of mutes, but never met one, and decided not to bring up the matter lest the fragile-looking child be humiliated.

Michaela knew all too well how that felt.

"Are you forbidden from the feast?" she asked instead.

Elizabeth shrugged, and then pointed past Michaela, her eyes wide and her mouth shaped into an O.

It appeared as though Lady Helltongue was preparing to torture the guests with another butchering of voice. Michaela groaned and dropped her head, her hands covering her ears.

"Can one *wish* oneself deaf, I wonder?"

Elizabeth Tornfield covered her own ears and bent at the waist, her mouth open in a silent guffaw and Michaela giggled. But she and her new young friend were spared from the lady's imminent screeching by Alan Tornfield himself.

"A moment, if you please," he interrupted with a handsome bow in Lady Osprey's direction. "I have an announcement before the festivities continue." Alan stepped onto the dais that held the lord's table with only a slight wobble and then smiled broadly at the crowd.

"I feel I must take this opportunity to address the sad news of our liege, Lord Magnus Cherbon's, passing, more than a year ago." Not even a murmur of sympathy answered the announcement, and Michaela was not surprised. It was no secret that all within the demesne had detested the Cherbon Devil and his greedy, merciless rule, and most had looked upon his death as a blessing. Elizabeth inched closer to Michaela's side and peeked around the curtain at her father as he continued his speech.

"Our lands have been without a master for too long a time, and so it is with a happy heart that I follow such sadness with a bit of a miracle: Lord Cherbon's son, my cousin, Roderick, is expected to return from the Holy Land any day, to take his father's place at Cherbon Castle."

At this, excited murmurs raced through the hall. Michaela caught only snippets of exclamations.

"Roderick, Lord Roderick!"

"So handsome . . ."

". . . not at all like his sire."

"However," Lord Alan said crossly over the animated whispering, "due to some rather . . . devastating injuries he suffered while on his pilgrimage, and dare I say, lameness of body"—the crowd gasped—"as well as terms of the inheritance set forth by Magnus himself, it is possible that the bequeathement of the demesne could fall"—Alan paused, and the crowd seemed to lean forward eagerly—"to none other than yours truly."

The hall erupted in surprised shouts and applause, and Lord Tornfield's smile was not a little prideful. He let the praise go on for several more seconds before raising his hands for silence once more.

"While I am, of course, saddened by the losses my cousin has suffered, I feel that tonight is a cause for celebration and merry-making. After all, it could only be a matter of weeks before I am removed to the northern part of our lands." The crowd responded with a collective moan. "So! Let us make the most of our time together with a bit of sport—a competition, if you will, of song. I shall grant a boon to the most accomplished singer." The crowd cheered. "We have already gratefully received Lady Juliette's offering."

Lady Juliette smiled widely about the guests and gave a saucy wink.

"Who dares challenge her?" Lord Alan looked over those gathered. "Oh, come on. Who will give it a go?"

For the better part of an hour, more than a score of guests, male and female, took their turn in the fun of the challenge. None were truly accomplished in their talent—a few even deliberately mocking themselves by singing bawdy limericks or reciting silly lines of verse—but none were nearly as bad as Lady Juliette, Michaela was relieved to hear. She and little Lady Elizabeth enjoyed each performance, hidden away behind the curtain, dancing each other in a circle with joined hands.

The most recent contestant, a young man of good family, took his bow amidst roaring laughter and applause and Lord Tornfield claimed the dais once more as Michaela fell back onto her stool panting and giggling.

"Oh, well done, *well done!*" he laughed, and raised his ever-present chalice in salute of the young man. "Who else? Who will be next? We can't let the fun end now!"

Michaela felt a tug on her hair again and turned to see Elizabeth pantomiming a palm away from her open mouth. Then she pointed at Michaela.

"Oh, no. I think not."

Elizabeth gave a mock pout then clasped her hands before her chest in a plea.

"Before all these people? They would devour me whole, Elizabeth. I haven't the talent for—"

"Lady Michaela Fortune shall sing!"

Michaela's stomach dropped into her bottom as her mother's warbly voice rang out through the hall.

"My daughter, where is she? Michaela?" Agatha's calls sounded ever closer, and Michaela could already hear the snickers and whispers from the crowd. "Michaela?"

Elizabeth gave her an unexpected—and surprisingly

forceful—shove, and Michaela sprang from behind the curtain, stumbling, stumbling, catching herself with one outstretched hand, nearly standing, before at last sprawling facedown on the flagstones.

"Oh, Michaela, there you are, dear," Agatha said in delight.

The guests made no effort to quell their laughter.

Then Agatha was at her side, pulling her daughter up by the arm. "Here we are, do get up, dear—and what has happened to your gown? No matter. Go on then, you have such a lovely voice." Then she leaned in close to Michaela's ear to whisper, "Think of the *boon,* Michaela! Mayhap a bit off the taxes. . . ."

"Oh, yes, Pudding—give us a song!" someone from the crowd goaded.

Michaela was very aware of her soiled dress, of Lady Juliette smirking in her direction, and of her mother's reminder of the Fortunes' growing poverty. Mayhap Lord Tornfield would grant a small reprieve, but . . .

Meanwhile, the crowd egged each other on.

"I dunno if we should have a verse from Miss Fortune— the devil might strike us all deaf!"

Michaela flung her hair out of her eyes and spun on the heckler. "I vow that if you can still claim even a bit of your hearing after that monstrosity of sound"—she said, and glanced at the shocked Juliette—"your tender ears should be quite safe for the rest of your life, devil or nay."

"Michaela!" Agatha gasped and patted her daughter's arm. "That was unkind."

Lady Juliette had regained her composure and now stepped from the crush with a malicious look. "Verily, Miss Fortune? 'Monstrosity of sound,' was it? Well, then, if the crowd judges your voice more worthy than mine, I shall grant you my own boon. Anything you wish."

Michaela raised her eyebrows. "Anything I wish?"

Lady Juliette looked to Alan Tornfield. "Do you consent to this wager, my lord?"

The lord was looking at Michaela as if he'd never seen her before, which was unlikely since she'd made such a scene of slippery pudding and broken pottery.

"By all means, ladies," he said in an amused voice. "Please, proceed."

For a moment, Michaela was frozen in the quiet, expectant hall, the guests regarding her blatantly. All eyes were pinned to her, the center of attention—a situation that never, ever turned out to Miss Fortune's advantage.

Someone coughed. Agatha Fortune smiled encouragingly at her daughter.

"Will you name a tune, m'lady?" the leader of the trio asked politely, if pointedly.

Michaela looked back at Juliette and saw the woman's smirk, as if she could sense how close Michaela was to forfeiting.

Think of the boon, Michaela! Mayhap a bit off the taxes. . . .

"We're waiting, Miss Fortune," Juliette taunted.

Michaela took a deep breath. "No music," she said to the lute player.

"Oh-ho!" Juliette laughed and clapped her hands.

"There was none written for this piece."

Juliette abruptly closed her mouth.

Michaela took a deep, deep breath as her mother stepped away, leaving Michaela in a circle of expectant guests. Alone.

Then she opened her mouth and sang as best as she could, her eyes closed, moving herself out of the smoky, humid hall of Tornfield Manor and imagining herself flying through the clouds, her arms outstretched like wings.

The tune had been taught to her as a young girl by the friar who traveled through the Cherbon demesne, originally written as a chant for monks. But Michaela turned it into a high song of sweet mourning, pouring all of her wishes and dreams atop the hurt and humiliation she'd been dealt—not only that night of the feast, but throughout her entire life—and creating a confection of song so pure and personal that she could feel her own tears press against her closed eyelids.

It was a longish piece, but she did not shorten it, relishing these few moments when, locked away in her own mind, she could give free rein to the one thing she did even passably well. The hall was wide and deep and tall-ceilinged, and each note ricocheted off the stones as she sang them, circling around and meeting each other to make a chorus of voices, it seemed.

As the last drawn-out word hung and then faded, Michaela reluctantly brought herself down from her fanciful flight and opened her eyes.

Everyone in the hall was staring at her as if the song had caused her to grow an additional head. Even the servants had stopped, frozen in their tasks of clearing the long tables and ferrying trays, and the silence following Michaela's song was perfect. Not even a breath stirred the air.

She felt her face start to heat and turned quickly to focus her attention on Lord Tornfield. He, too, was staring at her as if she were some strange creature who had slinked into his home, his mouth agape, and he didn't seem to notice that the chalice in his hand was loosing a stream of wine onto the toe of his boot.

Michaela said nothing, only waited for her judgment in the contest, feeling naked, vulnerable. As if she'd bared her very soul before all gathered.

Still, no one made any sound or movement as slight

as a sniffle or the shuffling of a foot. Michaela felt her throat closing.

Then, suddenly, the sound of two hands clapping vigorously cracked the awkward stillness, and Michaela turned her head to seek the applauder.

Elizabeth Tornfield had stepped from behind the musicians' curtain and was clapping as if attempting to break off both her arms. Her smile was the warmest Michaela had ever received from someone not of her relation, and the sight of this little girl, bravely risking reprimand at showing herself at the feast in order to praise her new friend, caused Michaela's heart to expand.

At least *someone* had liked her song.

His daughter's appearance obviously affected Lord Tornfield, as well, for he shook himself after a quiet gasp, dropped his now-empty chalice to the floor with a clang, and joined in his daughter's enthusiastic applause.

"Well done!" he shouted. "Oh, yes, well done, indeed!"

The rest of the hall added their own lukewarm praise immediately, and Michaela looked around at the guests, whispering to their neighbors while clapping and regarding Michaela from the corners of their eyes.

And then Lord Tornfield was off across the hall, still clapping, until he dropped to his knees before his daughter and embraced her, speaking in a low voice that was drowned out by the dwindling applause. In a moment he rose and led Elizabeth back to his place on the dais, helping her up the step as if she were an invalid. The murmurs of the crowd increased, and Michaela had the distinct impression that she was no longer the topic of gossip. She tried to squelch the traitorous relief she felt.

Alan Tornfield addressed the hall once more. "Do we have any other contestants?" After only a breath of a pause:

"I should think not, after that stunning, *stunning* attempt. I would declare Lady—Michaela, is it?—Fortune champion, lest there is any foolish enough to challenge her. No?" he asked, looking over the hall. Then his eyes, crinkling happily much like his daughter's, found Michaela, and his blond mustache twitched. "I believe you have earned a pair of boons, my lady." He held forth a long, courteous arm and bowed slightly. "Collect at your discretion."

"This is outrageous!"

Lady Juliette, of course. The woman stepped from the crowd once more with a swish and flounce of her fancy skirts and walked directly up to Michaela. "I'll grant no boon to a girl who gleans her talents from Satan! That song was clearly devil's trickery!"

Michaela felt her eyebrows draw downward and her fingers curl into fists at her sides. She had never before struck another human being, but in that moment she seriously considered it.

"Now, Lady Juliette," Lord Tornfield said mildly. "Certainly you knew the identity of the woman you challenged before she gave her try, and clearly, it is not Satan who stands before you now. This was all done in good fun, any matter. I'm sure Lady Michaela's boon will be a reasonable one." Although his words were friendly and advising, his tone indicated that the matter was not open to debate.

Lady Juliette's face glowed ghastly white. "Very well, *Miss Devil's Fortune*," she fairly spat. "What will your wretched prize be? And should you request something ridiculous, be forewarned that I will slap your face."

"Oh, my request will be very fair," Michaela rejoined, and moved even closer to the fuming lady so that her next words would be heard by Lady Juliette alone. "And *you* be forewarned that, should you dare strike me, I will drag you from this hall by your hair and call down the Hunt to steal your soul," she hissed, malicious glee filling her at teasing the woman so ruthlessly.

Devil, indeed. Good heavens.

"Name your prize, heathen," Juliette demanded through clenched teeth.

"Well, then," Michaela stepped back and looked down upon herself. "Since it is through your fault that my gown is hopelessly stained"—she let her eyes roam over the fine green velvet draping her rival—"I will have the one you are wearing."

Juliette laughed. "You're daft! This gown cost more than what your piddling hold brings to the demesne in a year!"

Michaela shrugged. "Mayhap you should have considered the value of your own possessions before you set about ruining another's."

"I'll not do it!" Juliette shrieked, looking to Lord Tornfield. "This is absurd!"

"It seems reasonable enough to me," the lord said. "And it was your challenge, Lady Juliette. I'm certain Lady Michaela will accept you sending the gown to her home by messenger. Surely she does not expect you to turn it over this night?" Lord Tornfield raised a questioning eyebrow to Michaela, and her heart pounded.

"Of course," Michaela acquiesced. "I shall look for it within the fortnight."

Juliette stammered. "I—I—" She stamped her foot and set her mouth in a pinched frown. "Very well, then. You shall have it." She made no attempt to mask her glare for Michaela. "Now, I'm certain you will understand if I bid you good night." She spun on her heel and swept from the hall, a few quiet snickers from the other guests escorting her out with her personal servants.

Lord Tornfield's commanding voice rang out again. "Have my fair musicians quit me as well? The night is far from over, my good men—let us continue the festivities in earnest! I have much to celebrate!"

The music immediately bloomed forth once more, and the crowd drifted away to refreshments or more private conversation, while Lord Tornfield beckoned to Michaela to join him and his daughter before the dais.

Michaela curtsied. "My lord, I am honored by your decision."

"Nonsense!" The blond man smiled, still keeping an affectionate hold on his daughter. "You fairly bested any and all—"

Elizabeth suddenly broke free from her father and threw her slender arms around Michaela's waist, nearly toppling them both.

"Oh, my!" Michaela laughed and squeezed the pretty girl, partly out of affection, and partly to keep the pair of them upright. Elizabeth continued to cling and so Michaela let her be. It was nice to be embraced.

"She seems to have taken to you rather quickly," Lord Tornfield observed. "How long were the two of you hidden away?"

"Not long," Michaela rushed to assure him, and wondered if the little girl was not clinging to her in order to avoid punishment. "I do hope you'll forgive Lady Elizabeth for disobeying you, my lord."

"I beg your pardon?"

Beneath Michaela's forearms, Elizabeth's shoulders shook.

"I shall . . . I shall forfeit my boon if it will prevent her from being reprimanded."

"Why on earth would I reprimand Elizabeth?"

Michaela felt her face heat. Must she always feel the fool?

"For . . . ah, attending the feast without your permission?"

Elizabeth drew away slightly and Michaela saw that the girl was *laughing*.

Alan Tornfield frowned at Michaela for a moment and then burst out in his own merry chuckle. "Lady Michaela, it has been my fondest wish for some time now that Elizabeth join the festivities of Tornfield. I assure you, she was hiding away of her own accord. Verily, this is the first time she has shown herself to anyone other than myself or the household staff since her mother passed."

Michaela knew she must look like a stunned ninny, but there was nothing for it. "Oh," was all she could think to say for a moment. "Oh. Well, then, I am pleased that she decided to appear, as well."

Elizabeth returned to her father's side and Alan Tornfield smiled as he drew his arm around the girl's shoulders. "Now, as for your boon—"

"My lord, if you please," Michaela interrupted. "I would request that my father's hold be granted some sort of small reprieve. Our harvest was scant last year—our village seems to be shrinking. I'd not ask the whole of our debt be forgiven, of course, but perhaps a small portion? Or an extension for payment in full?"

Lord Tornfield looked at her thoughtfully. "I am well aware of the state of your parents' distress, Lady Michaela. Indeed, all the land felt the pinch of Magnus Cherbon's rule, myself included. We were granted an unexpected reprieve by his passing, but now that Lord Roderick has returned, I do wonder for how long."

"I see," Michaela said, hearing the man's answer in his tone, if not his words.

"But perhaps we can reach some sort of arrangement," Lord Tornfield said suddenly, his thoughtful gaze flicking to his daughter. He looked back to Michaela's face and his eyes sparkled. "I am not an unreasonable man, after all."

Michaela didn't know what to say, so she said nothing. After a moment, Lord Tornfield spoke again.

"Perhaps you would consider taking a position in my household, in lieu of your parents' debt," he suggested slowly, and Michaela thought she might have seen Alan Tornfield's eyes take a quick appraisal of her body. Her stomach fluttered. "As Elizabeth's companion, of course," he added quickly. "I would not wish your reputation harmed."

Michaela wanted to laugh. Her reputation could be no further tarnished were she to walk through the streets of London stark naked. But then the essence of Lord Tornfield's suggestion struck home.

"My lord, are you proposing that the whole of my parents' debt would be forgiven, only for my companionship for Elizabeth?"

"I think . . . I think, yes. Yes." His words grew surer. "Lady Michaela, my daughter's happiness is most important to me. If she has some sort of quick affection for you, if you can draw her out of her shell—perhaps even coax her to speak once more—it is worth all the tithes in my holding." With these last words, Michaela saw the lord's throat constrict. "For each quarter that you reside at Tornfield Manor as Elizabeth's companion, the Fortune tithe will be dismissed. I know it is terribly boorish of me to reap favor from a boon that is yours, but will you accept?"

Michaela wanted to weep. Instead, she let a shaky smile curl over her face as she suddenly realized how terribly handsome Lord Alan Tornfield was. At his side, Elizabeth's face turned toward Michaela, hopefully expectant.

"I will," Michaela breathed.

Chapter Two

He was home.

Roderick's heart thudded in his chest like a war drum as Cherbon came into his view by way of the gatehouse. He reined his mount to a halt to collect himself, and leaned onto his right thigh to give his screaming left knee and hip a moment of rest from gripping the horse's side. Hugh Gilbert drew his horse even with Roderick's and stopped, the misshapen bundle bound to Hugh's back by lengths of wide, fine linen crisscrossed over his chest giving him a hunched appearance.

"This is it, is it?" Hugh said, and looked to Roderick with his usual sardonic grin. "Likely enough, I suppose."

During the long, long months of Roderick's recovery, the Hugh Gilbert Roderick had first met before Heraclea had slowly changed into a different man. Although to be fair, Roderick guessed that Hugh likely hadn't changed at all. The man he knew after the battle had been a desperate man, a guilty man—qualities taken on in a time of trial. The Hugh Gilbert who sat the horse next to Roderick's side was the true man. The man he had been before his pilgrimage and the man he was now. And although in those early days of sickness, Roderick would have never guessed that their lives would become so closely entwined, he liked the man Hugh Gilbert was, owed him a great deal, despite Hugh's protests.

And Roderick was glad that Hugh accompanied him now to his home. Roderick would have not admitted it under threat of death, but the sight of the soaring gatehouse of Cherbon Castle struck old, cold, weary fear into him. Even though he knew the Cherbon Devil was dead and buried more than a year past, Magnus's ghost seemed to reach out to Roderick from the mortar between the rough stone with bony, pointing fingers, and his deep, menacing voice seemed to ring in the ears of his son.

Failure. Failure!

Worthless, useless cripple!

You should have died instead of me.

But Roderick had not died, much to his own surprise, instead drawing morbid, determined strength from the news that Magnus Cherbon had met his own final judgment halfway around the world, ironically within the formidable and decadent walls of Cherbon. And now the Cherbon demesne was Roderick's—the Cherbon Devil reincarnated, in his own bitter mind, but for different reasons. Once, a desperate lifetime ago it seemed, this fortress had housed a frightened and cowed young boy, then a rebellious and angry young man. Now it welcomed an injured and embittered lord back into its cold arms. Roderick was home again, and unlike his hasty and solitary departure, he had not made the long return journey alone.

The bundle strapped to Hugh's back squirmed and gave a cross squawk.

"Yes, yes, Bottomless Pit," Hugh said over his shoulder.

"Nearly there. I vow you've wet me through to my front side."

The wind gusted, whipping the ragged remains of the Cherbon standards topping either side of the gatehouse tower into snapping strips. Ivy had laid siege to the imposing fortress and been left to run its mad reign unchecked, giving the walls stretching away to the north and east an abandoned, dangerous, wild appearance. The drawbridge was lowered, but there was no fanfare, no bustling serfs attending the castle's business either on foot or in cart. In the cloud-covered gloom of that rainy and cold afternoon, no harker so much as called out a warning.

Not even the sound of a footstep could be heard from beyond the curtain wall. Only the lonely wind, skimming the gray stones.

Roderick adjusted in his saddle onto his screaming left hip once more and clucked his weary horse over the drawbridge, wordlessly prompting Hugh to follow. Young Leo began to cry in earnest as they passed into the barbican.

The inner bailey of Cherbon was more derelict than its exterior. Vines ran their wicked, tangled maze here, as well, almost like a plague of vegetation had been visited upon the castle, and the old, crackling growth seemed a carpet of despair. Strewn about the ground were bits of broken furniture, barrels that had burst their staves as if dropped and left to lay where they had vomited their contents, now long picked over by scavengers. Shattered jugs and wedges of pottery—Roderick saw a jagged piece with the Cherbon crest cleaved where it had broken. He saw a length of once-costly and now weather-faded cloth— perhaps a piece of the drapery belonging behind the lord's table in the great hall.

Roderick walked his horse through the crackling,

crunching litter of the bailey, around the great tower of the keep toward the entrance of the hall. He stopped and put his back to the south wall, also covered in choking vines to the battlements and wallwalk above. Over the keep, between where Roderick stood and the hidden inner courtyard, a gossamer finger of wood smoke struggled to scratch at the low blanket of sky. A crow cawed. Roderick let the reins fall from his hands and grasped his left leg below his knee. Using his right fist, he beat his boot backward out of the stirrup, and prepared to lift his leg over the pommel.

Hugh was off his own horse in a blink, and Roderick felt a familiar pinch of jealousy at the man's ease of movement, even with stout little Leo strapped to his back.

"One moment, Rick. I'll get—"

"I can do it," Roderick growled.

"Don't be an ass," Hugh snapped, searching beneath the vines for a chunk of discarded firewood, left to rot where it had been dropped. He wrested it away from the greedy vines, Leo now silent, and brought it to Roderick's right side, where he stood the wide length on its end. "We've been astride all the day. With as stiff as you are upon dismounting, you'd break your only good leg. And then where would you be, I ask?"

Roderick had no reply, for of course, Hugh was right. He grasped Hugh's shoulder and stepped onto the wobbly wooden pylon. Holding his nearly useless leg aloft, he made the short hop to the ground, pain shooting up the muscles of his buttocks and to either side of his spine, all the same. Then, for naught but petulant spite, Roderick kicked the wood length over with his left boot and bit back the painful cry it elicited in his knee.

Roderick pulled the walking stick from the sheath that at one time had held his broadsword and extended it. Leaning heavily, he snatched up the horse's reins with wide, awkward sweeps of his free arm and tugged his mount toward the bailey well. Once there, he found that the bucket was missing several planks and the hemp rope had rotted nearly in two.

Roderick threw the useless garbage to the vines with a crash and a growl, where it splintered completely. He turned and jerked the horse toward the doorway of the hall, his stomach in painful knots.

He told himself it was not fear he felt. Only anticipation. Relief for the end of their long, long journey.

"Going in now, are we?" Hugh called as Roderick ducked through the doorway, pulling his horse onto the cobbled floors after him.

The hall was darker and, oddly enough, colder than the bailey, although a pitiful fire burned in the giant, square stone-lined pit near the end of the room. A remnant of the meters-long swags of drapery that had once ran the course of both long walls hung in one pitiful scrap there near the door, replaced with long swoops of cobwebs, gossamer threads of dirt, and crumbling vines straggling over the painted plaster murals set near the beamed ceiling. The floor was only marginally clearer than the bailey he'd left behind, the intricate pattern of stonework hidden beneath a thick layer of dirt and dead vines and broken furnishings.

Only the lord's table still stood aright, a lumpy pile of what looked like discarded cloth resting on its center. Whoever had built the fire had likely left it, Roderick thought, and he wondered if the person in residence was of Cherbon or just some wanderer who had stumbled upon the deserted castle in a spot of luck.

Behind him, Roderick's horse stamped and blew quietly, shaking him from the scene of destruction before his eyes.

His eyes sought the doorway at the opposite end of the room, leading to the kitchens and the interior well within, and was readying to limp in that direction when the pile of cloth on the table stirred.

"Harliss!" the lump of clothing shouted, and Roderick stopped. He knew that voice. "Roderick? Is that you, my son?"

Roderick wanted no one to ever address him as "son" again in that room, not even Friar Cope, but he limped around in a circle all the same. "Yes, Friar."

The older, rotund man immediately reached for the jug at his elbow. After a long swallow, he stood. "I'm glad you've returned," he said, as if Roderick had just come back from a day of hunting in the wood beyond Cherbon's walls. "Glory be to God. But, my son, your father is dead."

"Good."

The friar nodded. "Cherbon is yours."

"I know," Roderick said with a touch of impatience. "My horse thirsts." He turned back toward the kitchen doorway and was met by yet another ghost from his past, the ghost of the woman Friar Cope had called out for in the midst of his stupor, and the source of the knot in Roderick's stomach.

"Good day, Roderick," Harliss said in her thin, stingy-gray voice.

Before him was the woman who had sought to take the place of his mother, the nurse who had cared for him and reared him under Magnus's orders. Perhaps more skeletal, more gray, than when he'd left Cherbon, but still the same severe coif, the same dire gray gown and apron, the same permanent, disapproving frown. Her hands were clenched before her waist. How many times had those hands struck him?

When Roderick gave her no return greeting, she spoke again. "Do my eyes deceive me, or are you entertaining your animal in the great hall?"

"You will address me as 'my lord,' *servant*," Roderick stated flatly. "And yes, this is my animal, and yes, he is in the hall, although it is of no concern to you save that had you cared for the bucket in yon well, he would not be here. As it is, this chamber is akin to a sty, and were my father still alive, I'm certain you would be whipped." *Take that, you bitch.*

Harliss's knife-thin nostrils flared. "Oh, I do doubt he would resort to that. *My lord.*" Harliss turned her crone's face to Friar Cope as he puffed to a stop between she and Roderick. "Have you told him, Friar?"

"Yes, he has," Roderick snapped.

"No," Friar Cope wheezed. "Roderick—"

"So there *are* others about," Hugh said merrily as he entered the doorway, his voice rather loud for the large, quiet space. "They aren't transients, are they? I do so crave a hearty meal and Leo is—*my God!* This hall is a disgrace! No matter—I will go fetch my own mount and we shall have a pagan feast upon the floor."

Hugh had unbound Leo from his back and re-seated the toddler astride one hip. Harliss looked at the pair of them as if they were beggars, although Hugh's clothing was as rich as Cherbon's hall had at one time looked, and Leo wore a gown of silk and wool embroidered with gold thread, and tiny leather slippers upon his feet. He looked like a small prince.

The costume was the last gift Aurelia had given him. Roderick had watched her fashion it with her own hands.

"Wod-wick!" Leo shouted, and held his arms toward Roderick.

"He can't take you now, Wart. But do get down and have a run about," Hugh declared, and set the toddler on his feet. Leo immediately ran to Roderick despite Hugh's words, tripping as his feet became tangled in the dead vines, but catching himself with Roderick's long cloak, burying his face behind Roderick's knees.

Roderick struggled not to let his leg buckle under the slight but horrendously painful pressure of the boy's head.

"Cherbon *is* yours," Friar Cope continued, as if Hugh had not interrupted them. "But there is a condition to the inheritance, Roderick."

Hugh turned a frown to Roderick. "What kind of shit is this, Rick? *A condition?* Ridiculous. You know these two, I suppose?"

Roderick nodded, and the knot in his stomach threatened to snap. Of course there was a condition. Even from the grave, Magnus was intent on making certain his son was miserable.

"Cherbon's Friar, Cope," Roderick said through clenched teeth. "And my old nurse, Harliss. Where the other residents of the keep are, I know not."

"Ah, at last I meet Harliss the Heartless," Hugh said with more than a bit of frost in his tone. "I have heard much of your charity."

"I save my charity for those in need," Harliss sneered. "It is wasted on prideful, disobedient little boys."

Roderick pinned the old friar with his glare. "What condition?"

"Ah, well," the friar stammered, "in order to claim Cherbon, you must marry."

"Is that all?" Roderick said, the knot loosening.

"Ah, the lady must be of good family," Cope muttered,

searching the folds of his robes. "I have the directive here, somewhere. . . ."

"It matters not. Does the king know of this?"

"Of course, my so—my lord," Friar Cope corrected himself. "Magnus ordered a copy sent to him shortly after you departed for the Holy Land." The round man crossed himself. "But, my lord—"

Harliss spoke again. "Act not as though you didn't know he was ill, Roderick," she accused. "You abandoned your own father when you knew he would surely die!"

Roderick stepped toward her. "Whether you believe that I had no knowledge of his illness is of no consequence to me. But I am surely glad that he is dead. Magnus goaded and shamed me until I consented to make that damned pilgrimage." Roderick pulled back his hair from the side of his face, fully revealing the wicked scars that tangled over his skin, then snapped back his cloak, displaying his walking stick. "See you the treasures I reaped for my holy duty?" He thought he saw a glint of satisfaction in Harliss's soulless eyes. "And if you address me by my Christian name again, Nurse, *I will* have you whipped."

The old nurse's throat convulsed, as if she choked down her fury like vomit. "My apologies, my lord, if I overstepped my place." It was not at all sincere.

Behind him, Leo began to whine softly.

"Now," Roderick snapped, "where have the rest of the servants gone to?"

"There are yet a score at Cherbon," Harliss offered grudgingly. "They are in the chambers above—the only ones left much untouched by the pillaging."

"Roust them, lest I find them first. And the rest?"

Harliss's lips thinned to the point that they disappeared into her face. "Scattered to the villages—worthless muck."

"With much of Cherbon's possessions, I see. Fetch them today," Roderick commanded. "Immediately. Any who owes service to the castle and does not come at my word—by the morn—I will double their families' fines. Permanently."

Friar Cope gasped, but Roderick ignored it. "Should you fail me in this task, I will have you stripped naked and set beyond Cherbon's walls. By the morrow's eve, the bailey grounds, the lord's private rooms—*my rooms*"—he emphasized—"and chambers for Sir Hugh and Leo shall be cleaned and returned to a state fit for residence, or I will see each and every servant punished equally."

"Of course, my lord," Harliss fumed, but she did not move.

"What are you waiting for, woman?" Roderick demanded. "Go!"

"I was but going to ask, my lord," Harliss nearly whispered in her rage, "if you would have me attend"—her cold eyes went to the floor near Roderick's cloak—"your noble friend's child. I *am* Cherbon's nurse."

"He is not Sir Hugh's boy," Roderick supplied.

"The orphan then," Harliss said, exasperation tingeing her words.

"Leo is *my* son," Roderick growled. "And your claws shall not come within a meter of him, or I will have them mounted on yon wall. You are now a kitchen maid. Now, for the last time, be gone."

"Poof!" Hugh had the inappropriateness to shout. "Ha!"

Harliss left the hall with a crackle of vines.

"You have changed, Roderick," Friar Cope said quietly, sadly.

"Good day to you, Friar," Roderick said, and reached around to grab up Leo by one arm. His horse had wandered farther down the hall, and was now lapping at the tabletop, where it had succeeded in overturning the friar's jug.

"Before I go," the man said, and handed Roderick a rolled piece of parchment. "The decree. My lord, in order for you to keep Cherbon—"

"Yes, Cope, you've already said I must marry."

"Before your thirtieth birthday, my lord. If you do not, Lord Alan of Tornfield, your cousin, will inherit."

Roderick stared at the friar for several moments, thinking of his scars, his lameness, his hatred of everything that was Cherbon. He crushed the decree in his fist, wishing it was Magnus Cherbon's neck.

"Get to your useless chapel, Friar Traitor," Roderick said slowly, carefully.

"Roderick, I was no accomplice in this, you must believe—"

"And if you value your life, tread not in this hall again without my express summons."

Friar Cope bowed and fled without another word.

"Welcome home, Rick," Hugh said on a great sigh. "Would that we had stayed in Constantinople."

"No," Roderick said, quietly at first, as he looked around the ruined hall, one hand still clenched around Leo's plump arm, the other grasping the decree and his walking stick. "No. My father will not best me. It is nearly a year 'til I reach the age that Magnus set forth."

"You'll engage in this madness?" Hugh asked incredulously.

"On the morrow, if you'll assist me, Hugh, we shall send out the word."

"What word, Rick?"

"That the Cherbon Devil has returned. And he seeks a bride."

Chapter Three

Five months later
Tornfield Manor

"My lord, Lady Juliette of Osprey!"

At the announcement, Michaela's and Elizabeth's heads swiveled to look at each other, both with similar expressions of dread and distaste. Then they giggled silently and turned their faces back to their meal.

The woman came rushing into the hall, interrupting supper with her clicking, stiff slippers and swishing skirts. "Lord Tornfield, my apologies for bursting in on you without warning, but I felt I must come to you immediately!" She stopped before the dais, panting, and made a quick curtsey before smiling sweetly in Elizabeth's direction. "My dear."

On the opposite side of Elizabeth, to Michaela's left, Alan stood, wiping his mustache with a cloth. "Lady Juliette, you are always welcome at Tornfield Manor. You must tell me, what is the nature of your distress?"

Juliette gave a great, dramatic sigh and held forth her fist, gripping a wrinkled piece of parchment. A manservant ferried the piece from the lady's hand to Alan's, who shook it open with an intrigued frown on his handsome, kind face and read it silently.

Michaela and Elizabeth exchanged looks from the corners of their eyes.

The dark-haired woman had wandered down the table. "Miss Fortune," Lady Juliette at last acknowledged. "I trust you are enjoying your boon?"

Michaela nearly lost her good humor, being reminded of the fairly won gown. Juliette had kept her word and sent the green velvet to the Fortune hold, but when Michaela had opened the package, the gown was nothing more than a pile of strips, having been cut through all the seams and down the skirt and bodice with a very, very sharp blade.

"Oh, I'm enjoying it very much, Lady Juliette," Michaela agreed. Then she lowered her voice to nearly a whisper. "Why, just his morn, I marveled at how soft it feels against one's bare bottom."

Alan Tornfield let loose an abrupt, disbelieving laugh and raised his eyes from the missive. "I can scarce believe it. How did you come by this, my lady?"

"It was sent to Osprey by Cherbon's messenger only last month," Juliette supplied, rushing back to stand before the lord. "And I can assure you by my own vow that it is true—I have just come from Cherbon, and can attest to its sincerity."

Michaela saw one of Alan's noble, sculpted eyebrows raise, as if in sarcastic question.

Juliette fidgeted and blushed. "Only to see if it was true, of course. And it is!"

"I knew he sought a—well, no matter," Alan said mildly, folding the missive carefully and tucking it into his belt. "Although I would learn more from your visit." He turned to look at his daughter and then Michaela. "If you will excuse me, ladies. I'll return before your bedtime, Elizabeth."

"My lord," Michaela acquiesced, and watched him go, she knew, with longing in her eyes. He was so handsome. And kind, as well, to give that nasty Lady Juliette audience during his mealtime. The very epitome of nobility. And he was *so* handsome. . . .

Elizabeth elbowed her sharply in the ribs.

"Ow! Minx," Michaela whispered, and gave the girl a pinch on the arm.

Elizabeth grinned and then threw her head pointedly in the direction of her departing father. She shrugged her shoulders and raised her eyebrows, looking very much like Alan in that moment.

"I've no idea," Michaela answered.

Elizabeth pushed her plate away as if the sudden appearance of Lady Juliette had spoiled her appetite.

Michaela could not help but agree, and dropped her eating knife onto her own platter. Immediately, a servant appeared to sweep away the remains of the meal, and Michaela marveled at her new station in the Tornfield household. Although the Fortunes of course employed servants, they were few, with only a handful of people filling a multitude of positions. Many were the times that Michaela had cleared the Fortunes' table of the mealtime dishes and delivered them to the overworked and frazzled kitchen staff herself. She did her own cleaning of her chamber, and often helped with the monthly washing. She had no lady's maid at the Fortune home.

At Tornfield, she had two. And she'd not so much as stepped foot in the kitchens or wash house since she'd come. They frequently ate meat with every meal. There was even a garderobe on the second floor, near the sleeping chambers. She wondered if such rich living would make her slothful at times, but she sincerely did not care. The skin on her hands was growing soft and smooth, and no one here dared speak poorly of her, under warning from the lord himself. Except when Lady Juliette came to visit, of course, but what could kind Lord Alan do with such a spiteful woman not under his direct rule?

That handsome, kind, noble man . . .

"What shall we do before your father returns and you're off to bed?" Michaela asked, even the appearance of Lady Juliette unable to shake her feelings of contentment.

Elizabeth made the now-familiar pantomime for sing as the two girls made their way to a grouping of chairs near the large hearth, but Michaela shook her head, glancing the way Lord Alan had disappeared with the land's worst singer. She had no desire to push the limits of her and Lady Juliette's tense civility.

"Not tonight, Elizabeth."

Elizabeth crooked her arms and flapped her elbows.

"I am not a chicken," Michaela protested, giving the girl another fond pinch before flopping in a plush armchair—it was the lady of the keep's chair, a miniature of Alan's—which the lord had designated for Michaela's use.

She found it quite, quite comfortable.

"What of a tale instead?" Michaela suggested. "A fable? Perhaps a bible story—you've not heard Daniel in the lion's den for some time."

Elizabeth shook her head. Then she pointed to Michaela and then did the motions of pulling back a bow string.

Michaela groaned. "Not that silly one again."

Elizabeth clasped her hands before her chest and batted her eyelashes.

"Oh, very well. Such nonsense, though. Pull your chair closer so I'm not forced to shout." When Elizabeth's chair was nearly touching Michaela's, she began the story originally told to her by Agatha Fortune, one Michaela knew she must have recited to Elizabeth a score of times in the past five months.

"It was Yule's Eve," Michaela said, "and my mother and father had had a terrible row, although you would hardly think that's possible, looking at them now, would you? My father is said to have at one time been a very hard man, again, difficult to believe, I know," Michaela added, at Elizabeth's expected skeptical look.

"He'd been into his cups that night, and was entertaining a band of rowdy soldiers in the hall—shouting and breaking things and carrying on quite dreadfully, according to Mother. She was heavy with me at that time, and the great noise was keeping her awake. Well. She decided that she had had quite enough of Father's merriment and went into the hall to request that he bid his friends good night. She saw that they had the demesne's meek friar cornered near the hearth and were using him as a target to throw bones and rocks and bits of my mother's pottery at.

"Of course, she rescued the friar first by flying to his side—getting hit by a half-eaten leg of lamb for her trouble—and then demanded that my father's guests leave that instant. She told them all that they should be shamed of treating a man of God so poorly and that, were they not all careful, they'd be taken up by the Hunt as punishment. Well, my father was not agreeable to being ordered about his own hall by his wife, not to mention threatened with what he perceived as superstitious drivel, so he told my mother that if she did not care for the way he was entertaining his guests, *she* could be the one to leave."

Elizabeth was rapt, her knees drawn up in the seat beneath her gown, her fists before her mouth. She nodded quickly. *Go on, go on.*

"Well. It being night, Mother was in her rail and robe, but she had slipped on some old shoes to come into the hall and take the men to task. It was brutally cold, snow was deep outside the keep door, but so incensed was she that she thought to teach my father a lesson by going to the stables for the night, where the shepherdess kept a warm and comfortable shelter. She bid my father farewell and left the keep.

"She was no farther than the road when she heard the terrible calling of the hounds, and the sound of hoofbeats like thunder in the snow. Ever firm in her belief that God would protect her, Mother stood her ground, determined to get to the bottom of the legend that had everyone in the village terrified. Then the riders were upon her, and there was no time to hide."

Elizabeth covered her eyes for an instant, but then looked once more with merry excitement at Michaela.

"The next morn, my father, feeling the ill effect of his overindulgence, and no little remorse for his poor treatment of his wife, went in search of my mother. He looked in the stables first, as although he was—by his own words—a bit thick at the time, he knew it was the only place my mother could and would go where she and I would be safe. But the shepherdess stated that she had not seen sign of Agatha since the day previous, and she had not ventured out of her hut the whole of the night, for she had heard the baying of the hounds beneath her covers and was fearful of the Hunt.

"Well. At this, my father became concerned. As he left the shepherdess, he wondered where on earth his cumbersome and oft troublesome wife could have hidden herself away. That is, until he found the shoe in the center of the road. Mother's footprints led up to where the shoe lay and then simply . . . vanished."

Michaela had told this tale to Elizabeth many times since coming to Tornfield Manor, and she never embellished from the version told to her by her own mother, but it was here that the story deviated from the original version. Michaela still recounted the truth, but omitted the part where Agatha claimed to have been taken up on the horse of the Hunt's fearsome leader and lifted away into the sky.

This was a child's tale, after all. No need to frighten the girl with details that were—in Michaela's opinion—likely stretched to contain some sort of twisted moral. Michaela herself had lost enough sleep over the dreadful story, until she'd grown old enough to determine what was true and what was likely dramatic embellishment.

"It is said that my father and the villagers searched for sign of my mother for the next pair of days, without ceasing. On the third day, father took to the village chapel and fell to his knees, begging God to return his wife and unborn child to him. He prayed that he would perform any penance if his request was granted."

Elizabeth swept both palms away from her stomach in a wide mound.

"That's right. It was just then that my mother entered the chapel, nearly scaring the life out of my father. She was unharmed, but missing *both* shoes, and she said to him, 'Walter, you must never fight again. You must give your life to God as a meek and obedient servant, lest you and this child be taken from me as punishment for your wickedness.'"

Elizabeth held her palms up, a questioning look on her face.

"So he did. Father dismissed the men of the village who were reserved for fighting, hung his own weapons on the wall of our hall, and set to seeing only to the comfort and happiness of his wife."

Not willing to let even a word of the retelling slip, Elizabeth pointed to Michaela's bodice.

"Yes, and this, I nearly forgot." Although she hadn't truly forgotten, she simply didn't wish to bring it out. Michaela reached into the neck of her gown and withdrew the chain that held the small piece of metal, like a link from a chain shirt. She held it up for Elizabeth to see. It was blackened with age, thin and bent, but unbroken. Michaela had oft wondered, if it was a link of mail, how it had been connected to its mates, being whole and unbroken with no visible seam of weld. But she had never asked.

"This was the only thing my mother carried with her upon her return from her three-day absence. She kept it with her always and then, when I was born, placed it around my neck. When I was old enough to understand, she made me swear to never take it off, lest the Hunt return for me."

Elizabeth pointed at Michaela, and then hooked her index fingers on either side of her head.

Michaela rolled her eyes. "Yes, this is what the villagers say makes me the devil. Are you content now?"

Elizabeth nodded with an impish smile.

"Good." Michaela took Elizabeth's small, pale hand and kissed it. "Do you think I'm the devil?"

She shook her head and pulled her hand free. Elizabeth circled her crown with one finger and then flapped her hands near her shoulders.

"An angel, am I? Oh, I daresay that *is* the right answer."

Elizabeth made the sign for angel again and then spun her arms in wide, crazy circles before falling out of her chair with a look of feigned surprise.

"Oh, you little—!" Michaela screeched in a mockery of outrage, and fell upon the girl in an attack of tickling.

A masculine clearing of throat interrupted their play, and both girls looked up to see a smiling Alan Tornfield standing over them.

Michaela was completely humiliated to see Lady Juliette smirking at his side.

"Well, I must say that you were right, Lord Tornfield," Juliette said sweetly. "Miss Fortune does make a jolly nurse for your Elizabeth."

Elizabeth got up from the floor and fled the hall, leaving Michaela to struggle to her feet alone, her hand slipping off the arm of the chair but once.

"Oh, she's not Elizabeth's nurse, Lady Juliette," Alan said, and Michaela wanted to think there was a bit of chastisement in his tone. "They're . . . friends."

"Friends. Of course," Juliette accepted. "How fortunate for Elizabeth that her father has found such a generous . . . friend."

Michaela bit her tongue until she tasted blood. She would have chewed it off at the root with her own teeth rather than say something mean and petty in front of Lord Tornfield. Any matter, Lady Juliette continued.

"I hate to leave such entertaining company," she simpered, "but I have a long journey to my own hearth. Good night, my lord. I hope my visit has been informative."

"Enlightening, certainly. I will be in touch with you very soon. Good night, Lady Juliette."

"Miss Fortune."

Michaela kept her tongue firmly between her teeth as Juliette swept from the hall.

And then it was only Michaela and Lord Tornfield in the large, quiet room, lit by the hearth at her back. The flames bathed him in a golden glow and his hair, his mustache, his skin, looked like they were cast from that precious metal, even if his expression appeared unusually tense and preoccupied.

Lord Tornfield held his hand out toward her, and Michaela's favorite part of each day began as she wrapped her fingers around his forearm.

"Amen," Alan said in a quiet smiling voice, and then kissed the top of Elizabeth's head before rising from the edge of the bed. Michaela stepped to the pair and added her own kiss to the little girl's face.

"Happy dreams, my love," she said, and went round to the opposite side of Elizabeth's bed to help pull the embroidered coverlet over the girl.

Elizabeth blew kisses to them both as Alan carried the candlestick from the room, allowing Michaela to precede him through the doorway and then closing the door softly.

Michaela was filled with warm contentment as she and Alan walked side by side down the corridor to her own chamber—easily twice the size of her room at the Fortune house. In this comfortable, loving routine, Michaela liked to imagine that she was the Lady of Tornfield, that Elizabeth was her daughter, and handsome Lord Alan was her own husband. She gave a heavy sigh as she came to a halt before her door, a reluctant good night on her tongue.

"Lady Michaela," Alan said before Michaela could speak. "Would you indulge me a few moments of your time before retiring? There is something of importance I would speak with you about."

"Of course, my lord," she said immediately, her stomach aflutter at what could be so pressing that Lord Alan would retain her company after Elizabeth was abed.

"It is rather private. Would it be terribly untoward of me to request we converse in my apartment?"

Michaela's hand slid off the door latch and she fell—*hard*—into the door frame. Alan's arm shot out to steady her and a concerned frown creased his handsome brow.

"Are you all right?"

"Oh, yes!" She laughed. "I just . . . My hand slipped, is all." She shrugged, and felt like an idiot. "We can converse anywhere you wish, my lord," she said, trying to gather her posture and what was left of her pride.

"Thank you. Shall we, then?"

She followed him farther down the corridor to his door and stepped inside when he swept his arm toward the portal.

It would have been obvious to any stranger who entered that these were the lord's rooms by the masculine décor—dark burgundy draperies hung at the large window and around the bed, and rich fabric of that same hue covered the pair of tufted stools nestled under a small table along one wall. There were few frills, and the plush velvet seemed to breathe leather and musk. But Michaela did see a handful of signs that the chamber had once housed a female—a gilded hairbrush on a side table, a pair of dainty embroidered slippers at the foot of a painted wooden trunk—and her heart broke a little at the bittersweet feelings evoked by seeing such objects the husband had retained from his wife.

Several candelabras had been lit by servants earlier in the eve in preparation for the lord's retirement, and the fire crackled private secrets.

A perfect setting, in Michaela's mind, for what she hoped would be an intimate conversation.

"Please," Lord Alan invited, dragging one of the stools out for her and then setting the candlestick on the small table. "Forgive me if I seem a bit . . . foolish. I've not had a lady in this room since . . ."

"I understand," Michaela rushed to assure him as she sat. Thankfully, her bottom connected securely with the upholstered seat. "No need to apologize." The lovely, lovely man . . .

Lord Alan joined her at the table with a quick, boyish smile. It fled his face in a blink. "I want to tell you why Lady Juliette visited me this evening."

"Oh, *must* we talk about Lady Juliette?" The almost whining plea was out of Michaela's mouth before she could stop it, and she was mortified, even when Lord Alan smiled charmingly. "I am sorry. Do go on."

Alan seemed to relax a bit then, and pulled from his belt the rolled parchment Michaela had seen earlier, and handed it to her.

Michaela unrolled the missive and let her eyes scan over the thousands of tiny, intricate letters covering the page. It would take her an hour to read it in its entirety.

Lord Alan took pity on her. "The gist of the thing is this: Lord Roderick Cherbon, my cousin, has a stipulation he must fulfill in order to fully inherit Cherbon demesne."

"This says that?" Michaela questioned, and her eyes went to the page. She thought it odd Lord Cherbon would want such a private matter served up to his people for gossip.

"No. I say that, in confidence, to you," Alan clarified. "It is why I announced months ago that there is a possibility that I could inherit in his place."

"Oh," Michaela said, giddy that Alan considered her enough to confide this bit of close information.

"The stipulation is that he must marry a lady of good family before his thirtieth birthday."

"Oh, my," Michaela gasped, not really caring, but wanting to show Lord Alan that she found anything he said riveting.

"The problem *is in* this missive, and is clear to anyone who would read it, especially in light of Lady Juliette's information. Apparently, my once-sought-after cousin is finding the bride search a bit more of a challenge than he likely thought it would be. May I?" Alan took the missive from her, shook it open, and began to skim with squinted eyes.

"Announcement this day of . . . yes, yes—ah! 'Any unmarried lady of good, titled family who is in want of a husband should immediately report to Cherbon Castle. If Lord Roderick Cherbon finds such a woman agreeable after a period of no more than ninety days and can come to a mutual agreement of marriage, upon their wedding she will be legally granted one-fifth of Cherbon's holding to use at her own discretion. Please see Sir Hugh Gilbert upon arrival.'"

Michaela felt her eyes widen. "That certainly *is* strange," she said carefully.

"Don't you see?" Alan said, leaning forward on his stool, and Michaela caught her breath at his closeness. "No one will marry him now—he's a beast! He's trying to *bribe* his way to the inheritance!"

"A beast?"

"A beast," Alan reiterated. "He slinks about the castle with a walking stick and in a long black cloak, keeping his face hidden. He's frightened away each woman come to court him since his return to Cherbon. This missive only proves how close he is to losing the demesne."

"I see," Michaela said, although she did not. "What has this to do with me?"

"Your parents' taxes aren't the only ones in the land which can not be paid, Michaela," Alan said with a wry smile, and her heart stopped beating for an instant when he used her given name. "If I do not inherit Cherbon, Roderick will demand my dues and I cannot pay him. This manor—your parents' land—will be forfeited, and Elizabeth and I will lose you."

"Oh my heavens!" Michaela gasped. "Oh, no! I can't . . ." She stopped, took a deep breath. "What shall we do? You *must* inherit!"

He gave her a smile that nearly made the shock of his dire announcement worth it. "I know. And I have come up with an idea that will allow you to stay with us forever, if you wish."

"Oh, yes! Of course, I wish! Do tell, my lord."

"I have already set in motion plans for a grand feast at Tornfield in one month, and after that night, regardless of whether my cousin is successful in his search or not, we will be safe." He paused. "Do you trust me, Michaela?" His words were like a caress.

"Yes," she whispered.

Alan leaned even closer to her over the tabletop. "Elizabeth can not lose you. *I* can not lose you. You *do* wish to stay with us, don't you? Truly?"

"I do, certainly, I do." She leaned in as well, her bosom biting into the table's edge, but she scarcely felt it. "More than anything."

His lips hovered a scant inch from hers. "As do I."

Alan's head moved closer.

Michaela leaned more heavily on the table and tilted her head.

The table toppled onto its side, knocking both would-be kissers to the floor and spilling the candle onto the rug.

Alan shouted, jumped to his feet nimbly, and stamped out the flames.

Michaela wanted to die, right there on the floor.

He helped her up with a shaky laugh. "Ah, well. Best not to get carried away in an improper manner, eh?"

"Ha-ha! Yes," Michaela agreed. *No!* she screamed inside her head. *No, no, no! Let's get carried away. Please, let's!*

But he was already walking her to the door. "Shall I escort you to your room?" Alan asked politely.

"There's no need for that," Michaela reluctantly declined, trying not to let her eyes stray to the big bed at the far end of the room. "I know the way."

"Of course you do." Alan smiled. He paused, took her hand, and then leaned in to press his lips—his warm, soft lips!—to her cheek. "Good night, Michaela. I wish you the sweetest dreams."

She gave him a genuine smile this time as he ushered her from the chamber. "Good night, my lord," she sighed around her dazed smile, too late for Alan to hear though, as the door had already closed behind her.

Michaela skipped the whole way of the corridor to her chamber, and only tripped once.

But it didn't count because she was alone.

Chapter Four

"I'm not going, Hugh."

"Oh, Rick, *come on!*" Hugh Gilbert flopped into the wide armchair in Roderick's chamber. "We've not left Cherbon since our arrival. I'm bored out of my very skull. Do I not have a bit of distraction, I do fear I'll start digging out my own eyes for sport."

"Shall I have a spoon fetched for you?"

"Witty tonight, are we?" Hugh threw himself from the chair once more and approached Roderick where he sprawled on the floor, stretching rather ineffectively on his own. Hugh dropped to one knee and pressed Roderick's left shoulder to the floor while he twisted his hip to the right, a hand on his thigh for added weight. "Relax your shoulders."

"I am," Roderick growled, the muscles of his back feeling like hammered iron along his spine.

"Well, try to relax them a bit more, then. All right, other side." He helped Roderick to readjust. "Any matter, the invitation clearly stated that the feast is to be held partially to celebrate your homecoming. It's rather rude for the guest of honor to refuse."

Roderick grunted. "I'm quite certain Alan Tornfield would prefer me dead upon some muddy field, now that he has chance to win Cherbon. A feast in my honor—horse shit."

"Well, then, don't you at least want to see what he is truly about? Stand up—we'll work on balance now."

"No, I don't." Roderick struggled to his feet, slapping Hugh's hand away as he balanced on his good leg. Hugh handed him his broad sword to hold in his left hand. Roderick balanced it on its tip for a moment, to steady his swaying. "I could not care less what piddling scheme Alan thinks he's come upon. He won't take Cherbon."

"He may, if you don't cease frightening off every eligible lady who darkens our door," Hugh said testily. "All right then, sword out." Roderick slowly raised the tip of the sword from the floor until it was perpendicular to his body. "Good, good, Rick—steady! Honestly, one would think you'd at least *try* to impress a woman the tiniest bit. It's not as if it's difficult to do, the poor creatures. A kind word, a smile. Must you always slink about the keep like some great, growling ogre?"

Roderick swayed and returned the sword tip to the floor to regain his balance and sent Hugh a black look. "How would you have me move about, Hugh? Shall I dance?"

"That *would* be refreshing."

"Shut up."

"*You* shut up. Once more with the sword on this side." Hugh held his hands at the ready to catch Roderick should he fall. "It would not kill you to at least be cordial."

"I've tried cordial, or have you forgotten?" The sword fell and rose again, slowly, but more steady in his right hand than it had been in months. Roderick felt a pang at the taunting memories he held of swinging this piece of metal as if it were a hollow wooden stick. "My attempts were wasted."

"Your smiles were grimaces, your topics of conversation dour and macabre. You shout at the servants at all hours of the day and night. It's unsettling."

"Are *you* unsettled by it?"

"Of course not. But I'm accustomed to it. Let's get your boots and we'll work on swing."

Roderick lowered the tip of the heavy weapon and hopped backward to sit in the armchair just behind him while Hugh brought his boots. "Then the one who marries me shall also become accustomed to it." He leaned his sword against the chair and began the daily struggle with his footwear.

"There is no one left to *get* accustomed to it," Hugh nearly shouted, then dropped to one knee again. He sighed crossly. "Get off, I'll do it."

"No." Roderick slapped Hugh's hands away. "I can dress myself."

"I never insinuated that you could not," Hugh said. He watched Roderick struggle with his left boot. "Your thirtieth birthday is"—he paused, one thumb touching the fingertips of one hand—"one hundred ninety-two days away, Rick. What are we to do should you not marry?"

Roderick did not answer him, only grunted as at last the left boot slid fully up to his knee.

"Fine then. Let us forget this whole lot in England, Rick," Hugh said quietly, emphatically. "To hell with Magnus. To hell with Alan Tornfield. To hell with *Cherbon!* There is no love lost between you and this land, and nothing left for me to lay claim to beyond debt. Together we can return to Constantinople and rebuild our army— your name is likened to a legend there for your bravery!

Our fortunes can be reclaimed on our own terms! There we can be princes—*kings!* I don't know about you, but I've always fancied myself as royalty."

Hugh let the bold statements hang in the silence for several moments while Roderick studied the floor between his boots. When Roderick still had no answer for his friend, Hugh continued.

"Here, all we have to look forward to, at best, is your unhappy marriage to some horse-faced, cast-off spinster woman. At worst, you won't marry at all and the two of us—as well as Leo—will be tossed out on our arses. What will become of him then, Rick? At least if you marry he has a chance of an inheritance. Would you have him a beggar child?"

"I won't let that happen, Hugh."

"Then at least go to the feast at Tornfield tonight," Hugh reasoned. "See what Alan is about. Mayhap if you employ but a tiny—*tiny*—bit of charm, you could find your future bride in a setting not so dreadful"—he waved a hand, indicating Roderick's dark and gloomy bedchamber—"as all this."

Roderick thought upon the suggestion for several moments, but then shook his head. If he was going to be stared at, he preferred it be in his own home, where he could escape if he wished.

"No. I'll not change my mind. But—"

"Rick!"

"*You go,* Hugh, in my stead," Roderick clarified. "Extend my regrets to my cousin and find out what you can."

Hugh stared wide-eyed at Roderick, as if he couldn't believe what he'd just heard. "Verily, Rick? You wish me to go?"

"I do. Most dreadfully, I do, if only to have a reprieve

from your incessant nagging and physical torture upon my person."

Hugh's face split into a wide grin, and Roderick felt a moment's guilt in realizing that Hugh rarely showed his teeth lately beyond a sarcastic smirk to anyone other than Leo.

"Smashing," Hugh said, and shot to his feet. "Brilliant idea, Rick! I'll leave directly, and will return on the morrow." Hugh seemed to be spinning thoughts in his head, speaking aloud but not really expecting a reply. "I shall wear the green—no, *blue*—tunic. And my red cape and boots. Or the buff . . . ?"

"I'm certain you'll look very comely. Now, get out," Roderick growled.

"But, what of the physical torture? We haven't finished your exercises." Hugh frowned.

"If we continue, you'll not have time to ready yourself. I'm sure you wish to bathe."

"God's teeth—you're right! I smell like a goatherd." Hugh spun to the door then spun back to Roderick as if so caught up with excitement that he'd gone brainless. "But Leo—?"

"Send him to me before you depart. Surely we can stand each other's company for one evening."

Hugh grew still, even in the whirlwind of anticipation. "He'll like that very much, Rick."

Roderick waved him away and did not meet his eyes.

"I'll send him up in a thrice." A pause. "You're certain you can—"

"I'm not completely helpless, Hugh."

"Of course you're not," Hugh said quietly, and Roderick felt a pinch of humiliation at the placating tone. "I've never, never thought that of you—how could I?" Hugh sighed when he received no·answer. "I'll see you on the morrow, Rick—with gossip aplenty, I hope."

* * *

Michaela pulled Elizabeth along the corridor behind the kitchens, both girls with their hands over their mouths to stifle the giggles—well, Michaela's giggles. No merry sound came from behind Elizabeth's hand, although her mouth was pulled deep into her cheeks in a grin and her eyes sparkled. They stopped behind a set of tall wooden shelves, just before the doorway to the noisy, smoky, fragrant kitchen.

Michaela turned her head to Elizabeth with a finger to her mouth, then she pulled on one ear and pointed toward the doorway.

Listen!

"—take six of us to move this cake. Merciful savior, I've never seen such a prideful thing. To think of all the foodstuffs wasted on such a frivolous—"

"Oh, pooh! 'Tis been a fair piece of time since the lord's been s'happy. Good for him, I say. Huzzah to the lord and his new bride."

At Michaela's side, Elizabeth gripped her arm. Michaela turned to see the little girl's mouth hung open in a shocked O. Elizabeth snaked an arm about Michaela's waist as the two continued to listen.

"Huzzah, indeed. 'Tis scandalous, is what it is. I fail to see how he could just up and marry her, on this very night, with no time of betrothal! *Her!*"

"They've known each other long enough—why delay it, when all will be gathered tonight to witness it? And Lady Elizabeth is in sore want of a mother."

A disgusted snort. "Not of that sort, I daresay. A nasty bit of work, that one."

Elizabeth made as if to pull away from Michaela and charge through the doorway, but Michaela pulled her back.

"It is of no consequence what they say, Elizabeth," Michaela whispered with a smile. "What do we care for what they think, eh? The only thing that matters is that my suspicions were correct—and now we can be together, like a real family, forever."

The angry frown melted away from Elizabeth's face, to be replaced by a wondrous smile. She pulled away gently this time and did a slow spin with her skirts held out, her eyes closing briefly as if in rapture.

"You look beautiful," Michaela whispered. "Like a princess." And it was true. Michaela was doubly glad she'd created the new ensemble she herself now wore. Since Lady Juliette had stained her one good gown, and the lovely boon she'd won from the woman was delivered in pieces, Michaela had used a bit of imagination and combined the two. Now, her rose-colored satin skirt was quilted over with long, wide strips of the dark green velvet, strategically and evenly covering the stains. The colors alternated like a maypole and Michaela had to admit that the effect was striking. With the pieces of the green bodice, she'd fashioned a beautiful short, lace-up vest to go over her own gown, allowing her long, wide rose sleeves to show.

For the first time in her life, Michaela was thankful that her family had been too poor to employ a full-time seamstress.

Michaela hoped Lady Juliette had been invited to the feast so that she could see the rather ingenious use of the gown she'd sought to cheat Michaela out of.

It would be Michaela's wedding gown.

Elizabeth stopped her twirling and stepped close to

Michaela. She placed one small palm first over her own heart, and then reached out to touch Michaela's chest.

Michaela felt emotion well into her eyes. "I love you, too, Elizabeth," she whispered in a cracking voice. Then the faint sounds of strings being plucked into tune reached her ears and she hastily wiped at her eyes while donning a bright smile. "Let's carry on to the hall—the musicians have arrived and I don't wish to miss one moment of this feast."

Michaela just knew it was going to be the greatest night in the whole of her life.

The meal dragged on what seemed like forever, but Michaela didn't mind in the least. She was enjoying sitting at the lord's table, Elizabeth between her and Alan, the flood of the guests poured into Tornfield's hall admiring the three of them.

And her heart did an evil, prideful little dance to see Lady Juliette of Osprey indeed sitting at one of the front tables. Michaela made sure to acknowledge the wretch with a slight nod and sweet smile. To her surprise, Lady Juliette returned the gesture and even added an admiring glance at Michaela's vest.

Of course she will be only pleasant to me now, Michaela reasoned. *I will be her better, and the lady of the keep. Soon she will be a guest in* my *home.*

And it was then that Michaela decided to forgive Lady Juliette for all her past slights, and she felt a burden she'd not known she was carrying slide from her back.

Agatha Fortune was right—forgiveness was a happy balm to the soul.

As if to affirm the adage, Michaela's gaze swept to where

her parents were seated—at a table of honor, with Lady Juliette, no less. Michaela'd had no time to speak with her mother or father, but she made sure to wave several times and blow her father a discreet kiss from one finger.

They, as usual, looked very happy. As if they'd not a single care in the world.

The clang of dishes being cleared competed with the music, and was soon cushioned by the oohing of the guests. From the left side of the hall, two strapping young serving boys carried out an impossibly large tray, covered edge to edge in what had to be the biggest cake ever served outside of London. Elizabeth shot to her feet to look down upon the masterpiece as it was set slowly and carefully on a heretofore empty table before the lord's dais. Michaela—striving for an air of maturity—did not stand, although she did lean forward eagerly.

The shallow, wide cake was shaped like a battle shield, covered in swirls of pattern made from crushed nuts, mimicking perfectly the Cherbon crest, and decorated with the tiniest sprigs of late ferns and autumn leaves. Bouquets of dyed feathers and ribbon adorned the corners like fantastic fountains. It looked too beautiful to be a confection meant to be eaten.

When the cake was at last safely deposited on the table, the servant boys stepped away, Alan stood, and the guests broke into applause. Alan let them go on for a few moments, smiling and nodding his head as he looked about the blanket of expectant and curious faces. Then he raised both hands, begging silence.

"Good evening, friends. Thank you all for making the journey to Tornfield this night. It is with a light and joyful heart that I and my family"—he swept an arm to his right, indicating Elizabeth and Michaela, and Michaela's heart skipped—"welcome you to our home, to share in a very happy event."

Beneath the table, Elizabeth's hand snaked on to Michaela's thigh and seized her hand tightly. Michaela squeezed back.

"Of course I speak for us all in expressing regret that our liege, Lord Roderick Cherbon, was unable to attend tonight due to personal business that demanded his attention. I would have liked very much for him to be with us."

Surely he must be a saint, Michaela thought, *to speak such kind words about the Cherbon Devil. My husband is a good, good man.*

"But I will extend a hearty welcome to his first man, Sir Hugh Gilbert, also just returned from the Holy Land." Alan put his hands together and the rest of the guests followed suit as a dark-haired, tall, and slender man stood from the table where Lady Juliette and Michaela's parents also sat.

From Michaela's vantage point on the raised dais, it was clear to see the commotion Sir Hugh Gilbert caused within the female population. Michaela herself was surprised at the man's handsomeness, and his dress was superb—costly and fine. His black hair was trimmed close to his scalp, and he sported a very short beard—little more than heavy shadow, actually. Michaela could see the dark rim of thick lashes around his eyes from her seat. Below her, women companions craned their neck to catch a clearer glimpse of the stranger and then leaned their heads together, twittering excitedly.

And Sir Hugh seemed quite aware of the attention he was garnering, for as he spoke, he let his eyes stray from Alan's figure and rove over the appreciative crowd, as if he was a minstrel, readying to recite dramatic verse for an eager audience.

"My dear Lord Tornfield, Lord Cherbon wishes me to extend his deepest and most heartfelt regrets that he could not personally answer your gracious call to feast with you and your guests. He wishes for me to assure you all that he is ready to fulfill the void left in the demesne by his father's death, and as such, his many responsibilities oft keep him engaged. Rest assured though, that he is at your service should you but ask for his assistance." This well-spoken and dazzling man bowed slightly in Alan's direction. "Lord Tornfield, you have my own personal thanks for your gracious and warm hospitality." He sat.

Michaela saw a somewhat bemused smile come over Alan's face. "Sir Hugh, if you would indulge me, Lord Cherbon is not . . . *ill,* is he?"

Hugh stood once more. "Not at all, Lord Tornfield. The very epitome of health." He began to sit.

"Forgive me, but I—*we all*—had heard that he was wounded most dire in the Holy Land. I thought mayhap his injuries—"

Hugh stood erect again, slowly, and pinned Alan with what Michaela saw as an overly haughty look.

"I can assure you that any injuries Lord Cherbon sustained do not hinder his abilities to rule in any manner whatsoever. But I will most certainly relay your kind inquiry after his health to him. I'm certain he will be touched by your . . . concern." Sir Hugh sat once more.

Michaela could not help but feel slightly piqued—as though in some nearly undetectable manner, this Sir Hugh Gilbert had managed to chastise Alan in his own hall, at his own feast.

Michaela decided she did not like this man, handsome or not, one tiny bit.

Alan cleared his throat. "Very fine. Thank you, Sir Hugh." He looked back to the crowd. "And now, for the main purpose of our gathering."

All thoughts of the pompous knight flew from Michaela's head and her stomach clenched. She caught her mother's eye and winked. Agatha sent her a kind, if rather confused, smile.

"As you all know, my daughter and I have been on our own following the tragic and untimely death of my wife. Tornfield Manor has been lacking in a lady's touch, and my daughter lacking for the close bond of a mother. I mean to remedy that this very night."

At Michaela's side, Elizabeth was nearly bouncing in her seat.

"It is customary to gather all together for the announcement of betrothal, and in that I will not disappoint, save that the period of engagement for myself and my new bride will likely be the shortest on record. Friar Cope?" A robed man Michaela was well-familiar with materialized from the shadows of a perimeter wall and made his way to stand near the magnificent Cherbon cake. The audience gasped.

"Indeed." Alan smiled proudly. "For on this night not only do I announce my intent to wed, I will have it done before you all as my witnesses." The proclamation sounded strange to Michaela's ears but she paid it no heed, so consumed with joy and excitement was she.

Michaela wanted to gain her feet in anticipation of Alan's announcement, but restrained her anxiousness until his next words. She drew a deep, steadying breath.

"It is with great pride that I present to you all the next Lady Tornfield, Lady Juliette of Osprey."

For a moment, Michaela thought she'd misheard Alan because of the thunderous applause that vibrated the stone walls of the hall. But a croaking sound to her left, a sound that was quiet and strangled and should have been unheard in the din, cut through the roar of approval from the guests as well as the screaming in Michaela's own head. She turned her head slowly, slowly, as if in a dream, to see Elizabeth duck under the table and run to stand before her father, tears streaming down her pale face.

"Pa—" she croaked. "Pa-pa, no! You said the . . . *wrong name.* Michaela said . . . you were to marry *her!*"

The only sounds following the shocking words were the pounding of Michaela's own heart and the hushed breaths of the guests.

Then Lady Juliette stood from her seat, and smiled at the girl. "Come now, dear—your father would not marry Miss Fortune. You and I will get along brilliantly."

Alan, however had dropped to his knees before his daughter and grasped her shoulders. Michaela looked at his wide, welling eyes as if she were still caught in some lucid dream that was quickly becoming a nightmare.

"Elizabeth—you spoke! My darling girl, I—"

Elizabeth jerked out of his hands. "Say it's not true, Papa. You love *Michaela.* Say!"

Alan swallowed and his eyes flicked over Elizabeth's shoulder to Michaela, who could not seem to breathe at that moment. "I am marrying Lady Juliette, my love. But Lady Michaela will—"

"No!" Elizabeth shouted and then turned to Michaela, who could do nothing but stare back helplessly.

Then the little girl ran from the hall. Michaela wanted to follow her, but could not command her legs to move. Alan was still looking at her. The hall was deathly silent.

Then the clicking of heels caused both Michaela and Alan to turn. Lady Juliette stood before the table, her brows drawn slightly. "My lord, do you wish to postpone the ceremony?" she asked quietly. "I do not wish for—"

"No," Alan interrupted, and rose to stand. With one final, strangely pleading glance at Michaela, he joined Juliette and the friar, while Michaela's throat tightened, tightened, and the usually ignored metal link beneath her dress seemed to be burning a hole into her flesh.

And when kind Friar Cope cleared his throat and began to speak, when Alan took Juliette's hand, his back to Michaela, now sitting alone at the lord's table, Michaela's heart shattered into a hundred thousand pieces.

Chapter Five

Michaela took to her bed for two days, not rising to eat, to wash, and she made little reply to either of her parents who checked on her frequently.

The fact that she lay in the bed she thought never to cradle her again was enough to sink her into the very dregs of a deep depression. Each time her eyes opened from exhausted sleep, she saw and heard the events of the feast on her last evening at Tornfield Manor like some sort of sick, contrary dream that only occurred while she was awake.

She'd left that very night, returning to the Fortune household with her parents, not even taking time to pack her few belongings or seek out Elizabeth for a good-bye. She felt cowardly and traitorous for that. She had been too hurt, too mortified, too . . . destroyed.

She never wanted to leave this room again.

A soft rap upon her door caused Michaela to burrow deeper into her pillow and pull the covers up over her head. Perhaps if she feigned sleep, whoever knocked would simply go away.

"Michaela?" It was her father this time, and she heard the

creak of the floorboards as he stepped into the room, and then the door scraping to. "Are you awake?"

Michaela did not reply, squeezing her eyes shut beneath the canopy of blanket, praying he would leave her.

But she felt the mattress dip as Walter sat on the side of her bed.

"Your mother is very worried for you, child," he said quietly. "Would that you at least come take a meal so she does not think you to waste away to nothing."

"I hope that I do," Michaela said bitterly, thinking that she had not wanted to speak, but the words were out of her mouth before she could stop them. She knew her tone was childish.

Her father's hand was warm on her calf through the thin blanket. "Oh, Michaela," he sighed. "I know that you are hurt, and for that I am sorry. But hiding away in your chamber for years and years will not undo what has happened."

"I know that, Papa," she said. "But if I stay here, I don't have to face anyone."

"What have you to be shamed of?" Walter demanded. "You did naught wrong."

"What have I to be—?" Michaela snapped the covers off her head to look at her father, graying, portly, kind-faced. "I told Elizabeth that her father was going to *marry me*. I told her that we were going to be a family. And she believed me, trusted me. I made a fool out of myself before all the land. 'Poor Miss Fortune, that she would think a handsome man like Lord Alan would marry *her!*' 'Tis bad enough that everyone talks about us like they do. I'll never be able to show my face after this!"

"Nonsense," Walter scoffed. "You told no one save Elizabeth your suspicions, and what she said at the feast, everyone likely took as the innocent assumptions of a young, troubled girl."

"Oh, Papa," Michaela sighed. "You don't understand."

Walter gave her a smile. "I understand more than you think I do. I, too, know what it's like, having people say mean-spirited things about you and your family. Things that are untrue. Think you I am deaf, or slow-witted?"

"Of course not," Michaela said. "But it never seems to bother you, Papa. Me, it—"

"It crushes, I know. But Michaela," he implored, "the folk did not always hold the opinion of me and your mother that they do now. Granted, I was always looked upon with scorn, but for different reasons. Your mother, now, she was once highly revered and respected in the shire."

Michaela was intrigued. Her father had never spoken about the past, before Michaela was born. She held no hope that it would help her in her current situation, but she wanted him to keep talking. She sat up. "Tell me."

Walter nodded once. "I do not relish it, but all right. Perhaps it will allow you to understand a little better our station, and how we came to be here. Perhaps it will help you to bear your burden more easily.

"When your mother and I were married, you may be surprised to know that the only man I owed allegiance to was the king."

Michaela's eyebrows rose.

"Indeed. I was one of William's most favored lords, and he used me well. Not even to God—especially not to God— did I give a bended knee. I held a vast tract of land in the north of England for my loyalty, but before I could make a home there I was sent to Cherbonshire to help Magnus Cherbon gain control over his demesne for the king."

Michaela gasped. "You were in league with the Cherbon Devil?"

"I was, although I am not proud to say it aloud. Your mother's parents were vassal to Magnus Cherbon, and the instant I saw her lovely face, heard her speak, I knew I must have her.

"She was a godly woman, but light of spirit, sharp of tongue and wit. And lovely. Oh, my dear, your mother in her youth was dazzling. It was no hard task to convince her father to give her to me, a favored warrior of the king, and a man who was destined for greatness, even if he was rumored to be harsh and bloodthirsty."

Michaela couldn't help the chirp of laughter. "You, Papa?"

But there was no merriment in Walter's eyes. "Yes, Michaela, me. In assisting Magnus Cherbon, many a man went to his grave by way of the sword that hangs in our hall. I was ruthless in my ambition to become the greatest, most powerful lord outside of the king's court. Greater even than the man I aided, Magnus Cherbon. I remember all too clearly my vow to the king: 'A man a day by my sword until this land submits to your rule.'"

Walter looked down at his lap as if the memory shamed him. "And I kept my word. No trials. Pleas of innocence and for mercy fell on the ground before blood. And when I had succeeded, when Cherbon at last knew an uneasy and fearful peace, I knew my glory was at hand. I was to bide the winter here, in this house we live in, with your mother until the spring. William had granted me license to build a grand castle on my land in the north country. Your mother was heavy with you, and so after you were born and we saw that you would live, we were to make the long journey to our new home."

"But we never left."

"Almost, but no. No, we didn't." Walter sighed. "When your mother went missing that winter, for the first time in my selfish life I felt fear for another human being. I was mad with worry, and could only think of seeing her again, safe. It took me two days until I realized what I must do, and when I did, you were returned to me. I had made a promise, and one that I would keep."

Michaela knew a bit of this part of the tale, when Walter had knelt in the village chapel and begged God to bring his wife back to him. But she still didn't understand how this had anything to do with her own problem.

"My time in Cherbon was done, and when the spring came, we set out—the three of us, and my most trusted men. On our second day of travel, I was summoned to the king's court. He wanted me to assist in quelling a small up-rising en route to my lands. But the man he'd known before Cherbon was not the man who stood before him. I refused. I told him that I would never fight again."

"What happened, Papa?"

"Well, he did what any king in possession of good sense would do, faced with a subject who held valuable property and rights from him but would not fight." Walter raised his eyes. "He stripped me of my lands, and my license. Sent me back to Cherbonshire to live here, in the least of the holdings."

"That seems rather unfair," Michaela said in his defense.

"Not unfair at all. Generous, really," Walter argued. "He could have had me killed, my dear, for refusing him thusly after all the favors I had won. Instead, my punishment was to live out my days in the land I had painted with my own sword, under the distant heel of the Cherbon Devil. But it was your and your mother's punishment as well, you see, that affected me so much more deeply. Agatha ridiculed, you shunned. I am paying for my barbarity, still. But I know the truth, and so I am at peace.

"Which is what you need to accept, daughter," Walter said, at last bringing his shocking tale back to Michaela. "Your own truth. Hold it inside of you and honor what you know is right and fair and good. *You* are right and fair and good. Angels watch you, watch over you—I do truly believe. You will find your place in this life yet, Michaela. It has only not been revealed."

She felt none the more enlightened by her father's sad tale of loss and humility. In fact she was more piqued, and something was bothering her to no end. "But Papa, did not Magnus Cherbon wish to aid in your plight after you had helped him secure his own demesne? Surely he would repay you."

Walter chuckled. "Oh, no. Magnus was more than happy with the station I had been given. Although he'd heard that I had given up the sword, it always turned in his mind that I would one day take up my blade again. In a bigger hold, I could have revolted against him and usurped his place."

"Papa, truly?" Michaela said skeptically, although it was not like Walter to boast.

"Truly. I could have disposed of Magnus Cherbon within a week's time had I the will."

Michaela was stunned. And a little perturbed that her father had sentenced them all to this poverty and humbling station. Surely God did not wish them to suffer so?

"You will marry one day, Michaela," Walter continued. "And when you do, you will be removed from this place, into your own life. The life you lived at Tornfield was not yours—you were only borrowing it. You will forget what you now feel for Lord Alan."

"How I wish I could," Michaela sighed. Although she would have vowed she hated Alan Tornfield, she missed him desperately already, and hated herself for that. And Elizabeth . . . She felt a burning desire to repay Alan for shattering her dreams and ripping her away from sweet Elizabeth. "I hate him, Papa. He is a cruel liar and he played me false."

Walter tilted his head as if what his daughter had said interested him. "Did he, though?"

She did not want to meet his probing eyes and was glad when another knock sounded at the door, and Agatha entered, carrying a woven basket.

"Oh, Michaela!" Agatha set the basket at the bedside and grasped her daughter's hands. "You have come out of your burrow, at last!"

"Only for a moment, Mother," Michaela said as Agatha embraced her. "I still have yet to decide what I am to do."

"Of course, of course. And until you do, you may go through your things from Tornfield. They were sent over this morn by Lady Juliette with a note. Wasn't that thoughtful of her ladyship?" Agatha waved a hand toward the basket on the floor.

Michaela groaned and fell back onto the mattress, yanking the covers over her head once more. She wanted not one piece of anything she had so much as touched at Tornfield. It was bad enough that the now-hated rose-and-green gown lay wadded in the corner of her chamber. Her mother's voice taunted her from beyond the blanket.

"Oh, here are your nightclothes, and a pair of aprons, and—what's this?" Michaela heard the crackle of parchment. "My goodness, it looks a royal decree, 'tis so fancy!"

Michaela peeked out from the covers to find her mother

holding a wrinkled piece of parchment. She immediately knew what it was, and memories of that intimate night in Lord Alan's chamber flooded her so that she thought she would start crying once more. Oh, she hated, hated, *hated* that man!

"Burn it," she said, hiding once more. She had no wish to see the pathetic plea that had prompted Lord Alan to marry that wretched, nasty, beastly Juliette. And, un-Christian or not, she did not care in the least if Lord Roderick Cherbon ever found a wife!

Michaela snatched the covers down once more and all but ripped the parchment from her mother's hand. She stared at it a long time.

And then Michaela smiled.

Chapter Six

If there was one positive thing that had come from Alan Tornfield marrying, it was that his wedding feast had prompted three more ladies to come to Cherbon in hopes of becoming Roderick's very wealthy wife. Roderick suspected the women had been dazzled by Hugh's handsomeness and charm and had hoped that Roderick would be equally as engaging. But of the three newest ingénues, one had not had the courage to come over Cherbon's drawbridge after glimpsing the dark castle, and one had made it only to the bailey and the entrance of the hall before losing her nerve, leaving only one to successfully hear Hugh's interrogation and have her trunks installed in a chamber.

She had been here a pair of days, this new woman—whatever she was called—and Roderick had kept his distance, hoping that the girl would have space to accustom herself to the dank and morbid air of Cherbon before he thrust his own beastly presence upon her.

But time was running out for Roderick, and so two days was all he could allow her. They would meet today, and perhaps the face Roderick looked upon would be the face of his bride. Obviously she possessed more fortitude than the others—only one had been in residence more than two days, and that woman had been nearly three score—her hearing and eyesight failing.

Remembering that desperate spinster caused Roderick to chuckle darkly.

He found his chair at the lord's table in the great hall, pleased that his orders to have a roaring blaze in the square, open hearth had been obeyed precisely. He knew he was strict and unyielding with the servants, but Magnus Cherbon had obviously been correct in his method of handling the manor staff. The instant he'd died and left Cherbon unattended, the folk had turned savage, vandalizing and stealing from the very castle that had been their home.

A firm hand was called for, and Roderick was in prime mental condition to rule over his past—everyone and everything in it.

He stretched out his left leg to take the pressure off his knee in the quiet of the hall—he'd commanded that he was to be left completely and utterly alone when he was about during the day, unless he specifically called for attendance.

"Bellowed, rather," Hugh liked to say exasperatingly.

As if thinking of his best friend had produced him, Hugh came through the arched doorway that led from the east wing, Leo spinning his plump legs over the smooth stones before him in his typical dash-about fashion.

He would be three very soon, Roderick marveled to himself. Three years—nearly one year since he'd left his mother behind in Constantinople, so young that Leo had stopped crying for her long ago, likely remembered naught of her. But Roderick had not forgotten Aurelia—how could he? The little boy's joyful eyes over his wide smile reminded Roderick of Aurelia in that instant, and his heart did a traitorous skip.

"Wod-wick," Leo called, flying to the table's edge and catching himself just short of Roderick, his little fist gripping a table leg to swing to a stop. He always looked so eager. "Gooday, Wod-wick."

"Good day, Leo," Roderick said.

The boy edged closer, stretched out a hand tentatively, and patted Roderick's left leg gently. His face was hopeful. "Ee-oh sit now?"

"No," Roderick said, his discomfiture causing him to frown. "Not today. I . . . I am quite harried today with keep business. I'm sure you understand," he said gruffly, his words echoing in the empty room, across the empty table and empty floor.

"Run along to the kitchens, Maggot," Hugh said, taking the boy's hand and turning his face toward him. "See if you can't wheedle a biscuit from Cook to go along with your meal."

"All wite, Hoo," Leo said cheerfully, but looked back to Roderick before he left, his face growing solemn once more. "Gooday, Wod-wick."

"Good day, Leo," Roderick replied, and watched the boy dash to the opposite end of the hall.

"She's on her way," was Hugh's morning greeting as Leo left them. "Leo and I passed her in the corridor. Are you unnerved?"

"No, I'm not unnerved," Roderick scoffed. "Why would I be unnerved?"

Hugh shrugged.

"Is she comely?" Roderick asked suddenly.

"I daresay no," Hugh said, an eyebrow raising. "But she seems to have most of her teeth, so that's something."

Roderick huffed a mirthless laugh. Oh, what he had been reduced to! More money than the church and yet he was naught but a beggar in this arena.

Then Hugh set to his usual round of criticism. "God's teeth, Rick, must you wear that blasted cloak, always? And I thought you were to have Harliss trim your hair last night."

"That was your idea, not mine. I'd no sooner let Harliss near me with a blade as I would dash through Henry's court in my skin."

"Now, that I would like to see." Hugh chuckled.

"I wear the cloak because it's mine and I wish it."

"You wear it because you are ashamed. At least lower the hood when you're alone or with me. Christly goodness."

"I warn you, Hugh, you go too far." But Roderick shoved the hood back onto his shoulders, feeling uncomfortably exposed. In truth, he'd become so accustomed to his costume that he donned the covering out of habit and never noticed it.

"Someone must," was all Hugh said, quickly. Then his eyes darted toward the kitchen and Roderick turned to see a tall woman in a drab dress the color of old bones. Even from this distance, the figure was skeletal.

Already Roderick imagined that sharing a bed with the woman would be like being tossed onto in a pile of sharpened sticks. He sighed. In his condition, he'd never bed her any matter.

"Please, Rick—I beg of you—do not trouble yourself to frighten her. For all our sakes."

The journey to Cherbon was a long one—the miles and the hours tangling together and rolling along the rutted dirt road under Michaela's feet. But the time between when the sun had risen two hours into their journey until now when it was high in the sky had given Michaela time at last to think upon her impetuous—and perhaps childish—decision.

She was offering herself in marriage to the Cherbon Devil. Well, the son of the Cherbon Devil, at any rate. A scarred beast of a man now, according to Alan and the rumors slipping from everyone's tongues. It was to be a repayment, on many, many levels, in Michaela's mind, for not only would it crush Alan Tornfield should he not inherit Cherbon, but it would take from the coffers the coin Michaela felt was long-owed to her family.

Blood money. And no matter how grotesque, how foul, how brutish Roderick Cherbon turned out to be, Michaela had vowed that she would marry him. She had to. There were debts that demanded repayment.

Michaela was bone-weary of letting her own life run her over. She had tried to be a good person, a good daughter—obedient, meek, kind. And all it had gotten her was kicked and stepped on. Well, no more. She was a different woman now, with a different life just waiting for her at Cherbon.

Even so, wild imaginings of what awaited her at the demesne seat ran through her mind as if she were a young girl once more, scared of a summer storm, or the shadows across her bedchamber floor. And this new, mature woman was heartened that both her parents accompanied her in the family's small wagon on the long journey, Walter remembering the way still, although he'd not laid eyes upon Cherbon in years.

They topped a small rise and, ahead, looming like a foggy, black specter even in the brightness of midday, the jagged battlements and craggy inner keep of Cherbon rose out of the surrounding gentle countryside like its own malevolent mountain range.

The wagon rolled to a stop and all three Fortunes stared at the castle in silence, Walter being first to speak after a long, tense moment.

"Are you certain, Michaela?" was all he asked.

Michaela swallowed down the lump in her throat. "Yes, Papa. I'm certain." *But, please, let's go before I lose my resolve.*

In just shy of an hour, they clattered across Cherbon's lowered drawbridge, passing through vine-covered walls of the barbican that were easily twenty feet thick, damp with fog and moss and foliage as if enchanted. Here, at ground level, mist seemed to hang as if they had passed from the real world of the surrounding English countryside into a dark realm of fairy lore.

Though no one had called out to them as they approached the castle or passed under the raised gate, prompting Michaela to wonder that the whole place wasn't abandoned, they saw serfs aplenty about the bailey, busy with a myriad of tasks. But the wide inner grounds were eerily somber; no one spoke or shouted or called to a friend, no workday songs were sung. Even the clangs from what sounded like a smithy's shop were oddly muffled.

And everyone completely ignored the three people rolling through the bailey in the cart.

Walter was maneuvering their conveyance around the south side of the inner compound when the stilted silence of the bailey was breached by a muffled shriek.

The door to the keep flew open and a tall, malnourished-looking woman burst through the doorway in a billow of drab skirt, frantically snatching up the thin material while dashing away from the keep. She ran toward the cart seemingly as fast as she could command her legs, her eyes full of terror and her mouth pulled wide. She fairly flew past the Fortunes with nary a glance, and Michaela turned to watch the woman disappear into the dark throat of the barbican.

She jumped back to attention when the keep door slammed shut, echoing in the bailey.

None of the serfs had made a move to assist the woman, only stared in mild curiosity until she was gone. And then they had taken up their work once more.

"Michaela . . ." Agatha began in a warbling, worried voice.

But Michaela knew that if she allowed her mother to speak aloud the fears racing through her own mind, she would never descend from the cart and do what had to be done. She gathered up her skirts, the now-wrinkled decree from the Lord of Cherbon still gripped tightly in her fist, and hopped to the ground.

"Wait here," she tossed over her shoulder to her parents, and was proud of the calm, assured tone that came out of her mouth. She straightened her spine and marched toward the keep, ready to do battle with the devil.

And suddenly, the door was before her, tall and wide and thick and solid. And suddenly again, it was more than a door. It was her unsure future.

She knocked.

Michaela's hand had barely ceased rapping when the door began to inch open and a man's voice called out.

"Oh, changed your mind, have you? Well, that's simply too bad. You'll—" A sliver of a face appeared in the opening, half hidden in shadow. Their eyes seemed to travel past Michaela and scan the bailey behind her, as if looking for the fled woman. Then she was pinned by their gaze, sparkling in the darkness. "What do *you* want?"

Oh, he *was* going to be a nasty one.

Michaela gathered her courage and offered the missive to the crack in the door. "Lord Cherbon, I presume?"

The parchment was snatched from her hand and in a moment the man gave a shout of laughter. He seemed to address the hall behind him.

"We've another contestant yet, Rick! Poor little poppet—she thinks *I'm you!*" The door swung open wide. "Welcome to Cherbon, Miss Fortune."

Roderick still stood in the shadows, where he had been en route to his chambers when Hugh's greeting of their unexpected visitor reached his ears.

Was it some specter come to call? Hugh's odd sense of humor often prompted outrageous bits of nonsense from his mouth, but surely he would not jest so about welcoming misfortune to Cherbon.

They'd had enough of that bastard already.

But then the door swung wide, emitting the weak foggy sunlight from the bailey, and Roderick saw the woman silhouetted in the doorway. He stepped back onto the lowest riser of the stair, disappearing completely into the darkness of the tall corridor.

"Well, come in, come in!" Hugh commanded exasperatedly, sweeping his arm wide.

The woman hesitated and glanced behind her. "My trunk—my parents . . ."

"Are you of age?" When the woman nodded hesitantly, Hugh gave a put-out sigh and leaned past her to shout through the doorway, "I've no time at all to deal with you. Yes, yes, she'll be fine. Just toss the trunk over the side, then, thanks. Good day." Then he pulled the woman in by her arm and closed the door firmly.

Hugh all but dragged the woman to the lord's table, peering toward the corridor where Roderick was hidden away. "Oh, you've just missed him," Hugh lamented to the woman—little more than a girl, Roderick now saw. Hugh spun a low stool about, released the woman's arm and patted the seat. "Here you are," he said as he turned and flopped into Roderick's own chair, already reaching for a stack of parchment and quill.

The woman stood there for a moment, as if unsure she would stay, and Roderick took those spare seconds to look at her.

She was . . . enchanting. Her hair was blond, no . . . a reddish—no, *blond,* tied back at either temple and then together into one long plait. She was not slender, but not plump, her back smooth and trim in her gown. Perhaps a bit shorter than average.

Her profile mesmerized Roderick—softly rounded cheeks colored with a flush of disconcertment, brow wrinkled delicately, her mouth pinched into a stingy bud. Her ears were like tiny shells, pale and perfect.

Surely she could not be here to answer his call.

"Well?" Hugh demanded. "Are you going to sit or aren't you? If you've already changed your mind then you should run, run, run—your parents are likely over the drawbridge by now. I'm certain it's a long walk to"—he looked in disdain at her simple gown—"wherever it is you're from. Not Tornfield any longer, I reckon."

The woman stood there a moment longer. "Thank you for your concern, but I think I shall stay." Closer now to Roderick's ears, her voice sounded like a breeze over a rippling stream—refreshing and light and sweet. She sat.

"Very good." Hugh took the quill at the ready. "Name? I assume you are not legally called Miss Fortune . . . are you?"

"Lady Michaela Fortune," she supplied. "My parents are Walter and Agatha. We are vassal to the Tornfield hold, on the south most edge of the shire."

Fortune, Roderick thought to himself. *I know that surname.*

"Ah! So you *are* actually Miss Fortune." Hugh seemed quite pleased with that bit of information as he scribbled. "Age?"

"A score and one, come January."

"So, one score, *now.*"

Lady Michaela's mouth pinched again. "Yes. Sorry."

"Have you been or are you now married?"

"No."

"I daresay I already knew the answer to that one, didn't I? Ha! Children?"

"None."

"Sickness?"

"I beg your pardon?"

Hugh sighed. "The clap, leprosy, weeping sores, lazy eye—are you *ill?*"

"Oh. No. I'm quite healthy."

"Wanted by the law?"

"I should hope not!" she exclaimed as if horrified.

"I must ask, you understand. You'd be surprised how—any matter." Hugh lay down the quill and leaned back in the chair to scrutinize Lady Michaela Fortune. "The terms of the agreement, as you likely have already read—you *can* read, I assume?"

Roderick saw one slender eyebrow raise. "A bit, yes."

"Very good. Ninety *consecutive*—that means all-in-a-row, one-after-the-other—days at Cherbon, while your suitability as a potential bride is determined. During that time, you will assume the duties of lady and evaluate the compatibility between you and Lord Cherbon. If, at the end of ninety days—which I must tell you I doubt highly you will endure—all the criteria have been met and it is agreeable to both you and the lord, you will be wed. Your prize will then be legally recorded and dispensed. Do you understand?"

"Yes, I—"

"Good. Any questions?"

"Well, may—?"

"Fine. Sign here." He shoved the parchment and quill at the young woman who took them and quickly scribbled along the bottom of the page. Then Hugh snatched the items away once more before shooting from his seat and heading toward where Roderick still hid. "Come along, come along—I will show you to your chamber."

Roderick stepped from the stairs and ducked underneath the cubby behind them just before Hugh and a trotting Lady Fortune entered the corridor and swished above. The air behind the woman smelled like freshly mown hay.

"But my trunk—" the woman was arguing with Hugh's back.

"Yes, yes, I'm sure there are many valuables in it. We'll have it sent up. In the meantime you can make do with what the last one left about the chamber . . ."

Roderick stood in the darkness, his heart pounding, pounding, while the fresh, green fragrance of Michaela Fortune hung in the shadows around him like a warning.

Chapter Seven

The chamber was absolutely dreadful. Though sumptu-
ously appointed with expensive fabrics and furnishings,
Michaela felt smothered by feelings of despair and fear as
soon as she followed Sir Hugh Gilbert through the doorway.
She shivered so violently that she stumbled on her feet.

Hugh Gilbert cocked a wry eyebrow at her before continuing in the lecture he'd begun in the hall below. "Meals are
taken thrice a day. Lonely affairs, but the food is passable.
Necessary rooms are down the hall past your door about
three score steps. I'd use the one on the right if I were you.
The servants slip into the left-hand one—as if I don't
know—and their diet leaves a rather unpleasant atmosphere
to follow."

There was so much to take in, almost as if Michaela had
landed in a foreign country and had only an hour to learn the
customs of the natives. "Necessary rooms?"

"Oh, you know." Hugh sighed, and rolled his eyes to the
ceiling briefly before leaning forward and saying in a loud
whisper, "Where you go to tinkle."

"Oh. Oh!" Michaela flushed. "When will I receive Lord Cherbon?"

"When will—" Hugh broke off in a rather loud and rude laugh. "You won't receive him at all, poppet. When *he* is ready to assess *you,* you will be summoned. Until that time, simply go about your business."

"Assess me?" This man was grating on Michaela's good graces. "Like a cow, you mean."

"Oh, no, my lady," Hugh said, appearing horrified by the suggestion. "More like a horse."

Michaela wished for a large rock to chuck at the man.

"If there is anything you have need of that the staff cannot accommodate—which would not surprise me as they're hopelessly inept—simply send word. Sir Hugh Gilbert shall scurry-scurry to your side most obediently." His tone was mocking to the extreme.

"*Sir* Hugh Gilbert?" Michaela asked pointedly, eyeing the man's fine costume. Beyond fine—it was magnificent, with embroidery and deep velvet. Fit more for royalty than a lowly crusading knight. "Is that—"

Sir Hugh's eyes sparkled like deep, icy water and his beautiful lips thinned. "Yes. *Sir.* 'Lord of Nothing' is hardly impressive, is it?" He gave her a tight smile. "If you'll excuse me, I'll see that your trunk is brought up." He gave a mocking bow. "Miss Fortune."

The chamber door closed.

Michaela growled and spun on her heel, looking for any convenient object to hurl. But her loose, worn slipper slid from beneath her heel and tangled in the rug underfoot, wrenching her ankle and sending her to the floor with a cry. As she landed, she heard the odd sound of a musical giggle, like a child would make, and she rose up on her hands, searching the low shadows from floor level.

"Who was that? Who's here? Show yourself!" Michaela held her breath and listened, but heard not another whisper. A feeling of being watched tiptoed between her shoulder blades on icy feet.

Was Cherbon Castle haunted? It would explain the morbid surroundings, but Michaela did not think she could resign herself to sharing a bedchamber with a spirit, no matter how outrageous the prize.

How would she ever get undressed with any modesty?

"Hello?" she called quietly. She swallowed, and the sound was loud in the vast room. "Are you . . . are you a ghost?"

The giggle sounded again, from behind her. Michaela sat up quickly and turned just in time to see the little boy dash from behind a drapery to the door.

"Wait!" Michaela called, and struggled to gain her feet.

But the dark-haired child wrenched open the door and fled into the corridor on bare feet, leaving the door swinging wide behind him.

Michaela sat on the floor, undecided. Probably the child belonged to some servant of Cherbon, brought to the castle by his parent and warned to stay out of sight—it would explain the hiding. She looked about the dismal room, the despair seeming to seep from the very walls, then to the open doorway and black corridor beyond.

The boy, more familiar with the castle than Michaela, was likely already to the stone keep's heart on his swift feet by now. She'd never catch him.

Go about your business, Sir Hugh Gilbert had said.

If she was to become Lady of Cherbon, wasn't the manor's children—their whereabouts and unruly behavior—her business? Besides, she must learn the passages of her new home eventually. And finding the boy might lend her some insight as to the strange and unconcerned behavior of

the villagers. Perhaps she would even encounter the great
and lordly Lord Cherbon in her explorations.

Her stomach did a nervous wiggle.

Michaela gained her feet and marched into the corridor,
leaving the door standing open.

Roderick limped straightaway to his chamber, confident
that Hugh would soon follow, and he was not disappointed.
His handsome, dark-haired friend came through the door,
chuckling, not long after Roderick had settled into his
chair and began the struggle with his boots.

There would be no further need for the damned things
until nightfall, when he could move about the keep on his
own, now that one applicant had fled and a new one—
much to his surprise—had been installed. And this woman
was one Roderick wanted nothing to do with at this point.

She was dangerous to him, he could feel it. Dangerous,
but also essential to his survival.

Hugh closed the door, and as soon as the action was complete, he doubled over, his hands on his knees, laughing.

"I take it you find the new girl amusing?" Roderick
asked. He knew his tone was pissy, but he didn't care. His
heart still pounded in a strange and foreign way from
seeing Michaela Fortune, and it unsettled him. Roderick
told himself it was because the young woman was likely
his last hope to win Cherbon, and not at all because of her
smell, her voice, her oddly colored hair; how she had
seemed bold yet naïve in the way she'd answered Hugh's
probing and—Roderick had to admit—rude questions.
Perhaps it was simple honesty Roderick had seen in her,
but regardless, it was unsettling.

"Oh, good lord, yes!" Hugh gasped. He dragged his feet

to the side of Roderick's bed and collapsed on it. "This is just too, too good, Rick—*hoo!*"

"Are you going to tell me the why of it, or just lie there cackling on my bed?"

Hugh took a deep, steadying breath, chuckles still escaping him. At last he seemed to gain control over his mirth. "I know the chit, Rick—I've just seen her, four days past, at the Tornfield feast."

"She was at Tornfield?" Roderick yanked off his tall, stiff left boot with a "*Gah*—you bastard!" He tossed the boot to the floor. "As a guest?"

"Since she was seated at Tornfield's own table, his daughter between them, a guest of honor was my first assumption."

"Not so?"

"Not so." Hugh sat up, leaning on one long arm—his right arm, Roderick couldn't help but notice. Roderick could see the flexion of his elbow through his tight sleeve. "She was in Tornfield's employ as companion to his daughter."

"She was his servant?"

"Yes, and no," Hugh said, a chuckle creeping back into his voice, as if the memory tickled him. "Elizabeth Tornfield has been mute since her mother's death some time ago. Miss Fortune managed to coax the girl from some rather antisocial behavior and Tornfield was so thrilled that he offered her a position in the hold in lieu of her parents' dues. It seems the three of them grew rather . . . *close.* So close in fact, that Miss Fortune *and* the girl were under the assumption that Tornfield would marry *her.*"

"I vow you gossip more than the kitchen maids."

"Oh-ho, Rick, you disparage me unjustly! I did not come by this knowledge from gossip—Tornfield's daughter stood up in front of all the hall and objected to his marrying the

Osprey woman in favor of Miss Fortune, just as the ceremony was to commence! Everyone was completely humiliated!"

Something sharp twisted in Roderick's stomach. "You didn't feel this was aught which I should know?"

"Why would I?" Hugh protested. "I thought she was but a servant with rather ridiculous ambition. It was not more than a humorous anecdote at the time, and I know how little use you have for humor these days. I'd no idea until today that she was of noble blood."

Roderick grunted. *Fortune, Fortune* . . . Again, he searched his mind for a reference point for the name. He knew he'd heard it before, in connection with his father, but he could not place it.

"So what now, Rick?" Hugh asked, getting up from the bed and gathering up Roderick's discarded boots. He poured a chalice of wine and placed it in Roderick's hand. "A pair of days, and then you will meet her?"

The suggestion caused Roderick to break out immediately in a cold sweat. "I think not, Hugh," he tried to say evenly. "The longer we put this one off, the better."

"Hmm?" Hugh swallowed the mouthful of wine he'd taken from his own cup. "The reason for that being . . . ?"

Roderick stared at the floor, his head on his left hand, swirling the contents of his cup with his right, concentrating on the mastery of his muscles commanding the cup. After a long moment, he explained, although it pained his pride. Who else could he confide in if not faithful Hugh?

"She is my last hope to gain Cherbon," Roderick said quietly. "My thirtieth birthday is one hundred eighty-eight days from today. Should Michaela Fortune not stay—"

"So you *were* watching!" Hugh said with a grin as he

caught that Roderick had remained long enough to find out the girl's full name.

"Should she not stay, should something about me or Cherbon not suit her, Alan Tornfield will gain all."

"Would that be so very bad?" Hugh asked quietly, all foolishness gone from his tone as he knelt by Roderick's chair. "To let him bloody have it? I hate this place, Rick— you hate this place—"

"I don't hate—"

"Yes, you do!" Hugh said. "I can see it in your eyes—to walk where your father walked, to live in the rooms where your mother died, where you saw serfs and servants beaten and killed, where you yourself were so mistreated—it's eating you alive."

"It spurs me on," Roderick argued. "You can't understand, Hugh. It is my life's prize to call Cherbon my own. I must. I must right things—"

"Right things?" Hugh stood. "By engaging in the same tactics your father used?"

"I have not."

"You have! There is no forgiveness in you, Rick, for the servants, for me, or for yourself." Hugh spread his arms. "And Leo! God's teeth, he loves you so, and you act as though he doesn't exis—"

"Enough!" Roderick bellowed, and Hugh fell silent. "I will not warn you again, Hugh."

Hugh stared at Roderick a long time, and Roderick tried to see anger there, but he only saw . . . pity.

"I do apologize," Hugh said at last. "Forgive me, Rick. You may meet Miss Fortune when you feel it is the right time, of course. I am here to do your bidding."

Pity, pity, and more pity. It disgusted Roderick. He disgusted himself.

Roderick dragged himself from the chair and Hugh was immediately at his side as Roderick grabbed for the tall poster at the end of the bed. He waved Hugh away. "I've got it, Hugh—leave me." Roderick swung his body around with his arm and landed on the bed.

"Very well, Rick. Is there anything you've need of until you emerge this evening?" It was said in a light tone, but Roderick knew his friend was serious—and correct. He wouldn't venture from his chamber until darkness had a firm grip on the land.

Roderick shook his head, but then as Hugh started through the doorway, he called out again. "She's very comely, isn't she, Hugh?"

Hugh froze in place, glanced back over his shoulder.

"Miss Fortune, as you call her," Roderick clarified. "She's—"

"She's odd-looking," Hugh said shortly. "If you wish my honest appraisal. Clumsy. Desperate. Likely vengeful." He paused. "She should fit in well."

And then Hugh was gone.

Roderick turned over on his right side, but his arm protested and so he flopped onto his back once more. He stared up at the shadowed canopy, and it was not dark enough to suit him, so he covered his eyes with his forearm.

And he waited for night.

Michaela turned right outside the chamber door and headed down the corridor in the opposite direction from which Sir Hugh had led her, supposedly toward the rooms where "you go to tinkle." Michaela had taken advantage of the garderobe at Tornfield Manor, and she was pleased that

Cherbon boasted not one, but two of the convenient rooms. Since becoming used to living at Tornfield, Michaela now considered the appointments absolutely necessary, and she took a moment to duck her head in the doorways of both, almost to see if there were actually two.

There were, and Sir Hugh was correct—the room on the left had a most unpleasant odor.

She continued down the corridor, although she'd seen no further sign of the dark-haired little boy. The passage was wide, low ceilinged, and wound like long, discarded wood shavings from a carver's tool. And like the rest of Cherbon that she'd seen so far, the corridor was dark, dark, dark, even in what Michaela knew to be only late afternoon. There were sconces along the wall at convenient intervals, meant to be lit and dispel the gloom of the interior, but only every fifth or sixth staggered set was in use, the ones in between holding waxen stems that looked as if they had been deliberately broken off near the base. Twice, Michaela slipped when cylindrical pieces of wax rolled beneath her feet.

The absence of adequate light made for long stretches of corridor draped in complete darkness, the glimmer of a faraway candle Michaela's only guide. The stones seemed to breathe cold, and whisper sinister, moss-wrapped secrets that Michaela did not want to hear. She hurried between the light, not knowing if the darker shadows she passed were doors to other chambers, or black ghosts, waiting only for her to pause long enough for them to reach out cold, black arms and pull her into the stones to be devoured.

The corridor shrank into a narrow, steep stairwell, and Michaela would have most certainly tumbled to her death had she not been for once paying such close attention to the stones beneath her feet. Around the bend of the stairs, she saw a throbbing glow of light, she could hear muffled conversation, and the clanging of metal, slams, bangs, crashes. She could smell the lingering odor of bread that had been baked hours ago, and her growling stomach—and the promise of absolute light—spurred her feet down the steps.

She came out of the stairwell rather abruptly, indeed in the kitchen, and ran straightaway into the biting corner of a wide, long planked table set just off center in the room, where two women—one short and round, the other tall, thin, and gray—worked at chopping what seemed to be a mountain of vegetables.

And on a tall, spindly stool at the fat cook's side, the dark-haired little boy who had ran from Michaela's chamber sat, munching on a carrot.

Three heads spun to look at Michaela as she all but fell onto the table, sending several turnips wobble-rolling onto the floor, and within a blink the little boy had hopped from his stool and streaked through the opposite end of the kitchen.

"Wait!" Michaela called again, rather pointlessly, as the boy had shown her the soles of his feet before she even spoke. She pressed a hand to her waist where surely the morrow would find a long bruise from the table edge, and turned to the two women, who stared at her as if she was nothing more than a chunk of firewood, stood on its end. "Whose child is that?" she demanded.

Neither of them so much as blinked, although the tall, thin woman's lips grew even thinner.

"Hello?" Michaela waved her hands in front of her own face. "Have I gone invisible?"

"No, m'lady. You're quite solid. Good evening," the shorter woman said at last.

The gray woman dropped her eyes back to her task, abusing a turnip most viciously.

"That boy was lurking in my chamber, and would not heed me when I called to him," Michaela explained. "I would speak to his mother."

Now, the shorter woman began chopping as well, and Michaela felt as though she had just been left in the domed-ceiling room alone. The women's attitudes were sorely grating on Michaela's good graces, but she held her temper—they likely had no idea who Michaela was. But since Sir Hugh had given her leave to assume the duties of Lady of Cherbon, Michaela felt it best that she start with these women. It would not do for the hold's mistress to allow this sort of disrespect.

Careful, a meek little voice warned inside her head, *you thought to be Tornfield's lady, as well. And that did not quite work out as you planned, did it?*

"I am Lady Michaela Fortune," she offered. "I've come to marry Lord Cherbon."

Neither woman looked up from their work.

Michaela pressed her lips together for a moment. "'Tis possible I will become your mistress not long after the new year has come."

The round woman looked up briefly at Michaela with almost tired pity in her eyes. "I wish you well, m'lady."

The gray woman did not raise her face but snorted rather stingily.

Michaela's patience was nearly gone—the snort had done it. She had been laughed at her entire life, and refused to begin her life thusly at Cherbon Castle. She was a new woman, after all.

"Now listen here," she began. "I don't know who has trained you on the proper manner in which you speak to the mistress of the household, but I assure you that I will not tolerate this kind of insubordinance. Sir Hugh has given me leave to assume the duties of lady in this keep and I—"

The gray woman slammed her knife down on the wooden tabletop, causing both Michaela and the round cook to jump. The narrowed eyes she pinned on Michaela looked cold and mean.

"My lady," she said rather nastily, "should I take the time to bow and scrape to every classless, destitute chit what's come through Cherbon's great hall, I would complete not one of my duties."

Michaela felt as though she'd been slapped, but the gray woman continued before she could think of anything smart to say.

"Do you know—*my lady*—that you are number . . . hmm, let me see . . . ninety-seven, I believe. Yes, ninety-seven. Ninety-six women have come before you with hopes of seizing Cherbon's riches, and ninety-six have fled in terror after no more than two days. It is a disgrace to the Cherbon name, to parade strange women through here as if running a brothel, and I, for one, will not tolerate it!"

The round woman had stopped chopping, but she only stood at the table with her head down. Michaela thought she whispered something like, "Harliss, 'tis not your place."

"It *is* my place," the gray woman spat, directing her venomous words not to the cook, but to Michaela. "Regardless of Roderick's argument to the contrary, and I will not shirk my duty. *I never have* and I will never! Now, to answer your question—*my lady*—the little boy you saw hiding in your chamber, the one who would not heed your commands, is none other than Leo Cherbon, Lord Cherbon's son. I'm sure you understand his lack of attention to you, when he

has had no fewer than ninety-seven women vying to be his new mum!"

Michaela stood there for a long silent moment, shaking inside at the dressing-down and shocking information she'd just received. And although she wanted desperately to retreat to her dark, depressing chamber, or perhaps simply walk from the castle completely, Michaela was still determined to stay at Cherbon no matter what. This was only a small bump in her road. No matter at all, really. So she straightened her spine and looked the gray woman—Harliss—directly in the eyes.

"Is that so? Well, then I thank you, Harliss, for relaying the information to me. It is most enlightening. However, until number ninety-eight takes my place, you would be well-advised to address me with the respect due to my station and the name of Cherbon. I do not expect you to cow before me, but I will not tolerate rudeness or disrespect of any kind." And it was here that Michaela took a leap. "Should you spout such venom at me at any time in the future, I will see that you are dismissed."

Harliss looked as if she were carved from stone, but her eyes shot flaming arrows at Michaela.

"Do you both understand?" Michaela asked loudly, trying to keep the quiver from her voice with volume.

"Of course. My lady." Michaela was surprised the woman's teeth didn't fall from her lips, her jaw was set so firmly. The round cook at her side had not raised her eyes still, but nodded quickly at Michaela's question.

"Very well," Michaela said. "Now, where is Leo's nurse?"

"He has no nurse, m'lady," the cook offered quickly.

"No nurse? Who cares for him?"

"Sir Hugh, m'lady."

Michaela frowned. "There is no children's nurse at Cherbon?"

The cook looked vastly uncomfortable and gave no answer.

"There is a children's nurse, only she has been relieved of her duties," Harliss said.

"Well, that will not do at all," Michaela said. "Tell this nurse to come to me after breaking the fast in the morn. I will see that she is reinstated to her proper duties at once. Lord Cherbon's son can not be allowed to run about like a wild thing."

Harliss looked rather surprised, and Michaela thought she might have seen the corners of her thin mouth rise the slightest bit.

"I could not agree with you more. My lady."

Chapter Eight

Michaela was awoken from an uneasy sleep by a terrible crashing on her chamber door. Her bare feet were on the painfully cold floor and she was lurching toward the sound before her eyes were truly open.

She fumbled with the unfamiliar latch. "A moment, just a moment!" she shouted, trying to command her stupid fingers to work. At last the bolt slid free and the door was shoved open, knocking into Michaela and sending her to her backside on the floor. A very angry-looking Hugh Gilbert stood in the doorway.

"Who in the hell do you think you are?" he demanded straightaway, and Michaela noticed from her position on the floor the little boy snaked around Hugh's legs, his eyes red and puffy, his cheeks streaked with tracks of wet. Leo Cherbon had his lower lip caught between his teeth and his chest was hitching back quiet, dwindling sobs.

"I—" Michaela stuttered, sleep slipping from her fuzzled brain too slowly to take in the events. "Sir Hugh, what—"

He took a menacing step toward her, and pointed his finger. "Gather your pitiful belongings and be gone from

Cherbon within the hour, or I swear, as God as my witness, I will throttle you myself! Come along, Leo—we'll go have a good snotrag and some biscuits." He turned to go.

"Wait! Sir Hugh, please!" Michaela scrambled to her feet and flew to the doorway. Hugh stopped, but did not turn to look at her, although Leo Cherbon watched her with hurt, wary eyes.

"What is it?" he growled.

"Why are you dismissing me? What have I done? I've been in my chamber the whole of the night! I don't see how—"

"What have you done?" Hugh asked incredulously, and then spun on his heel to rush at Michaela, Leo still attached to his leg like a barnacle. She had to steel herself not to stumble backward. Once upon her, Hugh jerked Leo forward by his arm and pulled the hem of his gown up from his legs. A half-dozen thin welts marred the smooth skin of the baby's outer thigh, and Leo squirmed to the side, trying to escape Hugh's display.

Michaela gasped and her throat clenched painfully at the sight of the tiny boy's injuries. "Oh, my heavens—who—surely you don't think I did that to him!"

"Not with your own hand, no, but you may as well have," Hugh growled. He let Leo pull away and hide behind him once more. "It is quite obvious to me, Miss Fortune, that you have no desire to fulfill the requirements of the station of Lady of Cherbon by sentencing Roderick's child to such a devil, and your discernment in the arena of delegating duties to the servants leaves much to be desired."

"I don't know what—" And then Michaela recalled the conversation she'd had last evening with that wretched Harliss and the quiet cook. "Was it his nurse? I told Harliss she was to have Cherbon's nurse report to me this morn, not simply tell her to re-assume her duties!"

"*Harliss* was Cherbon's nurse," Hugh clarified. "And *this*"—he gestured toward Leo's leg—"is her preferred method of reprimanding a three-year-old who will not wear his shoes."

Michaela felt she might vomit, and her fingertips came up to press against her lips. "Oh my God," she whispered, her eyes finding Leo's face, which he promptly hid in Hugh's fine tunic. "Leo, I'm so sorry—I didn't know . . . Harliss didn't tell me . . ." She broke off and dropped to her knees before Hugh's legs, ignoring the knight now.

"Leo," she called gently, and in a moment, the little boy rolled his face slightly outward to appraise her with one eye. "Leo, I'm sorry." She placed her palm on her chest and tried to hold back her tears at the sight of the small, hurt face before her. "Lady Michaela is very, very sorry that mean Harliss struck you. I will never let her do that again, I promise, promise, promise!"

The little boy's shoulders hitched and he sniffed. "Harliss hurt Ee-oh. No soos."

"I know, I know." Michaela's own chest hitched, and a fury rose up in her. If the gray woman had been standing in the corridor with them in that moment, Michaela truly believed she could have killed her. "But she will not do it again." Michaela looked up at Hugh. "Leo was hiding in my chamber after you left last eve. I chased him to the kitchens and encountered Harliss. She led me to believe that Leo's nurse was someone other than her. I was only trying to do what I thought was right, Sir Hugh—you must believe me! Never would I want harm to come to any child! Especially one so small."

"When Lord Cherbon finds out about this, he will—"

"I will tell him myself," Michaela volunteered immediately. "It was my mistake, my wrong. I will admit to it and accept my punishment."

"He has no wish to entertain you at this point, Miss Fortune," Hugh reiterated, and although he still stressed the hated nickname, Michaela thought most of his anger had dissipated. "Leo and I will inform him straightaway. If he wishes you dismissed—"

"Then I will go," Michaela agreed quietly. Then she turned her attention back to Leo. "But I do hope I stay. I'd like for the two of us to become friends, Leo. Do you like to sing?"

Leo stared at her for a moment and then nodded ever so slightly.

Michaela smiled as if this bit of information surprised her greatly. "I do, as well! Perhaps we can play a bit later, if Sir Hugh agrees. We can go for a walk about the bailey and sing songs together. Would you like that?"

Leo nodded again, more enthusiastically this time. Then, to Michaela's amazement, he reached out a chubby hand and touched her hair briefly, as if it might burn him.

"You hair yong," he said shyly.

Michaela smiled a bit wider and gave him a wink. "Yes, it is long. And a mess likely, since I've just come from bed." She looked up at Leo's keeper. "All right, Hugh?" she asked quietly.

Hugh grunted. "Come on then, Puke. Perhaps you may visit with Miss Fortune later this afternoon, after you've had your lie-down." He turned to go but halted as Michaela rose to her feet, and his words were meant for Michaela's ears only. "If you *ever* do anything to endanger this child again, I will flay the skin from you. I think you're a walking disaster as it is, and not to last out the week. But

I will give you the courtesy of a warning this one time only, Miss Fortune. Do we understand each other?"

"No, we do not," Michaela whispered back. "I made a mistake, Hugh, and one that I will rectify to my own satisfaction this very morn. I don't care if you are Lord Cherbon's man—do not threaten me again, or accuse me of aught which you do not know as fact, or you would be wise to lock your chamber door upon retiring at night. If you are too put out by the duties your lord has charged you with to tolerate my presence, then you may tell him to deal with me himself, for the only way that I shall ever leave Cherbon is upon *his* word. *Good day*."

Michaela turned back to her chamber and closed the door before Hugh could respond. She threw the bolt for good measure.

Then she walked calmly back to bed, lay down carefully, and let her trembling overtake her at last.

"She is turning Cherbon inside out," Hugh said disgustedly, as he helped Roderick in his daily stretches. "I'm telling you, Rick—she simply will not do."

"Argh! Hugh, not so far—my leg is pulling from its socket!"

Hugh eased back immediately. "Sorry. I was throwing her out this morn, after the incident with Leo. I would have, too, did I not know how conniving Harliss can be. I'm giving Miss Fortune the benefit of the doubt."

"Very kind of you," Roderick said dryly.

"It is, yes. Although I must say that I'm impressed with how she handled Heartless."

Roderick raised his eyebrows, waited.

"She is now Cherbon's garderobe mistress."

Roderick chuckled darkly. "Fitting. Would that I had thought of that myself."

"Ingenious, I agree. But still, I fear she will not do." Hugh released Roderick's knee and gestured for Roderick to twist his hips toward him now. "She is . . . strange. Not at all what I expected."

Roderick lifted his knees up and over to his left, and sighed at the stretch. This side was always so much easier. "Cherbon is not exactly a den of normalcy, Hugh."

"True, but I don't care for her, any matter. She is brazen. And quite mouthy."

"Perhaps you see a bit of yourself in that?"

Hugh snorted. "She demands to see you on every unfortunate occasion of our meeting."

"That's not so strange," Roderick offered. "Haven't all the candidates expressed such a wish? To see the man they would marry?"

"They have, yes," Hugh said with patience. "But I believe Miss Fortune actually *means* it."

Roderick's pride stung a bit at that. But he let it go. Hugh was honest and blunt, and Roderick appreciated those qualities in his friend in every other aspect of their lives at Cherbon. He told himself he could not pick and choose where Hugh could and couldn't be honest. Roderick was no simpering maid who required his truths coated in honey.

"Where is she now?" Roderick asked, seeking to change the subject lest he be plunged into one of his dark moods.

"She is out in the bailey with Leo, picking flowers and singing," Hugh sneered. "I would have disallowed it, but he insisted. I doubt Miss Fortune will let any harm to come to him after my terrible dressing-down this morn—she seemed properly chastised. And it gives me a moment's peace. Let Cherbon have a respite as well, I say. She's not stopped since Harliss—ordering cleanings, whitewashings, new candles!" Hugh shook his head and chuckled. "There is such a thing as overenthusiasm."

Roderick grunted his assent but held his tongue through the remainder of the stretch. He was intrigued by Michaela Fortune, and damned his crippled self for preventing him from seeking her out in the light. He had little hope that she would stay, but her so-labeled overenthusiasm for keep affairs was heartening, and Roderick wanted to do nothing that might frighten her away. He wished he was more improved, more mobile, less scarred and hideous. Perhaps if he had the lights put out for the evening meal, and came in his hood . . .

But no. That would likely frighten her more. He would simply have to wait.

He could still see her in his mind, though, from his memory of her arrival, and his nightly forays. . . .

"I think it is good that she seeks to spend time with Leo," Roderick said as Hugh helped him from the floor and to his chair. "You're no child's nurse, Hugh."

"The two of us get on just fine."

"I know you do," Roderick said, accepting the chalice of wine that also held a powdered herb to help with the stiffness and pain he always felt after his daily torture sessions. "And I do not fault your care of him in the least. But your social life leaves much to be desired. You needed to beat the women from you in Constantinople—what sport do you have here?"

"*You're* to lecture *me* on entertaining lovers?" Hugh said. "Besides, you're forgetting the Tornfield feast— I fared quite well there that night." He winked at Roderick, and Roderick laughed.

"Good on you, Hugh. I should have known." He sat for several moments, contemplating his cup and waiting for the warm, tingling sensation of the powder to take effect. Perhaps there was more he could be doing to better his physical condition. Perhaps more work, more practice. "What do you think if I were to increase my exercises, Hugh?" he asked suddenly, before his nerve could leave him. "Perhaps I could get around a bit better?"

Hugh's eyes widened. "Do you jest? Rick—that is precisely what you need! I've been thinking of other things that we might do besides the stretches Aurelia showed us—things that are actually relevant to your station!" Hugh set his chalice aside and dropped to one knee at the side of Roderick's chair. "We could make use of the squire's practice!"

"Do we *have* any squires?"

"No, of course not," Hugh said, and waved his hand. "But the soldiers' quarters are still possessed of the rings, the dummies, the wooden weaponry! It would—"

"You'd have me play with child's things?" Roderick frowned.

"Think about it, Rick! The lighter weights, the simplicity of the exercises—your body knows how to do these things, we only need strengthen it!"

Roderick did think about it, and the more he did, the more the idea made sense to him. A crazy little bubble of excitement welled up in him, but he recognized it and burst it.

Hope had no place at Cherbon.

Hugh grasped his shoulder. "What do you say, Rick? Will you give me permission to have the props brought out?"

"Brought out, yes, but not in the practice arena. I don't wish for anyone to see—"

"Of course not," Hugh rushed. "I'll have them brought t—"

"No, no—*you* bring them, Hugh. At night."

"Yes, yes. I see. Where shall we—"

But Roderick already knew the perfect location for his childish, painful, humiliating practice before Hugh could finish his question. Where he was sure his father could watch Roderick take back the life he'd tried so hard to destroy.

"Take them to the ring on the knoll, near the stables."

". . . and they rode all the way to London town!" Michaela ended the song on a clap and Leo joined in enthusiastically.

"More!" the little boy demanded with his beautiful smile.

"Again? Leo, we've sung it a dozen times already!"

"No more?" He scrunched up his nose and then, as if the idea had just come to him, he grabbed up the scraggly bunch of mangled and wilted stems and thrust them at Michaela. "Fowwers?"

Michaela laughed. "I think we've picked all to be had today." The ragged greenery was little more than frilly weeds—all that was readily available as winter bore down on the land, but the picking of them had given the boy such joy, and Michaela felt her load lighten at just being with Leo Cherbon. The boy's very existence had been a shock at first, but Michaela was thrilled by the lord's young son and she hated to leave his company.

"Mayhap we can go about again on the morrow if Sir

Hugh will allow it, eh? But right now, I must return to the keep. I have chores to attend to, and you likely are wanting of a morsel to eat."

The boy's round face fell again, but only for a moment before he suddenly bolted to his bare feet in the grass and ran past Michaela, shouting, "Fire, fire!"

"Fire?" Michaela twisted around with alarm, but only saw Leo dashing toward a rotund figure in a brown robe.

Friar. It was Friar Cope, a man Michaela was most familiar with, having seen him recently at the wedding of Alan Tornfield and Lady Juliette.

She had hoped to escape that memory here, and she wondered with dread what the holy man was doing at Cherbon.

Leo hurled himself at Friar Cope's knees, and the kind man laughed and patted the boy's head. "Good day, Leo! What are you doing about alone? Where is Sir Hugh?"

"No Hoo. Aid-ee Mike-lah! Ee-oh pick fowwers!" Leo announced, thrusting his bouquet at Friar Cope and then pointing backward in Michaela's direction.

The friar allowed the little boy to take hold of his hand and pull him closer, and Michaela groaned inwardly at the pitiful little smile the friar gave her.

"Good day, Lady Michaela. I see the rumors I heard were sadly correct."

"Good day, Friar. It's nice to see you again." It wasn't. "What business have you at Cherbon?" she asked, choosing to ignore the subject of her own new residency there.

"No business, my dear. Only coming home, at last. Being the demesne seat, Cherbon is the base of my ministry."

"Oh, I didn't realize," Michaela said lightly, but inside she screamed in temper, pounded her fists and stomped her feet. Now she would be faced with the damning memory of Alan's betrayal and her own humiliation on a regular basis. "Welcome home, then."

"Thank you, my lady. May I sit?" The friar indicated the flattened patch of dead grass Leo had recently vacated, as if asking permission to dine at a grand table.

"Of course," Michaela said, although Leo was already tugging the man onto the ground by pulling on his hand with both arms.

"Fire sit—Ee-oh pick more fowwers!" And he was off a short distance away, perusing the buffet of weeds and grass for anything remotely blossomlike.

Michaela and Friar Cope sat side by side for several moments, watching the three-year-old in heavy silence.

"Michaela, my dear, what in Heaven's name are you doing at Cherbon?" he asked quietly.

"What am I doing here?" Michaela reiterated quietly, ruffling a palm over the crackly grass near her hip. "What am I doing here? Well, I hope to be saving my parents from poverty, is what I'm doing here. Since I was so recently relieved of my position at Tornfield. Which you obviously already know all about."

"You were not relieved of your position," Cope argued gently. "I've just come from Tornfield and you still have a home there, should you want it. Cherbon is no place for you—Roderick is no man for you to be setting your sights on."

The mention of Tornfield caused Michaela's heart to clench. "Why? Because I am the least of nobility in the whole of the land? Is silly Miss Fortune not worthy of such a grand home as Cherbon? Lord Roderick too lofty an ambition?" She knew she sounded defensive, but she didn't care—she was.

"Not at all," Cope answered. "You are very special, my child. I have known that since your birth. But this place is—" He broke off, looked around the deserted grounds, and Michaela knew he was seeing the vine-covered walls, the gloomy, abandoned atmosphere. "Haunted, for lack of a better word. Many sad and terrible things have taken place at Cherbon. And Roderick—he was not always the hard man that he is now. Indeed, before he left on his pilgrimage, we all had great hopes for the day when Roderick would take his father's place. A kind man, gentle, then. Fair in word and in deed. But I fear he has come to resemble his father in actions and rule so much that there is little that could be done to redeem him. He is scarred, and not only from his physical injuries."

"I didn't know Roderick Cherbon before I came, nor did I meet his father. So I shall reserve my opinion of him until I know him well enough on my own."

"But, my dear," Cope insisted, "so many women—most more experienced than you, if I may be so bold—have tried and fled. There is—"

"Ninety-six, to be exact," Michaela said lightly, plucking a short, rough leaf from the grass and rubbing it between her thumb and finger. "I am the ninety-seventh."

Friar Cope was quiet for a moment. "Your parents are worried for you. Your father, especially. He knew Magnus Cherbon—"

"Magnus Cherbon is dead, though, Friar," Michaela interrupted. "And I am getting along well enough so far. I must succeed here. There is no other hope for my parents, or for me."

Cope reached into his robe. "Mayhap this will sway you?" He handed Michaela a folded scrap of paper.

She didn't want to take it, but she did, and unfolded

it carefully. Her throat tightened at the familiar, dainty, scribbling script of Elizabeth Tornfield.

Dear Michaela,
    Why did you leave? I am sad. Lady Juliette is horrid. I hate her. Please come home. Please.
                                            Elizabeth Tornfield

Michaela hastily brushed at the tears on her face, folded the letter back and returned it to the friar.

"You don't wish to keep it?" he asked, his eyes wide.

"No, I don't. Thank you." She swiped at her nose with the back of her hand, not caring if it was uncouth. "Lord Alan would likely be much put-out that his daughter sent me that message. I assume you read it?" It was not an accusation, only a statement.

"I did, yes. And I do doubt that Lord Alan minds—he gave his blessing for me to carry the message to you."

Anger welled up in Michaela at the thought of Alan's attempted manipulation. "I shall forget I ever read it. And if you by chance happen to be asked to carry another to me, please do not."

"Michaela—"

"Leo!" Michaela called in a loud, shaky voice, standing and cutting off Friar Cope's sympathetic tone. The little boy turned his bright, eager face to her. "Come along—'tis time we returned to the keep."

Friar Cope too stood. "Do not begrudge Lord Alan his choice, Michaela. He was doing what he felt was best for all at Tornfield."

"Certainly. Which is why I am no longer at Tornfield." Leo dashed to Michaela's side, swinging himself about on her skirts. She reached down to seize his hand and began walking away from Cope without so much as a glance. "Good day, Friar."

"Gooday, Fire!" Leo twisted about to call back and wave over his shoulder. Then his little voice seemed directed upward. "Aid-ee Mike-lah ky-in'?"

"No, Leo." Michaela sniffed and did not look down at the boy lest the tears spill over her lashes. "I have something in my eye, that's all."

Chapter Nine

Something had greatly upset Miss Fortune, and Roderick could not help but wonder at the cause, as he was fairly certain it was not him.

She had cried herself to sleep; he could see that even in the almost complete absence of light of her bedchamber, staring at her still form on the mattress through the cleft of the bed curtains. Her face was turned toward him on her pillow as she lay on her side on the very edge of the mattress—as if she had stared longingly out—and she clutched a length of the coverlet to her face. The murky light from the faraway window illuminated her cheeks and hair just enough for him to see the puffiness of her eyelids and the downward turn of her mouth, even in the darkness.

Damned to shadows as he was, Roderick's night vision had become quite spectacular.

As he crept about, he had found no evidence for her distress in the chamber that had housed him through his boyhood. Everything was in its place, nothing strewn about in a pique of anger or despair. And perhaps 'twas only the hopeless feel of the room Roderick had always and still hated, but he didn't think so. Miss Fortune was unhappy.

He wanted her to be happy here. But he didn't know how to make it so. Indeed, in his longest memory, no one had ever been happy at Cherbon, save mayhap his father, and he had been a demon who found happiness only in others' misery.

Magnus had likely died ecstatic.

Roderick took a chance and crouched awkwardly at the bedside, his left leg held straight, his face mayhap only a foot away from the sleeping Miss Fortune's. In all the time since women had been coming to Cherbon in hopes of becoming his wife, Roderick had never made use of the secret panel of his old room. But since he'd first seen Michaela Fortune, it was as if he could not stay away from her. Although he could not bring himself to speak to her face-to-face—quite possibly sending her screaming from the keep in mad terror, like the last woman—this way he could look in upon her, mayhap glean some small piece of information that would aid him in keeping her.

His injuries had made him like the animal people rumored him to be—his night vision was superb; his hearing—despite his temporary deafness in one ear—was sharper than a bat's; his sense of smell so keen that he could tell an oak from a beech with his eyes closed. And he could smell her—loudly, it seemed—from where he crouched. Her fresh, green scent, like the newest heather crushed underfoot, and her sadness. It was a sweet smell, but rather sorry, like wet hay stacked in a stable and then forgotten.

"What happened?" he breathed, his own fine hearing barely even registering the words.

But she stirred, hummed a bit in her sleep, and even that sound was despondent.

Roderick waited until she was still again, and then rose to his feet slowly, soundlessly. He was pressing his fortune—

ha!—staying here, daring to even breathe in her presence. Should she awaken and find him—a beast of a man, scarred and broken—a black monster, she would be rightly terrified. Roderick was ashamed.

He slipped behind the well-oiled panel and into the tiny cubicle that led to the corridor of his own wing.

A week passed, and although Roderick continued his nightly visits to Miss Fortune when she was least aware, he was relieved to note that she no longer seemed to be crying herself to sleep. But a pair of faint creases had begun to etch themselves between her delicate eyebrows as if life for her at Cherbon was exacting a great toll and required her complete concentration.

He hovered over her for only a pair of minutes each time, trying to absorb as much of her as he could in the quiet dark, as if it would lend him insight to her person, her very soul. He wondered at her motives, both in coming to Cherbon and in staying, when no other woman had been able to bear the castle or its lord. But there was no revelation to be found on the smooth surfaces of her eyelids, and so each visit only left Roderick wanting, and this night was no different.

Hugh and Leo were waiting for him when he returned to his chamber, and as soon as he swung open the door, Leo scrambled to his feet from where he and Hugh had been lounging on the thick rug on the floor and ran to greet him.

"Good ee-binning, Wod-wick," Leo said, catching himself just before he barreled into Roderick's legs, but his smile was pure and wide and bright. He looked back over his shoulder at Hugh as if for approval, and Hugh nodded and winked at the boy.

"Good evening, Leo. How was your day?"

"Fun! But Aid-ee Mike-lah no pick fowwers and singed wif me today—busy-busy. But no soos. And no bad Harliss."

Roderick nodded seriously. Could it have been Leo that had upset Miss Fortune those handful of days ago? Perhaps something the boy had said? Her mysterious tears haunted Roderick still, and his concern of them troubled him even more deeply.

"Does Lady Michaela enjoy herself when the pair of you go about?" he asked the boy.

Leo nodded. "Sometime her get somefing in her eye, tho', and then her go to bed. Wod-wick pay soul-jer wif me and Hoo, now?" The little boy reached out tentatively, as if to take Roderick's hand.

"Not tonight, Leo." Roderick winced inwardly as Leo's hand stopped in midair and he snatched it behind his back. "I must speak with Sir Hugh for a moment and then I'm going to bed, as well. Should you also be?"

Leo was looking at the floor now. He nodded slowly and then turned to dash back to the rug and throw himself down amidst the wooden toys scattered there, his little back to Roderick. Hugh reached out and ruffled the boy's hair as he stood.

"You may play for a bit longer, Snot, and then it's off to bed with you."

"All wite, Hoo."

Roderick collapsed in his chair and Hugh dragged over another to join him. "It seems our Miss Fortune has received a letter."

"From whom? I saw no strangers about today."

"How could you? You didn't leave your chamber until after the evening meal, when most everyone had quit the keep."

Roderick shrugged.

"Any matter, the letter came last week, when Cope returned from Tornfield. He carried with him a message from Tornfield's young daughter, Elizabeth."

Ah. So there it was.

Roderick would not admit even to Hugh his secret trips into his childhood chamber, and because he knew Hugh could not keep even the smallest sliver of gossip to himself, Roderick could feign disinterest.

"How lovely for Lady Michaela," he said, letting an extra crinkle of sarcasm muss his words.

"They want her back."

The chalice Roderick was bringing to his lips paused, but only for an instant. He didn't think Hugh noticed.

"Oh?" He drank.

"Mmm-hmm. Seems Tornfield was more than a little surprised that Miss Fortune took off like she did. Apparently he wanted the chance to speak with her, explain some things."

"Well, too bad for him, then, isn't it?" Roderick paused. "Is she going back?"

"No. She's told me and Friar Cope as much. Says she'll stay here until you throw her out."

Roderick released the breath he hadn't known he'd been holding.

"Apparently her family is in such dire straits, and her pride was so badly bruised, she wouldn't have Alan Tornfield on a silver platter. She's determined to win you."

Roderick thought of Leo relating that Lady Michaela had gotten something in her eye and then gone to bed. Whatever was in the missive from the Tornfield girl had obviously been the thing that upset her, and Roderick was angry that he was just now hearing of it.

"Why are you telling me this at this late date, Hugh? Besides your usual penchant for salacious gossip?"

"I'm only warning you," Hugh said mildly, sipping from his own chalice that had been set aside earlier, assumedly when he'd brought Leo in for their nightly play. "And I only found out myself today. If Tornfield decides to press his suit and Miss Fortune is as in love with him as I suspect, she could be worn down. Perhaps she'll return to him after all."

Roderick grunted, and his heart pounded. "What? To live out her days as a child's nurse?" Roderick scoffed.

"No, Rick—likely as his mistress," Hugh explained patiently, as if the information did not faze him in the least. "Or whatever Miss Fortune demands. Besides her being modestly good-looking, I suppose, if you like the pale-faced, shepherdess type, you're not the only one keeping track of the days until your thirtieth birthday. 'Tis likely your dear cousin would try to woo Miss Fortune away if only to be certain you do not inherit Cherbon."

"That's ridiculous," Roderick spat. Then he looked at Hugh. "Isn't it?"

Hugh shrugged, took another sip. "I daresay I would not be surprised if more messages begin to arrive. And then it will be gifts, and minstrels, and on and on." He waved a bored hand.

"No more messages—for anyone at Cherbon—before they come through me. I will approve all correspondence."

"Miss Fortune is a step ahead of you in that area, Rick," Hugh said. "Her feminine pique already prevailed of the fat friar to deliver no more messages to her from Tornfield."

"Oh. Good." Roderick felt very unsure. "We should start my increased practices soon though, should we not? Perhaps if I'm well enough—"

"I do think it would be best. And who knows? Perhaps Miss Fortune will not be repulsed by you."

"Thank you, friend," Roderick said, and quirked an eyebrow.

"Now, Rick, come on—you know I didn't mean it in that way." Hugh reached over and gripped Roderick's forearm, but Roderick shrugged it away. "It's only that—"

"I know, Hugh." Roderick bent over and began the nightly struggle with his boots. "I tire. Do you move the squires' toys tonight?"

"Yes. As soon as Leo—"

"Very well. Good night, Hugh."

Hugh sat for a moment longer, as if he wanted to say something else, but Roderick's glaring glance caused him to rethink the wisdom of it. He sighed instead.

"All right, Rick. I'll leave you to your sourness." He rose, setting his chalice on a side table. "Come along, Grub. Nighty-nighty, doggies bitey. Say your good night to Roderick."

Leo reluctantly got up from the floor and dashed to stand before Roderick, who had to drop the laces of his boots to keep the tyke from barreling into him. As soon as his hands grasped the boy's small upper arms, Leo took it as an embrace and threw both hands around Roderick's neck.

"Good night, Wod-wick. See you 'morrow."

"Good night, Leo." Roderick felt awkward with the boy hung about him, but he patted his slender back dumbly before setting Leo from him. "Run along now," he said gruffly.

At the door, Hugh was smiling strangely. He held out an arm, shepherding the boy as Leo flew past him. The lad was forever running full tilt. "Oh, I nearly forgot," Hugh said, and leaned into the corridor. "Boil! *Leo,* stop! Wait for me, right there. *Don't move.*"

Hugh reentered the chamber and crossed to Roderick's chair, reaching into his fine tunic. He withdrew a folded sheet of parchment. "From none other than Miss Fortune herself. I told her you wouldn't, but as I've said, she is quite impossible." Hugh handed the square to Roderick, saluted him, and then left the room, closing the door on his shout of, "Leo! You little arse-tick! Come ba—"

Left in the disconcerting silence of Leo's impromptu embrace and the unexpected letter from the woman he'd just been spying on, Roderick sat staring at the missive for several moments. He took a deep breath and opened it.

> *My lord,*
>   *I do think it unseemly that I assume the role of Lady of Cherbon without your input on some matters. It is my most sincere wish that we are introduced properly, and discuss several aspects of my duties. I will await you in the great hall at noon, as Sir Hugh has told me of your abhorrence for mornings.*
>
>   *Respectfully,*
>   *Michaela Fortune*

Roderick read the missive through several times. No one save Hugh dared demand Roderick do anything anymore, and for the better part of an hour, while he struggled with his boots and removed his heavy clothes, Roderick fumed at the girl's audacity.

But then he recalled the tear-streaked face in the moonlight, and the instance of the Tornfield girl begging her to return—telling the old friar, no less, so desperate was the hold to have her back, and Roderick was torn.

Should he meet with Miss Fortune in the light, so soon after her arrival, it was very likely she would pack her belongings and be off to Tornfield by sunset.

Though should he refuse her, he could very well suffer the same outcome. For how long could a wounded bird such as she beat her beak on a cold iron piling? Especially when a comfortable nest called to her? Roderick knew she had not felt welcomed at Cherbon, by the serfs, by Hugh, and especially not by Roderick. Perhaps she found some little joy in Leo, but Leo was only a child. He could not be expected to carry the whole of Cherbon on his young shoulders.

You were, a small voice reminded him. *Who had a care for* your *childhood? Not your father. Not Harliss. Not your poor, young-dead mother.* But he shut the voice behind the heavy, black door beyond which it lived.

If Michaela Fortune had been so heartbroken by Alan Tornfield, and if she was as impossible and headstrong as Hugh related, Roderick did not see her returning to his cousin anytime soon. And besides, Miss Fortune need learn that no one commanded the Cherbon Devil. Not now, and not ever again.

The morrow's noon would find her waiting.

Chapter Ten

It was a strange feeling, sitting in the great hall at the lord's table all alone. The room was beginning to look much improved already since Michaela's arrival, ten days past: the stacks of tables and benches and armchairs at the far end were no more, the furniture now pulled out, polished and orderly before her. Candelabras shone from the center of each table, only waiting for a flame, along with small pots of lavender and rosemary each to either side. The floor was not only cleanly swept, but had been recently washed, and the room smelled a little like a wet cave—the scent was not unpleasant, but made Michaela shiver all the same, as if remembering some old nightmare.

The fire in the massive, square open hearth in the floor crackled at an acceptable level, built so that it could be grown at a moment's notice. She had ordered new draperies for the walls to adorn the whitewashing between the plaster murals, but they would not be ready for several weeks. She was content enough though, not having to look upon sweeping cobwebs, macabre swags of dead vines, and the black smudges of old soot.

So the great hall was well on its way to being restored to what Michaela suspected was its former glory—it was clean, orderly, and smelled pleasant. But it was obnoxiously empty.

It was noon, at least, she guessed. Likely much later than noon, were she to be honest with herself. Michaela had been sitting at the table for the better part of an hour, waiting for the appearance of Roderick Cherbon, with no luck at all. He had sent no reply to her message, either yea or nay, and so she had gathered up her optimism and waited. She must speak to him, about her duties, their future, Sir Hugh, Leo . . . everything. She was more than a little proud of herself for outlasting by far any other woman who had come to Cherbon, and she felt it was now past the time of initiation, when she should be granted the privilege of an audience with the lord of the demesne. Not an unreasonable request, and one that she thought she was owed after the hell Cherbon's other residents had put her through.

And still she sat alone, facing the doorway she expected him from, as the seconds turned into minutes and the minutes turned into another long, tense hour. Servants passed through the hall on swift, busied feet, and a pair of them had even inquired of her needs—a great improvement from ten days past. Still, Michaela was beginning to feel quite foolish the longer she sat alone, with no obvious purpose in the room, and no task to busy her hands.

What would she do if he simply did not come? If he cared so little that he would ignore her request? What would she do? Leave Cherbon? And what? Return to the Fortune hold until the family was thrown out?

Would she go back to Tornfield? To Alan, to sweet, lovely Elizabeth? How she missed them all, here in this dark, hopelessly grand castle, full of shadowy past.

Then the sound of hinges squeaking drew her attention, but not to the corridor she faced. The main entrance door to the hall opened behind her and she turned in her seat, wondering at the change in Roderick Cherbon's habits, to be out and about the keep grounds before dark. Michaela felt a queer mixture of dread and relief that she was at last to meet her intended.

But contrary to the twisted monster of her imagination that rumors had led Michaela to expect, it was a quite able-bodied man who entered Cherbon's hall. A blond, musta-chioed man, sweeping aside his rain-dampened cloak as he strode swiftly down the main aisle of tables toward her. A handsome man, with his jaw set, his eyes pinned to her.

It was Alan Tornfield.

"You will gather your belongings immediately," he said to her before he had even come to stand before the table, his voice surprisingly angry and unlike anything she had ever heard from him. "If you hurry, we can be returned to Tornfield before nightfall."

Michaela sat staring dumbly at him for a moment, at once not believing he stood in Cherbon's hall and at the same time so very happy to see him. "What are you doing here?" she asked faintly.

"Don't be ridiculous, Michaela—I've come to fetch you home. Now, do please hurry." He then walked around the table and reached down to seize her hand in his warm, strong fingers, and tugged her. His eyes darted to the far corners of the room. "Come—where is your chamber? I shall help you."

And then the memory of when she'd last seen Alan Tornfield crashed back upon her, and she snatched her hand away, leaving Alan to walk a pair of steps before re-alizing he no longer had hold of her.

"I will do no such thing! You have assumed too much, my lord, if you think me to accompany you anywhere, especially to Tornfield to reside alongside *your new wife!*"

Alan threw his hands up in the air. "So that *is* why you've run away!"

Michaela gaped at him. "Was there ever any question in your mind, the reason why? And I did not run away, I simply left! After the humiliating blow you dealt me before all the land, can you fault me?"

"No, you *ran away,* not giving me the chance to explain or the courtesy of a farewell!"

"Oh!" Michaela shrieked and shot to her feet. "You would speak to me of courtesy? Truly? Were you courteous when you decided to marry that wretched woman and bring her into *our home* without so much as a hint to me or your daughter?"

Alan stormed back toward her, his eyes afire. "I did what I did for us—for *you!*" he insisted, slamming his knuckles down on the tabletop before her. "Yes, Lady Juliette convinced me of the scheme, I admit—her own funds were aught that would save Tornfield! If I had taken you for my wife, Michaela, and Roderick had married, how would our dues be paid, hmm? That lucky ring you wear 'round your neck, mayhap? Is it made of gold? Is it silvered?"

Michaela was so furious and hurt, she could not gather a sufficient response before Alan continued.

"No. No, it's not. And then Roderick would have demanded his due, as is his right, and where would that have left us, Michaela? Tossed out of Tornfield Manor, that's where. Penniless. Who would care for us, support us, then? Who would care for your parents? My Elizabeth?

"But now, we can be free, without poverty's shadow

haunting us ever again! All you have to do is come home. Come home with me, Michaela."

"I can not—I *will not*—love another woman's husband."

"You prefer Roderick over me, then? Is that it? A malformed beast of a man who would take you as his wife only out of desperation?"

"Is that not why you married Juliette? Out of desperation? Or are you in love with her?"

"It is not the same."

"It is."

Alan shook his head. "It isn't," he said quietly. "I know you, Michaela. Unlike any other who walks this earth do I know you. I know your mind, your dreams—"

"Stop it!"

"—your heart. Roderick can never care for you the way I do, not if given a hundred lifetimes to try. I know that, as well."

"You are right. He will never care for me the way you claim to because he will make me his *wife!* You don't know what it's like, Alan, to live your entire life on the edge of acceptance, never being invited in or wanted despite who or what you are. Yes, Roderick Cherbon would likely have taken any of the other women who came to this keep had they stayed. But they did not stay, and *I* am here now, and I believe there is a reason for that. That is all that matters to me."

"What of Elizabeth? Would you see her punished for my sins? An innocent girl who loves you like she has loved no other woman save her own mother?"

"Get out."

"What do I tell her, Michaela? That you care so little for either of us that you'd choose the Cherbon Devil over us?"

"Get out!"

"She loves you. And I know you love me—I can see it in your eyes." To her surprise, Alan dropped suddenly to his knees before her, and took one of her hands in both of his. "Please, Michaela. Please. I beg you—come back to Tornfield with me."

Michaela stared down at the handsome face she'd grown so accustomed to, his features blurred by the tears in her eyes. Wasn't this what she'd always wanted from Alan? A confession of love, a helpless plea for her to return to Tornfield?

"You only want me now because I am here, Alan," she whispered, and each word pained her for its truthfulness. "It's not about how you or Elizabeth feel about me really—it's about Cherbon. It's always been Cherbon."

His brows lowered and he opened his mouth, but before Alan could speak, a rude bark of laughter from beyond him caused Michaela to jump and raise her eyes, spilling tears down her cheeks.

Sir Hugh Gilbert rocked on his heels, his hands clasped behind his back. "How touching. He's skipped the gifts and minstrels and went straight on to barging into your home himself, Rick. I believe I do stand corrected."

At Hugh's side stood a massive, crooked figure in a long black cloak and hood, like a giant Grim Reaper, shadowed and frightening and dangerous. All that was missing was a gleaming scythe and glowing red eyes.

Michaela realized she was seeing Roderick Cherbon for the first time, and her breath caught in her chest like a barbed hook.

He had not ignored her after all.

Roderick ignored Hugh's sardonic words, too caught up

with the sight of his physically perfect cousin—his rival
for Cherbon and now, very obviously, Michaela Fortune—
kneeling before the woman in his own hall.

She was in the same gown she'd worn the day she'd arrived, her hand still gripped by a surprised and foolish-
looking Alan Tornfield. Her cheeks were wet with tears,
and each streak slashed outrageous fury in Roderick.

Speak, you fool! he told himself.

But the sniveling man on the floor beat him to it, as he
rose and turned toward Roderick, and the shock on his face
as his eyes blatantly roamed Roderick's costume was hu-
miliatingly apparent. He dropped his eyes to the side and
bowed stiffly.

"Lord Cherbon, forgive me this intrusion."

"I will not," Roderick managed to growl at last, and he
was dismayed at the gravelly, choked sound of his words.
His voice belonged to a monster. "What business have you
at Cherbon?"

Hugh swept a hand between the two men. "Why, he's
obviously come to pay the dues he owes, Rick! Why else
would a man, so deeply in debt to his overlord, dare come
within a stone's throw of his sire's keep? He'd be daft!"

Roderick knew this was not the case, and he knew Hugh
recognized it as well. But for once, Roderick felt inclined
to go along with Hugh's childish goading.

"Leave your coin and go then," Roderick invited. "I do not
hold court this day."

To Roderick's delight, Tornfield looked instantly uneasy.
"I have no coin to leave you as of yet, my lord."

Hugh laughed. "Forgotten your purse, have you?"

Tornfield's eyes flicked hatefully at Hugh before
coming back to Roderick. The sop managed to pull his
spine straight. "I've come for Lady Michaela."

Roderick put his walking stick to use and drag-stepped the ten or so feet separating him from Tornfield, the woman still standing at the table behind Roderick's cousin, as if shielded by him.

That suited Roderick's purpose perfectly.

"You've come for Lady Michaela?" he reiterated quietly, still keeping the damaged side of his face turned into his hood.

Tornfield's throat convulsed and Roderick wanted to chuckle at the large gulp that came from the man. "Y-yes. That's . . . that's right!" He tried to stand up even taller, but although Roderick leaned on his cane, Tornfield was still the shorter by a generous two inches. "She belongs to Tornfield Manor, and I would that she accompany me there this day."

"Huh," Roderick huffed. Then he did chuckle low, and leaned closer to Tornfield's face, so that his quietest words would be spoken directly to the blond man.

"Lady Michaela . . . is my betrothed." Roderick barely breathed the words. "And therefore . . . she belongs . . . *to me.*" He paused. "Would you steal from me . . . *cousin?*"

"O-of course not, my lord," Tornfield stuttered, and seemed to want to step back a pace but remembered the woman standing behind him. "But surely you understand that Cherbon is no place for a woman such as Michaela— she is . . ." Tornfield broke off, swallowed again. "I have a young daughter, Elizabeth, who misses her terribly, and—"

"I, too, have a child, who has grown close to Lady Michaela," Roderick said easily. "A son. *Cherbon's heir.*" He let the statement dangle pointedly.

"Is that so?" Tornfield squeaked.

Roderick nodded slowly.

"Well, ah . . ." Tornfield cleared his throat. He seemed

to gather himself and attempt to puff out his chest. "Well, I'm very sorry to tell you, my lord, but Lady Michaela is in love with *me*. She came here only to punish me over a quarrel we've had, but she doesn't wish to be here any longer. I do apologize if this is an inconvenience."

"Oh, but it is an inconvenience," Roderick insisted quietly. "A grave, grave inconvenience to me, Tornfield." Without looking away from the blond man, Roderick said, "Do you wish to go, Lady Michaela?"

From behind Tornfield, he heard her musical, if petulant, reply. "I most certainly do not! This man is married."

Roderick let the visible part of his face relax into the closest proximity of a smile he could muster. "There you are, then. You have your answer."

"No. No! I do not accept that answer!" Tornfield squeaked. "She is only cross with me! Given time—"

"The time you will be given is the time is takes me to count one to five," Roderick said, letting the forced smile fall from his mouth. "If you are still here when 'five' leaves my lips, I will fall upon you and teach you some of the exquisite pain that I was learned of in my recent travels. I do vow that the experience will stay with you a very, very long time." And with that, Roderick turned his face fully toward Alan Tornfield, and delighted in the blanket of horrified fear that fell over the man's pale face.

"Oh my God!" Tornfield choked.

"One," Roderick whispered.

"Surely you do not mean to—"

"Two . . ."

Hugh stepped forward and leaned between the two men. "I can assure you that he does not jest. Not even the slightest sense of humor, this one."

Tornfield looked to Hugh, then to Roderick, and then let

his eyes flick over his shoulder at the silent woman behind him still.

"Three . . ."

"Shall I throw you—pardon me—*show* you out?" Hugh offered courteously. "I would so hate for blood to spill on those fine, fine boots of yours. Wherever did you get them, Tornfield?"

"I—I—"

"Four . . ."

Alan Tornfield spun on his heel and skipped—walked—ran from the hall, Hugh following along leisurely and calling to him.

"Are they calfskin? The color is divine! I have a short pair in crimson, myself. . . ."

And then Roderick turned to face the woman before him, remembering too late that his scars were no longer hidden by his hood.

Her clear blue eyes widened, she gasped, and her hands flew to cover her slack mouth.

Roderick waited for her scream.

Chapter Eleven

Michaela was unsure what she had thought Roderick Cherbon would look like, but it wasn't the figure that stood before her now.

Instantly, memories of overheard rumors melded with the reality in front of her eyes, and the wild tales of his injuries were largely confirmed. He walked—putting to rest the false rumors that he could not—with the assistance of a long, black-polished, bentwood cane with a wide palm rest that he gripped with his left hand. But the large, square boots on his feet witnessed that his legs had indeed suffered the lion's share of injury in the Holy Land. Especially his left knee, which seemed to be turned outward, while the boot pointed straight ahead.

His right arm was also bent and held against his side, his fist clenched as if it were made that way, had never felt the freedom of fingers uncurled. He was dressed all in black and dark gray, as if he'd searched the land for clothing boasting the deepest absence of color in order to attire himself wholly in the shadows he was rumored to be part of. His tunic was ebony, his undershirt, pitch; only his face and the thick, corded column of his throat flashed in the dark recesses of his hood, the cloak of which was also black.

And within that diamond-shaped cave of raven wool was the fabled countenance of the Cherbon Devil. Hollow-cheeked and pale, square of jaw but with a jutting, clefted chin. His lips were full, a hairline scar diagonally breeching the curved seam, as if it had once been thought to stitch his mouth closed forever. His nose was longer than most men's, topped by a pair of bumps on the bridge, and Michaela knew it had experienced severe trauma. A thick, flat scar found its wellspring between the craggy peaks of his nose, and swept over Roderick Cherbon's right cheekbone just past the outer corner of his right eye. A clean wound made with a sharp blade, it seemed, but the scar it left was long and puckered and white, and ran off to God knew where on the rest of his head.

Above the high cheekbones—one scarred, one smooth—sunken eyes regarded her as a wary animal would appraise an unwelcome visitor to his lair. And it was there that Michaela became hopelessly mesmerized, fingertips pressing her lips almost painfully into her teeth while her heart pounded, pounded, pounded, until she thought she could hear its echo in the silent hall.

They were green, yes, but that humble word was not enough. His eyes were a spring leaf; the palest emerald; a tidal pool cupped by white sand in the morning sun. Sparkling, clear green, jeweled, dewed, glassy . . .

"Do I shock you?" he growled at her, and his tone held no little self-deprecation, aided by the slight lift of one corner of his mouth. It was as if he found her reaction amusing.

"Yes," she whispered, the word muffled still by her hands. She felt not at all like herself, and the only thing she could compare her state to was when she was lost in a song. She let her hands slide slowly from her mouth. "You . . ."

"I?" he prompted, his tone turning slightly harsh. "Yes, Miss Fortune? What is it you want to say? That I am hideously crippled? Scarred? Yes. I am. But surely you'd heard the rumors before you came."

She shook her head faintly. Why couldn't she seem to gather her wits? "No, you—"

He arched the eyebrow over his ruined cheek, seemed to turn his scars toward her more deliberately. "I'm not crippled?"

"Well, yes, you are, but—" Michaela squeezed her eyes shut for a moment and shook her head. When she looked at him once more, she felt only slightly more able to speak coherently.

"You have the most beautiful eyes I've ever seen," she breathed, and then felt her face heat as his features grew even more hard, shuttered.

"What are you about?" he growled. "Is it your game to try to play me against Tornfield? Is that why you're here? For if it is, you may pack your things and be the hell gone from my sight. I do not engage in such sport, especially with those I find to be beneath me."

Michaela felt her head draw back as if he'd struck her. Suddenly, his eyes weren't quite as beautiful as they had been only a moment ago.

"I beg your pardon?"

"You can beg all you damned well please, but I issued that missive for one purpose and one purpose only: to gain me Cherbon. If your presence engages some other itinerary of your own creation, you can bloody well take it elsewhere."

"Why are you angry with me? I did not call Alan Tornfield to Cherbon. I've stayed longer than any other woman who had come here dared, and I've spent that time fulfilling my duties in a keep and with servants who have been left to run wild. I assure you, my lord, that if my motive was to return with Alan Tornfield as his mistress—"

"It was good enough a position for you before he married," Roderick scoffed.

"You know nothing about my time at Tornfield!" Michaela insisted. "And I find your assumptions quite distasteful!"

"Oh, there are likely many things about Cherbon—both the man and the keep—that you will find distasteful, Miss Fortune." Roderick almost chuckled. "Would that you accustom yourself to it now to save yourself any future insult."

Michaela pressed her lips together as she struggled to regain hold over her temper. "Lord Cherbon, I requested your presence here because I have want to speak with you about our arrangement and the running of this hold. I thank you for coming, albeit quite tardily—"

Then he *did* laugh. "My appearance is not in answer to your summons, Miss Fortune. And our arrangement, as you call it, was set forth quite clearly by my missive and Sir Hugh Gilbert. There is nothing more for you to know." His eyes flicked about the cavernous room. "You are fulfilling your duties satisfactorily, thus far. If there is aught you do that I do not agree with, rest assured that I will have it undone." He took firm hold of his walking stick. "Now, if you'll excuse me, I was en route to other business before I stumbled upon your touching encounter with my cousin."

He turned to lurch away.

"Lord Cherbon, *wait!*" Michaela stamped her foot on the last word. He paused but did not face her. "I find it most unusual that a man would be so disinterested in the woman who is not only to be his wife, but stepmother to his son! Especially a noble man who has kind intentions toward his future family. I—I must insist that we have regular communications if we are to both find success in your endeavor to hold Cherbon."

The black-cloaked figure slowly turned, and when he looked at Michaela, his face was a stone mask of fury that caused her to back up a step.

"Mayhap it has escaped your notice, Miss Fortune, but I am not a *kind* man, not a *noble* man. You would do well to guard your person about me instead of worrying what I intend for my son, like some beggarly, weeping, useless nun. I care not one bloody shit for what you insist. If the way I run Cherbon does not please you"—he extended his cane past him—"*there* is the door. It works perfectly well as an exit as it does an entrance." He clack-stumped his way from the hall, lurching like a black, mythical creature.

Michaela stood alone once more in the silence of the grand and somehow melancholy room and wondered what in the name of God she was doing at Cherbon Castle.

As soon as Roderick had passed through the doorway from the great hall and lurched into the bailey, he regretted his harsh words to Michaela Fortune. More than regretted them—he felt as if he'd just personally ended any chance he'd ever had of keeping Cherbon. He stopped at the well and braced his hand against the timber support.

And he could still see her cheeks pinkening in her otherwise creamy face, as if each hateful word he'd said to her—about her—had been a blow in itself.

Not that he cared that he had possibly hurt her feelings. It wasn't about that, of course. Only Cherbon. Only his obsession.

Roderick turned back toward the hall and recrossed the short span of dirt he'd already come over—what would have taken an able-bodied man only seconds, took Roderick more than a full minute. He flung the door wide in his self-fury and stomped inside.

The hall was empty. Of course.

He thought for a moment of following her to her chamber but quickly dismissed the idea. She was likely packing her things now, and by the time he made the long and arduous journey to his boyhood room, she would be gone. He couldn't very well chase her, as Alan Tornfield had done. And besides, he could not think what he would apologize for. He was what he was now, for good or for ill, forever and ever, amen, if you would. His time in the Holy Land had sealed that covenant.

Roderick made his way back outdoors and up the twenty or so meters along the south wall to come around the corner of the keep. Across the eastern expanse of bailey, between bustling serfs who never once glanced his way—as they had been warned against—Roderick saw Hugh coming through the north-east gate of the outer wall, riding one horse and leading another.

Roderick would be worsened physically by the ride, he knew, but mayhap it would clear his mind.

Any matter, he would take any chance he could to ride over the lands that would now likely fall from his possession very soon.

Michaela slammed the chamber door so hard that it bounced in its frame and swung back open to crash against the wall. She attacked the slab of wood, marched it back into its proper place, and slid the bolt so forcefully, she scraped blood from three of her knuckles.

"Oh—*dammit!*" She yelled the never-before-used expletive and brought her fingers to her mouth. She decided then and there that she should curse more often. In all her life, she had obeyed her mother's instructions on a proper, chaste manner of living. What a lady did and did not do. And where had it gotten her? No one had ever *treated* her like a lady. Where were her riches, her due respect? She had been laughed at, ridiculed, reviled in her home village, whispered about at Tornfield. Now she was in the company of a man she at last realized was the beast he was rumored to be, and she had no choice but to stay and put up with it.

Cursing had felt good. And so she would continue. Often. And she would strive to learn even more vile words to add to her vocabulary. Surely Lord Cherbon would prove useful for something other than a heavy coffer, after all. What did it matter if she cursed and blasphemed? Who would hear her?

"Bloody shit," she tested on a whisper, borrowing the phrase from her surly intended.

No bolt of lightning struck her dead in the dismal room. No thunderous reprimand from Heaven caused her to fall prostrate to the floor. So, emboldened, she thought to raise her voice a bit.

"Damn bollocks, then!"

Again no fiery pit opened beneath her slippers, but a little giggle from behind her did cause Michaela to shriek and jump.

Leo Cherbon sat cross-legged in the middle of her bed,

his hands over his mouth and his eyes laughing louder than his chirp.

"Leo, what are you doing in here?" she demanded, her face heating like a fired iron.

Immediately, the little boy's forehead creased into concern and his eyes shone as if an unseen tap had been set free behind the thick, black lashes.

"Aid-ee Mike-lah cross wif Ee-oh?"

"Oh, no, no!" Michaela rushed to the bedside and climbed upon it to kneel before the boy. "I'm not cross with you. You just surprised me. Are you supposed to be in here?"

This brought the mischievous smile back to his face and he shook his head slyly. "Ee-oh no lie-down today. Hoo gone!" He held up his hands and his eyes widened as if it was a grand mystery where Sir Hugh could have possibly vanished to.

"Hugh's gone, eh?" Michaela looked sideways at him, but couldn't help but grin. He was irresistible.

Leo nodded. "Ee-oh have his lie-down wif you." And the boy flopped down on his side and snuggled into Michaela's pillows.

"Oh, why not?" Michaela sighed, and climbed up to the head of the bed. Immediately, Leo inched closer to her and reached out a little hand to grasp hers. He slid his head back to look at her and smiled as if she had just given him a pony covered in cakes.

"Why cross?"

"Why am I cross?" The little boy nodded and snuggled in even further, as if he expected a wonderful story. Michaela sighed. "Well, that is a very good question, Leo. Why am I cross? Let's see. Well, I suppose I am cross with your father."

"Wif Wod-wick?"

"Yes, Roderick." Michaela frowned. "Is that what you call him—Roderick?"

Leo nodded again. "Wod-wick big."

Michaela thought there were several words she could add to the boy's description of the Lord of Cherbon, but she refrained, once again falling back on her mother's lessons of propriety. He was only three, after all.

"Yes, he is. Leo, do you not ever call Roderick Father or Papa?"

Leo shook his head. "Wod-wick."

"Why?" Michaela could not understand this strange habit between a father and his very young son. Mayhap if Leo were ten or twelve, but not three.

Leo shrugged. "Wod-wick say, 'My name Wod-wick.' But Hoo say 'Wick.'"

Michaela nodded this time. "Yes, Sir Hugh does call him Rick, doesn't he? But would *you* rather call him something else?"

Leo seemed to think about that very deeply for one just out of swaddling. "Ee-oh *wather* say Papa."

"Do you think you would be scolded for calling him Papa?"

Leo shook his head and giggled. "Wod-wick never scold Ee-oh. Ee-oh love Wod-wick."

"Well, then, if that's what you wish to call him, and Lord Roderick doesn't mind, then you should call him Papa."

"Yes?" Leo asked, his face brightening as if it had never occurred to him.

"Yes, I think so. Most certainly."

Leo nodded as if they had decided something very grave. "But Ee-oh no see Wod-wick."

"No?"

"He no pay wif Ee-oh. Busy, busy, all time."

Michaela felt her eyebrows raise. "Would you like to spend more time with Lord Roderick?"

The little boy's eyes were huge and sad and he nodded slowly. "Love him," he reiterated. "Bess of all."

He loves him best of all. Michaela felt her heart was breaking. *The poor, misguided, abandoned baby.*

"Well, then," she said to the little boy, drawing him close and cuddling his warm body to hers, "the two of us shall work on showing him that together. What do you say to that?"

"Yay," Leo yawned. "Shh, Aid-ee Mike-lah. Ee-oh seep now, all wite?"

And it was all right with Michaela, for she had many things to think about. She stroked Leo's silky hair as he began to snore quietly.

A plan was forming in her mind.

Chapter Twelve

She was still at Cherbon.

When Roderick and Hugh returned from their ride, Roderick made use of the secret panel to confirm his suspicions, not taking any great pains in his increased stiffness to be quiet. He'd shoved open the wood trapdoor ahead of his cane and tromped inside, expecting to see a chamber abandoned with the detritus of flight.

His breath caught in his chest and brought his clumping footsteps to a gritty halt. What he'd seen instead was Miss Fortune enjoying an afternoon nap, her arm protectively around Leo. Both were snuggled together like rabbits and sound asleep. Miss Fortune stirred only slightly—rubbing her red-gold hair on her pillow—but amazingly did not wake.

Roderick dared not take another step into the room. It was late afternoon, and should either of them wake, they would clearly see the Lord of Cherbon caught before the open panel like the cowardly sneak he was. But although he would not enter farther, neither could he retreat. He felt his brows lower into a hard frown, and strange, almost nauseous feelings swirled in his stomach. Perhaps it was only the pain resulting from his punishing ride; perhaps it was missing the noon meal. But Roderick definitely felt a thick, mucousy lump stringing from his throat to his gut. Staring at the pair on the bed seemed to cause it to grow, a curiosity to Roderick, to be certain.

What a fool you are, Miss Fortune, he said in his mind, clearly hearing the derisive pity of his silent thoughts. For a breath of time, Roderick had almost respected Michaela Fortune for having the nerve to stand up to Alan Tornfield's machinations. But now, after Roderick had spoken so hatefully to her and still she remained, his opinion changed.

She must be a greedy, desperate, prideless fool. But Roderick could perhaps relax a bit again—if Miss Fortune had stayed through his scathing rebuff, 'twas likely she would stay through the end.

The lump grew again, and this time, it had the taste of fear swirled inside of it, but for what reason, Roderick could not fathom. He had no time to think upon it though, as a pounding exploded upon the chamber's proper door.

"Miss Fortune!" It was Hugh. "Miss Fortune, open the door immediately! *Miss Fortune!*"

Roderick slipped behind the panel and out of the room just as Miss Fortune's feet began to pedal the light covering from her legs. Hugh had parted from Roderick upon their return to seek out Leo and was obviously distressed that the boy was not in his chambers as expected. The image in Roderick's mind of the woman and child curled together and in the glowing afternoon light accompanied him from her chamber, and the lump in his stomach seemed to lengthen into the long rope loop of a noose.

* * *

It wasn't that Michaela was beginning to like Sir Hugh Gilbert at all, but she did smile at the memory of his handsome face, more than a bit at a loss, when she had offered to take Leo for the remainder of the day.

He had agreed, and even though he'd left Leo with a gruff admonition, "Mind yourself, Vomit, that I do not receive a report of bad-lad behavior from Lady Michaela."

"All wite, Hoo."

Michaela would have wagered her portion of Cherbon's riches that the knight already missed the boy.

And how could he not? Michaela had only known Leo for little less than a fortnight, and she was delighted by him. After their shared "lie-down," they took a turn about the bailey for more "fowwers" and a song or two. On a knoll past Cherbon's wall, near the stables, and crowned by a low, spreading, bony tree and one spindly cross, Michaela had spied a black, hulking outline, crouched on the ground in the glowing afternoon light.

It could only be Roderick.

His posture was odd, still, and Michaela wondered what called him to that desolate knoll to assume such a reflective pose.

Graves, perhaps? His father's?

But then Leo was tugging on her hand, dancing impatiently in a bent-knee squirm, and so Michaela reluctantly left the bailey to escort Leo up to the garderobe for a tinkle. There was no sign of Roderick when they descended to the kitchen well for a washup before the evening meal, which they ate side by side, chattering all the while as if they were contemporaries discussing the business of the day. Michaela pushed the image of the hulking man and his mysterious activities from her mind and gave herself over to Leo's full attention.

She was fascinated by this young person, no longer an infant but not yet the solid little boy he would become. A wonderful combination of learning and innocence and Michaela drank it up like honeyed wine.

Although she sought to concentrate on Leo in the present, she could not help wondering about the boy's mother—where was she? What had happened to take her out of her son's life? What had been her relationship with Roderick Cherbon? But Leo was little more than a baby who was unable to answer such adult inquiries, and so Michaela tucked her curiosity away as she took his small hand and led him from the hall. Night was upon Cherbon, and 'twas time to seek out Sir Hugh for Leo's bedtime, as she had promised earlier.

"Ai-dee Mike-lah sing to Ee-oh?"

She smiled down at him in the dim light of the corridor—many of the candelabras had been supplemented with additional tapers at her request, but there were still gaps.

"If Sir Hugh agrees, certainly." The stones in the keep were beginning already to radiate their sinister chill and so she turned the boy down the corridor to her own chamber. "Let's stop so that I may get a wrap and then we shall ask him together."

They were nearly upon her door when Michaela noticed it standing wide-open. She pulled Leo to a halt, and crouched down with a ready *Shh!* when he turned questioning eyes to her. Together they walked quietly to the doorway and stopped.

Michaela felt a sick fury billow up in her at the sight of Harliss riffling through her trunk, muttering crossly, and Leo immediately ducked behind Michaela's legs upon seeing the skinny old woman.

"Harliss!" Michaela barked, causing the hag to raise up

with a start and bang her head on the propped lid of the trunk. "I assume you have a very good explanation for being in my chamber, not to mention snooping in my personal belongings."

"I beg your pardon, my lady," Harliss said stiffly. She closed the lid of the trunk slowly, deliberately, and began to walk toward Michaela. "Ah . . . a chamber maid has misplaced her . . . *ring*. And I thought mayhap she had dropped it while tidying your chamber."

Michaela's eyes narrowed. "As no one has any need to clean the inside of my trunk, I doubt the ring would be there. If there even *was* a ring," she added pointedly. "Which maid has made this claim?"

The woman attempted to sidle past Michaela in the doorway. "I forget what she is called, my lady. Excuse me. I'll be about my duties."

But Michaela stepped before Harliss, denying her escape.

"I don't think I will," she said. "Excuse you, that is. I've had enough of your lies and tricks, Harliss. If you value your place at Cherbon, you will tell me the truth of why you were in my chamber."

"It was but a misunderstanding, my lady," Harliss insisted, and then tried to move past Michaela again, going so far as to push a shoulder into her.

Michaela reached out and stayed the woman with a tight grip. "You're not going anywhere until you admit you were snooping on me! Are you a thief as well as a liar?"

"Take your hands off of me, you filthy beggar!" Harliss screeched, jerking away from Michaela, all false servitude gone from her voice. "I care not one whit for what Roderick and that beggarly Hugh Gilbert say. You are *not* my mistress and I will not tolerate your whorish pawing! I was at Cherbon before you were even *whelped,* and I will take no further orders from you! You are a disgrace to the Cherbon name!"

Michaela was disquieted by Harliss's sudden fury, but because Leo was still at her side, quaking in fear, Michaela sought to rise to her station.

"Attending the garderobes not suiting you?" she asked mildly. "You should have better learned your place, then."

"It is *you* who does not suit me," Harliss growled. "And make no mistake, as soon as I am able, I will see you *thrown* forcefully from Cherbon—disgraceful, disrespectful Roderick and his little dunce of a bastard as well! *Then* we shall see who rules what."

"Oh, I think not," Michaela chuckled, although the wild look in the old woman's dull eyes was more than unsettling. Michaela was beginning to think that Harliss was quite disturbed. Whether it would be considered overstepping her duties or not, Michaela did not want such a dangerous, unbalanced old woman anywhere near Leo. "I am putting Leo to bed. When I am finished, I shall seek you. It would be best if you had your belongings already packed, for next time we meet, you are taking your leave of Cherbon. Permanently, with or without your possessions."

Harliss cackled. "You have no power here. Go back to your sty, sow, and wallow in the filth Roderick has spread while you can. There is no one at Cherbon who can move me—I'd like to see any who claim to, try!"

A dark voice rumbled from the shadows of the corridor. "I do believe I shall take that challenge, Harliss."

Michaela spun to face the voice as Leo dashed from her skirts, crying, "Wod-wick!"

He stepped from the blackness of the stone passageway, his awkward footsteps only now audible. His hood was back and for the first time, Michaela saw long waves of thick, chestnut hair. His green eyes sparkled maliciously in the flickering candlelight.

Harliss made a strangling sound before laughing again. "You'll lose! I have *tenir* here, set out years ago by your father. My place at Cherbon is secure as long as I live, whelp!"

Roderick, too, chuckled, and if Michaela had thought Harliss's mirth to be evil, the Lord of Cherbon's was positively black.

"Your death can be arranged," he suggested.

Harliss gasped. Her gray eyes narrowed. "You don't have the bollocks!"

"While there are many parts of my person that are indeed damaged, I can assure you that those are not," Roderick said, and Michaela felt an uncomfortable heat wash over her face at his crude words.

Roderick angled his chin slightly over his shoulder, fully revealing the twisting scars over his face in the candlelight. "Hugh!" he bellowed.

In moments, the sharp clickity-clickity of Sir Hugh Gilbert's boots came from the blackness. "Yes, Rick? What is—? Oh, for fuck's sake!" He was rolling his eyes as he emerged from the deepest of the shadows and stopped near Roderick, but Leo stayed wrapped around his father's leg. "Which one has done it this time?" he asked, looking pointedly between Michaela and the seething old maid next to her.

"Take Leo to his chamber—Lady Michaela and I need tend to a rather unsavory matter that I would rather he not be witness to."

"Oh?" Hugh said interestedly. "Tsk-tsk, Heartless. Done it now, have you?"

"Shut your filthy mouth, you—you . . . hanger-on! Leech! Common slut!"

Hugh's eyebrows rose as he pried Leo away from Roderick and scooped the boy up to sit in the crook of his arm. "I rather like that last one. May I use it?"

"Hugh," Roderick chastised in a low voice, as if warning him not to further antagonize the mad old woman.

"Yes, yes—all right. Let's go, Slug. Nighty-nighty, doggies bitey." He turned to duck back into the shadows, but Leo stretched out an arm toward Michaela.

"Aid-ee Mike-lah sing to Ee-oh, Hoo!"

"Not tonight, Louse. She and Rick have rubbish to dispose of. You'll see her on the morrow."

"'Night, Aid-ee Mike-lah!" Leo waved.

"Good night, Leo." She tried to give him a smile, but it was hard, knowing that in seconds she would be left alone in the dank passage with the two most frightening people she'd ever known. "Happy dreams."

"Good night . . . *Papa!*" Leo's smile was as wide as his face, and Michaela saw Roderick Cherbon freeze, his own features emotionless.

The man seemed momentarily stunned, but recovered quickly. "Now," Lord Cherbon growled, bringing his attention back to the gray woman, "would you gather your own things, or shall I have them thrown out after you?"

"You are stupider than you appear," Harliss sneered. "I've already told you, your father has set a *tenir* for—"

"I know about your *tenir*," Roderick cut her off. "You indeed have a *servile* position in the Cherbon demesne as long as you live."

"Ha!" Harliss crowed in Michaela's face. "See? I'll not be going anywhere, Misfortune!" She didn't even bother making the derogatory moniker two words.

"Oh, yes. I daresay you will," Roderick said smoothly. "I've decided to kill two crows with one boulder, as it is. You'll complete your *tenir* with Cherbon, Harliss—at Tornfield Manor."

"What?" Harliss screeched. "You can't—"

"I can, and I will, and consider it already done. Tornfield is Cherbon's and therefore fulfilling of your charter. You may live out the rest of your wretched days there, or be off Cherbon's lands forever. Your decision." He shrugged and then leaned against the stone wall, to give his leg some relief, Michaela suspected, and she wondered oddly if it pained his injured arm to press against the cold stones so. "But know that if you decide to take your leave of Tornfield, you will be breaking the charter, and I will be under no obligation to preserve your position—or your life."

"Your father was right—you are a vile, loathsome, spineless worm!"

Roderick shrugged again, the motion awkward against the stones. "Then you should be glad to be quit of me. You have a quarter of an hour. Lady Michaela and I shall meet you in the hall then, and see you gone."

Michaela started and her eyes widened, but she nodded once sagely, as if she had been in on the scheme all along.

"You will regret this," Harliss hissed, pointing a bony, gray, trembling finger at Roderick. In an instant, that cadaverlike appendage was aimed at Michaela. "You, as well, Misfortune!"

"I may regret many things, Harliss," Michaela said calmly, "but your departure from Cherbon will never be one of them."

"We shall just see!" And with that, the gray old woman spun on her bony heel and scurried into the blackness.

Michaela's heart beat one hundred times before Roderick

Cherbon spoke. "Shall we carry on to the hall, Lady Michaela?" he asked courteously, if in a growling voice full of forced patience. "I would not miss Harliss's leave, and I have come to agree with your idea that the two of us should speak."

Michaela swallowed. "You have?" She hadn't meant for the words to come out in a squeak, but there they were.

He nodded, straightened his posture, and then seemed to pause. Whatever had given him a second thought was obviously of no import, for he held out an arm for her to proceed him.

"After you."

Michaela nodded swiftly and set her mouth in a grim line as she started off down the corridor, Lord Cherbon's stumping footfalls chasing her.

She prayed that she would not trip in front of him. If the enormous man fell on her, they would both have need of a cane.

Chapter Thirteen

"So you plan on seeing this through to the end, do you?"
Roderick had not wanted the words to come out as an accusation, but he was unpracticed with speaking to a woman—
indeed, he was unpracticed in speaking to any other, save
Hugh or Leo—and so he let the words hang without apology.

Lady Michaela's forehead creased. "Well, yes, of course.
Why else would I still be here?"

Roderick merely nodded and grunted. He realized that his
hood was still thrown back onto his shoulders, and his hands
clenched against the reflex to reach up and jerk the heavy
black wool over his head. What did it matter now? She had
seen him in the hall at midday, and just now in the candlelight of the corridor. The damage was done.

Still, Roderick felt painfully exposed.

"I saw you with Leo—unlike Alan Tornfield, I do not
expect you to take the position of nurse at Cherbon."

"I understand that. I enjoy being with Leo, though. He
seems to benefit from a woman's company, do you
not agree? With . . . ah, with his mother . . ." Michaela let
the sentence dangle unfinished and her cheeks flushed,

obviously curious yet uncomfortable with the subject of Leo's mother.

"Yes, I do think time spent with you will benefit him." Roderick was not even remotely interested in broaching Aurelia with this strange young woman yet. "You have my blessing to keep his company as much as it pleases you. When you tire of him, send him to Hugh."

Michaela's frown returned, this time intensified, as if she was not at all pleased with Roderick's generosity with the boy. Then her eyes narrowed for an instant before her mouth turned upward in a sunny smile.

"Perhaps you would care to join us in the afternoons, my lord? Leo speaks of you ceaselessly and I know he would be delighted with your company. Our habit has been to walk about the bailey, but we could go anywhere—"

"Are you slow, Lady Michaela?" Roderick growled, his strained decorum creaking and splintering at her outrageous suggestion. She wanted him to walk with them? *Walk?* In the *bloody afternoon?* Surely she was not so dimwitted as to have missed his staggering, lurching, humping gait, his twisted leg, his walking stick, his destroyed face, his weaker arm. Was she deliberately goading him into admitting his failures of person?

"Am I slow? Well, yes, I suppose, I am." Michaela looked nonplussed and seemed to think for a moment. "Certainly, I can't go very fast because Leo's legs are so much shorter than mine, but ofttimes he does run, and then I daresay I am a bit quicker."

Roderick stared at the naïve look of hope on her face for a long moment, and then laughter burst from him before he had chance to squelch it.

Slow! Oh, bloody hell!

"I don't see what's humorous about that," the woman sniffed. "But I'm glad I amuse you, my lord."

Roderick swallowed down the foreign sensation of chuckles, even though her prickliness did make him want to laugh all the harder. What kind of woman was this?

"You do amuse me, Lady Michaela," he said, his words once more acceptably gruff. "Which is the only reason you still remain at Cherbon. Alas, I fear the running of the demesne leaves me little time to play about the bailey with a woman and a child, but, please, do so yourselves as often as you wish."

The woman's head drew back slightly. "Very well. Then should we meet in the hall?"

"What? When?"

"On the morrow? At the noon meal? The day after?" She held her palms toward him, as if offering him a compromise. "Or we could talk in your chamber, or mine, or—"

"About what?"

"*About what?* About . . . well, about everything."

"Aren't we doing that now?"

"Well, yes, but the everythings do vary day by day, do they not?"

"You want us to speak on a daily basis?"

The woman frowned at him and folded her arms across her bosom. "Don't you?"

"No!"

Her mouth dropped open. "Well, that is simply not acceptable," Michaela Fortune said, and then set her lips to match the tone of her words.

Roderick couldn't help but laugh again. The things that came from this woman's mouth!

"I am sorry if you find it thusly, Lady Michaela, but I

have neither the time nor the inclination to converse about matters that have no bearing on my duties."

"No bearing on your—" Now her fists went to her hips. "Your *son* has no bearing? The woman who is to be your— have you forgotten that we are to be married, my lord?"

"I have not, no." How could he forget, especially now, facing her with her color high, her oddly colored hair shining in the candlelit murkiness of the empty hall? She was innocently sensual in her anger, and it only served to remind Roderick of his failings. He wondered suddenly if Alan Tornfield had enjoyed her in his bed. Obviously he had, to have come so boldly for her.

Who would not covet a face and body such as hers?

She stared at him for a long moment, and then her anger seemed to fall away. "Lord Cherbon, certainly we would not pretend that either one of us are in this situation out of tender feelings for the other. I answered your announcement out of a need to save my family from poverty—from Cherbon's own fines, ironically—and, yes, a petty part of me wants to be certain that Alan Tornfield does not inherit the demesne. Your goal is to see your home secured to your name."

"I had nearly forgotten. Thank you."

Her eyes narrowed. "I would make a point. Even though we have been brought together for dire reasons unique to each of us, I will not sentence myself to a lifetime of estrangement from the man who is to be my husband and the father of my stepson, who I am very quickly coming to adore. I will not do it."

Roderick was confused. "What are you saying, Lady Michaela?"

"I am saying that if you can not bring yourself to give me the modicum of respect that your family deserves on a daily basis"—she took a deep breath—"then I, too, shall take my leave with Harliss."

"Surely you jest."

"No. I do not. Lord Cherbon, although this is initially a marriage of convenience for both of us, it would still be a marriage, and I see no reason why we should not foster at least a partnership between us."

She had him by the bollocks now, and Roderick wasn't sure when it had happened. In all of his meetings with Michaela Fortune, it had been *him* in control, *his* holding the prize of Cherbon's riches, which she so desperately needed, over *her* head. How arrogant was he to not have thought her to turn the tables on him and realize his needs were just as desperate—if not more so.

He needed Michaela Fortune, and in truth, he was intrigued by her. He wanted her to stay. He wanted to see her with Leo—even if from a distance; wanted her to continue working her magic on the cold, dark keep, its grandeur long-ago forgotten in place of misery and tragedy and sadness. But her challenge also transported Roderick back in time more than four years, when his father had given him his own ultimatum.

You will go to the Holy Land, make something of yourself, or you will be set from Cherbon. I'll not have you useless here—battle will strengthen you or kill you. I care not which, but one would be preferable over the other. Coddled, spoiled, weak as you are—you deserve not one stone of Cherbon.

The memory of those stabbing words, which after a lifetime of scorn should have not so much as pinched, wounded him again, angered him, brought back the resentment.

Roderick noticed he was clenching and unclenching his fists, and the longer Michaela Fortune stood there with her chin tilted at him, her gaze resolute, the more her image blurred and melted with the memory of Magnus, standing in nearly the same spot. And instead of hearing Lady Michaela's reasoning, he heard his father's damnation.

He was before her quicker than he would have thought his lameness would allow, so quickly that Michaela had no chance to flee. He grabbed her upper arms and pulled her to him, startled for an instant at how petite she was when just beneath his gaze. She tilted her face up, and although there was a flash of fear in her eyes, her stubborn jaw remained set, as if she was not going to let her intimidation of him show.

Roderick had to break her. He could not let her have the upper hand—it was too dangerous to his mind by far.

"You want to be my wife then, in truth. Is that it?"

She swallowed as if preparing to speak, but then simply nodded.

"You'd have me in your bed?" Roderick leaned his mouth near her cheek and the scent of her exploded around his head, making him dizzy. He could tell she was holding her breath, and he pushed his suit farther, leaning so close that his lips were only a whisper away. "A beast of a man, ruined, savage, who would tear you to pieces before a kind word fell from his lips?"

Her breath shivered out of her and to Roderick's surprise, her shaking voice sounded in his ear as loudly as bells from a Roman cathedral.

"Not a ruined man. *My husband.*"

He pushed her away as if she were afire, and Roderick's heart galloped like wild horse hooves. Michaela Fortune's chest heaved, and he could see the tiny, curling tendrils of her hair trembling where they had escaped around her face.

Not a ruined man. My husband.

"She's tried to abscond with the silver, Rick." Hugh's voice cut in like a bucket of icy water on the coals of Roderick and Lady Michaela's confrontation, and they both turned to see Hugh Gilbert with a large woven sack in one hand and a struggling, cursing Harliss in his other. They were standing in the far doorway that led from the servants' rooms and Roderick wondered how long Hugh had been there.

Neither Roderick nor Michaela spoke, and so Harliss jerked free from Hugh's grasp and stormed toward the pair, a much smaller sack in her own clawlike fist. She said not one word as she swept by them and to the door, although her eyes shot flaming arrows at them both. She swung open the heavy oaken slab and vanished into the night.

She didn't bother closing the door.

Hugh ambled over, a curious look on his face as he took in the pair. "I gave her leave to take one of the old mares—hope you don't mind, Rick."

"No," Roderick answered. He could not meet Michaela Fortune's eyes, but he could not take his gaze from her, concentrating instead on the long rope of hair that swept over her shoulder, near her chin. "It's fine, Hugh."

Hugh smiled his most dazzling and bowed low before Michaela. Roderick knew more than a pinch of jealousy as he was once more faced with the fact that his best friend was handsome, charming, and whole.

"Miss Fortune, I must relay Leo's appreciation of your time with him this day. He barely stopped chattering about Aid-ee Mike-lah and fowwers and such nonsense long enough for his eyes to close. So, for your generosity, you have my thanks, as well."

"I enjoy spending time with Leo very much. There is no

need to thank me as if I've performed some distasteful chore," Michaela said, her nose held slightly in the air. Then, without warning, her gaze pinned Roderick, and the question in her eyes was unmistakable. "I imagine we shall be in each other's constant company if I become his step-mother."

Roderick felt impotent here between these two beautiful, undamaged people in his home. Challenged, dared, pressed. Was he a fool? Perhaps.

"I shall see you tomorrow evening, Lady Michaela. After Leo is abed. In your chamber."

Michaela nodded once, and a ghost of a smile flitted about the corners of her lips. "I look forward to it."

Roderick wanted to flee as quickly as he could, and he cursed himself for leaving his chamber without his walking stick. As he limped past Hugh, his left arm swinging wildly to balance his lurch, he gave not so much as a good night to either of them. Hugh's eyes narrowed suspiciously.

Roderick heard his father's triumphant laugh in his own head as he slinked from the hall.

Michaela fell into the nearest chair feeling as though she could vomit as Roderick stomped from the hall. She knew her demands had not pleased the man, and she was so, so very glad her ruse had worked.

What a stupid, stupid, foolish risk she had taken by issuing that rash ultimatum! And to have been brought face-to-face with—in the very clutches of—that large, powerful man with his sparkling green eyes, talking in that low, gravelly, mesmerizing voice about the bed they would share, and whether he would rip her to pieces within it . . .

She was completely surprised that she had not fainted.

She was also surprised when Sir Hugh Gilbert—whom she had forgotten about as soon as Roderick had left—scraped back a chair across from her at the table. The look on his face was an odd combination of interest and confusion and, of course, amusement.

"You think you have him figured, do you?" Hugh asked quietly, propping a high, sculpted cheekbone against his fist.

"What? No. No, I don't think that at all," Michaela grumbled, thoughtlessly mirroring Sir Hugh's pose.

"Good. Because you don't," Hugh said without apology. Michaela flashed him a glare before he continued. "You want to try and win him, is that it?"

"Would you please go away?" Michaela groaned. "I have no desire to discuss my personal motives with you, Sir Hugh."

Hugh held up both palms and leaned away from the table. "Fine. I am simply trying to help. I would think you to welcome assistance from the one person at Cherbon who knows Rick better than any other, but"—his chair skittered back on the stones as he stood—"I can see that my help is neither desired nor appreciated. So, forgive me for my impudence and good night, Miss Fortune." He turned to go.

Michaela sat with her head resting on her fist as she reluctantly mulled over Sir Hugh's words. Of course, the exasperating man was right—who else knew Roderick better than the man who had lived through battle with him? Traveled from faraway foreign lands back to Cherbon, and who now stood by his friend's side faithfully, helping to raise Leo as well as resurrect Cherbon from the ashes?

Michaela raised her head. "Were you *offering* to help me?" she called into the shadows after Hugh, half hoping that he was already too far to hear her.

He was not.

The man materialized from the gloom like silky smoke, but remained on the perimeter of light. "Well, I wouldn't have brought it up otherwise, would I?"

Michaela frowned. She still did not like Sir Hugh Gilbert, although she didn't know why. So she asked the first question that came to her mind.

"Why would you want to?"

Hugh slowly walked back toward the table, his hands hidden behind his back. Again, he was dressed as if for a morning at the king's court, and Michaela had to admit that he was a beautiful man, although she was surprised to realize that she found Hugh Gilbert's appearance lacking next to the Lord of Cherbon's. Hugh was perfect, sculpted, charming; Roderick Cherbon was towering, dark, breathtaking.

"If Rick loses Cherbon, I have no home," Hugh said quietly. "I took debt upon everything I owned to join in the crusade, and when I came back with nothing to repay my creditors . . ." Hugh shrugged then the sardonic smile was returned to his face. "I fear I have few skills useful to trade. I dress fairly well, I can pen a decent rhyme, and I sit a horse better than any man in this land. But, where would that take me, eh? A traveling balladeer, perhaps?" He chuckled and shook his head. "I am but a frivolous decoration anywhere other than Cherbon."

Michaela nodded. It made sense, although it did strike her as darkly humorous that so many were dependent on Cherbon Castle for their very lives. Perhaps the lord himself, most of all.

It was possible that she had judged Hugh Gilbert too soon and too harshly.

"A friendship between us may be to the benefit of all," Michaela mused aloud.

Hugh's eyebrows rose. "It may, indeed."

"All right, then. What can I do?" Michaela asked.

Roderick was just finishing up his fourth cup of wine in little less than an hour when Hugh rapped lightly on and then opened his door.

Roderick knew his friend would come. Hugh could not possibly retire for the night without sharing some comment about the evening's events—he'd explode before the cock crowed.

Although Roderick valued Hugh's friendship—indeed, Hugh was the only friend he had since coming home to Cherbon—Roderick dearly wished he could spend the long dark hours alone, mulling over his predicament with Lady Michaela Fortune.

Miss Fortune, indeed.

"Never a dull moment, is there?" Hugh asked brightly, coming to flop in the chair next to Roderick's and helping himself to the carafe. "I do vow, Rick, there is more intrigue here than at Aurelia's brothel."

Roderick snorted, and drained his chalice. Hugh obliged him with more wine.

After Hugh took a long, noisy drink, he sighed contentedly. "So, are we to continue the exercises tonight? I know you're likely sore from the ride, but it will do you good to warm up your muscles, perhaps ease the stiffness."

"Not tonight, Hugh," Roderick said, having completely forgotten about their new schedule of creative torture. "I'd be useless in the ring—my leg . . ."

"Your leg, my arse," Hugh scoffed. "I do believe Miss Fortune has you in a humor."

"No, she doesn't," Roderick argued childishly, not wishing to discuss his feelings for the woman with Hugh.

"No?" Hugh challenged. "Any matter, that one's trouble, Rick. I know our time is running out, but I believe you would do better to cut Miss Fortune loose and take your chances on another arrival—any other. Marry the next one immediately, I say, warts and all."

"What have you against her?" Roderick asked. "She's younger than three score, not hideous, and *she's* here *now*. It appears to me that she is as good as any other. You've nagged at me enough over driving women away—I find it odd that you would encourage me to do that very thing with this one, Hugh."

Roderick's friend was oddly quiet for a long moment. "You find her attractive, then?"

"What?" Then Roderick snorted again as he realized his friend had picked up on only one thing he'd said—that Michaela was not hideous. "Of course not."

"Planning to take her to bed, are you?"

"Hugh," Roderick sighed.

"Your pride would be all that prevented you," Hugh cut in. "But, whatever you say, Rick. Besides, I don't think Miss Fortune would actually throw you out of her bed."

Roderick's head spun around quickly. "No?"

"Oh, don't look so hopeful. I do believe she is somewhat of a trollop."

Roderick laughed. "Oh, bloody hell, Hugh!"

"Laugh if you will, but . . ." Hugh shrugged and raised his chalice to his lips.

Roderick grew solemn once more. "What would lead you to believe that? Desperate as he is, I doubt my cousin would be so eager to have a trollop in his home, keeping his daughter company."

"Well, Miss Fortune slept with him, and they weren't married—not even betrothed, so . . ."

"How could you possibly be certain of their intimacy?" Roderick demanded, wanting to think that perhaps his fears about Miss Fortune's relationship with Alan Tornfield were unfounded.

"Oh, come on, Rick—it's all anyone at Tornfield could talk about at the feast! Why do you think she was so humiliated when he wed that other woman? They were quite predictable—Tornfield accompanied Miss Fortune to her chambers each night, after the daughter was abed."

Roderick said nothing, trying to digest this new bit of information. After a while, he said, "Whatever happened between Lady Michaela and Tornfield before she came to Cherbon has no bearing on the present or the future. She chose not to return there, so I can assume anything between them is over."

"Assume all you like, but Miss Fortune is in love with him," Hugh said easily. "If you marry her, it will put you in quite the awkward position, having your wife take your cousin for a lover."

"You are too dramatic, Hugh."

"Am I? What of when she begs you for Alan Tornfield's pardon for his dues? When she flaunts their affair both here and at Tornfield? You'll be the laughingstock of the land. For all we know, her presence at Cherbon is naught but an intricate scheme concocted by both she and Tornfield."

"She won't go back to Tornfield." Roderick didn't know how to explain it, but he felt in his gut that whatever feelings Michaela Fortune had for Alan Tornfield had been but juvenile daydreams which he had dashed in a most rude, adult manner when he'd married another. And Roderick simply did not believe that Alan Tornfield would find it in his own best interest to plant Michaela—as a lover or otherwise—in the lair of the Cherbon Devil.

"All right, perhaps not Tornfield," Hugh conceded. "But a woman like that likely won't keep a lonely bed for long."

Roderick shrugged. "I care not. She can take a lover if she so chooses, as long as she's discreet."

"And bear another man's child for you to rear?"

Roderick sent Hugh a swift, dark look.

"I'm simply saying, Rick, your generous nature can only be tested so far." Hugh stretched out his legs and drained his cup. "Trust me, Miss Fortune's first order of business will be to have you wrapped securely around her bitty finger, under the brilliant ruse of the two of you becoming best mates. It wouldn't surprise me in the least if she went so far as to seduce you."

Roderick laughed harshly, even though the idea of Michaela Fortune's seducing him to her bed stirred his manhood. He shifted in his chair. "Oh, I do doubt she'll go that far."

"I don't know, Rick—she seems quite desperate," Hugh said, and Roderick felt as though his friend had punched him. It was one thing for Roderick to think such low thoughts of himself, to himself, but quite another to hear them from the mouth of his best friend.

But Hugh swept right over the slight as if it had never been. "You know—I'll wager one silver piece that when next you two are alone she tries to get you to kiss her."

"What?" Roderick laughed, thinking to himself how close he had come to doing that very thing before Hugh and Harliss had appeared. And how very much Roderick had wanted to kiss her. "Hugh, you are too much."

"Scared you'll lose? Or scared I'll win?" Hugh taunted

with a grin. He dug inside his tunic for his small leather purse and then jerked open the laces. "Come on then." Hugh slapped the small silver coin down on the table between their chairs. "Put your coin where your convictions hide, Lord Roderick Cherbon, you devil!"

Roderick couldn't help but laugh. "All right, all right! I will take that wager, Sir Hugh Gilbert, Lord of Nothing."

"Bloody right." Hugh held his hand across the tabletop and coin toward Roderick, and Roderick readily grasped it, sealing the bet. "Now, off your arse—I have torture to inflict, and you sorely deserve it after the way you treated poor Heartless. Let's go, Rick."

As Roderick struggled to his feet, he realized once more how lucky he was to have Hugh for a friend. Blunt and crass or not, it was because of him that Roderick lived now. And Roderick would forgive Hugh Gilbert any little slight.

Chapter Fourteen

Although having Leo for the afternoon was a great distraction, Michaela could still feel the thorny knots cinching tighter and tighter in her stomach as evening drew ever nearer.

She had demanded this meeting, and now she had no earthly idea what they were to talk about. Of course Hugh Gilbert's advice gave her a good start: seek to be his friend. Ask questions about his past and show interest in his family, his father, and the time he was away from Cherbon. Be bold with his person. He might balk at first, Hugh had warned, but she must be relentless in her pursuit.

Very well. Michaela would be relentless.

If she did not collapse in terror at his first growl.

"Aid-ee Mike-lah sing to Ee-oh tonight, yes?" the little boy demanded from beside her on the bed, drawing Michaela blessedly out of her own head. They had been playing with Leo's collection of wooden animals, and a menagerie of four-legged creatures lay scattered across the covers.

"Yes, of course," Michaela acquiesced. "But your papa is to come and speak with me once you are off to sleep, so we'd best have a song or two here, in my chamber, before Sir Hugh comes to fetch you. All right?"

"All wite." Leo dropped the cow in his hand and snuggled closer to her, laying the side of his face against her bosom, and it brought a warm smile to her face. He was so precious. "Sing about the aid-ee and the sip."

"The lady and the ship?" Leo nodded against the fabric of her gown. "It's rather morbid for bedtime, but all right." She cleared her throat and began the song by humming the refrain before singing the first verse.

"There was a young maiden from Surrey, who loved a young man of war. He went far away in a hurry, on a ship that followed a star. She begged him and cried for his leisure, but the young soldier paid her no heed; he left for a promise of treasure, his heart had been conquered by greed.

"Hoo-lah, hoo-lah! My lady awaits him, down where the sea meets the shore; Hoo-lah, hoo-lah! She'll wait there forever, for a ship that will sail there no more."

Through three more verses, telling of the loyal maiden and her greedy lover's fate—the violent storm, the watery grave for the heartless fellow, Michaela sang the sad song, and Leo grew more limp against her. She held him close and dropped her voice to nearly a whisper as she finished the final refrain. "Hoo-lah, hoo-lah! She'll wait there forever, for a ship that will sail there no more."

"Well, if that doesn't give the lad nightmares, I don't know what will."

Michaela jumped, causing Leo to stir in her arms and sit up. She had been so immersed in the song and the feel of the little boy against her that she had not heard her chamber door open or Hugh Gilbert enter. Her stomach did a funny tumble when she saw Roderick Cherbon looming in the doorway behind him. Fledgling friendship or nay, Michaela sent Hugh a disapproving frown.

"What?" the knight implored, coming to the side of the bed and holding out his arms for Leo. "We knocked. You obviously didn't hear us with all your caterwauling. Hello, Slime. Had a good day, have you?"

"Yes, Hoo. Papa!" Leo pushed aside Hugh's arms and slid from the bed on his backside, his feet running toward Roderick before they had met the floor properly. The little boy once more launched his arms around Roderick's long legs beneath the cloak, and although Michaela saw the pained look on Roderick's face, she was oddly pleased that he dropped a hand down to Leo's back. The pats were awkward, but they were pats.

"Leo," Roderick replied gruffly, "why are you calling me Papa, of a sudden?"

"You my papa, Papa," Leo said simply and Michaela let loose the silent breath she'd been holding against Leo confessing her part in the Papa business. "And Aid-ee Mikelah say call you what I call you. Papa!" Leo tilted his head back and grinned up at Roderick.

Michaela cringed as Roderick shot her a questioning look, but she was spared any further comment as Hugh took firm but gentle hold of the boy. "Let's go, Weevil. Nighty-nighty, doggies bitey."

"'Night, Papa."

"Good night, Leo."

"'Night, Aid-ee Mike-lah."

"Good night, Leo. Dream happy dreams."

As the man and boy quit the chamber, Hugh gave Michaela an exaggerated wink and a smile, and it bolstered her courage.

Until the door closed and she was left alone in her dark, quiet room with the Cherbon Devil.

Relentless, Michaela reminded herself.

"Good evening, my lord." She sent him what she hoped was a friendly smile, although her nerves were making her lips tremble. If he looked too closely at her, he would think she had palsy.

Even though he had spoken readily enough to Leo, Lord Cherbon's reply was little more than a growl. He still stood near the door, as if he expected their initial meeting to last only moments, so that he could make a ready escape.

"Won't you come in?" Michaela asked, indicating with one hand the small pairing of table and chairs near the hearth. Michaela had ordered the fire built to blazing, so that even though the few candles illuminated the darkest corners of the chamber and the bedside where she and Leo had played, the brightest spot in the room was the warmest.

And also the most intimate.

Roderick Cherbon's permanent scowl was barely visible in the deep recesses of his hood, but Michaela could see the crevasses on either side of his mouth deepen. His arms were crossed, and his walking stick dangled from the crook of an elbow. "Forgive me if I do not," he began. "Is there aught which—"

His hasty excuse was cut short by a soft rapping on the door, and Michaela sent up a silent prayer of thanks for the interruption—some of the servants in the hold were actually beginning to heed her on nearly a regular basis.

"My lady," the voice of the maid called through the door. "I've the tray ye called fer."

"Pardon, my lord." Michaela smiled sweetly as she moved nearer to Roderick, causing him to do the very thing she expected—and desired: he moved away from her, farther into her chamber. Before she opened the door, Michaela saw Roderick turn his back to the room, facing the roaring fire.

Michaela took the tray from the maid with a smile and murmur of thanks and kicked the door closed with her heel before walking carefully toward the giant black shadow near the table. She stumbled over the edge of the rug, but caught herself with a gasp as plates rattled threateningly. She had to remind herself to smile despite the urge to roll her trembling lips inward and bite them still when he turned to apprise himself of her progress or impending crash.

"Here we are," she said cheerfully, setting the tray of fresh bread and wine and a slab of white cheese on the table.

Lord Cherbon's hood twitched as he glanced down at the table, and then the dark oval of shadow faced her. "Did you miss the evening meal?"

"Ah, no. No." Michaela tried not to stutter. It was quite difficult—the man was the most intimidating person she'd ever met, not to mention entertained alone in her bedchamber. "But I know you have the habit of dining late, and I thought perhaps we could enjoy a light repast together while we talked."

"I'm not hungry." He turned back to the fire, his posture rigid.

Could he really dislike her so much, already?

"All right." Michaela struggled to keep hold of her nerves. She reached for the carafe. "Perhaps some wine, then?"

"*I don't want any bloody wine, either!*" Lord Cherbon barked, causing Michaela to jump and the wine coming from the mouth of the carafe to overshoot the chalice and splash over the entire tray. The vessel slipped from her hands, despite her attempts to grip it even tighter, somersaulted over the bread, and clanged to the floor, where it rolled away in the darkness.

"Now look what you've made me do!" she shouted, her embarrassment spurring her words before she had time to think upon the implications of them.

"I made you do naught," Lord Cherbon growled. "I didn't wish this meeting, and I don't wish to be here now. I do not appreciate being dictated to in my own home, and you can be assured that my generosity is at its very end. Save your hospitality, Lady Michaela, and if you have aught to say to me, I beg you, do get it out."

It was the final straw for Michaela. Despite her resolve to be a stronger, more willful woman now that she was at Cherbon, the strain of being here was simply too much on her brave façade. Alan Tornfield had been right: Cherbon was no place for a woman such as she. And that thought set loose the first tears. Covered in wine, trembling from fear and nerves, at her own end and not caring what Lord Roderick Cherbon thought about it, Michaela sat down hard on one of the chairs and dropped her head onto her arms, sobbing to her deepest humiliation.

"You are a h-horrible, h-horrible man!" she wailed into the tabletop. What did it matter now, what she said to him? No one at Cherbon had any care for others' feelings, and if Roderick Cherbon wanted to throw her out for voicing her misery, then so be it.

"I don't know why you seem so shocked," Roderick said gruffly. "I told you as much myself."

She ignored his defense. "All I've done at Cherbon since my arrival is try to better this hold. I've tried to friend Leo, even that . . . that obnoxious Hugh Gilbert!" She found her stride then, and raised her head to swipe at her eyes with the heels of both hands. "I miss my mother and father—I've no one to talk to here save a boy who has not even seen three years! I've put up with surly and disobedient servants—not to mention Harliss, herself—and all the while I've had to retire to this wretched, horrid, sad room to spend my evenings alone, wondering why the man who might one day be my husband will have naught to do with me or his son or anyone who does not . . . who does not dress in red calfskin boots!"

Michaela drew a deep breath, blew it out in a whoosh, and wiped her nose on the hem of her skirt. At least she was no longer trembling. She fully expected Roderick Cherbon to turn on his heel and stomp from the room, but he remained before the fire, motionless.

"Do you also miss Tornfield?" he asked gruffly, and Michaela nearly fell from her chair in shock.

She was taken so off guard that she answered honestly. "I do. Lord Alan and Elizabeth . . . they grew to be like family to me. I have never been happier in all my life than when I lived at Tornfield Manor."

"Then why did you flee there? Why did you not return when Tornfield invaded my home and begged you like a spineless coward to return?"

Her throat constricted again. "That is absolutely none of your business."

"It was because he cuckolded you, was it not? You were his lover and yet he chose to marry another, setting you aside like rubbish."

Michaela was so outraged she could not speak.

"It matters not to me," Lord Cherbon continued mildly. "You may take a lover, if you wish."

Michaela could barely choke out, "Why, thank you, my lord."

Her sarcasm was obviously lost on him, for he merely shrugged. A long pause fell between them, and during that time, Michaela realized that this was the longest and most civilly Roderick Cherbon had spoken to her since her arrival. He still had not moved from before the fire, as if he were made from the same heavy stones that comprised the hearth.

"Will you?" he asked suddenly, turning that black oval of hood toward her again.

"Will I what?"

"Keep a lover."

What a strange, strange place Cherbon was. And what a strange man, as well. He had her so confused by the way his topics of conversation flitted from one thing to the next. Michaela shrugged, because she didn't know what else to do.

"I've not made up my mind." She let another pause stretch out between them before asking, "Is it your wish that I do so?"

The black hulking figure jerked. "If it pleases you. Lord Alan, mayhap?"

"Lord Alan is married, remember?"

The hooded figure seemed to look at his feet. "But you would also be married."

Michaela nodded, and she couldn't help but feel that Roderick Cherbon was testing her, trying to draw information of a mysterious nature from her. "Indeed I would be." Perhaps it was his manner, to see the strength of her mettle. If so, then she would return the favor to him. There was little more damage she could do at this point.

"What if you become my lover . . . Roderick?" Just saying the words caused her heart to race, and she could feel the flutter of her own pulse, like a tiny bird thrashing against the curtain of her throat.

Lord Cherbon was entirely motionless, and for the time it took Michaela to count twenty, he neither moved nor spoke.

At last she sighed. "But, alas, that would not do, either."

Roderick's profile twitched her way, and his hood shifted the smallest measure, throwing a bar of stuttering gold across his ruined cheek.

"Why is that?"

Michaela smiled. "Because you would be a married man, as well."

The rough curve of his scar lifted on his cheek, like a craggy cliff shifting, sliding, into the rocky field of a shadowy grin.

"Indeed, I would be," he said.

Before her bravado could slip away from her, Michaela stood and stepped to stand perpendicular to the Lord of Cherbon. To her surprise—and her fearful excitement— he, too, turned, so that they stood facing each other, little more than a handsbreadth apart. Michaela looked up into his once more darkly shadowed face, and before she could hesitate, she reached up with both hands and pushed the hood back from his head.

He flinched, but Michaela paid him no heed, letting her arms go back slowly to her sides and her gaze rove over his face, his scars, his full lips, his beautiful, dazzling eyes, sating her curiosity as she'd not had chance to since first seeing those green depths. The only sounds in the room were their breaths meeting and swirling together before dashing toward the crackling flames to be washed up the chimney.

"You dislike this chamber?" he asked suddenly, quietly, and Michaela watched his mouth as he spoke.

"I loathe it," she admitted.

Roderick nodded. "It was my boyhood room. I, too, detested every moment in it."

"Little wonder no other women stayed, if this is where you interred them."

Roderick's mouth curved into a smile, but jerkily, as if the motion was still largely foreign to him. "You may move, if you wish."

"Why did *you* detest this chamber?" Michaela asked, wondering at the childhood Roderick had endured at the hands of Magnus Cherbon. She tried to imagine Roderick as a young boy, a tawny-haired Leo.

But it had been the wrong thing to ask. Roderick's face closed down with a nearly audible slam, and he made to move away.

But Michaela grabbed his forearm, realizing too late that it was the arm that had been so dreadfully injured. She felt, rather than heard, his intake of breath, and eased her grip, although she did not let go completely.

"Does it hurt?" she asked on a whisper, indicating with her eyes where her fingers rested, but quickly realizing that the question could mean so very many things.

"At times," Roderick whispered back. "But not often, now." His answer, too, was infinite.

Moving slowly, as if approaching a baby rabbit instead of a huge, dangerous mass of a man, Michaela raised her hands once more to his face, this time, laying her palms alongside his cheeks. She brushed his long scar with her left thumb.

"This?" she asked.

He shook his head, only a twitch.

She moved her right hand, drawing her forefinger lightly down the bridge of his nose. "This?"

Again, he shook his head.

Michaela's eyes went to the diagonal scar spanning his mouth, and she touched it with both thumbs, looking into his eyes and raising her eyebrows in silent question.

"No," he answered.

Michaela let her hands slide past his ears to the back of his neck and pulled gently. She rose up on her toes and pressed her lips to his cheek, then to his nose, then to the thin white line over his lips, warm and smooth and soft. Then she let him go.

He stared at her for a long moment and then a rather unexpected snort came from him and he shook his head.

"He's always right," Roderick murmured.

"Who is always right?" Michaela asked with a frown.

"Exactly." Roderick drew his hood up once more and moved away from Michaela toward the door, his walking stick cracking impatiently.

"Good night, Miss Fortune," he said gruffly.

"But—"

"I'll see you tomorrow evening," he said, cutting her off as he swung open the door, slipped into the corridor, and left her with nothing but its solid slam and a mess on her floor.

Michaela sighed. "Bloody hell."

Roderick stumped through the maze of corridors toward his own chamber as fast as his crippled, useless body would carry him, and the entire way, his father's cawing laughter rang in his ears. His mouth was set painfully against his teeth as he stomp-dragged-stomped, his lips still feeling the warm burnish of Michaela Fortune's kiss.

Fool, fool, fool . . .

Yet all the while, his stomach clenched with traitorous excitement.

Fool!

He neared his door, and threw it open into the wall, startling Hugh from his usual post-Leo-bedtime lounge in one of the tall armchairs.

"God, Rick! Now look—you've made me spill wine on my best tunic," he spat, brushing at the red droplets splattered down his front.

'Twas the second time in an hour Roderick had been accused of such a thing.

Roderick clomped to his wardrobe, jerked open one half of the doors with his free hand, and cleared a shelf of miscellany with one swipe, revealing his small coffer of incidental coin. He threw open the lid, fished out a coin, and turned back to Hugh, leaving the wardrobe swinging wide.

Roderick nearly destroyed the table, slamming the piece of silver down. As it was, the tabletop let loose a splintering sound and wrenched to the side, causing Hugh to snatch at the coin before it slid to the floor.

"I'll be in the ring. You can join me or no." Roderick turned to stomp from the room, not caring if Hugh followed.

To hell with them all.

As he disappeared into the black corridor, he missed Hugh clenching the coin in his hand, and the satisfied smile that spread over his mouth.

Chapter Fifteen

"You must wear your shoes, Leo."

"No! No soos."

"*Yes*. A proper boy must not go about barefoot. The keep floors are like ice—you'll catch a chill."

"No soos!"

Michaela sighed as the little boy struggled free from her lap and dashed across the floor to collapse at his pile of toys scattered on the rug. She tossed the small leather slipper into the air and let it fall.

Forget the fool she'd made of herself with the lord of the keep last night, she couldn't even get a three-year-old to wear his shoes. How ever was she to make a proper lady of Cherbon? At any minute, she expected a smug Hugh Gilbert to appear, carrying the message that Roderick wished her to take her leave posthaste.

She hoped Hugh *would* show his handsome, smirking face. She was in this awkward predicament now, thanks to his insane advice. Perhaps his little scheme had worked flawlessly to seduce countless simple maidens, but with an argumentative, looming, wounded man—no. Most certainly it had not.

She had to get away from the keep for a while, clear her head, and give herself time to think.

She stood and gave a loud, dramatic sigh. "Well, then, I suppose I shall see you later this afternoon."

He paused his chubby hand, holding a mounted soldier that had previously been intent on leveling the surrounding toys, and turned curious eyes up to her. "Where you go, Aid-ee Mike-lah?"

"Oh, I'm only going for a walk about the bailey. Too bad you shan't be able to come with me and keep me company."

Leo shot to his feet, the mounted soldier left to the revenge of his fallen victims. "Ee-oh go, too!"

"No, I'm afraid not." Michaela shook her head sadly. "You see, it is too wet for a lad to go about outdoors barefoot. And since you don't wish to wear your shoes . . ." She shrugged. "But I'll come and see you when I get back, all right?" She started for the door.

"No, no, no!" Leo wailed, and Michaela turned to see the little boy scavenging around on the floor, seeking the mate to his slipper. "Ee-oh has soos! Ee-oh has soos! Wait for Ee-oh!" He fell onto his backside with a huff as he struggled to pull on the leather shoe.

Michaela smiled to herself and went to him, dropping to her knees. "Shall I help you?"

"Yes." Leo all but threw the shoe at her in his haste.

"Yes, what?"

"Pees."

Michaela cupped his cheek in her palm, pleased with both the boy and herself. "Very good."

Perhaps she wasn't so stupid after all.

It was only a matter of moments before Michaela and Leo were free from the oppressive darkness of Cherbon Castle, roaming the open bailey in the chilly, breezy sunshine. They were just coming around the northeast side of the keep when the familiar round form of Friar Cope emerged from a small, nearly hidden doorway.

"Fire Cope!" Leo shouted, as usual, pleased to see everyone he happened upon, and ran to the holy man.

"Good day, Leo. Keeping Lady Michaela busy, I see." He raised his eyes to Michaela. "Good day, my dear. How are you holding up?"

"Oh, quite well, Friar," Michaela lied. "Off on another mission?" she asked, eyeing the saddlebag seated on his shoulder.

"Another round through the demesne, before weather is upon us." He looked briefly to the sky as if expecting a blizzard at any moment. "Have you seen Lord Roderick today?"

"No, not yet," Michaela hedged, wondering if she would see him tonight as Roderick had promised. She tried to stamp down the nervous excitement the thought provoked in her.

"Perhaps you should seek him out," the friar suggested mysteriously. "He has audience with a man whom I'm certain you will be very pleased to see."

Michaela could not stifle her groan. "It isn't Alan Tornfield, is it?" Heavens, that man had caused her enough trouble, and if the Lord of Tornfield had come to speak to Roderick again, Cherbon's mood would be the blackest of black upon the blond man's departure.

The friar shook his head. "I cannot say. You must find out for yourself—they're in the chapel." He nodded toward the door he'd come from and began to walk away, ruffling Leo's hair. "God be with you both."

Cherbon Castle had a chapel? Of course, it made sense if Cope made his residence here, but there were no church services that Michaela was aware of. No servant had mentioned it, and neither had Hugh Gilbert or Roderick. Not even Cope, himself.

"Oh, Friar, wait!" Michaela called. She had just remembered an important question nagging her mind that the friar may know the answer to.

He turned, but continued walking backward, holding a palm up. "Press me not, Michaela. Lord Cherbon is put-out enou—"

"No, it's not about the visitor," Michaela rushed, thankful the words caused the older man to pause. She pointed to the faraway knoll, just visible over the curtain wall. "Are those graves?"

The friar's gaze turned to follow Michaela's arm, and he nodded. "Yes. Eight of them."

Aha! Michaela said to herself, pleased that her instincts had been correct. "Who is buried there?"

Friar Cope glanced at the keep, as if expecting condemnation. "Magnus Cherbon, Roderick's father; Dorian Cherbon, Roderick's mother. And six of their seven children. Good day."

Friar Cope turned once more, and in moments had disappeared through the northeast gate, toward the stables and the place where Roderick Cherbon's entire family, save the son that now stood against her skirts, lay dead.

"Lord Cherbon, I beg of you," the old man said to Roderick with a frown. "The friar is gone now. I know where the box is, and it will cause no harm to the altar. If you'll only let me prove—"

"Lord Fortune," Roderick growled, already at his wits' end with his betrothed's father. "I care not one whit what damage might befall this waste of space in my home." He looked around the long, tall-ceilinged, ornate room, grander even than the great hall, with scorn. "My refusal though, is twofold: I will not be party to any such religious superstition you have deluded yourself to be truth. And I will not allow exhumation of an item laid buried by my father. He was an evil man, and aught that he touched was also thusly. Let it stay buried."

"You don't understand." Walter Fortune shook his head impatiently. "Lord Cherbon, I knew your father well—and yes, he was an evil, black-hearted man. But the thing he buried here, he did as a kindness for me—for my wife and daughter. For Michaela. I must have it back—it cannot remain within the same walls as her. It is too dangerous, for everyone here at Cherbon. Especially you, my lord."

"Had you forgotten of this item when you delivered your daughter to my doorstep, Fortune?" Roderick challenged. "Perhaps in your haste to secure her place—and yours—in my coffers?"

The old man flushed. "No, sire. I had not forgotten. I simply doubted that Michaela would stay."

Roderick snorted and then studied the intense old man for several moments, thinking to himself. *Fortune, Fortune. Walter Fortune . . .*

Something about his wife, wasn't it? Something she'd lost or she'd cursed . . . ?

Roderick caught a slight flash of light out of the corner of his right eye. When he turned his head, he saw nothing, and attributed it to one of the annoyances brought on by his injuries.

Any matter, Roderick still could not place the old man in his memory, which was no wonder—Magnus had not lowered himself to speak to his son often, unless it was to berate or shame him or his mother. "Is it valuable, this thing you seek?"

Walter shook his head. "No, my lord. No value at all. It's likely turned to dust after these score of years, yet I cannot risk—"

"Where is it, exactly?"

The old man threw a nervous glance over his shoulder, toward an alcove where an enormous stone carving of a winged warrior astride a rearing horse loomed to the left of the chapel's altar.

"Buried under the only perfectly square stone beneath the horse's raised hooves," Walter almost whispered, and to Roderick's amusement, the old man began to withdraw a long, thin, iron bar from his tunic, of all places. "I can easily pry the stone loose and have—"

"No," Roderick interrupted, shaking his head. "If it is a part of Cherbon, it belongs to me."

"But look upon it, my lord," the old man rushed. "If you feel it is of value, I will leave it to your guardianship. But I swear to you, it is useless to anyone other than m—"

The old man's plea was interrupted by the sound of a scuffle near the vestibule—where Roderick had thought he'd seen a flash of light. Had it been someone slipping in through the doorway?

Walter Fortune had heard the whispering, too, and his pose mirrored Roderick's.

"Who's there?" Roderick demanded. "Show yourself!"

Leo dashed from the shadows, his happy face coming

into kaleidoscope view from the stained-glass windows set high into the walls. Roderick groaned as the little boy ran to him, knowing that where Leo went, also trod—

"Papa!" Michaela Fortune's face was a wash of surprise and pleasure as she saw her sire standing before Roderick, and she rushed to the old man and threw her arms about his neck. "How wonderful that you've come! Is Mother with you, as well?"

"Hello, my dear," Walter said, forcing a smile and returning his daughter's embrace, although the look he gave Roderick over Michaela's shoulder seemed to beg: *Do not tell her.*

"No, your mother is at home. I only thought to look in upon you and see how you fared at Cherbon." He drew his daughter away and looked her up and down. "You've thinned out a fair bit, I'd say."

"Perhaps," Michaela replied dismissively. "Leo does keep me rather busy. Papa, this is Lord Cherbon's son, Leo. Leo, this is *my* papa, Lord Fortune. Say your manners."

Leo took a half step away from Roderick's legs and bowed his chin down to his chest. "Gooday, my lord."

"Good day, Leo." Walter smiled at the boy and then his eyes went to Roderick's. "A fine son you have, my lord. You must be protective of him."

Roderick grunted.

"Will you stay, Papa? A day or two, mayhap?"

"No, no, I'm afraid not." Walter Fortune looked at his daughter, but Roderick knew the old man's next words were for him alone. "I will be back, though. I cannot leave my only child's side for long."

"Oh, Papa." Michaela smiled. "But you're not leaving this moment, are you? Surely you've only just arrived!

The journey home is lengthy, and you are no longer the freshest of men."

Walter Fortune sent his daughter a mock frown. "I'll thank you to mind your pert tongue, young woman." Then he let his daftly kind smile shine through again.

Roderick wondered how this man, seemingly so innocuous and simple, could have been connected in any way with Magnus Cherbon.

"But you are right. I would rest my bones this night and be off with the dawn. We all might share a meal together, in good will." Walter looked to Roderick while Michaela clapped her hands together. "If it meets with Lord Cherbon's approval, of course. There are some matters I still have need to discuss with him."

As far as Roderick was concerned, the conversation he'd had with Walter Fortune comprised the whole of their palaver, and he would not entertain the impotent old fool's fanciful hunt again.

Hunt . . .

The word triggered a catch somewhere deep in Roderick's mind, but he swept it aside as nonsense, choosing instead to address his betrothed's sire.

"You need not my permission to stay, Fortune—Cherbon is your daughter's home now, as well. But I do not take meals in the hall, so . . . enjoy." Roderick turned to Michaela, his eyes wanting to land and linger on those lips, whose feel and texture he still remembered so vividly from her folly last night. "If you'll excuse me, Lady Michaela."

"My lord." Michaela bowed her head slightly, and Roderick wondered if it was his imagination that showed him Miss Fortune's eyes straying to the location of his own mouth.

He moved, but had forgotten the accessory about his knee that was Leo.

"Turn me loose, Leo. I have matters to tend to."

"Ee-oh go wif you. Ee-oh go wif him papa."

Roderick looked up at Michaela pointedly, expecting her to intervene as Hugh would.

She only stared back at Roderick, a cryptic smile on her full, pink lips.

"Leo, you . . . I have—" Roderick tried to think of an excuse—any excuse—that would put the boy off. It shouldn't have been hard to think of a reason that would seem plausible to a three-year-old, but when Roderick looked down into the wide brown eyes, so like the beautiful, exotic Aurelia's, the greasy knot filled his throat again, and it seemed to dam logical communication between his brain and his mouth.

Roderick looked at Michaela, knowing her silence was purposeful. She would not rescue him—bloody hell, it was likely she had put the boy up to it.

"You'll come and get him in one hour," Roderick growled.

"Of course, my lord. From where shall I fetch him?"

Roderick searched his mind. His only plans after being rid of Walter Fortune had been to retire to his chamber— he was dreadfully unused to being about in the daylight.

"We shall be in my accounting chamber." Roderick reached down and pried the boy from his leg. "*Let go* that I might walk without you underfoot." Roderick started for the rear of the blasphemous chapel in his pathetic, stomp-drag manner.

The sound of clattering feet soon caught up with him, and Leo dashed around to his other side in order to slip a hand into the folds of his cloak.

"We go count all you money, Papa?"

"Yes, Leo," Roderick sighed. He would have to speak to Hugh about the subject matter he discussed with the three-year-old. "We're going to go and count all of my money."

Chapter Sixteen

The time between when Roderick had left Michaela and her father in the chapel and when she awaited him in her chamber that night seemed to span three days.

Would he come as he'd said he would? Or had his parting words to her been only a nod to courtesy? She didn't think so—the Lord of Cherbon seemed to care little for niceties or the sparing of feelings, Michaela knew firsthand.

She'd hoped to ask him if he indeed planned on visiting her chamber again when she'd gone to fetch Leo, but the only persons she'd encountered in Cherbon's monies room were Leo and a smirking Hugh Gilbert. And while disappointed that Roderick had vanished on her—and Leo—yet again, Michaela had taken the opportunity to complain to Hugh about his method of drawing Lord Cherbon from his shell and gaining his confidence.

But Hugh had not seemed put off in the least by Michaela's angry—if hushed, for Leo's sake—accusations. He'd assured Michaela that he knew "Rick" better than anyone, and that his plan would work.

"Relentless," he reminded her again, and then with a wink, suggested, "Bolder! Push him."

So now Michaela sat in one of the chairs by the hearth once more, only this time she shivered with every chill that raced across the floor, and tucked her bare feet under the hem of her skirt.

She'd taken off her shoes.

She hoped that was bolder.

The rap on her door caused her to jump and gasp, a hand to her chest. Michaela took a deep breath and blew it out before calling as calmly as possible, "Yes?"

The door opened and there he was, tall and wide-shouldered in his draping black cloak, his walking stick kicked out to the side of his shadowed outline, and at the memory of the green eyes she knew were hidden in the darkness of his hood, the roughness of his upper lip, the tight smoothness of the scar on his cheek; remembering the smell of him, the largeness of his person when Michaela stood in his shadow, the thought of the young, lonely boy he used to be, visiting the graves on a nearby knoll, caused her heart rate to treble.

He came in without invitation this time, Michaela was pleased to note, and shut the door behind him.

"Good evening, my lord," Michaela said.

Roderick Cherbon grunted.

Michaela smiled at him and stretched out her legs as she poked her frozen toes from beneath her skirt. She did think her feet quite pretty. For feet, of course.

His hood flicked down at the movement, and then raised to address her face once more.

"Have you lost your shoes?"

Michaela felt the heat wanting to creep up into her face, and was glad her back was to the fire—mayhap it would shadow her embarrassment.

"No, I—I felt more comfortable taking them off this evening," she said, a trifle defensively even to her own ears. She felt the need to disconcert the massive man now more than ever. She let her voice go husky. "I like . . . I like the feel of the fire on my bare skin."

He crossed the floor in his deliberate, careful manner, showing Michaela how much skill and balance it took to move a body of such grand dimensions. He stopped a pair of paces from her and with the hand not holding his walking stick, pushed back his hood. Immediately, the fire threw green sparks into those breathtaking eyes.

"Then should you not turn your feet toward the fire rather than to me?"

She thought she almost saw him smile, and Michaela choked on her own humiliation.

"I was . . . they . . ."

But he spared her any lame excuse by sitting in the chair opposite her. He dwarfed the medium-sized piece of wooden furniture, but his posture was graceful.

Michaela wondered what the muscles of his arms and shoulders looked like beneath his shirt. What they would feel like under her palms . . .

"What would you speak about this evening, Miss Fortune?" Roderick asked, reaching for the carafe of wine on the table. He paused, one eyebrow raised. "No bread? No cheese?"

Michaela shook her head, shocked when he poured himself a chalice of wine and then held the carafe toward her own cup as if in question. "Yes, thank you. No, you said you didn't—"

"I've changed my mind," Roderick interrupted her. "Have a tray sent up tomorrow night. Now, our chat . . . ?"

"Oh, yes." Michaela was now so confused that she had no

idea what to say to the man. He had discomfited her to the point that she wasn't certain she could take a drink of wine properly. "Ah . . . how was Leo for you this afternoon?"

"Fine." He took a sip from his chalice and looked into the flames, momentarily hypnotizing Michaela with his profile.

"You—" She shook her head slightly to clear it. "You weren't there when I came to fetch him."

"Yes. I know."

Michaela frowned. "Where were you?"

Then Roderick did look at her and his expression clearly conveyed his displeasure with her question.

"Have you seen your father settled?"

"Yes. He'll take his leave upon the morn." Michaela bit her lip for a moment. "He said he had yet to speak with you further. Did you—"

"Lord Fortune and I have said all to each other that needed to be said. I am certain the next time we meet will be at our wedding."

Hearing those words from his lips caused Michaela's stomach to clench. *Our wedding!*

Well, at least as of this night, he still planned on marrying her. And the thought of that event blessed her with another subject to broach with him.

"Shall we be married in the chapel?"

His look of distaste was unmistakable. "Do you wish it?"

"Of course. It's very beautiful."

"Is it?" Roderick turned his face back to the fire once more and grunted. "It can be arranged. I care not."

"I see," Michaela said. "You have some quarrel with Friar Cope, then."

"Had I a quarrel with Cope, 'tis unlikely he would yet be breathing, let alone making his home at Cherbon." Roderick held his chalice just before his lips. "The chapel is simply naught but a waste of space. A wedding will put it to some use, I suppose." He sipped.

"A waste of space?" Michaela was intrigued. "Mayhap you would not consider it so were it used for its intended purpose."

The fire had taken hold of the stout logs beautifully by now, and Michaela's toes—hidden from the lord's gaze under the table, unfortunately—were toasty warm. The chamber was growing quite close.

Roderick laughed harshly. "Then it would serve as a waste of time, as well."

"What a sinful thing to say," she said, picking up her own chalice. "For shame, Lord Cherbon." She took a drink, her eyes never leaving him.

"I've had my fill of religion, Miss Fortune," Roderick said evenly. "Or have you not heard of my *holy pilgrimage?*" He spat the words like a curse.

"Of course." Michaela knew she was getting closer to the core of this man and she clearly heard Hugh Gilbert's voice in her ear, pushing her to push him. "I've heard of your bravery and selflessness, as well."

"You have no idea," he murmured, and then drank again.

"You're right," she conceded. "I don't." She let the silence lay between them like broken glass, one of them not caring enough to pick up the pieces, the other too frightened she would end up bleeding. "Perhaps if you told me about it, I—"

"No."

It really was growing warm in the chamber, and for a mad instant, Michaela wondered if Sir Hugh would think her bold if she took off her overdress. The heat was making her slightly reckless.

"Might I ask you about your family, then?" she tried.

"Your mother? Your . . . your brothers? Sisters? I'd know Leo's lineage for when he grows older."

"My mother is dead. I have no brothers or sisters. I am all Leo needs know about."

"But Friar Cope said—"

"Cope has a habit of dramatic embellishment."

Michaela felt herself frown. "My lord," she started.

"Why do we not talk about your family, hmm?" Roderick's face swung to hers suddenly, and Michaela could not help but gasp at the glimpse of ferocity she saw flash in his eyes. "Since you've come to Cherbon, your sire's name has seemed familiar to me, and yet I could not place him. But upon his visit today, I began to recall—a scandal, if I'm not mistaken. Something about your mother claiming to be stolen away by the Wild Hunt. Isn't that it?"

It was Michaela's turn to stiffen. "That's all nonsense. My mother is—"

"Mad?" Roderick suggested coolly. "Or an idiot?"

"Don't speak that way about her," Michaela snapped. "You know her not!"

"So she was lying. There was no Hunt." Roderick swirled the contents of his cup and leaned back in the chair. "The servants say you were spawned by the devil himself—that 'tis why you're called Miss Fortune; bad luck seems to follow you."

"You obviously are in no humor to have a reasonable discussion with me this evening." Michaela stood, hoping Roderick would take her cue and leave.

He did not. "Either you believe her claims, or you do not. One makes you the daughter of a deranged old woman who ruined her family, the other . . ." Roderick shrugged. "Miss Fortune."

"My mother is not a deranged old woman."

"So you believe her?"

"Yes!" Michaela shouted. "I do believe her. Is that what you wanted to hear?"

Roderick's eyes bored into hers. "Yes."

Michaela had never been so deeply disturbed, admitting to the strange rumors that surrounded her parents with this wounded, mountain of a man who had no use for God. She felt as if something wild and dangerous was whirling inside of her, seeking a way to be free and wreak its havoc.

"Tell me of *your* mother," she challenged, beyond all good sense. "Of the graves on yonder knoll. I've seen you there."

Roderick shrugged, as if the subject had little meaning for him. "My mother was Dorian Cherbon. She died when I was nine years old. Besides Magnus's, the other graves are my sisters—six of them, each dead before they had lived a month."

Michaela could not help her gasp.

"Now," Roderick said smoothly, quietly, as he reached for the carafe and refilled his cup, "is that what *you* wanted to hear?"

"You were raised by your father, then?" Michaela answered his question with one of her own, because although the answers he'd given her did not bring her joy, they were indeed what she had wanted to hear. "No one has so much as a kind word to say of him."

"Because there are none," Roderick offered. "Everything you've heard about him is true, and likely worse. So, yes, I was raised by my father, if that's what you'd like to call it. Him, and Harliss."

Michaela pressed on. "Is that why you . . . why you seem so distant with Leo?"

"What in bloody hell are you talking about?" he

growled. "The manner in which I interact with Leo is none of your concern."

"It is if I am to be your wife and Leo's stepmother," she argued quietly. "My father, he was nearly broken by the thing—whatever it was my mother believes happened to her before my birth. By association, it has broken a part of me, I daresay. You . . . you have been broken by—"

"Everyone is broken, Miss Fortune," Roderick said, and then he did stand. "It's only a matter of who retains all their pieces still." He came to her, standing so close she could feel the added heat of his body, and it made her sweat. "And I do not. I left them behind in a bloody room in Constantinople. So it's of no use trying to fix me."

"I don't want to fix you," she said, noticing how her voice had gone breathy.

His eyebrow rose. "No?"

She shook her head. "I want to know you—to understand you."

"What I am is what you see." Roderick held his arms away from his sides and they seemed to stretch from one wall of the room to the other as he loomed before her. "A beast. The new Cherbon Devil. Broken, scarred. Rather unpleasant."

Michaela shook her head again, but the movement was slight, so mesmerized was she by his very presence, the energy rolling off of him. She stepped closer to him, as if drawn.

"Are you going to kiss me again?" He gave her a dangerous grin, the scar on his cheek going white by his eye like a warning.

But she could not heed it. "I think I shall." She licked her lips. "Do you mind?"

For one who was so deliberate in his movements, Roderick had taken her into his arms within the span of a blink, and this time, it was he who kissed her. Roughly, wetly, his mouth open and his tongue invading her. Michaela could only cling to the front of his tunic, her head spinning, her heart racing, her breath flown somewhere beyond the keep. The feel of him was intoxicating to the point that she felt she'd been drugged.

Then he let her go so suddenly that she nearly fell over, gasping, her body afire and not from the blaze in the hearth. He turned and grabbed up his walking stick and then faced her once more.

"I believe our palaver is finished for the night, Miss Fortune. Bid your father farewell for me on the morn." He stomped to her door, opened it, but paused before stepping through. "And be sure to remember the tray for tomorrow night."

Then he was gone.

Michaela was at last able to move, but the best she could manage was to bring her fingertips to her lips where the Lord of Cherbon's mouth had touched hers.

He was forever leaving her.

Roderick stormed through the dark, twisting corridors, lurching into and bounding off of the walls like a wounded animal, and with great growls swiping at the intermittent candles fastened to the walls. Alone at last, finally allowing himself to feel his thrashing heart, his shaking muscles, his anger, his—

Fear. His fear of the glow-haired woman he'd just left. His fear of the way she made him feel when he was with her.

Roderick didn't want to feel. The feeling part of him was dead, and that suited him perfectly. What business was it of Michaela Fortune's to try to resuscitate a part of him so damaged that its form would be a mockery of life? Sick and twisted and destroyed. Just like himself.

What a fool he was, behaving with her the way he would have behaved with a woman three years ago. Playing the seducer, as if he had anything other than wealth to offer. As if he could ever allow himself the whole comfort of her bed, her body. He had only duped himself for that short time in her chambers—when Roderick had kissed her as a man would kiss a woman, when she had responded to that kiss, he had foolishly forgotten.

He hadn't consciously known where he was going in his angry flight through the interior of Cherbon until he stopped, breathing hard, before the ornately carved doors of the chapel. A single, fat candle gutted on each side of the portal, but Roderick allowed the flames to stand, using their meager light to make out the Latin words carved on the lintel:

A porta inferi erue Domine animas eorum.
From the gate of hell deliver their souls, O Lord.

The words were almost enough to give Roderick pause, but he shook off the last remnants of superstition left buried in the deepest parts of him from his childhood, and threw open the doors, crashing them back against the stones and causing the candle flames to flap parallel to the ground. He stormed down the center aisle toward the altar. There, he stopped, his chest heaving like a bellows, as he looked around the murky shadows for a tool.

He grasped the altar railing with his free hand and heaved himself up the step, not glancing once at the twenty-foot-high crucifix over the tabernacle. In a moment, the long candle snuffer was in his fist and Roderick tromped back down the step, to the left of the altar as quickly as his ruined body would carry him. He lifted the snuffer high over his head and swung the dangling, bell-shaped end down in a whistle of air against the edge of the stone railing as hard as he could. The harmless bell flew into the blackness of the chapel with a ring and diminishing clinks, leaving a long, pointed, gleaming spear in Roderick's hand.

In a moment, he was standing before the stone statue of the winged rider, and save for the fact that Roderick was not astride, Roderick knew his and the inanimate man's poses were similar—warlike, vengeful, each brandishing a stave meant for destruction.

"You are mighty now, eh?" he growled at the cold, smooth stone eyes. "Only wait until someone rams a poison-tipped lance through your leg. See if your God rescues you then, *or the men you fought so hard to save!*"

With his last words still ringing in the stillness, Roderick threw his walking stick to the ground and stabbed the broken snuffer precisely into the packed joint around the only perfectly square stone beneath the horse's front hooves.

Roderick scraped and jabbed at the hard dirt, eventually dropping to his right knee, his crippled leg stretched awkwardly before him, almost straddling the stone beneath the rearing stallion. In a moment, he fitted the mangled tip of metal beneath the lip of the thin square and pried. It raised easily and slid away into the darkness under the rider.

Roderick threw the snuffer aside with a clang, his breaths bursting from him like angry shouts. He leaned forward, ignoring the screaming pulling in his thigh and knee, to brush away old dirt, as dry as sand, and his palm skittered across smooth wood. His fingertips sought the corners of the box buried in the floor and he worked it loose from its grave, setting it high up on his good thigh.

The box was not nailed shut, nor was the lid fastened

with anything at all, so that it lifted away easily when Roderick tested it.

Lying on the bottom of the box with no adornment, no letter of explanation or indication of ownership, was one old, limp, brown leather shoe.

Chapter Seventeen

Michaela was hunted by horrendous nightmares once she finally surrendered to sleep. Terrifying dreams of flying through gray-black smoke and clouds shading gloomy battlefields, catching glimpses of death and blood and mangled bodies piled on sand, on heath, on mud, in forests, and in dark, deep valleys. Wars and revolts, screaming battle horses and cries for retreat; whistling arrows and flaming projectiles smashing into fiery hell spread out like a disease over the earth. Hoofbeats, baying hounds, hoofbeats, flapping of wings, hoofbeats, hoofbeats, carrying her away forever . . .

She had never dreamt anything so grisly, and the visions stayed with her upon waking, so that she was only partly present while bidding her beloved father farewell the next morn.

Walter Fortune, too, seemed preoccupied, and pressed repeatedly upon Michaela to take care, and to come home if she felt the slightest urge at all.

"You need not stay here," Walter insisted in a low voice, his usually merry eyes solemn and intense. "The three of us, we shall manage."

But Michaela didn't know how to tell her father that she feared her heart was already ensnared by the two Cherbon males who resided in the gloomy castle, and so she only agreed with the best smile she could muster, and waved him through the barbican.

She had just entered the hall when Hugh Gilbert hailed her, coming from the doorway that led from the kitchens, a biscuit-wielding Leo happily in tow.

"Miss Fortune!" he called with a grin. Joy seemed to pour from the very fibers of his fine saffron tunic and Michaela could not help but wonder suspiciously at the cause of his jubilant mood. "Just the woman I was searching for."

"Sir Hugh. Good morn," she said coolly, and then crouched down with a ready smile before the boy. "Hello, Leo. Have you a bite for me? I've not had my breakfast yet and I am near to famished."

Leo giggled and held forth his soggy biscuit. Michaela leaned forward with her mouth opened wide, and then at the last minute, fastened her teeth around Leo's slight forearm.

"Mmm! Delicious!"

The boy giggled. "No bite Ee-oh, Aid-ee Mike-lah!"

"Oh, dear—I *am* sorry. But you are so sweet, I couldn't help myself." She tweaked his nose and then stood.

Hugh still wore his smirk, and he bowed low to Michaela. "I commend you, my lady."

Now Michaela was truly worried. "Why? What have you done?"

Hugh laughed. "Ah, it's not what *I've* done, but what *you've* done. I don't know what it is, but Rick came to his chamber in the most dreadful mood last night!"

Michaela felt her frown deepen. "Well, I don't see

what's so jolly about that. Obviously my advisor leaves much to be desired in his tutoring."

"No, no! To the contrary," Hugh insisted. He tugged on a lock of Leo's hair. "Go and play by the hearth, Stench. I must talk to Lady Michaela for a moment."

"All wite, Hoo."

"You must continue exactly what you're doing," Hugh said as soon as Leo was out of earshot. "You've got him on the run, I'd wager, and that's precisely what Roderick needs."

Michaela looked at Hugh for several moments, wondering what this man was about. For some reason she didn't want to let him know that it was Roderick who had been the aggressor last night in her chamber. Certainly, it had been Michaela's plan to move a bit closer to Roderick, but he had beaten her to the punch, kissing her like that. In a way Michaela had never hoped to be kissed.

"Is that so?" she said evasively.

"It most certainly is," Hugh agreed with a sage nod. "He barely said two words to me last eve, and when he did speak, it was akin to a bark. You must tell me, what happened?"

Michaela thought for a quick moment. "Oh, little more than what you advised. I—I took off my shoes. Asked him about his mother and . . . and his dead sisters."

Hugh's eyes widened to the point that Michaela feared they might pop free of the man's handsome face. "Verily?" he all but crowed. "Oh my, *yes*—that's *perfect!* No wonder he—" Hugh broke off, seemed to do a bit of his own thinking and then drew Michaela close by her elbow, as if they were great confidants. "Dorian Cherbon was a loony and—"

"A loony? Why would you say that? Did you know her?"

Hugh looked a bit confused for a moment. "Well, what

would *you* call a woman who tied a yoke of stone around her neck and walked into the sea? Hmm? *Sane?*"

Michaela felt the bottom drop out of her stomach, but Hugh continued as if he'd told her only what they would be having for supper.

"He's most nobly pissed this morn, of course," Hugh said rapturously. "So much so that I am being sent to Tornfield to collect its dues!"

"Oh?"

"Yes. And while I'm gone, you should finish him off. I must admit that Rick often depends on me overmuch. To shield him from things he finds . . . unpleasant."

Michaela's frown threatened to collapse her face, and she wanted to tell Sir Hugh that Roderick hadn't seemed to find her unpleasant in the least while he had been kissing her. But she held her silence.

"I'll likely be gone a pair of days—my appearance will catch your old lover off guard and he'll need scramble to produce such a large amount of coin. Meanwhile, you must hound Rick, press him to tell you more. Perhaps . . . perhaps—*yes!*" He leaned forward with a mischievous glint in his eyes. "Go on and invite him to your bed!"

Michaela drew back. "What?"

"What does it matter? You're to marry him any matter, and it's not as if you're a virgin, eh?"

Michaela had slapped his face before it occurred to her to do so.

Hugh looked shocked for a bit of time, and then his damnable grin returned. "Well, that was unexpected."

"Don't assume things about my person, Sir Hugh. It's rather unhealthy for you."

"So I see," the man replied mildly. "Any matter, I do apologize, but you see what I'm saying, do you not?"

Michaela had the distinct feeling that were she to follow Sir Hugh's advice, Roderick Cherbon would close himself off to her permanently. In the time she had come to know the man, it was quite obvious that intimacy was aught he was uncomfortable with, especially when it was pressed upon him. But then why would Hugh suggest she do such a thing? What was this game he played?

"I think I do," Michaela said carefully.

"Grand," Hugh said, looking relieved. "And when he refuses you, as I must warn you, he undoubtedly will, that's when you should inquire about Aurelia."

"Aurelia?" Although she was offended that Sir Hugh would think Roderick to find her so distasteful, Michaela couldn't help but be intrigued at the mention of a woman's name. "Who is she?"

Hugh's smile was so cool, snow would not have melted on his tongue. "Why, Leo's mother, of course."

Roderick sat alone in his chamber, brooding at the dire state of his life.

He was obsessed with the woman he was to marry in only a few short weeks.

Under ordinary circumstances, that would have been rather fortunate. However, he was no ordinary man, and Michaela Fortune was no ordinary woman. Roderick knew he could never bring himself to take his own wife to bed. Could not bear to see the pity in her eyes when she would look upon his misshapen form, and the thought of his own awkward attempts to make love to her left him in a cold sweat.

Clothed, and at a distance, he could still remain a man in her eyes. But in the closeness of a marriage bed . . .

And then there was the woman herself, and the strange story of her family. The shoe Roderick had unearthed in the chapel sat in its box in his wardrobe, and seemed to call to his imagination and curiosity.

Why would Walter Fortune be so desperate to regain a worn, leather shoe? Roderick couldn't help but guess that it had something to do with his wife's outrageous claims of the Wild Hunt, but in what way? And how could a shoe— not even a pair of shoes, as it was—be dangerous?

It disturbed Roderick that he was dwelling on matters of no direct concern to him. He'd given up empathy in Constantinople, after his last conversation with Aurelia, and vowed that once he stepped upon English soil once more, his only thoughts were to be of his own preservation. His and Hugh's and Leo's. To hell with everyone else.

Which is why Roderick knew now that he most definitely should not marry Michaela Fortune. Hugh had been right. Roderick should have sent her on her way immediately after their first encounter and married the next woman to appear at Cherbon, on the spot. *Any* woman besides her. *Any other woman.*

Because Roderick *wanted* Michaela. And he knew that she was not the type of woman to give and never ask for anything in return. Her needs were many and hungry. She'd already said she wanted to understand him, to know him. Noble enough sentiments in words, but if Roderick let her in, there was no way she could ever truly love him as he was. He would see the revulsion in her eyes, the shock and the pity, and it would kill him.

God, how he hated his weak self! He was unfit to marry Michaela, unfit to be Leo's father, unfit to rule Cherbon. His own father had been right all along, damn his evil soul to hell. Dorian Cherbon had saved herself a lifetime of this pain and grief by taking her own life, but Roderick also hated her for leaving him alone.

No one wanted him as he was. No one except his friend Hugh, and Leo. They were the only ones he could trust.

And so he would take out his anger and frustration on Alan Tornfield, the man who had held the one who was just out of Roderick's reach, and then thrown her away. The blackest part of Roderick's heart hoped dearly that Tornfield had no coin to give Hugh—Roderick would have his head mounted in Cherbon's bailey. And that thought, at last, made Roderick smile.

He turned his head as a rapping sounded on his door. Likely Hugh, forgetting a bit of this or that, or asking one final time if he could run Tornfield through just for sport.

"Come."

The door opened and to Roderick's dismay, Michaela Fortune stepped into his room, Leo dashing around her and running to Roderick's side.

Thank God he'd had Hugh help him with his boots before leaving.

Michaela seemed hesitantly curious about the room as she entered and closed the door almost to behind her, but she kept her gaze focused on Roderick. He recalled clearly his rash behavior with her the previous evening, kissing her surprise away in her bare feet, and Roderick felt his face warm.

"What do you want?" he asked, hearing his own abruptness. "I thought you knew my chamber was private."

"It—" Michaela seemed to swallow. "It's a beautiful day, my lord. Leo and I would like it very much if you would join us for a turn about the grounds."

The woman was daft! Asking him once again to walk

about as if he were an able-bodied, whole man. *Walk!* Next she'd want a footrace with him.

"No, thank you," Roderick said. "Leo, lean not on my—"

"Please?" Michaela stepped closer to his chair, and Roderick thought he could see a look of desperation that had never before darkened the depths of those blue eyes.

"Pees, Papa?" Leo mimicked.

The less he was in Michaela Fortune's presence until they were wed, the better. He already knew he could not control himself around her. Hell, he didn't even seem to know who he *was* when he was around her. And Leo forever clung, clung to him like—

"Very well." Roderick heard a voice that sounded remarkably like his own saying, "But only for an hour. I'm quite harried today."

It *was* a beautiful day. The morning's chilly dampness faded under a benign winter sun and the stones in the walls around the bailey radiated the bright, meager warmth back at the trio in a protective bowl. Serfs hurried in crisscrossing paths of chores, and several times, a servant nearly fell over their own feet at the sight of the large, cloaked man walking in their midst.

When they were halfway around the keep, Michaela had thought to shorten and slow her strides to maintain pace with him, but was rather surprised that his gait was nearly as quick as hers, thanks to his long legs. Leo was keeping a loose orbit around them both, dashing away to collect bits of nothing from the grounds—a rock, a stick, a long length of purple vine hiding in vain beneath the south wall—and then presenting his treasures to each of them in turn.

Michaela glanced out the corner of her eye at Lord

Cherbon's face. He had his hood raised still, but in the brightness of the bailey, she could see the paleness of his skin, the tight line of his mouth, his concentrated frown. His green eyes seemed faded in the daylight, with fatigue, or . . . something she could not give name to.

"Are we going too quickly for you?" she asked.

"Of course not!" Roderick barked, jamming the tip of his walking stick into the dirt with each step.

"You needn't shout at me," Michaela said mildly. "I don't malign you for a simple limp, my lord."

Roderick laughed, but the sound held no real humor. "'A simple limp,' says she," he muttered.

Michaela's eyebrows rose, but when no further explanation came, she shrugged and let her eyes go to the pebbles and hoofprints in the dirt before her slippers overtook them. They were coming upon the northeast gate, where beyond lay the stables, and the knoll of graves, as well as the edge of Cherbon's cliff, where a path led down to a stingy, rocky sliver of beach. Michaela looked at Roderick again.

"Leo and I often sit on the rocks overlooking the sea— he enjoys tossing pebbles over. . . ."

"It makes no difference to me," Roderick growled, and Michaela wondered why he had even agreed to accompany them if he was going to hang on to his foul humor the whole of the time.

But she gave a smile anyway and the two of them followed the little boy through the gate, where the dying grass swooped in a long swag away from the forest and along the road to where the jagged, gray rocks stood lined like sentinels. Roderick went more carefully up the slope that led to the cliff, but Michaela did not hover to him, choosing instead to let him make his own way without audience. She found a rather level swell of ground only a few paces farther and sank to her bottom, her legs crooked to one side, and leaned on her arm.

Roderick reached her in only a moment, but remained standing, staring out over the wind-tossed waves of the infinite ocean.

"Stay back from the edge, boy," Roderick barked, his frown deepening. "Leo!"

"All wite, Papa!" Leo's wind-softened answer flew back to them.

Michaela smiled to herself over the concern Roderick was showing for his son, and then she remembered what Hugh Gilbert had told her this morning:

Well, what would you *call a woman who tied a yoke of stone around her neck and walked into the sea? Hmm?* Sane?

What a fool she was, leading an already reticent man to the very site of heartbreaking tragedy. She may as well have gone up yonder knoll to dance a jig on his family's graves. Michaela was so aghast, she could not bring herself to speak.

His voice startled her. "Why do you believe your mother?"

"Beg pardon, my lord?"

"Her story about the Hunt," Roderick clarified. "What convinces you about the tale as truth?"

"You would have to know my mother," Michaela said, picking at stingy bits of dying grass in front of her hip. "She is . . . the most godly woman I have ever known. Anyone who knows her would say the same, although many do take her tale as a bit of an exaggeration. She devotes herself to God, to the welfare of others. She is a fine lady of our hold. It matters not to her that the folk whisper cruel things behind her back. 'They don't know the truth, as we do, Michaela,' is her excuse for them. Always."

"They think her quite mad, do they not?"

Michaela stopped the harsh denial before it could leave her mouth, calling to mind once again the terrible things Sir Hugh had said about Dorian Cherbon.

"Yes," Michaela said at last, quietly. "Yes, some do."

"But you don't." Roderick let the statement stand between them like a challenge.

"She has never, ever lied to me. And she believes it so thoroughly." Michaela hesitated only a moment before reaching into her bodice and withdrawing the chain. "She placed this about my neck only moments after I was born."

Roderick stared down at her and the warm metal between her thumb and forefinger for several moments before cocking his right leg, steadying himself with his walking stick, and slowly coming to rest upon the ground at her side. Without asking permission, he took the link in his own giant fingers, and his eyes found hers, reflecting the murkiness of the sea.

"'Tis a piece of mail."

Michaela nodded. "She told me it was a gift from the Hunt leader, and that I should never take it off."

He studied the metal again, and Michaela studied Roderick.

"It's old," he said. "Not English. Quite finely made."

"Is it?" Michaela shrugged. "I don't know. I don't care, really. I hate it."

Roderick nodded as if he understood, and let the link fall back on its chain. "Why are you to never take it off?"

"Oh, some such thing about two possessions . . . I've forgotten most of it, really."

"You just obey her. Even though that is the very object which the folk say curses you."

Michaela nodded. "I love her."

Roderick seemed to think for a very long time, watching

Leo playing on the rocks. Once the little boy looked back at them and waved, his fist clenched.

"Ee-oh find a snail!"

Michaela smiled and waved back.

"What is the other object?" Roderick asked suddenly.

"Sorry?" Michaela had forgotten what they were talking about, sitting so close to Roderick, feeling his warmth as the cold breeze rushed over the water, hearing Leo's playful chatter.

"You said there were two possessions."

"It doesn't matter," Michaela said. "It's never been found. Lost to time, I suspect."

"What *was* it, then?" Roderick pressed, and he reached over to lift the link from the bodice of her gown once more, his fingertips sweeping aside her hair to grasp the metal.

Michaela found that her breathing had ceased. His presence, his very person, was fascinating. His head was leaned toward her, so closely that she could see the threads of auburn and chestnut in his hair, the flecks of ice in his glacier-green eyes. How she wanted to thaw those eyes!

"A shoe." The answer came out as a whisper, and Roderick's hand stilled against her chest, over her heart.

"What?"

Michaela cleared her throat, and wondered if he was going to kiss her again. She greatly hoped that he would.

"A shoe. My mother's shoe. She lost it that night and it was never found."

Roderick's eyes were pinned to the metal link against his palm. "And you have no idea what will happen if this link and that lost shoe are brought together again?"

Michaela tried to laugh, even though a chill overtook her and a flash of the nightmare she'd endured last night raced over the shushing gray waves to comb through her hair like claws.

"The Hunt will come and carry me away, I suppose." She leaned closer to him, knowing it was bold, but not caring. She needed his strength, his vast, dark strength to keep the illogical fear away. "Will you protect me, Roderick?"

He looked into her eyes, and something there frightened Michaela more than the remnants of an old superstition. A hardness, a burden, a dangerous promise. He dropped the link back against her gown, and brought his palm alongside her jaw—it was rough and warm and large.

"Of course," he said, his lips dipping into a frown. "Of course I will, Michaela." His eyes went to her mouth and he leaned in slowly, placed his lips upon hers with infinite gentleness.

Michaela eased into his chest, bringing her hand to the front fold of his cloak, and let his kiss melt her. It was unlike either of their other two kisses, not hesitant, not demanding—*real*.

And it was growing deeper. Michaela could smell Roderick Cherbon's skin, wanted to touch his beautiful face, run her hands through his hair. Her hunger for him was sudden and growling and enormous. But his arm had come around her shoulders, locking her to him helplessly and she could not reach him. She felt, rather than heard, the low hum deep in his throat, of desire and arousal, and it nudged Michaela's heart over the edge.

He wanted her.

And was she lost to him already? This wonderful, amazing, damaged man with a past darker than Cherbon itself? The Cherbon Devil, who kept no close allies save a man whom Michaela suspected had ulterior, selfish motives? Roderick, who held himself away from his only son—was it because of the way his own father had treated him? The lack of a mother to love either of them?

Heat crept over her skin beneath her gown, gooseflesh prickled deliciously; she heard her own purr. . . .

And then they were both knocked flat as Leo fell upon them, giggling, "Kissy! Ee-oh kissy, too!"

Roderick grunted and gave a soft curse as he fell upon his right arm, and Michaela was quick to pull the little boy onto herself fully.

"Leo, stop kicking! You'll bloody my nose!"

The boy laughed gaily in response and then reached up with both play-dampened, gritty palms to frame Michaela's face before planting a wet, slippy kiss somewhere in the vicinity of her eye.

"Ee-oh kissy Aid-ee Mike-lah!"

She couldn't help but laugh, and bestow her own kiss upon the boy's mouth. "You are beautiful, Leo," she sighed. "I love you."

The boy looked at her with wide, wide brown eyes. "Do?"

"Yes, I do."

"That's right," Leo said adamantly, nodding as if she had given him the correct answer to a riddle. "You love Papa, too?"

Michaela looked to Roderick, who was still propped on his side, looking rather uncomfortable. Her heart broke a little that the man neither rushed to put the boy's innocent question off, nor would he look directly at her.

Michaela smiled at Leo and spoke low, as if imparting a great secret. "Yes. I love your papa."

"Me too!" Leo whispered.

And then Roderick was jerking himself to his feet with amazing speed. He took up his walking stick without a glance at the woman or the child on the ground. "I must return to the keep. A number of things I—" He broke off, still not meeting Michaela's eyes. "Good day to you both."

Michaela sat up with Leo on her lap, a heavy sigh on her lips. Once again he'd fled her. Fled his son. This was no way to begin a family.

Her eyes followed Roderick Cherbon for the several moments it took him to stomp away and disappear through the curtain wall.

"No," she said softly to herself. "No, I will not allow it."

"What you say, Aid-ee Mike-lah?"

Michaela stood, shook out her skirts, and took the boy's hand. "Come along, Leo—we're going after your papa."

Chapter Eighteen

"My lord!"

Roderick heard Michaela calling to him as he dragged himself across the hall, and he was more than a little perturbed that she had followed him. Did the woman never know when to stop? He didn't want to see her, or Leo. Didn't want to speak to either of them. He wanted to be alone in his chamber.

He was nearly to the stairs now, and did not slow his pace.

"My lord! *Roderick!*"

At this he did stop, turned to her, and growled, "Yes, Lady Michaela? Is there some matter of great import just come up?"

She was walking quickly toward him, Leo's wrist in her grip, his little hand flapping as he tried to wave it at Roderick. The boy was grinning. Michaela was not.

"Yes. Yes, there is." She came to a halt before him, her breasts rising and falling rapidly with her breath. In the hollow light of the hall, she seemed to glow: her skin, her hair, her eyes. As if she was a figure from one of the stained-glass windows of the useless chapel.

224 *Heather Grothaus*

Yes. I love your papa.

Roderick sent her what he hoped was his most threatening frown. "Well?" he bellowed.

"You promised us one hour," Michaela said. "It was quite rude of you to abandon us as you did."

"Abandon you?" Roderick scoffed. "Surely you are no infant, Michaela, that I can not leave you and be about the business of this keep. You have Leo, and he has you."

"We wanted *you,* my lord," Michaela insisted, and at her words, Roderick didn't know whether to laugh or curse at her for the fool she was.

Leo pulled free of the woman and stepped to Roderick, holding forth a chubby fist. "Ee-oh bring him snail to him papa. Here, Papa."

Roderick looked down at the boy, so eager, so hopeful.

"I don't want it. I've no time to play about with filthy creatures like a child, Leo." And Roderick heard Magnus Cherbon's tone in his own voice.

The boy's features instantly crumpled, like the undermined wall of a tower, and his brown eyes welled with shimmery tears.

"Papa don't want Ee-oh's snail?"

Roderick could almost feel the ripple of fury coming off of the woman before him.

"Oh, that is quite enough," she said between her teeth. "Come along, Leo—we shall go to the kitchens and see if Cook has some tidbit for you before the noon meal."

Roderick's relief was nearly crushing. "Good day," he said stiffly as the woman turned with the boy once more in her grip.

Michaela had spun back to face him in a flash. "*Not* good day," she hissed at him, and her eyes were murderous.

"I am not done with *you,* my lord. Once I see Leo tended to, I shall join you in your chamber."

"I think not," Roderick said mildly. "I have—"

"I care not for what imagined tasks you've set yourself to in your hiding place. You *will* speak with me."

"You don't command me, Lady Michaela," Roderick warned.

She arched one eyebrow at him and then took Leo toward the kitchens, her skirts swishing, her voice carrying over— gaily back to Roderick as she replied to the boy.

"Oh, no, Leo—of course your papa loves you. It's just that he's deathly frightened of snails."

Roderick turned toward the stairs once more and hurried up them as quickly as he could drag his damned crippled leg. Perhaps he could reach his chamber and lock the door before the lady arrived.

And then he could cower inside like the wretched, spineless, miserable thing he was.

Michaela's heart pounded in her ears like angry waves on the hull of a ship, but she ignored it, drowning it out with her fist falls on Roderick Cherbon's chamber door.

"It is I, my lord. Open, please."

No response.

She was shaking, both with fear and outrage. It was quite possible that challenging this volatile man would lead to her own destruction, but for Leo's sake—and for the sake of all their futures at Cherbon—Michaela would be brave. She raised her fist again and beat on the door, her other hand turning the long, thin piece of metal. Would she be brave enough to use it?

"My lord! I'll not go away until you speak with me, so you may as well let me in."

Still no response save her trilling pulse.

She looked down at the shank in her hand. Sir Hugh had given it to her before departing for Tornfield—in case Leo was being impish and bolted himself in his chamber. Michaela was quite certain the man had never dreamed she would use it on the lord's own door.

Roderick would be most put out with Sir Hugh upon his return.

"I'm coming in!" she warned, giving him—and perhaps herself—a final chance.

With an exasperated huff, Michaela scraped the piece of metal into the seam of door and wall and wrenched it about as if she was stirring a bowl of porridge. She pushed.

Nothing.

She manipulated the thin metal bar again, heard a clink that sounded likely, but before she could try the door once more, it swung inward suddenly, ripping the shank from her hand and dragging Michaela over the threshold to land in a pile at Roderick Cherbon's feet.

"Who gave you that?" he demanded, spying the long bar lying on the floor and swiping it up with a growl. He looked at it disgustedly then threw it to the ground once more, muttering, "Hugh."

Michaela scrambled to her feet with as much dignity as she could muster, then quickly darted around the large, cloaked man before he could herd her back into the corridor. But Roderick seemed to have no intention of evicting her from his room, as he slammed the door closed with an ear-ringing crash.

Michaela had to fight down her whoosh of breath as he

advanced on her. She squared her shoulders and raised her chin.

But he only limped past her to one of the oversized armchairs. It was as if, for all his show of keeping her away, he wanted her here.

"What do you want, Miss Fortune?" he asked gruffly, falling into his chair with a grunt. "A feast? All of us to play draughts or pony? I fear I'd be rather outmatched, even against a small boy and a woman."

"I want to know why you treat Leo so poorly."

Roderick's head turned to her as if she'd asked him why water was wet.

"Why I—" Roderick began.

"And"—Michaela interrupted—"and why you seem to . . . to like me one moment, and then push me away the next."

Roderick glared at her for an instant, and then looked away, muttering, "You're daft. I don't know what you expect from me."

"You are breaking Leo's heart—he loves you so! All *he* wants from you is your time, your attention. To know that you love him!"

"Do I not provide him with a home? With people to care for him? Is he not safe, well-fed, happy? He's not beaten, is he?"

"He's not a dog, my lord! He's a little boy, whose heart is broken because his father pretends he doesn't exist!"

"There are worse things," Roderick growled.

"Are there? Do you treat him that way because that is how Magnus treated you?"

Roderick bolted from his chair and grabbed up his walking stick but, instead of using it to bolster himself, he brandished it like a club, limping toward Michaela.

"No! Would that my father had only ignored my existence! Instead, he hounded me endlessly, reciting my failures, my weaknesses, until he had forced me on that damned pilgrimage that *nearly took my life!*"

Michaela forced herself to stand steady despite her watery knees.

"What you are doing is just as bad, my lord," she said, and she could hear the tremble of her own voice.

"I can assure you it's not." Roderick towered over her now, his hood thrown back against his shoulders, his hair tangled over his cloak, his eyes glowing green fire. "Any matter, I am no one for Leo to idolize. I can not teach him to ride, to fight, to be a man. Is that what you wanted to hear, Miss Fortune? Are you, too, like Magnus, in insisting that I acknowledge my shortcomings?"

"I am not your father. And you have no shortcomings in my eyes," Michaela said on a quick breath. He had no idea of his own worth. Looking up at him this way, his large, powerful body poised as if to devour her, Michaela wanted nothing more than for Roderick to kiss her again, as he had by the sea.

To kiss her, and more.

His beautiful mouth drew into a sneer. "You're either a fool or a liar."

"A fool perhaps, but no liar. Why is it so difficult for you to accept that I find you a fine man? Why do you see yourself as unlovable?"

"You're trying too hard, Miss Fortune." Roderick gave a poor imitation of a chuckle. "Once we are married, you will have your coin. There is no need to court me like some maiden."

"I'm not courting you, you stubborn bastard!" Michaela

shouted and stamped her foot. "But it would certainly not kill you to do so for me!"

"You are wasting your time, waiting on that."

"What about Leo?" Michaela pressed, reaching out for his cloak when he would have turned away.

Roderick shook her off, flinging his fist still gripping his walking stick in a backhand manner. "What of him?"

"Can you not show him the least bit of kindness? Can you not love *him?* If I am but a means to an end for you, if you could never love me, I beg you: break this legacy of hate passed down from your father, Roderick! Leo is *your son!*"

Roderick hurled his walking stick at the hearth, where it shattered in an explosion of a thousand splinters. *"He is not my son!"*

The silence that fell in the room after Roderick's proclamation was perfect. Roderick's back was to her now, and Michaela's head was spinning. What did he mean? That he did not claim Leo?

"I don't understand," she began. "Are you saying that—"

"I am saying"—Roderick's voice sounded in a way Michaela had never heard the lord before: tired, beaten, sad. "That Leo is not my issue. Not of my blood. Not my son."

"But"—Michaela felt a great longing to sit down, but the closest chair still seemed too far for her legs to carry her. "Everyone says . . . Sir Hugh—"

"Everyone thinks he is my son, and that is the way it must be. For Leo's sake," Roderick said. "I knew Leo's mother when I first arrived in Constantinople. Aurelia. She was a prostitute. And I did indeed lay with her."

Michaela's heart tripped at that confession, although she didn't know why—all along she had assumed Roderick had made love to Leo's mother. She wondered at the jealousy she felt now.

"But it was before I even arrived in that city that Leo's true father had come to her. I met him, you know—he fought in my company, although I did not know his name at the time."

"He abandoned them? Au . . . Aurelia and the baby?"

"No. He never returned to Aurelia to know about Leo. He was killed at Heraclea, along with most of the other men. Only Hugh, myself, and a handful of others who were swift of foot survived. Aurelia liked to think that—had he known, had she sent word to him earlier—he would have cared for them. But . . . the man was a titled lord, with a family of his own."

"But how then did Leo come to be with you and Hugh? And why would you claim another man's son as your own?"

"When I was injured . . . the surgeon did not think me to live. He would do nothing more than give Hugh a draught to ease my suffering. Hugh took me to Aurelia, and she saved my life."

"And then she simply gave her son away?" Michaela heard the disbelief in her own tone.

"Aurelia loved that boy with her whole heart. Never would she seek to be parted from him. But she had no other choice."

"Why?"

"She was dying." Roderick at last turned from the hearth and fell into his chair again, as if all the energy had been drained from him. "When Hugh brought me to her, she was already failing. She'd contracted some sort of a fever, and it had spread . . . spread to"—Roderick broke off for a moment. "She opened her robe for me once—when she saw that I would live and she would not. Her . . . breasts were purple and black, and swollen. The whites of her eyes, yellowed. She knew she would do well to see us depart Constantinople.

"And who then would care for a dead prostitute's bastard? No one. Aurelia knew that. Leo would have been left an orphan on the streets of that city, prey to the slavers and pedophiles. She begged me to take him with me when I left. To care for him as if he was my own. It was to be the payment for my life, and I gladly accepted the debt. The circumstances of Leo's birth were no fault of his. He was a babe—innocent. And yes, the son of one of the most beautiful and kind women I have ever known."

If Michaela had thought she may be in love with Roderick Cherbon that morning, now she was certain of it. Her heart was breaking for Leo, for his poor mother, for Roderick.

"But why claim him as your son? Was it not enough to bring him with you? Give him a place in your home?"

"No. If . . . if my own illness had suddenly returned and I had died, Leo would have no claim to anything at Cherbon. He would be in the same position as in Constantinople— mayhap worse off. I made that promise to Aurelia, knowing she would likely be dead before Hugh and I and her son gained England, and I will uphold it until my last breath. Before King Henry himself, I will swear that Leo is my son. So be it."

Roderick Cherbon sat in brooding silence, in the same chair, wearing the same cloak and boots, but in Michaela's eyes, this was a different man. A man of such honor and compassion that she had once thought only her own beloved papa to compare. The sacrifice he made for this woman and her son—lovely, innocent, beautiful Leo. Yes, the boy was precious, and Michaela loved him, true, but what Roderick had done, he had done knowing that if ever he had a son of his own blood, Leo would remain Cherbon's heir.

Roderick Cherbon loved Leo more than Michaela could have ever possibly guessed. What a fortunate, fortunate little boy.

"Leo needs to know," Michaela said quietly.

"That he is not my true son?" Roderick shook his head. "I think not, Miss Fortune."

"He *is* your son. *You* are his father. So be it." Michaela walked to stand behind Roderick and hesitantly laid her hand on his right shoulder. "But he desperately needs to know that you love him."

"I *care* for him," Roderick clarified, turning his head slightly and Michaela knew he was looking at her hand on his shoulder.

Michaela nodded, even though she knew Roderick could not see the motion. He could not so much as speak the simple word that described how he felt, so damaged was he. Let him have his time with it, then. Roderick Cherbon could be healed—his heart as well as his body.

She brought her other hand to his opposite shoulder, squeezed. "Do you think you might also come to care for me one day, my lord?"

She felt him stiffen slightly under her hand.

"Perhaps," he conceded gruffly. "But if you're looking for a proclamation of undying affection, you might as well bugger off. 'Tis not my manner."

"I see," Michaela said easily. She was kneading the tense muscles of his neck and shoulders, thrilling at the wide, hardness of him. Such a generous, vulnerable heart beneath the fierce appearance. Michaela was glad Roderick could not see her face, for she knew it must be softened with emotion. He would likely toss her out of his chamber on her bottom.

But to her surprise, Roderick reached up with his own right hand to grasp Michaela's. She curled her fingers around his and let her left hand drift up to his hair, her fingers raking it back from his temple.

"But I will try, Miss Fortune. With Leo. If it will please you."

Michaela felt her smile to the tips of her ears and she leaned down, placing her mouth near Roderick's ear. "It will please me very, very much, my lord. Thank you." She pressed her lips to the high, rough ledge of his cheek. She pulled away, but only slightly, and Roderick turned his face toward her.

He leaned forward and kissed her mouth, softly, his lips barely touching hers, and so Michaela flicked her tongue out to taste him.

In the fraction of a breath, Roderick had released Michaela's right hand to turn her and pull her over the arm of the chair onto his lap. Her arms snaked around his neck like the wild vines that had once claimed Cherbon, and Roderick kissed her as if he would consume her. His arms cradled her, his hands cupped her shoulder and buttock, and Michaela buried her hands in his hair, holding him to her, claiming him as her own, at last.

She heard Roderick's growl, and even though it was still frightening to her, this wild, animalistic part of him, it excited the untamed part of her own core, and she wanted to be taken by this beast, owned by him, marked by him.

His hand cupping her buttock slid up over her stomach and covered her breast, and he kneaded there, as she had worked his muscles. Only Roderick's touch was not meant to relax, and it didn't. Beneath her hip, Michaela could feel

the hardness of his erection, and an instinctive part of her
wanted to swing her legs around and straddle the Lord of
Cherbon's lap. She felt as though she were on fire inside,
and that Roderick's body was the only cure—

After he had burned her to ash, of course.

"I want you," she said against his mouth, smashing her
lips against his, mumbling her words, nibbling at him, licking him. "Roderick, please . . ."

His hand left her breast and traveled down to the L of her
trunk and legs, where her gown had caught between her
thighs. He slid a flat palm into the seam, and when he
touched her there, even through the thick wool, Michaela's
whole abdomen clenched.

"Yes," she sighed. "Roderick, take me to your bed."

He said nothing, only claimed her mouth again as his
fingers snagged a fold of her gown and slid the heavy skirt
up, slowly, until it bunched around her hips. His fingers
found her, wet and aching, and he touched her again, invaded her, until she was arching her hips and moaning
words she could not understand into his mouth. He was answering her, but she could not understand him either.

In a moment, Michaela's world went white hot, ear shattering and silent in the same moment that her climax took
her. As she gasped her way back down from the pinnacle,
she covered Roderick's face in small, breathy kisses, giggling, and surprisingly not at all ashamed at her present
state of seminudity on his lap.

Things were going to be much different around Cherbon Castle, Michaela thought.

"Have you finished?" Roderick asked calmly.

She pulled back to look at him. "My lord?" She gave
him a smile. "Why? Is there more to come?"

"I'm afraid not. But perhaps now you'll stop acting like

a mare in heat and nipping at me ceaselessly. Get up, Miss Fortune, my legs are asleep."

A knife through her heart would have been less painful, and Michaela quickly brought herself to her own feet. She stood there for a moment, looking at him as if hoping he would smile and turn his words into a tasteless lover's jest.

But all he did was wipe his hand on his pants. He glanced up at her, his face ruddy. "Was there anything else?"

"No," Michaela choked.

He raised an eyebrow and looked pointedly at the door.

Michaela lifted her chin and made her way from the room with as much dignity as her legs—still shaking from the release he'd given her—would allow. But once in the corridor, his door closed firmly behind her, she found she could not go any farther. She backed up against the stones across from his doorway and slid to her bottom, never feeling so low, so worthless, in her life. She was so stunned, tears would not come. She only sat staring at his door for what seemed like an hour, shaking, shaking, at what he'd done to her.

And then the first horrendous crash fell, causing her to jump and scream, but her cry could not have possibly been heard in the din that followed. It sounded as though a battle was being waged in the lord's chamber—wood splintering, pottery crashing, and Roderick's own ragged yells. The screech of furniture on stone; ringing metal as it bounced off an unknown object.

Nay, not a battle—a full-on war, with Roderick Cherbon playing both armies.

Michaela rose to her feet and approached the door, jumping when some heavy object met its ruin against the thick wood. She stood before it, raised a palm slowly to place it against the door, as if trying to feel the man beyond it.

After several moments, amazed that the storm continued when there could not possibly be anything left to destroy, Michaela backed away from the door and walked slowly down the corridor, her thoughts pained and tangled, the sound of the Cherbon Devil's anguish haunting her steps.

Chapter Nineteen

The next morning, sitting amidst the ruin that was his chamber, too fatigued to even begin the struggle that putting on his boots meant, Roderick was shamed to the very depths of his black soul—a feeling he hadn't experienced in years.

When he'd taken out his anger on his belongings the previous night, he'd told himself he was angry at Michaela Fortune, for pandering to his impotence by pretending she desired him. Or for playing the harlot with him, flaunting her sexual experience. Or for drawing from him the truth about Leo and Aurelia when he'd wanted no one else to know.

But in the cold light of morning, when the heat of emotion had cowardly fled him, Roderick knew he had been furious at no one save himself. Of his own fear. His pride. His vanity. He'd wanted to make love to Michaela, and when she'd all but begged him, he had convinced himself that he would, and damn the consequences. But seeing her spread before him in the height of her pleasure, the creamy skin of her perfect legs, the muscles and flesh soft and rounded and rich, her caution and self-consciousness tossed aside, Roderick had gone stone-cold terrified.

Terrified of losing her. If not as his wife, then simply that abandoned side of her, that sensual side that yearned for his body. Once she had seen all of him, she would never want him—would never look at him in the same way again. No woman had ever looked at him like Michaela Fortune had, not before the battle, and certainly not after. The broken part of Roderick needed those looks, those words, he feared, to survive in this half life he'd been left to at Cherbon.

He could not make love to her. And yet he could not abuse her so, he knew. And he didn't want to—God! She was beautiful and perfect—perfectly flawed. The way she stumbled and tripped and stuttered and dropped any item unlucky enough to be a moment in her grasp. Leo loved her, and as mistress of the keep, she had excelled. Whenever he was near her now—verily, whenever he so much as thought of her—his hunger for her grew so that he forgot himself. He said foolish things, hurtful things, meant to drive her away and protect himself. But Roderick knew that if he continued to push her away, to hurt her so, she would eventually stop coming back, and she would take with her what little remained of his own heart.

He could see no solution. He wanted Michaela, more than he wanted Cherbon, more than he had ever wanted anything. But he felt that whichever path he chose—take her body or no—he would drive her away. For one would leave her wanting, and the other would reveal fully the horror that was himself.

He must marry her quickly, then. After they were wed, if she did leave him for whatever reason, at least he would still have Cherbon—a place to live out the rest of his wretched life. A place for Leo to be safe, until he too could flee to a brighter future than what Roderick had been dealt.

Perhaps if Roderick tried to please Michaela in other ways once they were wed . . . perhaps it would be enough for her. With Leo, for instance. And she'd said she loved Roderick. Was that possible? Roderick doubted it. Likely it had been but an empty nicety to placate Leo. For the first time since lying in the long, smoky hospital in Constantinople, Roderick wished for a higher power to make its presence known, to guide him.

At least when Hugh returned, he might have someone to advise him.

And what was he to do about the ridiculous old shoe, resting silently in its box in his wardrobe? Of all the objects in Roderick's chamber now mangled and splintered and destroyed, the crumbling wooden box remained intact on its shelf. Perhaps he would give it to Michaela, as a peace offering. Or to show her that she had naught to fear from her mother's old superstitious tale. She could take off the metal link she hated so desperately, too—the thing that had made her Miss Fortune.

It was a good gift, he decided. His way of a pathetic apology. And the only one he had to give her.

Roderick looked down at the floor, where the thick, heavy walking boots he was sentenced to while in the keep rested, and he decided to forego them for his riding boots instead. Yes! He may have to go ahead of them at first, seek a stable hand to help him mount, but he would take Miss Fortune and Leo riding today, and give her the shoe then.

He braced his only other walking stick on the floor—spared because it had been hidden under his bed—and heaved himself from the chair after several false starts, grabbing for the posters on the bed as he slowly and awkwardly made his way across the field of detritus that was his floor. Once at his wardrobe, he dug with his right hand through the pile of ruined clothing until he touched the smooth leather of his boots. Raising up, he found himself eye level with the crumbly old box.

Roderick tossed his riding boots to the mattress behind him and slid the box from its shelf. He hopped backward to the edge of the bed and sat, laying his cane alongside him, the box resting on his lap. He lifted the lid and looked upon the shoe again.

It was tallish—more of a boot, really. Rich brown leather—Roderick guessed deerskin—worn nearly to the thinness of cloth. He picked it up from its resting place and held it before him. He frowned. This was no woman's shoe though—the sole was long and wide, the ties rough and thick, for a man's hand.

A mad urge seized him when he noticed the shoe had been fashioned for the right foot—his undamaged foot.

Looking about the chamber—as if anyone would be about to see him—Roderick pushed the box off his lap to rest near his cane. Taking care with the worn leather, he pulled the boot onto his right foot and calf—it slid on as if greased, like sliding his cock into a woman for the first time, and Roderick groaned as a shudder overtook him. He laced the boot quickly, as if he'd done it hundreds of times, as if he knew the crudely punched eyes and turns of lace intimately.

When it was done, Roderick stretched out his right leg before him, admiring the sight of his long, muscled appendage in a boot cut from such pliable skin. He had forgotten what a normal leg looked like—his own leg, no less. And his heart galloped like hoofbeats the longer he stared. The longer he stared, he could hear the screams of the horses. And hounds—were there not hounds howling? Surely there was no ringing in his deadened ear that could mimic such a mournful sound.

The hoofbeats pounded louder, harder, faster, their reverberations singing through Roderick's muscles, and he felt himself rising from the bed to stand, even against the voice in his head screaming, *You'll fall, you fool! You'll fall!*

Roderick stood. He stood, and then he took a step. And another.

And on the bed, beneath the box in which the damned shoe had been interred, lay his walking stick, forgotten.

And unneeded.

Michaela was sitting at a table in the great hall, Leo at her side, a variety of foodstuffs and other miscellany before them. Michaela leaned her head on her fist, her rib cage pressed against the edge of the table as she regarded the boy and pointed with her free hand to a ragged cattail, burst open like a summer storm cloud.

Leo crinkled his nose and then looked to Michaela. "Wite."

"White, yes. Very good." She smiled at him and then pointed to a pile of dried raspberries. "And these?"

"Wed," Leo answered immediately.

"Spot on. You're very clever, aren't you?"

He nodded with a grin.

She slid a circle of dried carrot toward him. "What about this?"

Leo's little brows drew down in concentration as he searched his mind for the correct word. "Oh . . . ohr—"

"Orange, is it not?" came the deep male voice from not very far behind Michaela and she raised her head with a start, her heart tripping even as Leo scrambled from the bench.

"Papa!" Leo wrapped himself about Roderick's legs as

if flung from a slingshot, and Michaela waited for the chastisement she was sure would come from Roderick, but it never did.

Actually, he was smiling. A strange smile, even unused as Michaela was to seeing it. Intense, bright—a bit frantic, perhaps.

He looked down at the boy. "It's a difficult word, is it not? Orange."

Leo nodded. "Ee-oh like wed."

"I should say so . . . red is much shorter." He looked up at Michaela and those green eyes were all but glowing at her. "Lady Michaela is a fine tutor, though. I had no idea you knew your colors."

Michaela could not return his smile, remembering his treatment of her the day before. Even though she had heard his anguish, she would not forgive him so easily.

"We've only started lessons today."

Roderick's eyebrows rose and she realized his hood was thrown back. In the daylight. "I am impressed." He patted Leo's head and Michaela thought the boy might swoon.

He carried no walking stick, but then Michaela remembered its destruction in his chamber. His boots were different today than the black ones she was used to seeing. These were slimmer, with a more pointed toe, although still more bulky than typical riding boots.

Her confusion deepened when Roderick Cherbon bent both knees and crouched before Leo. He seemed to wobble a bit, but balanced himself with little effort.

Michaela had never seen him do that—did not think his left leg was capable of it. Since coming to Cherbon, she had never seen it bent as it was now.

"Leo, I've a fancy for a ride this morn. Would you and Lady Michaela care to join me?"

Michaela heard Leo gasp and she thought for a moment he would choke on his tongue.

"Ee-oh wide on Papa's hohse?"

Roderick nodded.

"Wif him papa?"

Roderick laughed. "Yes. Now run along and fetch a cloak of some sort. We'll wait for you."

The boy set off from the hall in a dead run, whooping with joy.

"Leo, do you need help?" Michaela called, but he was already gone, leaving her alone with Roderick.

He rose, slowly, carefully, but without a wobble. When he looked at her, his smile was gone, but still his eyes glowed like firelit gems. Michaela's cheeks began to burn and so she dropped her gaze.

She heard his footsteps drawing near, and when his boots came into her line of sight, she had just enough time to notice how lessened his limp had become.

What in heaven's name . . . ?

Then he crouched again, this time before Michaela, and took her chin in his large, warm fingers. "Michaela," he began quietly.

She jerked her face free from his grasp, aghast at the tears she felt welling in her eyes.

He did not take her chin again, but covered both her fisted hands in one large palm. "Michaela," he said again. "I'm sorry."

It didn't even *sound* like Roderick Cherbon—not the words, not the tone of voice.

"You're only apologizing because you think me to leave now. But I'm staying—I have no choice, do I? Your precious Cherbon is safe."

His other hand joined his grip on her and he squeezed.

"I'm not apologizing only because I hope you'll not leave—although that is what I hope. I'm apologizing because I've treated you horribly, and I want to make amends. To you and to Leo. Won't you help me, Michaela?"

"That's all I've *done,* is try to help you!" She snatched her hands from him, unused to his kindness and not certain how to respond to him. The hurt she still felt was coming out as anger, but she clung to it, lest he switch back once more and smash her floundering hope. "All I've received for my efforts is punishment."

Roderick rose up enough to perch on the bench next to Michaela and he sighed. "You were right. The things you said to me last night. The way I treated Leo in the past was in part due to the way my father treated me. I don't want that for him. I want him to look back upon his childhood with fondness. To remember a father, and a mother"—at this, Michaela looked up at him—"who had only his happiness in mind. You and I, we can do that for him, can we not?"

Michaela knew she was staring like a ninny. She nodded faintly. "What's happened to you?" she blurted.

Roderick gave her a boyish smile, but in his green eyes Michaela thought she might have seen a flash of something akin to fear. "I . . . I don't quite know. Something, though. Is that all right?"

Michaela opened her mouth to speak—although what she would have said only God knows, because Leo came into the hall once more at a dead run, wearing one of Sir Hugh's fancy, embroidered wool undershirts. The hem came to his ankles and the sleeves flapped about him like wings as he pumped his arms. It looked like a rather fancy gown.

"Ee-oh weddy, Papa!" He was not slowing as he raced toward Roderick, and Michaela felt a collision was imminent.

But at the last moment, Roderick stood, his arms out, and scooped the boy up midstride, swinging him away from the table in a circle. Leo's hiccoughing laughter rang in the tall, dark hall like ghostly chimes.

"Well then, let's be off!" Roderick announced gaily. He looked down at Michaela and smiled. "My lady?"

Michaela tried to return the smile for Leo's sake, but all the while, her heart jarred her chest like hoofbeats on a packed winter road, her throat felt frozen tight with snow, and she was afraid.

That evening, soaking in a large, round copper tub before the hearth in her chamber, Michaela smiled at her earlier fear. How like her old self to be wary at a turn of good fortune in her life—there had been so few of them, she saw any change for the better as a bad omen.

Silly, silly girl.

She still had no earthly idea what had marked such a dramatic turnabout in Roderick Cherbon, but at this point she did not care one whit. The entire day had been a dream—riding through the country at Roderick's side, an ecstatic Leo fronting his father's saddle. The man had been busy with preparations beforehand, obviously, because the horses had stood ready at the stables, and Roderick's saddlebag had been filled with provisions for their holiday over the land: skins of wine and milk; bread and cheese and a pudding; a whole, cooked chicken, which Roderick had quartered for them with a small dagger hidden in his right boot; heavy blankets to spread on the ground and guard them from the chilly damp.

They were away the whole of the day, riding and exploring, talking and laughing and taking time down from their mounts for Leo to run wild. Now Michaela's body was feeling the effects from her long hours astride, but she relished each twinge as a souvenir from her and Roderick's first day as a truly betrothed couple. She could not have been happier.

Roderick was off putting Leo in his bed for the night, with a promise to return to her after he'd had his own wash. Although Michaela was more than pleased with this change in the Lord of Cherbon, she hoped to finish her bath and don proper clothing before Roderick appeared—memories of their previous encounter in his chamber still haunted her, and she wanted nothing to ruin what was left of the day.

She had only finished rinsing the last film of soap from her when a soft rap fell on her door. Before she could call out a warning, the door opened and Roderick slipped through the slit of shadow beyond, closing himself quietly inside the room.

Michaela slid down in the tub, until the water touched her chin and the copper rim was her horizon. "It seems you've caught me unawares, my lord." Her bare knees were poking from the water like stepping stones, but she could not pull them under. She lamented her earlier reckless splashing about.

He didn't seem surprised in the least to find her in the bath. As a matter of fact, he crossed the room as if out of habit and sat at the small table before the hearth, his body comfortably sideways to her, and poured himself a chalice of wine. His hair was damp, long, combed back from his face and down his fresh shirt, leaving a long strip of wet between his shoulder blades.

He wore no cloak at all, and for the first time, Michaela saw that his shoulders really were *that wide*—it was not a trick of the black material he draped himself in.

His pants fit him snugly, his left leg still twisted, but oddly it seemed not as severe a malformation as she'd noticed before. His right leg was perfect in the close black material. He still wore the riding boots.

"Did you enjoy yourself today, Lady Michaela?" He took a sip of wine, admiring the snapping flames to his right, as if giving her time to become accustomed to his presence.

"Certainly," Michaela said. "And I do believe it was the happiest day of Leo's life."

Roderick nodded thoughtfully. "He is not difficult to please, is he?"

"No." The water was growing cool, but Michaela was unsure how to go about lighting from the tub. Would she be embarrassed if he turned to watch her?

Would she be disappointed if he didn't?

She snaked an arm over the rim of the tub for the long length of linen folded on the stool, shook it to its full length in same moment as she stood from the tub with a fall of water.

"If you have no objections, I'd prefer for us to be married right away," Roderick said, and she held the cloth before her just as he turned his head.

She stood there, unwilling to risk exposing her more private parts by stepping foot over the tub. A chill rushed up her back, both from the coolness of the chamber and his statement.

What had happened to this man after she'd left his chamber last night?

"I have no objections. I'll send for my parents right away."

Roderick turned back to the fire, as if sensing her need for a moment of privacy, and she hurried from the tub to don a wrapper as he continued to speak.

"I've already taken the liberty. Cope should be returned

from his rounds in a day or so. We can be married in the chapel, as you requested, and celebrate the Yule Tide season as a family."

Michaela knotted the belt of her wrapper, her stomach mimicking the motion at the mention of the fateful holiday that had haunted her since her earliest memory. Her continuing nightmares, too, did little to help, as they stayed with her in all the waking hours, vivid and terrifying, as if warning her. She paused a moment before retrieving the linen once more to address the locks of hair escaped from the knot atop her crown. She stepped her icy feet into her slippers and approached the man at the table, still rubbing at her neck and face with the towel.

When she stood near him, he turned to look up at her. His face seemed to be shadowed by worry, or perhaps it was only a trick of the flames beyond.

She had to know.

"My lord, about last night . . ."

"Sit down, Michaela. Please." When she had sat, he continued, his green eyes pinned to her, never wavering. "I am a cripple," he blurted without warning, and his tone was neither self-deprecating nor defensive. "And there are parts of my body which . . . which I'd rather you not see."

Michaela frowned. "I don't understand."

"I know you don't. My behavior last night . . . I forgot myself, to put it quite simply." He shrugged and his gaze skimmed over her thin robe. "You are a very beautiful woman, Michaela. Sensual. Desirable. Giving you pleasure reminded me of my failings, and what I am incapable of as your husband."

A thread of fear began to twist around Michaela's throat, tiny and cutting. "What are you saying, Roderick?"

"I am saying that we will never make love."

"What?" Of all the things Michaela feared he might say to her, this had been the very last she expected.

"We have Leo," Roderick continued in a mild tone, ignoring her shock. "He is my heir, and you will be the only mother he ever remembers. I believe we can be happy that way."

"This makes no sense, my lord," Michaela stuttered. "In one breath, you tell me how desirable I am to you, and in the next you tell me you don't want my body?"

"Oh, but I do want your body, very much," Roderick said without apology. "But I would not expose you to—"

"You look quite fine to me," Michaela interrupted. "And I myself heard you tell Harliss that there was nothing wrong with your . . . with your—you know." She waved a hand toward his waist.

"That is true. But you cannot understand my . . . scars. My deformities. The sight of them would change me in your eyes, and I cannot allow that. We can pleasure each other in different ways, if you wish. Or, my offer still stands for you to take a lover."

"If I—?" Michaela shook her head. "You think me to disparage you for your scars? When I think so little of the ones that are visible? You would deny me the full partnership of a marriage? My own children? You would share your wife's body with another man?"

"I want you to be happy, Michaela," Roderick said. "I want us to be happy. And the scars on my face and arm are but lovely decoration compared to what you do not see."

Roderick had never hurt her like this. Not in all the harsh words he'd thrown at her since her arrival at Cherbon, not after the way he'd discarded her from his lap last night. To make her feel as though she were so shallow that she would refuse him because of his injuries—what kind of woman must he take her for?

"How can I marry you, knowing that I will never be your wife, in truth?" she asked incredulously. "Our marriage would be little more than a farce! If the king found out, you would lose Cherbon!"

"No," Roderick argued. "No one need know what does or does not go on in our bedchamber." He looked down at his left leg. "Mayhap one day . . ." He shrugged. "But I would that you not get your hopes up."

"I don't know what to say." Michaela sat, staring at him, the linen cloth twisted in her fist on her lap. "I am greatly insulted by this."

"I did not say what I have to insult you," Roderick said lightly. "Because I enjoyed this day, as well. And would have many more like it. Can you not take this good part of me that has returned? Take it and let us both make the best of it?"

Michaela stood. "I don't want only the good of you, Roderick. I want all of you."

"I can not offer that. For both our sakes."

She looked at him for a long moment, but could think of nothing more to say to him. Nothing that would perhaps convince him that what he was asking of her was of an impossible nature. "I need to be alone."

Roderick stood, not even bracing a hand on the table for support. "I understand. I do hope you will consider it, Michaela. Would you like to go about again on the morrow? I'm sure Leo would enjoy it."

"Yes. Yes, that will be fine, of course," she said distractedly. She felt surreal, as if nothing made good sense any longer.

He nodded. "Good night." Roderick crossed the floor with no noticeable limp at all now, and slipped from her room.

Beneath her robe, the metal link was cold against Michaela's skin, and she felt hunted.

Chapter Twenty

Roderick felt better than he had in years; since before his arrival in Constantinople, since . . . ever, really. The cold winter sun shone prisms in his frosty breath over Leo's—properly hooded, this time—head, and at his side sat Michaela on her own horse. She was singing them away from the castle wall, down the road that led toward the sea, and her voice was angelic.

She must have sung the song to the boy before, for Leo joined in sporadically. It was a lovely duet. Roderick was mesmerized.

Not a word had been breathed between him and Miss Fortune about their discussion of the previous night, but Roderick could see the faint purple streaks in the delicate hollows of her eyes, and could feel the distance she'd placed between them.

She would accept it. She must.

Because Roderick could feel himself improving. It was madness, he knew. Or magic, or devilish sorcery, mayhap. He didn't understand it, and he didn't care. A maddening idea had seized him that perhaps once day, his entire leg . . .

But he would not let his thoughts go there in the day-light. He still wore the old brown leather shoe on his right foot, under his own bulky riding boot. He'd not taken it off since first donning it, and he had no plans to.

Walter Fortune would never know the boot still existed, and to hell with his crazed ideas of the fabled Hunt. Non-sense. Impossible.

Isn't what's happening to you now impossible?

The shoe was Roderick's now. It was in his home, had been meant for him to find, he was certain of it.

Miss Fortune finished the last chorus and Leo ap-plauded enthusiastically.

"Here, here!" Roderick added. "Well done, Lady Mi-chaela."

She gave a dainty bow over her pommel. "You both are too kind."

"Oh, no, your voice has no equal. I am certain of it," Roderick argued. "I've traveled quite far, my lady, and I assure you it is exquisite."

Leo nodded. "Aid-ee Mike-lah sing pity, Papa."

"She most certainly does." Roderick cupped the tiny head below his own chin with one palm, rather amazed at how good it felt to carry the boy on his lap. "Where should we be off to, now, Leo? The shore?"

"Find nuts!" The boy pointed over the horse's head to where the road twisted into the heart of the forest, and Roderick's left foot itched madly.

As if she sensed his discomfort, Michaela turned a slight frown to him, her hand going mindlessly to her bosom. "There likely are none left, Leo. Perhaps—"

"Nuts!" Leo said again. "Pees? Ee-oh see skurls!"

Michaela was afraid of the wood, Roderick could tell, and the relentless sensation in his left boot warned him.

But his right boot spurred him. There was no need to pander to such nonsense. It was his wood. A harmless tract of forest.

"Just for a little while, Leo," Roderick said, hoping the confidence in his voice would put whatever worried Miss Fortune to rest. "And then it's back to the keep for your lie-down, all right?"

"All wite, Papa."

Roderick urged his mount forward with a smile for Michaela, entering the woodland road as if passing into a cave, even though the arching branches overhead were long bare. It was several moments before he heard the clop of Michaela's mount following them.

A thousand eyes seemed to be watching Michaela, from every knot of wood, every black mound of soggy leaves. She could hear Leo's carefree chattering to Roderick up ahead, see his short arm dart out from one side then the next of the large man, pointing at this or that with awe and excitement.

But traveling slowly, warily behind them, Michaela's head swiveled at each creak of wood, each rustle in the underbrush, as if she was keeping watch over the males ahead, although what she was protecting them from, she did not know.

Her most recent nightmare bloomed fresh in her mind, more sounds than images: the pounding hooves again; screeches and screams; dogs baying at a hidden, malevolent moon; the growls of some hungry creature, searching for fresh, warm blood. . . .

Michaela's heart thrashed in her chest, and part of her wanted to spur her mount forward to the safety of Roderick's

side, even though she was still hurt and angry over his ultimatum of the night before. But another part of her warned
her—in her mother's voice, no less—to not get too close to
Roderick Cherbon in this deep, quiet wood. It was dangerous, dangerous. . . .

And then the hair on her arms stood up as the rumbling
in her head was matched by reverberations in the road itself.
Ahead of her, Roderick pulled his mount to a stop, turned
his horse sideways in the middle of the road. As Michaela
looked at him, she saw her own emotions reflected in his
strong, scarred face: alarm, bewilderment, panic.

She was not imagining the hoofbeats. And they were
getting closer.

Roderick's horse half reared on its hind legs, causing
Leo to squeal with delight, and Roderick had to fight the
beast down. "Michaela, go back!" he called, his voice
commanding and yet unsure at the same time. "Hurry!"

Michaela's muscles tensed, ready to pull at the reins of
the dancing mare, but Leo's small face poking out of his
hood caused her to kick the horse forward, calling, "Give
me Leo!" even as her mount jumped toward them.

"There's not time!" Roderick cried. "You must flee the
wood now, Michaela—"

She skidded her mare sideways and the two mounts
crashed together, pinning Roderick's left leg from the knee
down between the two barrel chests of the horses.

Roderick did not so much as cry out.

"Give him to me!" Michaela demanded. "Give him to
me, now! Hurry!"

The hoofbeats were all around them now, shaking the
tree limbs and jarring the bits of detritus on the road.
Michaela reached for the boy in the same moment that
Roderick was pushing Leo off his saddle by his rump, the

little boy looking bewildered and frightened. He landed across Michaela and scrambled up her front to straddle her, his little arms around her neck like a noose.

"Now, go!" Roderick shouted. *"Go!"*

But it was too late. Both Roderick's and Michaela's heads swiveled to the bend in the road ahead, as the swelling of hooves broke in announcement of the arriving riders.

Michaela wrapped her arms around Leo and whispered, "Dear God, protect us!"

The sleek muzzle of a jet-black steed strained around the bend, steamy breath snorting from its nostrils, his rider tall and slender and clothed in the garb of a black knight. This craven stallion was instantly joined by its companion: a low, shaggy, white—

Pony.

"What in the name of fuck?" the black rider cried, and reined his horse to a halt, causing the stallion to scream indignantly. He threw back his coif.

The imposing rider on the dire-looking steed was none other than Sir Hugh Gilbert, Lord of Nothing.

And on the dainty little pony to his side rode young Lady Elizabeth Tornfield.

Roderick didn't know whether to kiss Hugh, or strangle him. His heart was pounding so in his chest that he thought it to explode.

Had he expected to be descended upon by the Fortunes' fabled Hunt? And Michaela had been as frantic to get her and Leo away from the road as had Roderick. Did she fear the same? He didn't know, didn't dare ask. But the maddening itch in his left boot had at last faded away to nothing once more.

"Lady Michaela!" the young girl cried, and kicked her pony into a run.

"Hello, Hoo!" Leo shouted, and waved a chubby arm at the black-clad rider.

Still at Roderick's side, Michaela gasped. "Elizabeth! What in heaven's name are you doing here?"

In seconds, the two small parties of riders were joined. Michaela handed Leo, arms already outstretched, to Hugh before dismounting and meeting the Tornfield girl in a consuming embrace. The little girl was sobbing uncontrollably.

"Hello, Pus," Hugh said to Leo, and returned the boy's embrace with a half smile. "The pair of you out for a jaunt with Miss Fortune, eh?" At these words he turned a raised eyebrow to Roderick. "Very cozy, Rick. How in holy hell did you manage to mount? Surely you didn't have a stable hand help you—Miss Fortune, was it?"

Roderick waved the man's question away with a careless hand, not prepared to answer Hugh now. In fact, he'd given no thought at all as to how he would explain his vastly improved condition to his friend. He dreaded the moment when Hugh would see him walk, or insist on helping him remove his footwear.

"What's the girl doing here?" Roderick growled, glancing at Tornfield's daughter still entangled with Michaela.

Hugh rolled his eyes and sighed. "She followed me, the sneaky little brat."

"Why didn't you return her?" Roderick asked in exasperation. The sight of Michaela so obviously happy to see the girl caused a nauseous swirl of unreasonable jealousy in Roderick. He wanted Michaela to have naught to do with her damnable Tornfields—especially not now, when they were so close to wedding.

"What? And waste more of my time?" Hugh shook his head. "I would have had to stay on another night, and she would have only followed me again. Persistent thing. I tell you, Rick, she was *determined* to reunite with her beloved Miss Fortune. Any matter, her father and stepmother aren't far behind us. They can take her back themselves. I'm sleeping in my own bed tonight, right, Worm?" Hugh tweaked Leo's nose and the boy giggled.

"Wite, Hoo."

"Tornfield's on your heels?" Roderick asked. He should *brain* Hugh. "Why could you not simply wait for them to catch up to you, then? Jesus, Hugh—I've no patience for this."

"Ha! No, thank you." Hugh laughed. "They've screeched and bellowed after me the entire way. I've dealt with them on my own long enough for my tastes. Besides, Harliss rides with them." He gave an exaggerated shudder. "They seem to get on with her quite well. Shit-rat mad, the whole lot."

At the mention of Harliss's name, Leo clung to Hugh's tunic, but his head turned to Roderick. "Her get me, Papa!"

Hugh beat him to answering the boy. "She wouldn't dare, Squid. I'll chop off her head and have it in a stew, first."

Leo looked unconvinced, and sent worried eyes back to Roderick, as if seeking reassurance.

"She shan't touch you, Leo," Roderick said, and was certain to look directly into the boy's eyes.

Leo's thin chest gave a great heave and he patted Roderick's shoulder. "All wite, Papa. All wite."

Ignoring Hugh's look of wary suspicion, Roderick turned his attention back to Michaela and the Tornfield girl—for a mute, she certainly did seem to talk a lot. Michaela was on her knees in the dirt, holding both of the girl's hands in her own while the blond child sobbed and hiccoughed around her words, pleading over something or other.

The sight worried Roderick.

His dread only increased when, again, rumbling hooves echoed down the corridor of the tree-lined road, and in a moment, a trio of riders appeared.

"Don't let them take me from you," Elizabeth begged as the riders came into view. "*Please,* Michaela!"

"Elizabeth, you must go home with your father," Michaela said, as gently as possible. She sympathized with the girl's dislike of Juliette, but Michaela knew that Alan Tornfield loved his daughter to distraction, and would never let anything bad happen to her.

Well, that's what Michaela *thought,* until she turned her head and saw Harliss accompanying the Tornfields.

"Oh, and they've brought Nurse, too!" Elizabeth sobbed. "She'll be so disappointed!"

"Nurse?" Michaela asked in disbelief, and her head turned to find Roderick. The giant man only stared down at her, his earlier, strange, but most welcome joviality vanished. Michaela looked back at Elizabeth. "Your father has installed *Harliss* as your *nurse?*"

"*Of course* he has!" Elizabeth wailed, jerking on Michaela's hands. "That's what you wanted, isn't it? I know you sent her to take care of me, and she is lovely, but I want *you,* Michaela!"

Michaela knew her mouth was hanging open. She must speak to Alan immediately—and Juliette, as well, if need be. The Tornfields must not allow Harliss near any child, but especially not Michaela's dear Elizabeth.

Good heavens, she and Roderick had sent the evil woman

there as little more than a slave—not to be a respected family servant. The very thought made Michaela queasy.

"Elizabeth Tornfield!" Alan shouted as he brought his mount to a halt and swung down to the road. His face was ruddy beneath his blond hair. "I shall take a *switch* to you, young woman!"

"Papa, no!" Elizabeth cried, and darted behind Michaela, who rose to stand.

As Alan walked toward her, his blond hair seemed dull in the cloud-covered wood, his mustache ridiculous, his shoulders narrow. The skin of his face was perfect, unflawed—adolescently soft looking.

Even his stride wasn't as manly as Michaela remembered. He had no heroic limp to speak of at all.

Alan stopped midway between where Michaela unwillingly sheltered Elizabeth and where Hugh and Roderick still sat their mounts.

"I beg pardon for this, Lord Cherbon," Alan said stiffly, with a bow to match, in Roderick's direction. "But I did call to your man—several times, actually—to stop. When we would start to gain on him, he would spur his mount."

"You called?" Hugh said airily, eyes wide. "I'd no idea."

"It is of no consequence," Roderick growled. "Take your daughter and go, Tornfield."

Lady Juliette urged her mount forward, her smile showing all two hundred of her big teeth. "Elizabeth, dear, you frightened us all so! Let us go home together—I am certain we can work everything out."

"No!" Elizabeth shrieked from behind Michaela still. "You are not my mother! I hate you! I want to stay with Michaela!"

"Elizabeth!" Harliss snapped on a gasp. "That is a dreadful thing to say—you will apologize this instant!"

Michaela turned slightly to catch Elizabeth's reaction and, to her surprise, the girl looked properly chastised.

"I'm sorry, Nurse."

"Not to me," Harliss clarified, and her gray eyes sparkled, her gray teeth flashed behind tight lips. "To Lady Juliette."

"I'm sorry, Lady Juliette."

Juliette's smile faltered, but only for a moment. "It's quite all right, my dear. We still have some—"

"But I don't want to go back with them, any matter," Elizabeth insisted, cutting off her stepmother's attempt at magnanimity, and turning pleading eyes to Michaela once more. "I want to stay with you! Don't you love me anymore? You didn't even answer my letter!"

"Elizabeth, Tornfield Manor is no longer my home, and your place is with your father and Lady Juliette. I am to marry Lord Cherbon and live here with him and Leo."

"*And* Sir Hugh," Hugh chimed in sunnily.

Michaela only threw him a black look.

Harliss got down from her mount and made to approach Michaela and Elizabeth. "Elizabeth, listen to me—"

On Hugh's lap, Leo whimpered and hid his face.

"Not one step closer, Harliss," Roderick growled. "You're frightening my son."

For an instant, a glimpse of the old Harliss soaked through the false exterior, but she covered it up again with amazing speed.

"Forgive me, Lord Roderick," Harliss simpered. "Hello, Leo. Darling, *darling* boy." Then she turned to Elizabeth again. "We've discussed this: Lady Michaela can not be your companion any longer. She has come to Cherbon to care for little Leo, there, and I'm sure you can see that he is very, very much loved by her. She is to be *his* mother, you understand."

The explanation should have been benign, but Michaela felt the twist of words as easily as a knife. She knew they cut Elizabeth.

"But I had her first!" Elizabeth cried. She looked up at Leo and then back to Michaela. "It's because of him that you won't come back, isn't it? You love him more than me."

Alan raised his face to the sky and sighed. "Elizabeth, don't do this." He stepped forward and took his daughter's arm. "Come along, now. You have caused enough trouble, and we are going *home*."

"It's true, isn't it?" The girl glanced back at the gray old hag as if for reassurance.

"Elizabeth, I *do* still love you. You are very, very dear to me."

"But not dear enough," the girl spat. "I'm not as dear as that sweet little *baby*, am I?"

"Ee-oh no baby!" Leo laid one palm against Hugh's cheek, forcing him to look into his eyes. "Hoo, Ee-oh no baby, wite?"

"Absolutely not," Hugh cried in outrage. "You are a properly grown pain in my arse."

"No baby." Leo turned his glare to Elizabeth and stuck out his tongue.

Michaela could not help the chirp of laughter that escaped her. It was very poor timing, though, as Elizabeth glared at her with bottomless humiliation in her eyes, and her chest heaved with entrapped sobs.

"Very well, M-Miss F-Fortune. Good riddance to you!" She turned and flounced back to Harliss, who readily took the girl into her long, gray arms.

The pain of Elizabeth's rebuke stabbed at Michaela, but perhaps it was better for the girl to be angry now. Angry perhaps, but Michaela needed to ensure that she would be safe at Tornfield.

She reached out for Alan's arm as he turned to go. "Lord Tornfield," she said in a lowered voice. "About Harliss—"

"Oh. Yes, of course." Alan turned and bowed stiffly again in Roderick's direction. "Thank you, my lord, for sending Nurse to us. She has proven quite able and we are very pleased with her."

"Harliss was not sent to you as a nurse, Tornfield," Roderick said. "The woman was relieved of her position at Cherbon due to outrageous acts of insubordination, treachery, and the endangering of my own son."

Alan looked shocked. He glanced back at Harliss, whom Michaela saw shake her head almost imperceptibly.

"I see," Alan said, slowly.

Lady Juliette had the bad taste to add her opinion to an already-strained conversation. "Oh, well—you know, some humors are simply not compatible. She is working out quite splendidly for us, my lord."

Michaela looked to Alan a final time. "I implore you, as a friend, and for Elizabeth's sake—"

"Leave it, Michaela," Alan said in a low voice. "We're fine—as are you, apparently." It sounded like an accusation.

"It was likely Harliss who urged Elizabeth to run away," Michaela insisted in a whisper, but it was not low enough.

Alan shook his head and walked back to his horse.

"Is that what you think, Miss Fortune?" Harliss asked in an amused tone as she helped Elizabeth onto her saddle. She brushed her hands and then approached. Michaela stood tall, even when faced with the evil woman. "Perhaps you should ask Sir Hugh why he would suggest Lady Elizabeth ride her pony to the bridge with him, then, hmm? Perhaps it is not I who seeks to lure you from Cherbon, although it is true that I don't think you deserve such a grand prize, either. Perhaps someone else, someone who has given you advice on your situation, seeks to rid himself of your presence for his own benefit, and thought to use your weakness for Elizabeth to his advantage?"

Michaela looked over at Hugh as Harliss stood face-to-face with her. Sir Hugh looked decidedly uncomfortable, and Michaela became furious.

"Hugh?" Michaela heard Roderick say, but her attention was brought back to Harliss, whispering in her face words meant for Michaela's ears alone.

"I warned you not to trifle with me, Miss Fortune, and I am not finished with you, by far. With any of you," she emphasized. "When you think to cross me again, remember this: cold water does not trouble me, and my arms are very, very strong."

"You're mad," Michaela said, hearing the tremble in her own voice. The woman made absolutely no sense at all, and it was terrifying.

"Yes," Harliss hissed with a smile. "Quite. You must be, to bear what I have in my life."

Then she turned and was scrambling up onto her horse like a gray insect.

"Good day, Lord Cherbon, Lady Michaela," Alan Tornfield said. "Again, I apologize for any trouble."

"Think naught of it, Tornfield," Roderick answered. "Of course you are all welcome to attend the wedding. Next week, likely. I'll send word." To Michaela's ears, the invitation sounded like a goad.

Alan nodded stiffly and then turned his horse and led the members of his household back down the woodland road until they had all disappeared.

It was Roderick's voice that stirred Michaela from her stare.

"See that Miss Fortune and Leo are returned to the keep safely, Hugh." He looked to the sky and Michaela noticed it had gone cold, ash gray, the exact shade of Harliss's eyes. "A storm comes on quickly and I have business to tend to." Then he spurred his mount into a gallop and was gone.

Michaela let her eyes pin Hugh Gilbert, who held a now-sleeping Leo cradled in one elbow against his chest. "You brought her here, didn't you? Elizabeth. For once, Harliss spoke true."

"Don't be silly," Hugh scoffed. "And you haven't been following my advice, obviously."

"Obviously," Michaela sneered as she gained her own mount with some difficulty. "If I had, I doubt I would be getting married in a matter of days, or that Roderick would be spending so much time with his son."

Hugh looked as if Michaela had slapped him. "It's a phase. It will pass. You don't know him as I do."

"You're right, I don't know him as you do. And I don't think you know him at all." Michaela nodded her head toward the road. "I'll follow you."

Hugh arched a sardonic eyebrow at her, but nudged his mount forward all the same. "This should be amusing," he muttered.

"Oh, I doubt you find anything about it funny in the least."

Chapter Twenty-One

Michaela was unwilling to let Hugh from her sight for even a moment, lest he try to cowardly escape from the discussion she was determined to have with him, and so she followed him to Leo's small but lavish chamber and oversaw him placing the boy in his bed for a late nap. Beyond the boy's room, thunder rumbled like a whispered promise of punishment yet to come, and Michaela knew Roderick was correct about the impending storm.

She watched Hugh's gentleness with Leo, the ruffling of his hair, the tucking of the thick coverlet securely under Leo's chin, nestling into the crook of Leo's arm a ragged, stuffed, appendageless doll. And even though she was furious at Roderick's closest friend, she realized that Hugh and Leo truly loved each other, and it made Michaela a bit sorry for what she was about to say to him.

But not sorry enough to not say it.

Hugh straightened from the bed and seemed to give an exasperated eyeroll to see Michaela still standing near the doorway.

"You don't give up, do you?" he whispered, and walked past her through the doorway.

She followed close on his heels, pulling Leo's door to softly after her. "Was it not you who told me to be relentless?"

Hugh walked down the corridor ahead of her and threw his hands over his head. "Absolutely no concept of context!" He glanced over his shoulder. "Very well, then—where would you give me your fierce dressing-down for whatever atrocities you believe I've executed against you, Miss Fortune?"

"Your chamber is closest, is it not?"

A score more paces and Hugh shoved open a door on the right side of the corridor. Michaela realized that Sir Hugh's room lay between Leo's and Roderick's, and she was not at all surprised. She followed him into the room.

All of the suites at Cherbon were lavishly outfitted, from the architecture itself to the rich furnishings, but Hugh's room was luxurious to the extreme. It seemed as if he had taken bits from all about the keep—from about the world, really—to decorate his private space, and Michaela imagined the room would rival many a royal chamber.

There were wide, upholstered benches and armchairs, their velvets glistening in the dim light and tossed over with rich throws and cushions; thick, sculpted rugs in vivid colors Michaela had never seen covered the whole of the floor, giving the room a close, hushed atmosphere, and she felt as though she was walking on a dense mattress. The bed was draped in what appeared to be bright silks, with more shiny cushions and throws tossed about and slinked over the edges of the mattress. Bright, polished weaponry—some pieces quite strange—adorned the walls, between elaborate tapestries depicting scenes of men in battle, of old Roman gods, of people in various stages of undress. Giant, dyed feathers and dried grasses stood in tall ceramic urns. The room had a sweet smell of lingering incense and Michaela had to admit that she was quite jealous of Sir Hugh Gilbert's home at Cherbon.

"I am rather surprised you took it upon yourself to help Rick mount a horse. Looking at you, one would not think you had the strength." The man flopped down in one of the upholstered chairs, tossing one leg carelessly over the arm. He laced his fingers together over his chest and regarded her with weary amusement. Outside, the rain arrived on Cherbon with a roar.

"I likely don't," Michaela answered. "Roderick mounted on his own."

Hugh's eyebrows shot up. "Obviously he had a stableman assist him before you arrived."

"No, we all—he and I and Leo—arrived at the stables together. I saw him mount. He seemed to do quite fine—why would you insist he need help?"

"I don't know why you're lying to me but—"

"I'm not lying to you! Ask him yourself."

"Fine! I will! Now get on with whatever you have to say before I throw you out of this room. You're terribly annoying, Miss Fortune, and I have had quite my fill already of annoying women." He sighed and leaned his head back against the chair, his eyes closing as if already dismissing her.

Michaela felt there was no need to dance around the subject. "Why do you hate me? What have I done to offend you so, Sir Hugh, that you would set out to sabotage not only my own efforts at Cherbon, but Roderick's very future at his family home?"

"Oh, spare me," Hugh muttered.

"No, I shan't," Michaela insisted with a frown. He

wasn't going to quip his way out of this. "You lured Elizabeth Tornfield here with hopes that she might persuade me to leave Cherbon, didn't you?"

"You're paranoid, Miss Fortune," he scoffed.

"I am not! You gave me advice under the guise of 'helping me,' and each time I followed it, Roderick moved farther away!"

Hugh held up both palms and raised his eyebrows. "Then you obviously executed my advice incorrectly. Proof that you are no woman for Roderick Cherbon," he said simply.

"I am the *only* woman for him," Michaela insisted. "And how dare you think to take upon yourself the machinations of his life! You are supposed to be his closest friend!"

"I *am* his closest friend."

"No! No, you're not!" Michaela stepped toward him, her fists clenched at her sides to keep from throwing something at him. "A friend would seek to aid Roderick in gaining everything he desires, everything he needs—not plot against him to keep him weak and miserable."

Hugh laughed. "*You* are the interloper here, Miss Fortune. I have known Roderick for more than three years. I have been through battle with him, sickness, seen him over Death's very threshold and back again. If there is one of us in this chamber who knows what Roderick needs, well"— he looked her up and down—"it is certainly *not* you. I know you've fooled yourself into thinking you might one day come to love him, but in truth, all you will be good for is making him miserable."

"I already love him," Michaela said fiercely.

Hugh seemed more than a little shocked for several moments. But he recovered, and his smug look returned. "You may *think* you do, but you don't truly know him. He is a wealthy novelty for you, and perhaps a bit of a charity. But for myself, for Leo—the three of us have a history together. You can never surmount that. You're an outsider."

"Perhaps I was when you departed for Tornfield, but no longer," Michaela challenged. "He's sought *me* out in your absence, confided in *me*."

Hugh smirked. "Really? And what great secrets did he impart, hmm? What he wanted for his din-din?"

"He told me about Aurelia. That Leo is not his son by his blood."

"Well, that *is* impressive, I concede. But it's hardly something that you would not have learned eventually, any matter." Hugh shrugged. Then his eyes narrowed, and a wicked gleam came into them. "Has he told you he will never make love to you?"

Michaela's face burned. "Yes. But I believe I can change that. It's only . . . only reluctance due to—"

Hugh laughed uproariously. "You can't change that, ducky! Trust me, that condition is most permanent." His face sobered. "You think you've got him though, don't you? That you and he and Leo are going to be one jolly family, and Miss Fortune will right any little trouble Lord Cherbon seems to have, isn't that it? Thank you so very much, Sir Hugh, for devoting your life to this man and his son, but now that I'm here, we have no further need of you. Good day and good luck. Well, I will tell you now, Michaela"—Hugh rose from his chair suddenly and advanced on her—"you will *never* do it. You can *never* know the man he was before Heraclea—how unlike his father he was when he came to battle."

His very stance before Michaela seemed to challenge her. "Did he tell you, when we engaged, all of us were nearly starved, our supply routes having been cut off for weeks? There were few horses left for the soldiers to fight on because we *ate them,* Miss Fortune. We were ambushed in our camp, in the dark of night. Most men were slaughtered before they could gain their feet and flee, and the ones who did escape—myself and two generals included—could only do so because Roderick mounted his own horse and rushed into a band of attackers alone. A score of Saracen soldiers on horseback, armed with lances and swords, swarmed 'round him like beez-z-z-z." He let the last word draw out maliciously. "I watched it—weaponless, helpless! They dragged him from his horse and only left him because they thought him dead. Roderick Cherbon's last act of self-lessness saved my life."

Michaela's throat was so tight she could barely force words through it. "But did you not also save his? By taking him to Aurelia?"

"What I did was no noble act. I had already lost everything, I had nothing to go back to. No home, no family, all my friends were dead, save the man who had saved me. Roderick was the only sane thing left to cling to. Him, and then Leo."

"You saved Roderick's life so that you would have someone to support you?"

"I wish it were as simple as greed! I took him to Aurelia so that he might live, yes, but I needed him to live so that I could spend the rest of *my* life trying to repay him for what he did. My life, at last, had meaning, purpose." Hugh stepped closer to Michaela. "Every move Roderick makes, every word he utters, every curse at me, every slight now for you, stems from that battle. From what he lost when his father forced him on that pilgrimage. Roderick was never like Magnus—the man who drove Dorian mad, mad enough to kill herself, leaving her only surviving child in the clutches of those *monsters*. And now Roderick reckons it was he who had it wrong all along—his father was the man in the right. *I* am the only one who can change that, for *I* am the only one who knows what he's been through."

"Noble sentiments, Sir Hugh," Michaela said. "But I don't believe it. Roderick needs a woman—a wife. He needs softness in his life now, and I can—"

"You can't be his woman, you stupid bitch! He won't let you!"

"He will in time!" Michaela insisted. "Because *I love him,* Hugh! I've told Roderick as I will tell you: they're only scars! I don't care—"

"They're not just scars, Michaela!" Hugh roared, and Michaela thought she saw a welling of tears in Hugh's cold eyes. "His leg is *gone!*"

Michaela went stone-cold in an instant, and chills overtook her skin. "Why . . . why would you say such a thing, Hugh?"

"Because it's true." There *were* tears in Hugh's eyes—cold, angry, resentful. Guilty. "A handsbreadth below Roderick's left knee—*nothing*. Gone. No foot, no ankle, no calf."

"That's impossible," Michaela whispered.

"*I was there* when they took it. *I held him down.*"

"But he walks! His boots—"

"His left boot is a construction. Wood, wool—leather straps to above his knee. That's how I know you lied to me when you said he mounted his horse alone—what's left of his leg and the boot he wears has not the strength to see him into the saddle, and to mount with his right is impossible; his left leg has not the flexibility to raise up and over."

"But he *did* mount alone, I saw him!" Michaela felt she had been flung back into one of her nightmares.

"You likely saw what Rick wanted you to see, is all. And that is why he will never make love to you. He is not whole. He feels he is no longer a man—can't mount a horse properly, can't fight. He would never let you see him like that. Only me. *Only* . . . me, Miss Fortune."

"But he"—Michaela swallowed hard. "He's destroyed his walking stick. He no longer uses it! Since you've been gone—"

"I don't know what game you play, but I will not allow it to continue," Hugh growled, and for the first time, Michaela knew a growing fear of this handsome, lanky man. He was furious with her. "You don't deserve a man like Roderick Cherbon, and I will not let you have him!"

Michaela huffed a nervous laugh. "Why, Sir Hugh, it sounds as though you yourself are in lo—" Michaela broke off abruptly as Hugh Gilbert's face paled and he turned away from her.

She brought a hand to her mouth for a moment, as the pieces fell into place. *"You're in love with him,"* she whispered.

After a moment, he glanced over his shoulder at her, although his eyes fell short of her face. A slight, sad smile lifted the corner of his mouth. "Guilty," he said quietly.

"Oh my God." Michaela walked past Hugh to sit upon one of the upholstered benches. Her legs would no longer support her. "Does he know?"

Hugh laughed. "Of course not. What kind of fool do you take me for, Miss Fortune? I know that any affection Rick holds for me is not . . . is not of the same nature as my own. But I don't care. I only want . . ." He trailed off with a wave of his hand.

"You only want to be with him," Michaela supplied.

Hugh nodded. "It is enough for me. Him and Leo. Perhaps you are not so stupid, after all."

"But if you know that he will never—why can you not let me have a chance to make him happy, as a woman can? As Roderick wants?"

"Womanly affection—bah," Hugh scoffed. "Overrated. You don't know that's what Roderick wants."

"I do. He's shown me, in his chamber, and mine," Michaela said gently. Oddly, she no longer wanted to hurt Hugh, but he must know that Michaela would not give Roderick up. She loved him, too.

He looked toward the long windows of his chamber, dark save for the shocking flashes of lightning. "What are you going to do then, Miss Fortune? Out me? Tell Rick my sordid little secret so that he might loathe and detest me and throw me from Cherbon? Would you see me ruined to the very end?"

"He wouldn't," Michaela said. "He cares for you too much, Hugh. But, no, I will not disclose your secret."

Hugh glanced at her again, and Michaela thought he no longer looked like the smooth, polished man she had known him as. He looked lonely and shaken and sad, and Michaela felt his rejection from where she sat.

"Thank you, Miss Fortune."

"But I will not stop trying to win him," Michaela said. "We are to be married, and I would have him as my husband in truth. Perhaps the three of us, you and I and Leo, we could give him the happiness, the friendship he deserves?"

"Perhaps," Hugh said. "But you know it would never work for long."

Michaela frowned. "I don't understand."

"One man, two lovers—messy business." Hugh let his

sardonic smile slip onto his face briefly. "He must choose one of us."

"I agree," Michaela said. "And when he does, we must honor his choice."

"You're saying that if Rick sends you away, you'll go?"

"I'll go," Michaela promised.

"Even though it means the ruination of your family, and that Rick will likely be forced to leave England with Leo and me?"

"I'll go," Michaela repeated solemnly. "But you must agree that, if he chooses me, you will no longer try to interfere in our relationship, or sabotage my efforts with him. I would not see you turned away from Cherbon for what you've done for Roderick and Leo, but should you force my hand, Hugh . . ."

Hugh gave her a sad smile. "I'll not force your hand, Miss Fortune. I do have *some* pride left."

Michaela rose and stuck out her hand. "We are agreed, then?"

Hugh clasped her fingers and looked directly into her eyes. "You weren't supposed to fall in love with him," he said quietly, and then released her hand. "But we are agreed. Now, how are we to go about finding out about his . . . you know." Hugh did a shuffling dance.

But Michaela was already on her way toward the door, and unwilling to tell Hugh the nature of her desperate mission. She paused, her hand on the latch, to look back at him. "You'll mind Leo if I'm not back before he wakes?"

Hugh frowned. "Of course. I daresay I've been doing it longer than you have and am leagues better at it, any matter. I'm rather surprised he has not come for me already because of the storm."

Michaela smiled. "Thank you, Hugh."

"Miss Fortune," Hugh called as she was just slipping into the corridor, and she paused. "What are you going to do?"

Michaela closed the door softly.

The corridor was black, icy and damp, but beneath her gown, the link was warm against her skin. Had Michaela withdrawn it on its long chain, she would have seen its glow.

The storm beyond the thick walls of the keep was worsening and every stone-jarring boom of thunder caused her already-pounding heart to shudder in her chest. There were no windows in the dark corridor, but for once, Michaela was glad of it. She thought that if she was made to look upon the startling, dazzling lightning, she may just die of fright.

Michaela had the distinct feeling that this was no normal storm. She could feel its malevolent heaviness creep through the corridor along the inky seam of floor and wall, as if watching her with gray eyes, trailing her, waiting for the opportune moment to strike, to stop her from doing what she intended.

In a moment, she stood before Roderick's door. She laid her cheek against the wood, her eyes closed, straining for any sound from beyond. But the thunder was coming in waves now, thwarting her. Like the relentless hoofbeats of a hundred horses carrying their vengeful riders from the darkness, it crashed louder with each report, perhaps now only as far away as the black bend of the corridor.

She let her fingertips skitter down the smooth wood to the latch of the door and opened it in the masking silence of the thunder.

Chapter Twenty-Two

Roderick let the lightning lash him as he lay on his bed, as if the white-hot flashes would cleanse him of his damned uncertainty, of his fear of his own life waiting for him beyond his safe chamber—what he was, what he was becoming.

His nonexistent left foot itched madly again, and it took everything he had not to spring his body together on the mattress and claw at his boot, or dig his heel into the coverings. It was madness, *madness,* and he knew it.

He had still not removed his boots, and now he was afraid to. More afraid of it than he had ever been in the whole of his life. He was fairly certain of what he would find if he did: the same thing that had been there when he pulled the boot on.

Nothing, of course.

But what frightened him was the possibility that once he removed the boot, the sensations he'd felt for the past two days, the increased mobility he had, would vanish. As if, by taking off the boot, he would renege on his part of the bargain he had unknowingly entered into with some dark force.

He could not lose his leg again. Not when he was just beginning to feel like a whole man once more. He didn't know how he was going to explain it to Hugh, who would surely interrogate him. Hugh was the only soul at Cherbon who knew the terrible secret of Roderick's left boot, and Roderick could not put his friend off for long.

What of Michaela Fortune? When and how would he ever tell her? Would he even be forced to? It was madness, he knew, to consider that his leg was . . . regenerating. Madness! But Roderick could *feel* it—the flesh, the bone—and it gave him the insane idea that one day, one day, he could mayhap be the husband to Miss Fortune that he wanted to be. A father to Leo. Cherbon's lord.

Roderick threw his forearm over his eyes with a cry as another blinding flash of lightning stuttered across his bed. He wanted his mother. A woman he had not seen in a score of years, whose memory was soft about the edges, whose features were blurred by time and pain. He could see her lying in her bed—she was forever in her bed—her long hair caught under her shoulders, her face pale, her eyes dim. She had been Roderick's only source of comfort in all the early years of his young life, even as constantly ill as she was. But his mother had been wrong in her convictions all along . . . and Magnus had been right, once again. Roderick *was* weak. He felt the madness turning in his brain, catching in his chest like a heavy sob, and the itch, the constant itch . . .

"You're a big boy now, Roderick, I know," she said to him. "But not so grown that you mayn't come and sit with me, hmm?"

He climbed readily upon her bed, a large lad for nine years, and lay down carefully next to her. She was so slight, smaller even than Roderick himself, and he was mindful of her frailty.

But she raised her pale white hand and laid it along his face, gave him a rare smile—her strength was so little now.

"You are my most cherished possession," she whispered. "My greatest accomplishment. I love you so very, very much."

The lightning flashed and thunder growled menacingly, as if something black—or mayhap only gray—was biding its time beyond the curtained bed.

"If I must go away, will you be all right?"

"Where are you going, Mother?"

She stroked her thumb lightly along his cheek—and to Roderick it felt like a soft, budding leaf, cool and fragile.

"Your father is a hard man, Roderick, this you know. And though he thinks you weak, like me, I know differently. You are strong. A strong boy, who will be a strong man. Stronger than Magnus."

"Stronger than Father?" Roderick didn't think that was possible. Magnus was a mountain, a world unto himself.

Dorian nodded, her hair making a shushing sound against the pillow. "He senses that your strength is different from his and it frightens him. Magnus is strong in his body, in his will. You, my love, my beloved, are strong of heart." She touched her forefinger to his bony chest. "And that sort of strength can change not only Cherbon, it can change the whole, whole world."

His mother drew a shallow breath. "If I must go away, do not think unkindly of me. I am as your father accuses— weak. And I am so very tired, my love. I cannot bear another . . . I cannot bear it, you see."

Roderick did not see. "Where would you go, Mother?" he asked again. "May I come, too?" He did not like this conversation—it frightened him. He wanted to lie here, in the soft quiet of his mother's presence forever. It was the only place in his world he felt safe. If she were to go away, he would be left only with his father, and Harliss the Heartless. . . .

"One thing you are to remember always: I love you. I love you, Roderick, as God loves you. Wholly. And perfectly. And should you one day wonder that I did not love you enough, would that you think of God to remind you. And if ever you think God has forsaken you, would that you call me to mind. One day, you will understand this."

Roderick didn't understand it at all, but he nodded anyway, so as not to upset his mother. She needed her rest.

She smiled at him again. "Now"—she reached her arm farther across his body and Roderick felt her weak tug. He aided her by moving closer, so that their bodies touched and they lay eye to eye on her pillow. She stroked his hair away from his forehead, over and over. "Let me look at you for a while. You may sleep if you like."

Roderick nodded, snuggled down into the pillow that smelled of the soap the maid used on her hair, and also her tangy, sour illness. His mother slid her head forward and pressed her lips to his.

Roderick smiled at the happy feeling in his belly, and although he tried very hard to keep his eyes open, to look into his mother's eyes and hold on to that happy feeling, she was stroking his hair again, and he could feel himself sinking down into sleep. . . .

The crashing thunder shook him awake with a child's cry of "Mother!" and he looked around the dark bed.

Dorian was gone, the blanket that had covered her now tossed over Roderick's legs, the mattress, the pillow still carrying the slight impression of her body, her head.

His mother had gone away.

And Roderick would never see her again.

* * *

The lightning flashed over his mumbled cry, his tormented writhing. Why would he call to mind such a terrible memory, tonight of all nights? He had not thought of Dorian Cherbon's last hours on earth for many years, and tonight his mother's words haunted him in time with the throbbing itch of his left foot.

She had been the only person in the whole of his life to say she loved him.

Until Leo. And Michaela Fortune.

He had failed them all.

Roderick threw his fists into the mattress at his side and gave a ragged howl of pain, his eyes squeezed shut against the horror that swooped around him like the storm flying beyond the keep.

"Roderick," a woman's voice whispered, and he thought for a moment that madness had at last fully claimed him.

But when he opened his eyes, the lightning stuttered across one half of Michaela Fortune's face as she leaned over him.

"It's all right," she said, climbing onto the mattress, across his body. She kissed his cheeks. "I'm here now. I'm here."

Michaela didn't know if Roderick had been dreaming, but as she lowered her head to next kiss his mouth, the lightning showed her his face and his eyes were wild. She touched her lips to his gently. He didn't fight her, but neither did he respond.

She was straddling him awkwardly, her skirt pulled tight over his abdomen and around her thighs, but she didn't want to move just yet—he needed to get used to her touch, the weight of her body atop his.

"I'm here for you," she whispered in his ear. "For all of you."

"You're making a mistake," he growled back, an animal so weary from his ensnarement that the worst he could do was a frightening sound.

She shook her head. "No. I have made many mistakes before—some I admit were with you. But not this night."

"I can't love you. Not like you want me to. I don't even think I can love Leo." His voice caught, as if he would weep.

"I want you to love me—and Leo—however you can. That is enough." Then she kissed him again, more deeply. He still did not respond. She raised her head only slightly, whispering the words into his mouth as the thunder crashed around them. "And until you can, I will love you both enough for all of us."

This time when she kissed him, he kissed her back.

Michaela let her hands come up from the mattress to frame his face, allowing the weight of her upper body to sink onto Roderick's chest. He felt thick and hard and strong beneath her, and it filled her with an odd sense of power, to have this giant of a man beneath her, almost at her mercy.

Almost.

Roderick's hands came gently, hesitantly, to Michaela's rib cage and she wondered if he could feel her heart thrashing against his palms. His fingertips began a gentle exploration of her sides, to the sensitive areas under her arms and at the curve of her breasts.

She was nervous to her very core. In all her wild imaginings of what her first time with a man would be like, she never thought it would be she playing the aggressor. It was as if she was taking her own virginity, and again she felt the headiness of power.

She raised up, sitting fully on his hips now, and after

giving him a moment to protest—which he did not—she
eased one side of her wide, scooped bodice down over her
shoulder. She slid her arm from the gown and then pushed
the other side down. In a moment, the upper part of her
gown was gathered around her waist, and her nipples
puckered in the chill of the dark room.

The lightning flashed again, revealing her nakedness,
and beneath her, Roderick gasped.

"You are beautiful," he said, his voice full of wonder
and despair, too. "Too beautiful for me."

Michaela shook her head, and then reached down for
his hands. She placed them on both her breasts, closing her
eyes at the contact. His skin was so hot on her chilled flesh
that she expected to hear a sizzle. After a moment, she
commanded him, "Raise up, my lord. Take off your shirt."

He froze for a beat of time, but then used his elbows and
then his hands to bring his face to hers. He jerked his shirt
over his head and had seized Michaela's arms and pulled
her back down to the mattress with him before his shirt
had time to hit the floor.

If she had thought his hands on her bare breasts was delicious, the sensation of his naked torso pressed against her
transported Michaela into another world. The hair of his
chest and trailing down his stomach felt like soft grass on
warm, solid earth. And when he kissed her again, she
could feel each twitch of his powerful muscles, each thrum
of blood in his veins. His arms around her felt as immense
and solid as the very sky, the storm raging around them,
certain and relentless and, yes, frightening.

She broke away from his mouth with no little effort and
struggled to the side of him, placing a hand on his chest
when he would have risen. In a moment, she had shimmied

out of the rest of her gown and kicked it from the bed into the dark. Her hands went boldly to the ties at his waist.

"What are you doing?" Roderick asked gruffly, a hint of amazement in his voice.

"What do you think I'm doing?"

"Making a mess of my laces likely," he said.

Michaela chuckled and flung the long ties up onto his stomach. "You do it, then."

In the murky darkness, she could see him shake his head. "This is a mistake, Michaela."

"No, it isn't." She was tired of waiting for him. Reaching behind her toward his right boot, she felt for the cold hilt of his hidden dagger.

Roderick became instantly alarmed as she moved to his feet. "No—stop—"

But she had the blade in hand before he could rise, and with one swift flick of her wrist, she drew the dagger's sharp edge up the center of the ladder his laces created. Aided by his erection, his breeches pulled apart soundlessly, save for the whoosh of breath that came from the Lord of Cherbon, himself.

Michaela tossed the blade over the edge of the bed and it disappeared into the darkness with a clang.

The lightning flashed again, two, three times, rattling the blackness of the bed. Michaela glimpsed Roderick's face, pale and creased and worried, yet drawn with intense passion and need.

"I can never be the man you want me to be," Roderick warned her, each word wracked with pain and shame.

"You already are." Pulling apart his breeches fully, his manhood sprung free, Michaela threw her leg over Roderick's hips. She took him in her hand, despite his strangled,

"Michaela, wait," and without giving herself time to be afraid, Michaela sank onto him.

Her cry mingled with Roderick's—pain and wonder and fear. She settled onto his length with difficulty, but did not relent until she had taken him all. She paused for a moment as the throbbing pain receded and then slowly, she began to ride him, the link around her neck swinging in time to her movements, out over Roderick's face, making a warped ring of shadow when the lightning flashed.

He caught it in his hand, pulled her forward onto his chest once more.

Michaela writhed atop Roderick, keeping him enslaved by her body. Bringing her hands to her neck, she lifted the chain over her head and placed it over Roderick's in one fluid motion. She kissed him deeply before pushing herself aright and sinking onto him fully once more.

Roderick brought his hands up, his arms crooked at the elbows, as if in surrender to her, and Michaela laced her fingers in his. The metal link rested in the center of his breastbone, and seemed to glow brighter with each flash of lightning, bright white rays bursting from it like a small, fantastic sun. With each ebb and flow of movement, Roderick kept time with his sighs, his groans, and the vulnerability of him sped Michaela's passion, prompted her to rock her hips faster. Making love to Roderick tonight was not for Michaela's pleasure, but she could feel a tightness winding in her, an urgent need for something, something . . . and she raced toward it.

She felt him grow inside her, heard his groans drawing out, longer and longer, his panting taking his words and tying them into unintelligible knots, and she knew that his time was very near. She was close, too, so close, and so she rode faster, deeper, letting loose her own throaty cries as she felt him in her very core, it seemed.

And then it started for her, an expanding around his length, slowly, infinitely, as if time had stopped, and then in a wink, her whole body, her whole world collapsed in with a crash and she cried out, froze.

Roderick gave a guttural yell and strained his hips upward, driving into her one time on his own, deeply, and his passion, too, erupted.

The link fell dim once more.

Michaela slumped to Roderick's side, feeling him slip erotically from her body. They lay in the dark together, without words, chasing their own breaths, for a long time.

Finally, Roderick spoke.

"Why did you give me the link? Your mother told you—"

"To never take it off, I know," Michaela finished quietly. "But that was before I had you to protect me. Remember, on the cliff, you promised to protect me. And I believe you will."

"I remember. But, Michaela, I cannot protect you as a proper husband should. I . . . it is the same reason why I would not make love to you. Why I abhor the thought of being naked in your—"

"Roderick, I know," she whispered.

"No, you don't. You can't possibly—"

"I know." Michaela pulled his head to look at her. "I know about your leg." He simply stared at her, and she saw his throat working as he swallowed. "Hugh told me."

"You knew . . . you knew before—" He let the question trail away, but Michaela knew what he was asking.

"Yes, I knew before we made love."

Roderick made a growling sound, and looked away from her. "Why?" he rasped. "Why have you done this?"

Michaela sat up, propped on one arm. "Because I love you, Roderick. And I wanted to show you are a man, *the man,* to me and for me. The man I want as my husband, in every way. Your scars, your injuries, they make you perfect to me."

"Stop!"

"No, I won't stop," she said gently. "You must know this before either of us can continue. I made love to you tonight so that you could see that you are not just a weighty purse to me, or a more noble title, or a grand keep. I want you for who you are, right now. And if you want me, then you will take me for who I am, right now. You will love me as a wife, true. If you can not do that, after all that we have shared, then I can not and will not marry you."

He was quiet for a long time. "You leave me with a very difficult decision."

"Oh, I hope it is not so very difficult." She tried to smile in the darkness. "My parents should arrive on the morrow— mayhap the day after. Either we wed, or I return home with them. It is your choice." She kissed his cheek, the closest part of his face to her, and then rolled over and rose from the bed.

"Where are you going?" he demanded, and Michaela wanted to think she detected a note of longing in his voice.

She pulled her gown over her head. "To my chamber, to wash and to sleep. You need your time to think, as do I. I will see you in the morn."

He humphed, and this time Michaela's smile was genuine. She came around the side of the bed and kissed his mouth properly.

"Good night, Roderick. Sleep well. I love you."

He didn't answer her, but she hadn't expected him to, and so she turned and quietly left his room.

* * *

Roderick lay for a long time in cold, sweaty fear after Michaela had left. Perhaps what she said was true. Perhaps she could accept him for what he was, and perhaps he was even some sort of a man still, in her eyes, at least.

Fear made him sick at his stomach. Fear of losing all that was wonderfully appearing just within his reach.

He tugged the sides of his ruined breeches together as best he could and rose to a sit. Michaela had missed cutting the bottom two rungs of lace and so he restrung the leather together sufficient to retain his modesty, then swung his legs over the side of the bed. He pushed with his arms and stood.

His left boot crunched sideways under his weight and Roderick spun his arms madly in the air, black dread rushing up his throat and blinding him as he began to topple to the floor. The feeling in his leg was gone, gone! He turned and grabbed at the bed with a cry, but clutched only at gossamer throws that slid with him to the ground.

Roderick's head struck the frame of the bed painfully, dazzling him for a moment, his right ankle twisted under him and as he at last crashed fully to the floor, Roderick realized that he had lost his leg once more.

The metal link around his neck was the last thing to hit, and it did so with a tiny, echoing clink before his wide-staring, disbelieving eyes.

Chapter Twenty-Three

Michaela was sore and aching and more hopeful than she had ever been in her life as she made her way down the black corridor to her chamber.

She had made love to Roderick, and he had let her. Things were going to be all right, after all. She realized then that it was Yule's Eve. They would be wed in a matter of days—perhaps she could even count the time in hours—and then she and he and Leo would become a family. It gave her an instant's frown about what was to come of the situation with Hugh—Michaela had spoken true when she'd told him she didn't wish for him to go, but she also knew what it was like to care for someone who did not return the emotion. Michaela could not have stayed at Tornfield Manor after Alan and Juliette wed, so it was very unlikely that Hugh could withstand seeing Michaela and Roderick together, as man and wife, for the rest of his days.

It would devastate Roderick if Hugh left.

She wondered for a moment if perhaps Hugh's feelings for Roderick might one day fade, change, as her own feelings for Alan had. But then she shook her head with a sad smile. Michaela knew her feelings had changed because of Roderick and distance, time to see who Alan really was, and that he was not the man she'd daydreamed into being. Hugh held no such illusions about Roderick—he knew his warts, and loved him in spite of them. Mayhap because of them. And Leo . . . heavens, how Leo loved his Hoo.

But now was not the time to think of such depressing possibilities. Michaela wanted a wash and a bite to eat and the rest of the evening to herself. She walked past her own door to head toward the hall and give instructions for water and a tray to be brought up. Perhaps she would have the same sent to Roderick's chamber, as well. A small gift for him.

She was nearly to the top of the stairs when she heard the commotion: a man shouting, a woman—the voice sounded like one of the maidservants—arguing fiercely with him.

"You can't go up there, my lord!"

"Get out of my way, woman, or I shall dash you down the stairs! I'll search this entire keep alone if I must! I know she is here!"

Michaela froze, a hand to her throat.

The man's voice belonged to Alan Tornfield.

He came upon the upper floor just then, and Michaela saw his wild, rain-soaked hair and clothes, the stricken look in his eyes as his gaze fell upon her. The maidservant was hanging on to the back of his cloak as if pulling vainly on a stubborn mule.

"Michaela, thank God! They're with you, aren't they? Say they are!"

"Alan, what in heaven's—it's all right," she said to the maid and waved her away. "Who are with me? My God, you're soaked through!"

"Elizabeth!" Alan gasped, trying to gulp down great

breaths of air. "And Harliss, as well. They're here, aren't they?"

"Of course not. Why would they be? Harliss is banned from Cherbon." The tiniest drip of fear fell onto Michaela's neck, as if snuck through the stones by the powerful storm still raging beyond Cherbon's walls, or flung from Alan's drenched form. She stepped toward him, reached out a hand to take his arm. "Come downstairs with me and you can explain. I'm sure—"

"There's no time!" Alan shouted, flinging her hand away. "If they're not here, they must be in the storm somewhere, lost!"

"What are you talking about?" Michaela's dread increased. "Weren't they with you on the way back to Tornfield?"

Alan fell back onto the corridor wall, his eyes squeezed shut. "Elizabeth ran off again, presumably to you. Harliss seemed to be close on her heels when they disappeared into the storm."

"Juliette?" Michaela asked, the reality of what Alan was telling her not quite sinking in.

Alan opened his eyes and his head came away from the wall, his face sickly pale in the flickering gloom of the corridor. "We were closer to Tornfield so I sent her on. In the black, the rain, I couldn't track Elizabeth and Harliss while keeping Juliette safe. She . . . she feels Elizabeth is gone because of her and now . . . I've lost them all!" His chest hitched under his soaked clothes.

"My God," Michaela breathed, hearing each rumble and flash beyond the keep as if amplified now. "All right. It will be all right. I'll go and alert Lord R—"

But her decisive speech was cut off by another voice in the blackness. "There you are, Miss Fortune." It was Hugh, and in a moment he materialized in the circle of candlelight. "Leo with you, then?"

"What?" Michaela said, her heart freezing to a halt.

Hugh frowned at Alan Tornfield, still leaning against the wall as if unable to stand by his own power. "It was *you!* I'll have you whipped, dog, for invading the lord's son's chamber!"

Alan gasped a strangled breath and slid down the wall to a slumping seat.

"Alan hasn't been to Leo's room, Hugh," Michaela choked, and she prayed her horrific suspicions were wrong, wrong, wrong.

"Well, someone was there who's only just come in from the rain—the floor is a deluge." Hugh's frown deepened as he looked between Michaela and Alan. "Where is Leo?"

Alan cried out and shook his fist. "Elizabeth, why? How could you?"

"The Tornfield girl's abducted Leo?" Hugh shouted, but before Alan could admit to the possibility, Michaela stepped to Hugh, her hands out.

"No, Hugh, I think it is much worse than that, I'm afraid—Elizabeth's run off, but Harliss was with her."

A squealing breath came from Hugh.

"Nurse will protect them," Alan argued. "She loves them both and—"

"I tried to tell you in the wood, Alan!" Michaela shouted. "Harliss is mad! She is mad for revenge on us all, and the surest way to get that revenge is through our children! She is evil, deranged!"

Alan was sobbing quietly in his heap on the floor and Michaela turned from him in disgust. She expected to see Hugh crazed with worry, but the man's beautiful eyes were hard, determined. His jaw was set and he seemed poised to action.

It was little wonder Hugh had saved Roderick's life in the Holy Land. How had she ever thought this man insincere?

"Take this blubbering mess and go search," Hugh commanded. "Call to any servants you see en route, but do not tarry to rally more. I will warn Roderick and we shall join you."

"Yes. All right, Hugh," Michaela readily agreed, so thankful that Hugh Gilbert was who he was.

He looked to Alan. "I vow to you, Tornfield, I vow to you by all that I hold holy in heaven and on earth, if Leo bears one bruise, one scratch—if he has so much as caught the sniffles from your asinine judgment, I will see your blood spilled over my boots by my own hand!" He looked back to Michaela, and she knew in that moment that Hugh meant every word to the center of his soul. "Go!" Hugh shouted as he turned on his own heel and raced into the black.

Michaela ran to Alan's side and yanked on his elbow. "Get up, Alan. If you value those children's lives and your own, *come on!*"

Roderick had forgotten how to walk with his cane and in his heavy prosthesis in two short days, as if he had only just lost his leg for the first time.

He lurched and crashed his way through the maze of dark passages of Cherbon, dizzy from the bash on his skull he'd suffered, and also the shock of the night.

Michaela had made love to him. She loved him. And she wanted him in spite of his hideousness, but now he could no longer pretend. What had happened to the power of the old boot he still wore? Why had it failed him, now of all times, when he had started to believe that he could pretend he was whole, could love Michaela as she deserved to be loved, as he wanted to love her? For those short, sweet days, Roderick had been a man once more, and now . . . now—

He was nothing but a beast again. A pathetic, growling, thrashing animal, unfit to love. Unfit for a family. Unfit to live.

He stopped, braced his forearm on a wall and waited with his eyes closed for the paralyzing trembling to ease. He could never face her like this again. Not when he had shown her he could walk, mount a horse, swing Leo about and toss him in the air with ease. Hell, the way he'd improved the last two days, Roderick was beginning to fancy a battle again, and thought of challenging Hugh to a mock contest. Roderick pulled away from the wall and lurched on down the corridor aimlessly.

But not now. No, now he could do none of those things, and it made him useless. Impotent. Pathetic. She had said she loved him, but that would change. In time, she would grow tired of his indigent state, his tottering, and she would seek her comfort elsewhere.

And now that Roderick loved her, had tasted her as the wife she would certainly be—warm and loyal and passionate—he felt his guts were being pulled slowly from his abdomen.

Perhaps this was how his mother had felt, before she walked into the sea and left him forever. She too had been ill, tired. She too had left someone she loved behind, thinking perhaps he was better off without her.

Had he been better off? Had Dorian Cherbon done the right thing in taking her own life?

A cold chill swept up Roderick's spine and Michaela's metal link, forgotten beneath his hastily donned shirt until now, began to itch against his skin. He stopped to scratch at it mindlessly, and then looked at where his crippled leg had dragged him to. The candles eternally guttering to either side of the ornately carved doors, the Latin words accusing from the lintel:

From the gate of hell deliver their souls, O Lord.

A rage built in Roderick, unlike any he had ever known, at his father, at his infirmities, at Aurelia for being ill, at Leo for being so innocent, at his mother for leaving him, at Miss Fortune for having the stupidity to come to Cherbon in the first place, to love him.

Roderick flung open the double doors with a roar and threw himself into the dark chapel, as if charging down the throat of a dragon.

Michaela knew she was a fool for dashing into the storm in nothing more than her gown and slippers, but she could not bring herself to pause even long enough to find some sort of cloak to throw about her.

Leo was out there. Leo and Elizabeth, both in Harliss's clutches.

Thankfully, Alan had recovered from his self-pitying puddle in the corridor and now ran at Michaela's side, the two of them clutching hands to maintain some sort of reference in the crashing, black world of water that was the storm around them. The terrain was treacherous in the freezing downpour, turning ditches of dying winter grass into deadly sluices, where rabbit holes and animal paths gaped suddenly underfoot, as if to take the desperate pair by surprise and swallow them whole.

As the lightning flashed, they could see the sea beyond, tempest and foaming, the waves lashing up the height of the cliffs themselves, it seemed. The sight of the black water, slashed with foamy gray arms grasping blindly for prey, any prey, caused Michaela's blood to run colder than the rain.

Alan jerked her to a stop. "Michaela!" he shouted, and crouched down. He picked up some small object and rose, holding it toward her. It was a tiny leather slipper.

Leo's shoe.

No soos!

Alan must have known by her face that the shoe belonged to Leo for he did not hesitate a moment more, tugging Michaela's shocked body into motion again.

"They must have gone toward the cliff," he shouted as they both ran and slid through the narrow valley. "Is there aught about for shelter there? A fishing hut perhaps?"

Michaela shook her head, but then realized he could not see her in the darkness. "No! There's a path that leads down to the water, but . . . nothing else!" Behind her, Michaela could feel the graves on the knoll watching them. Perhaps Dorian Cherbon particularly, as one who had taken this path long ago, to her own death. "There is little beach, Alan, and if the tide—"

Alan pulled her forward once more. "There is no other place they could have gone. They may be trapped on the cliff face!" They stumbled toward the rocky V, where the path disappeared over the cliff and down its jagged skirt to the thrashing hem of the sea.

Once at the head of the steep, zigzagging path, they stopped to look down. The tide was indeed on its way in, and the slender strip of rocky beach that was often visible was now covered over by a depth of foamy water. Michaela knew it would rise to the middle of the cliff at its highest point.

The children would not have gone this way on their own.

When the lightning flashed again, Alan gave a hoarse cry. He tore his hand free from Michaela's and dropped over the edge of the cliff onto the path, scrambling over the sharp, loose stone.

"Alan!" Michaela cried into the screaming wind, but he did not stop, did not slow. Why hadn't Roderick come yet? Michaela was terrified, and in need of his solid presence.

She swiped at the streams of icy water dripping into her eyes and followed Alan, keeping close watch on the boundary of water and rock that rose steadily with each crashing wave, rolling ever upward to meet them. The wind howled around the cliff like ghostly, hunting hounds.

Once he had come to a swaying halt before the altar, Roderick did not know what else to do. He'd not had any plans for coming to the chapel, and did not know why he had.

Small oil lamps to either side of the tabernacle gave a glow to the gilded surfaces and threw in shadowed relief the enormous crucifix suspended above. The very stones of the ornate room breathed old incense, and for a moment, Roderick was lost to two years ago, to the long hospital room in Constantinople, where another enormous crucifix had lorded and the smoky cologne had choked his raw throat.

Roderick gagged at the memory of incense-tinged blood in his mouth, of the ringing in his ears and the throbbing of his face, the way his leg had felt as though it was continuously on fire without being consumed. And then there was Hugh's gaunt, pale, worried face, seeking to champion Roderick's cause when all Roderick wanted was to slip away into death, away from the incense and the pain and the mocking crucifix. To a place where he might at last see his mother, and where he was sure to never see Magnus Cherbon again.

How he had prayed before Heraclea! How he had begged God to spare his men and lead them to a righteous victory; and yes, to finally make his father proud of him, to praise him and say, "Well done, my son! Well done!"

But God had answered none of his prayers. His men had been starved, ill, and then slaughtered. When Roderick had sought to save some of them—any of them—he had nearly paid with his own life. And all the sacrifice had earned him was the loss of his leg, his manhood.

Would that he had just damned died!

At least Magnus had not been alive to receive him at Cherbon once more, the ultimate failure, now.

Roderick threw his walking stick at the high tabernacle with a roar. "Why could you not just kill me outright? Why give me this suffering first? Why saddle me with a boy not of my flesh, who does not know it and who looks to me as his father? Why place before me the one woman I could love for the rest of my life and then leave me unable to be the man she deserves? Why? *Why, damn you!*"

Then Roderick dropped to his right knee, his left leg held out straight to his side, and he toppled sideways, catching himself with his right arm. His sobs shook him and he let his ragged breaths echo in the tall, quiet chapel, his pathetic keening. "Have I not suffered enough? Have I . . . have I not loved and then lost enough for your greedy wishes? Must you punish me yet? Punish the only souls on this earth I could bring my dead heart to open for? Aagghhh! I hate you, you bastard! Come on—come on then, and finish me off!" he gasped, feeling his tears and snot running down his face. "You can do no more to me now— send me on to hell, if you would! Only set the rest of them free of me!" His last words came out a choking, trailing sob, and he let his head fall to the cold stones before the altar, his shoulders shaking violently as he wept, purging himself of the poison in his wretched soul.

And then it was if the candle flames in the chapel were guttering to their ends at last, the golden glow fading, fading to soft, cool black. Roderick's sobs were dying with the light, and in the buzzing chaos of his brain, gentler memories called out to him.

My most cherished possession, his mother whispered. *I love you so very, very much, Roderick . . . as God loves you. Wholly. And perfectly. You are strong of heart . . . that sort of strength can change the whole, whole world.*

And Hugh: *I owe you my life, Rick, and I will spend the rest of my days trying to repay you for it. You will never have a more steadfast friend, this I vow.*

And Leo: *You love Papa? Me too!*

And finally, Michaela: *You promised to protect me. And I believe you will. I love you, Roderick. You are the man I want as my husband, in every way.*

All those he loved, and who in return loved him. Their unique memories grasped hands and danced circles teasingly around Roderick's brain, confusing him.

Why, why could he have not returned from Constantinople whole? Why, if their pilgrimage had been such a holy one, had his company perished, sending him back to his home, defeated, a half man?

Had you not been so injured, would you have ever seen Aurelia again? Taken Leo away from his inevitable poverty and death?

Would you have returned to Cherbon with Hugh at your side?

Would you have been forced to hold contest for a bride, finding no woman in all the land brave enough to pursue you save Michaela Fortune?

Roderick knew the answer to each question was no. Had his and Hugh's company been successful at Heraclea, they would have gleaned their spoils and returned home, Hugh able to pay his debts and regain his lands, Roderick eager to show Magnus his reward. Hugh and Roderick would have parted ways in Constantinople and likely never seen each other again.

No midnight drinking binges, or sarcastic comments about the poor state of Roderick's life—mocking him, then defending him, encouraging him. No crimson calfskin boots, clicking into his line of vision, demanding he get up and about. No one to share the worst of the memories with.

No dark-eyed scamp, dashing about Cherbon, his laugh ringing carelessly as he threw himself upon Roderick as if seeing him each time for the first time.

No Miss Fortune, her angel's voice bringing a soft femininity to Cherbon's black walls, her clumsiness so endearing, so entertaining. Her shapely body boldly pressed to his, making a virgin's love to him to bravely prove her true heart. How she loved Leo, and sparred with Hugh, and stood by Roderick's side against Tornfield, against Heartless, against the storm of memories that haunted him here at Cherbon. She had brought magic to him, in more than just the old worn boot still strapped to his right leg.

None of these people—the only people, save his mother, whom Roderick had ever truly loved—would be in his life now, had he not lost his leg and nearly his life on that fatal pilgrimage. The most remarkable individuals that he would have likely ever known, with or without his injuries.

Would he trade one of them for his leg? To have his scars magically healed? Was just one of their lives worth one short length of flesh and bone?

"No," Roderick cried hoarsely from his prone position

on the hard, stone floor before the altar. The light was returning now, slowly. "No," he repeated.

Roderick raised his head and he felt a final tear jump from the corner of his eye as he raised his gaze to the towering crucifix, but it was not a tear of self-loathing, or of regret as the others had been.

It was revelation.

"Forgive me," he whispered, awestruck.

And then Roderick heard the crash of the chapel doors behind him, and the rapid clicking of heels on stone.

"Rick!" Hugh cried. "Rick, thank God! What in holy hell are you doing hiding in—I thought I was mad to check, but—" Hugh broke off as he dropped to one knee beside Roderick and began pulling him to his feet. Roderick could feel Hugh's tremble. "Are you injured? Where is your cane? Hurry, hurry!"

"What is it, Hugh?" Roderick asked, taking in Hugh's lined and ashen face. He braced himself with one hand on the stone railing while Hugh scrambled behind the altar for Roderick's discarded walking stick.

"Alan Tornfield returned to Cherbon—his daughter ran off again, with Harliss, and we have reason to believe they came here." Hugh slapped the walking stick into Roderick's hand and jerked him forward. "Leo's missing from his room."

Something in Roderick froze just then, and the coldness seemed to radiate throughout his entire body. He jerked to a stop. "Leo?" he repeated hoarsely.

Hugh swallowed hard. "Yes, Leo. Now, do come on, Rick—Tornfield and Miss Fortune have already gone into the storm, and we must hurry to join them." He pulled Roderick forward again.

The old fear gripped Roderick once more. "Hugh, how can I—I can't walk—"

"Yes, yes!" Hugh barked irritably. "Don't you think I know that by now? Pathetic cripple, no leg—*I understand, Rick!* But you got on well enough to mount a horse the other day, so please do shut the fuck up now and let's go— Leo's life is in danger, and likely Miss Fortune's as well, if Harliss is involved."

Roderick said not another word, only shook off Hugh's arm, leaned into his cane, and lurched from the chapel more quickly than he ever had.

This was his test, then. Not a test from God—Roderick felt he had already survived that trial—but a test for himself.

It was time for Roderick to prove himself, *to* himself.

Chapter Twenty-Four

Alan was almost to the item he sought—Michaela saw it now, too: a long, once pale blue ribbon, now dark with rain—when his right foot slipped on a loose rock and sent him sliding down the side of the cliff.

Michaela screamed, thinking that in a moment, Alan Tornfield would meet the rising, crushing sea and be no more, leaving her alone in the storm on the trail of a madwoman.

But he did not go over into the sea. Instead, he landed on his side on a sliver of a shelf only ten feet below Michaela. She picked up the ribbon and crushed it together with Leo's shoe, not wishing to let one item of the precious young people out of her sight, and then carefully scrambled farther down the treacherous path to Alan's side.

"Alan! Are you all right?" There was not enough room to crouch, so she leaned into the rock and over him, the sea mist sliding over them like frozen slush. The tide was just below them now, and in moments the breakers would sweep them both from the cliff face. "Alan, you must get up! The water—"

"I think I've broken my arm," he groaned, and began to struggle to his feet.

Michaela held out the hand not clutching Leo's shoe and Elizabeth's ribbon and the slick rock for vain purchase.

"Get back, Michaela," Alan shouted. "You'll have us both drowned!"

Michaela scrambled back up the path, to where the ribbon had been found. Alan joined her in a moment, his face as white as the lightning striking the sea, and cradling his right arm. He looked to a small overhang where the ribbon had lain. A narrow, black opening sheltered underneath.

"Is it a cave, you think?" Michaela asked.

Alan nodded. "I can only hope. Either that or . . ." He glanced over his shoulder at the crashing waves that were ever advancing on them both. "I can't go in—with my arm, I'd be useless to fight off Harliss or bring the children out. We'll have to wait for Hugh and—"

"I'll go," Michaela said immediately, shoving the tiny shoe and slip of silk into Alan's chest. "There's no time to wait—look at the rocks, the tide mark. The water will invade the cave as it rises and they could all be drowned. Go back up, Alan, and make sure Roderick and Hugh see where we are when they come." Michaela crouched down and readied herself to enter the cave, but Alan held his uninjured arm before her chest.

"Michaela, no! What if—"

"Just go, Alan!" She pushed his arm away and ducked inside the pitch-black throat of the sea cave.

The waves were louder inside than without, pounding against the cliff and vibrating through the hard rock as Michaela crawled down the tunnel, narrow and sloped toward the heart of the land. Once the tide rose, the sea would rush inside like a river, filling up the cave. Her heart beat so fast in her chest that she could not discern the rhythm, a riffling of blood at once. She could hear nothing but the waves, and her heart.

"Leo!" she called as she crawled. "Elizabeth! Answer me!"

"Mike-lah!" the precious little voice called, sounding scared and weak and frantic, and Michaela threw herself down the slick slide of rock toward it.

A flicker of meager light heralded the opening of the passage just as Michaela splashed onto the floor of the bottlenecked cave. She scrambled up to a crouch and what she saw nearly caused her to vomit.

Leo was indeed inside, sitting in Elizabeth Tornfield's lap, both children clutching at each other in a depth of stagnant, murky water. And standing hunched near them was Harliss, a long blade in one hand and an even longer, thick torch in the other. Michaela knew in that moment that the woman was truly mad. The gray cloak she'd worn earlier was gone, revealing the costume beneath: an intricate and costly-looking gown and robe, soaked with water now, and her thin, gray hair was done in a clumsy, sweeping plait around her head, as if she were playing the part of a noble lady who would hostess a grand feast. The ensemble was much too short for the tall, bony woman, and hung on her skeletal frame like a bad jest.

"How lovely that you would join us, Miss Fortune," Harliss cackled. "But where is Roderick? It is him I want."

"He's not here. 'Tis only I, and Alan Tornfield. He's just outside. He's . . . he's hurt his arm."

"My papa?" Elizabeth choked.

"Shut up!" Harliss shrieked at the girl, and then turned her eyes back to Michaela. "Roderick knows, though, doesn't he? That I have them." She jerked her head toward the children, huddled together in the water on the floor.

Michaela nodded. "Hugh was calling for him as I left the keep." She took a step toward Leo and Elizabeth. "Are you both all right?"

"Stay back!" Harliss screeched, and splashed through the water at Michaela with the dagger outstretched, coming to stand between her and the children, the point of her blade dimpling Elizabeth's cheek. "Take one more step, and I shall cut her throat. I don't need her alive— either of them. Roderick will not know until he is arrived, and then it will be too late."

"All right," Michaela tried to answer calmly, and took a step back. "All right, Harliss, I won't move. But why not let them leave? I'll stay in their place until Roderick comes."

Harliss laughed, a frightening little giggle. "Oh, of course. So that you could try to overpower me once they've gone? No. As a matter of fact, my lady, I've changed my mind." Harliss gestured toward the children with her blade. "Please, won't you take a seat next to the girl?"

Michaela did not like the look in the woman's gray eyes, but felt it was far better to be close to Leo and Elizabeth than not, and so she dropped into the icy water at Elizabeth's side, wrapping an arm about them both and drawing her knees up to make as much of a barrier between the children and Harliss as she could.

"Lovely," Harliss crooned. She leaned the torch against the wall of the sea cave, and the flame spluttered and spat at the damp. Michaela prayed it would not go out. Then the woman picked up a coil of rope lying in the water and advanced on the trio. She threw it at Michaela's head and it stung her cheek where it slapped wetly.

"Wrap it around yourselves—all of you together, tightly,

now—and then give me the ends. I'll not have you trying anything clever once his lordship arrives."

"You want me to tie us up?" Michaela asked.

Harliss blinked. "Why, yes."

"No!" Michaela protested. "That's mad! If the tide comes in, we won't be able to get loose quick enough."

"I . . . know!" Harliss screamed, her eyes bulging from their sockets. "You'll either do it, or I'll start letting blood—the littlest snot's first! *Do it!*"

"All right, all right!" Michaela shook out the rope and looped it loosely around them all.

"Tighter," Harliss commanded, and gestured with her blade. "And once more. Now, one end to me."

Michaela was forced to hold the other end of the rope while Harliss made a pair of knots. Of course the snare would not hold the three of them should they try an escape, but it would entangle them and slow them down just enough that Harliss would have time to use her blade, perhaps fatally.

And if the cave flooded . . .

Michaela stopped the thought before it could blossom, and pulled the children closer to her.

"Ee-oh scared, Mike-lah," the little boy whispered, his head tucked under Elizabeth's chin. The two seemed to have completely overcome any animosity they'd once held toward each other. "Papa no come?"

"Yes, Leo," Michaela whispered and tried to smile. "Your papa will come for us. Just wait. He'll come."

Harliss backed against the wall and grabbed up the torch once more, her eyes on the tunnel leading to the cliff, and smiled her mad smile. She began humming a soft tune.

Please come, Roderick.

* * *

Roderick was terrified as he dragged and lurched over the stormy swells of land between Cherbon and the sea, Hugh never breaking pace with him, encouraging him wordlessly.

What if they could not find them—any of them? What if Leo and Michaela were taken from him forever by Harliss? Perhaps it was to be his punishment for his refusal of their unconditional love, for his damned vanity.

Then he would truly know what it was to have lost all.

The lightning flashed and Roderick saw the black outline of a man on the horizon of the cliff ahead, waving one arm madly, then running toward him and Hugh. His voice called out, shouts that were no louder than a whisper in the roar of wind and rain and surf.

"—here!" his voice called. "We're over here!"

They met Alan Tornfield, and he spun on his heel instantly, leading them back toward the edge of the cliff, his face chalky, his arm cradled across his stomach.

"Have you found the children? Where is Michaela?" Roderick demanded, his words coming out as gasps.

"We think they've taken shelter in a sea cave— Michaela—"

"A sea cave?" Hugh shouted. "You fool! The tide will—"

"I could not stop her!" Alan shouted back just as they met the head of the treacherous path. "She would not wait, fearing that they would be trapped. I would have gone in her stead, but I think my arm's broken."

"I'll break your fucking neck!" Hugh screamed.

Roderick felt as if all the blood had drained from his body, staring down at the brutish waves pounding the rocky cliff. He ignored Hugh and Tornfield—Hugh could kill him if he wished, for all Roderick cared. He braced his cane between two jagged boulders and slid awkwardly down onto the path.

"Rick, wait!" Hugh scrambled after.

Roderick inched along the path, his back to the sea, leaning into the cold, slick rock.

"It's just there!" Tornfield called from beyond Hugh. "Right before you, Roderick, under the ledge!"

Roderick saw the canopy of rock over the narrow opening just as a wave washed under his useless left boot and it slipped from its hold. Roderick cried out, grasping for purchase, and his cane fell from his left hand, tumbling away soundlessly into the surf now at his toes.

He could not go into the cave with his boot. It was weighty, unwieldy. Roderick turned his face against the rock to look back at Hugh.

"Undo the boot, Hugh."

"Rick, no! You mustn't try to—Jesus! You'll all be drowned!"

"They are my family!" Roderick roared against the screaming wind. "Hurry, Hugh!"

After one brief, painful look, Hugh bent down, his dagger drawn, and slashed the thick straps of leather hidden above Roderick's knee and down his dumb calf. Roderick stepped out of the boot, feeling two stone lighter, and hopped a careful step closer to the cave.

Hugh attempted one final plea. "I'll follow you in—you may need help getting—"

"No," Roderick said. "I know this cave from when I was a boy. The tunnel is small—we cannot risk a jam." Then he called past Hugh. "Go above, Tornfield, and call to anyone you see." It was an empty hope, the storm having likely driven everyone indoors, but Roderick wanted Tornfield out of the way.

The waves were splashing up his right calf, now, causing him to sway with the sea. In moments, the water would breach the slot in the cliff. He looked at his best friend again. "Hugh, try to stay as close as you can without being washed away. I'll send them up, one at a time."

"What of Harliss?" Hugh asked, but when Roderick gave him no answer, Hugh's throat convulsed, and he handed Roderick his dagger. "I shan't move until I see your face again, Rick, I swear it. Godspeed."

Roderick crouched down and squeezed into the opening of the cave, like a cold crypt, a rocky, watery coffin.

The cave swallowed the first small wave with a gulp, sending a splash of cold, salty spray over Michaela and the children burrowed into her side. Elizabeth screamed, and Leo began to whimper.

Michaela looked to Harliss, still hunched against the dripping wall with her sputtering torch. She had not seemed to notice the first invading wave, staring at the mouth of the tunnel and muttering low under her breath.

"Harliss," Michaela called. "The tide is coming in— we must go now, else we'll all be drowned."

"You'll not go anywhere, Miss Fortune," Harliss said distractedly. "Shut up."

"Surely there must be some other way to gain what you desire," Michaela persisted, her panic increasing as another trickle, then a belching wave washed into the cave. The water was perhaps twelve inches deep over the entire floor, and would rise quicker and higher with each successive flow. Soon, it would be a continuous river of sea, choking the cave, drowning them all. "The children are innocent— I beg you, let them go while there is still time."

"Michaela!" Roderick's voice boomed into the close space from the tunnel.

"Roderick!" she screamed with all her might. "Harliss has a blade!"

The gray old woman rushed to Michaela and hit her with the back of her fist, gripped around the hilt of the dagger. Michaela felt her lips split against her teeth and warm blood flow around her gums.

Elizabeth shrieked again and Leo began to cry in earnest. Another thicker, heavier wave washed into the cave with a strange glug, and then Roderick was tumbled onto the floor. Michaela gasped when she saw his leg, ending in nothing below his knee, where his pants had been sewn short.

He had come for them on his own, as he was.

And he was big and strong and powerful and beautiful.

He looked at her for only an instant before Harliss was upon him, swinging her blade in a downward arc toward his back, her deranged squeal ricocheting off the slick cave walls.

But Roderick threw off her attack with a long, thick arm, knocking Harliss back into the wall with a cry of rage. He rose to his right knee, wielding a blade in his right hand, and Michaela recognized Hugh Gilbert's jeweled dagger. His eyes widened as he looked at the gray old woman.

"Where did you get that gown?" he choked.

"You like it? You know it was Dorian's—you remember it, do you not?" Harliss showed her gray teeth. "Of course you do. We found you in her bed afterward, didn't we? It was the last thing you saw her wear."

"Where did you get it?" Roderick shouted.

"Why, I took it off of her," Harliss simpered, and looked down to admire her bony frame. "Such a beautiful dressing gown, I couldn't abide it being ruined by seawater. I wore it often, in the privacy of my own chamber, and your father's. He never noticed it was hers, you know. He paid so little mind to her when she was alive."

Roderick screamed in rage and Michaela saw his face transform with his fury, his agony. And she remembered the words Harliss had spoken to her on the wooded Cherbon road: *When you think to cross me again, remember this: cold water does not trouble me, and my arms are very, very strong.*

"You killed her," Michaela whispered. "You killed Dorian Cherbon."

"Well, I can't claim all the glory," Harliss said with a girlish tilt of her head. "She walked into the water of her own accord, determined at first. But I'm afraid her nerves got the better of her and I had to . . . *help her* see the thing through to the end. It was what she wanted, you must believe. She was *weak*! Too weak for Magnus, too weak for Cherbon. She knew it."

Roderick sprang at the woman, who sidestepped deftly, splashing through the water that was now more than two feet deep and rising quickly. Harliss flashed her blade against Michaela's throat.

"Stay back," Harliss screamed. The water was flowing in as if it were being washed over a mill wheel. "You'll get what you deserve at last, now! *You ungrateful whelp!* All your father would have given you, and you spat on it! You mocked him, went against him at every turn, clinging to weak, fragile Dorian. He needed a son and you failed him! That's why he placed the condition on your inheritance— so that mayhap your weak blood would be strengthened through your heir. He would rather have given Cherbon away than to see it fall to your uselessness."

"Magnus failed *me,* Harliss," Roderick countered. "He made my life a nightmare with his demands and cruelty, the way he treated my mother. I could have never pleased him, then or now."

"Because you are weak!" Harliss screeched, her blade biting into the thin skin over the bone behind Michaela's ear. "I could have helped you," she said then, her voice going keening. "I loved your father—he was a great and powerful man. And I tried to love you, too, Roderick. I wanted you to be my son, and you called me . . . *Heartless,*" she gasped.

"You tortured me!"

"I was trying to help you, can't you see? Dorian *wanted* to die! She left you! But I never did! Not when you railed at me, cursed me. When you abandoned your father for the crusade, and came back a cripple!" She looked down at his half leg. "I held him when he died, I listened to his death rattle, his wept requests: 'Roderick, my son. Where is Roderick?' he said. It was humiliating what he was reduced to in his last moments—weakness. With no one strong enough to stand with him, save me. Even when he was gone, I stayed at Cherbon, when *everyone* else fled. I kept your home for you, and you sent me away! I devoted my entire life to Cherbon!"

"You only wanted to take my mother's place—to be lady," Roderick accused.

"Is that so very bad?" Harliss demanded. "To want to marry the man you love? Bear his children? I'd hoped after Dorian . . ."

"Magnus never married you though, and he never would have. You were beneath him. Good enough for a lonely bed and to mind the chores, but not to give his name to. You were common."

"No! He didn't marry me because of her and then because of you—because you hated me!"

"I hated you, yes. But you delude yourself if you think Magnus would deprive himself of anything he wanted because of me, or anyone else, for that matter. He used you, Harliss, just as he used everyone."

"No!" she shouted again, and the dagger in her hand splashed into the water. Michaela felt it land against her hip. Harliss had not seemed to notice that she was no longer armed as she held out her empty palm to Roderick.

Michaela fished her hand down by her side. She grabbed the blade and felt the edge cut into her fingers, but she did not loose it. The water was to her breasts now, up to Leo's and Elizabeth's shoulders. Their lips were blue, their wet hair plastered to their skulls, their eyes wide and frozen as they pressed their cheeks together. They were no longer trembling and Michaela knew they were both running out of time. She brought the dagger to the ropes, now underwater, and began to saw clumsily.

"I only want what is due me," Harliss keened. "I have cared so well for Cherbon and I only want to return." She began to slog through the water toward Roderick. "It's my home," she whispered. "I want to care for your son. Perhaps he might learn to call me Grandmamma. . . ."

"Never," Roderick choked. The water lapped around his neck where he was braced against the cave wall for balance.

The ropes floated away and Michaela pulled up on Elizabeth and Leo, helping them raise their lolling heads out of the icy, salty water, pouring in now in great washes and crashes, creeping higher and higher up Michaela's body. In moments, the cave would be filled, dark with sea and death.

"Please, Roderick," Harliss begged, coming ever closer to him.

Michaela saw his eyes flick to the tunnel and she understood. She pulled the children through the water, behind Harliss, the sloshing waves masking their escape.

"I'll kill us all, then," she threatened. "Then we will be together for eternity—together always. . . ."

"Never," Roderick whispered again. And then he shouted, "Michaela, go!"

Harliss threw her head back and let loose an ear-piercing scream and then swung the lit torch at Roderick's head. Michaela lifted Elizabeth, Leo still clinging to the girl, in the same moment that the water rushed in. She held them both near the cave's ceiling where mayhap a foot of air remained. The mouth of the tunnel had disappeared beneath the water, but they could not see it any matter. The torch was drowned in that instant, the cave now pitch, and roaring with sea.

"Hold your breath, hold your breath! Pull yourselves along the rocks and then swim as hard as you can! Someone is waiting for you," Michaela said into where she could still feel their warm breaths, and she prayed silently that someone *would* be waiting to pull the children from the water, before they were washed out to the endless sea. "I am coming right behind you!" And then she pushed them toward the tunnel, pushed them as far up it as her arms could reach.

Michaela turned, her neck crooked and her face pressed against the ceiling. She could not see and dare not go any farther lest she become disoriented in the crashing darkness and never find the tunnel again.

"Roderick!" she croaked, and her voice crashed against her own eardrums.

There was no answer, only the water, and the darkness. And then Michaela felt a clawed hand grab at her thigh, talons puncturing the skin, and she knew Harliss was upon her. Michaela kicked as hard as she could, and her foot found soft, sick purchase before the hand turned her loose.

I must see that Leo is safe, Michaela sobbed in her own mind. *I must protect Roderick's son. I must protect Elizabeth.*

She found the sides of the tunnel with her hands, and kicked from the floor as the water glugged in a final time, deafening her as it pressed against her ears and filled the cave to its capacity and more, the backwash helping to suck Michaela up, up, up and out into the vastness of the open ocean.

And then someone had a grip on her hair, pulling her up, her breath bursting free of her lungs and the rain stinging her face. Michaela reached desperate hands up to her scalp, clawing for him who held her, and Hugh Gilbert's slender, strong fingers seized her wrist.

"Where is Rick?" Hugh shouted, even as he hauled her up, gasping, onto the ledge above the cave. "Michaela, Rick!"

"I couldn't find him!" she choked, seawater and sobs, her busted mouth and the dreadful cold halting her words. "He fought with Harliss, and then the cave flooded—*it's flooded, Hugh!* And Roderick is still—"

Michaela screamed as a rogue wave crashed her against the rock and nearly took her feet from beneath her, but Hugh kept his footing and steadied her. He looked into her eyes for only a moment, and she saw desperation, determination. Reckless and fearless resolve more solid than the cliff they stood upon.

And then Hugh stepped from the ledge, dropping into the water like a pylon, and was gone beneath the black sea.

* * *

He was going to die.

Rolling beneath the cold heavy water, his one leg worth little to kick and move himself upward, water rushing in upon water to push him back down the tunnel. His fingers slipped from the slimy rocks, cutting his palms and tearing away his nails.

His lungs would burst soon, and then he would take in great gulps of the icy, salty sea, sink back into the cave to bob and twirl with Harliss, who was likely already dead. He'd lost his grip on her and she'd found him no more beneath the black water.

He tried again. As the suck of water drew him forward, he kicked, scrabbled in his boot in the slow-motion action forced upon him by the heavy waves, and his numb fingers sought purchase. But then just as quickly, the ebb turned to flow once more, and he was pushed down, down, down . . .

Roderick let go, and he felt the pressure of the bubble of air leave his body with his scream. His arms stretched out before him, floating as he drifted backward.

Good-bye, Michaela. Good-bye, Leo. Hugh, Hugh . . . good-bye.

Something latched on to his ear. And for a moment he thought it was Harliss, but he paid it no mind. His thoughts were fading, fading, now, and he was growing warmer, at last.

Then his jaw was scraped, then loosed. His hair, then his neck was seized, then his shirt. Strong fingers dug into his armpits and with a whoosh of water, he was pulled up. A foot kicked into his stomach, treading water. And again. The rocks on the side of the tunnel bashed him, bit him, cut him.

But Roderick didn't care, couldn't feel it. He became one with the black.

Chapter Twenty-Five

She left the children huddled together in the wet, sobbing, as she helped Alan fish Hugh and Roderick from the icy clutches of the sea. Roderick was limp, lifeless—his green eyes hidden behind purple lids, his mouth blue in his white-gray face.

How they carried him up the cliff, Michaela would have no recollection. But when they lay him on the frozen, dead grass, when Hugh collapsed at his side, weeping violently and wheezing and coughing and beating upon Roderick's chest, Michaela could only stare.

"Papa!" She heard Leo's weak cry behind her, and Elizabeth's shushing, shuddering answer of, "No, love. No, Leo, stay here with me now. There's a good boy."

Roderick was dead.

"Rick!" Hugh strangled, and shoved the great mass of him onto his side. Roderick's arm flopped lifelessly onto the ground, and Hugh pounded his back mercilessly. "Get it out, you stubborn son of a bitch! *Rick!*"

Alan was staring down, helpless. He turned his head

slowly to Michaela. "His leg . . ." he choked. "I . . . I had no idea."

Michaela just shook her head quickly, pressed her knuckles into her bruised lips and rocked on her knees. She crawled to Roderick's side, laid her palm along his cold, stiff cheek. The muscles of his jaw felt seized, locking his teeth together. Hugh was weeping openly, his harsh sobs bursting from him with each blow to Roderick's back.

Michaela placed the heel of her hand on the front of Roderick's chin and pushed. His mouth opened.

"Yes," Hugh gasped. "Yes, stick in your finger—gag him!"

She did, and in seconds, a great wash of slimy, warmed water poured forth from Roderick. Gallons and gallons it seemed, and his chest heaved, his stomach lurched and bucked as his lungs fought for a chance to draw breath between the surges.

And then he was choking, gasping, coughing. His body jerked and twitched and he seemed to fight for a half hour to draw one whole breath.

But at last he did. He breathed. And both Michaela and Hugh fell over him, Hugh pulling Roderick up to lean back against him, one arm crooked around his neck, the other across his chest. Hugh's eyes were closed and he laid the side of his face against Roderick's, tears streaming from his eyes. Hugh kissed Roderick's cheek, the wet hair over his temple, his ear, shaking with his sobs.

Michaela grasped Roderick's corpse-cold hands in her own and peered into his face. "Roderick, can you hear me, my love? Open your eyes, Roderick—look at me! You've done it—you've saved us! Me and Leo and Elizabeth, we're all safe."

But he only lay against Hugh limply, his chest rattling a memory of seawater.

A blur streaked past Michaela and Leo threw himself against Roderick and Hugh, crying, "Papa! Papa! You all wite? Papa!" The small white hands grasped Roderick's face, smashing and pinching the long, lean cheeks. "Papa, wake up! It's Ee-oh!"

Roderick's eyelids fluttered open, and his gaze was dull and gray in the night. His lips parted on a gasp.

"Papa loves you, Leo," he croaked.

Michaela at last let the sob in her throat find its wretched, relieved voice and her head dropped into her hands as Roderick raised an arm limply and pulled Leo into his chest, Hugh opening his arm to encompass both the man and the boy.

"Ee-oh love him papa!" the boy wailed into Roderick's soaked tunic.

Michaela felt Alan come to her side, and she looked up to see him with his uninjured arm around Elizabeth, the girl's face hidden in his side, hands tucked away, her narrow shoulders shaking.

"I'll go back to Cherbon, and fetch a cart for the lord," Alan said solemnly. "I should take the children with me, don't you think?"

"No go!" Leo cried and clutched Roderick tighter. His hysterical sobs turned into a wracking cough.

"It's all right, Leo," Roderick wheezed. "Go with Lord Alan to the keep. I'll be right behind you."

"No, Papa! Ee-oh stay—"

Roderick held the boy away from him slightly and looked into his face. "*I promise, Leo*. Go get a change and a biscuit, and you may sleep with Lady Michaela and me tonight."

Leo coughed and sniffed. "Both?"

Roderick nodded weakly and tried to smile.

Leo drew a deep, wheezing breath. "All wite, Papa." He backed off Roderick's lap and stood, then threw his arms about Michaela. "Aid-ee Mike-lah come, too?"

"Yes, Leo. Of course I will."

The boy grew very still, and his whisper sounded directly into Michaela's ear. "Ee-oh call you him mama now. All wite?"

Michaela thought her heart would burst. "I would love that very, very much," she choked, and squeezed the little boy tight to her.

Leo kissed her cheek. "All wite, Mama." Then he stood and held his arms up to Alan, the gesture one of complete trust. "Ee-oh weddy now."

Elizabeth let her father go and Alan scooped up Leo awkwardly but without hesitation.

"My thanks, Tornfield," Roderick rasped.

Alan looked down at Roderick, and his chin gave the slightest flinch. He bent a knee and sank to the ground in homage, his hand keeping tight to Leo's slender back. "It is my deepest honor, my lord."

Elizabeth held out a hand to Michaela and she took it. The two exchanged smiles.

"I shall see you at Cherbon," the girl said, and her whispering voice held a note of maturity that Michaela had never heard before.

Michaela nodded, and squeezed her fingers before letting her go, and she watched until the man and children disappeared into the night.

A hand seized her arm and Michaela was turned around, into Roderick's chest, and in an instant, she was weeping once more.

"I love you, Michaela," Roderick whispered. "So very much. Please, please forgive the fool I have been!"

Michaela shook her head and then raised her mouth to kiss Roderick's lips, the thin line of scar so familiar to her now, and precious. She leaned back. "I have loved you since the moment I first saw your beautiful face."

He kissed her again, not with the heat of lovemaking, but with a passion that transcended it. One that had no need of spoken promises or vows of forever. In that kiss, their hearts spoke to each other wordlessly, and eternity was understood and accepted humbly.

When Roderick pulled away from her, it was to turn to Hugh, and Michaela let him go willingly. They both owed Hugh Gilbert so much. . . .

"Well, you've done it again," Roderick said.

Hugh swallowed noisily, and tried to revive his devil-may-care grin. It fell largely short. "What now, Rick?"

"Saved my life. That's twice, Hugh."

"Seems to be an annoying habit of mine, does it not?" Hugh reached out and gripped Roderick's arm, but Roderick pulled the man into his embrace.

"You are the truest friend I have ever known, Hugh," Roderick said. "I have greater love for you than I would a brother."

Over Roderick's shoulder, Michaela saw Hugh's eyes squeeze shut, tears coming from beneath them, but camouflaged in the rain that was now little more than drizzle. His mouth was held tight, pulled wide.

"As I do you," Hugh managed to bite off. "Never forget that," he whispered.

Then the two men drew apart and Hugh rose. "I should go," he said. "Tornfield may need assistance, and . . ." He let the sentence trail away. "Will you be all right here, Rick?" He turned to Michaela. "Miss Fortune?"

"Go, Hugh. Get dry, have a drink or twelve. We'll be right along after," Roderick said, and Michaela nodded, her stomach in a knot of worry.

Hugh stepped to Michaela and took both her hands. "All right, I'm going then," he said, a trifle loudly, Michaela thought, but when she looked into his eyes, she knew.

"Don't, Hugh," she whispered. The agony on Hugh's face was nearly too much for her. She had not thought she could possibly have any tears left, but there they were again, hot and painful in her eyes.

"Take care of them both, Miss Fortune," he said in a low voice. "I leave them in your care—the two people I love best in this world. They are everything to me."

"Hugh, please—what will I tell him?"

"Tell him naught. I would rather he hate me for thinking I simply abandoned Cherbon for the trouble of them both, than scorn me for the truth." Hugh brought up a slender forefinger to brush at Michaela's lips where Roderick had kissed her, and as he looked at her mouth, his brows drew together in a frown.

Then slowly, hesitantly, he lowered his head and pressed his mouth to Michaela's, and she kissed him back, held her palms to either side of his whiskered face.

"What's the meaning of this, I ask?" Roderick demanded in mock outrage. The pair pulled apart slowly, and Hugh had a sad smile on his face. "I should think you have enough skirt chasing you without molesting my intended, Hugh."

"Right you are, Rick," Hugh said, hanging a smile on his face and turning. "But you know I could not help myself. Perhaps Miss Fortune would run away with me."

Roderick laughed. "Ah, yes—a lovely title: Miss Fortune, Lady of Nothing."

They all laughed for an awkward moment.

"Well, then." Hugh began to walk backward, as if he could not take his eyes from Roderick—wanted to look at him as long as possible. He gave a carefree wave. "I'm off. Take care, the pair of you. In coming back to the keep, and all."

Roderick returned his wave. "See you in the hall, Hugh."

Hugh gave Michaela a smile—genuine and heartbreakingly handsome. Her fingertips were at her mouth, so she simply turned them outward at him.

"Farewell, Hugh," she whispered, too low for anyone but God to hear.

And then he was gone into the black night, and Roderick's voice called to Michaela. "Come here, woman, and keep me warm—I fear my teeth are to rattle from my very head."

She turned to him with a smile and sank at his side, wrapping her arms about him. They had sat like that for what seemed a very long time when Michaela opened her mouth to inquire of his injuries, but the sound of pounding hoofbeats stopped her.

Roderick looked up into her face, his own frown mirroring Michaela's. "Tornfield would not have sent riders, surely . . . ?"

"I . . . I don't know," Michaela began.

But the hoofbeats sounded like no gentle manor beasts, roaring instead like the wild poundings of stallions and mighty war steeds. And there seemed to be thousands of them, shaking the very ground beneath their seats.

Then the howling rushed down upon them on the wings of the sea wind, a hundred hounds' voices, hungry and seeking, as if they ran from Michaela's nightmares into reality.

"No," Michaela breathed, as the culmination of her life prepared to come crashing down around her and Roderick both.

It was Yule's Eve.

And the Hunt had returned for Michaela, at last.

Chapter Twenty-Six

Roderick sat very still for several moments, clinging to Michaela, thin and soaked and frozen through, and feeling the reverberations of the approaching riders in the very air around them both. He could not comprehend what was happening.

"No." Her whisper was incredulous, terrified.

Beneath Roderick's shredded tunic, the metal link began to burn against the skin of his chest.

It could not be. It was a myth, a ridiculous superstition.

But then his eyes squinted against the silver and gold glow growing between the treed blackness of the forest road, not quite touching it as it moved and bloomed between the arching branches. A sizzling wind preceded the light, and it smelled of incense and blood and . . . coin.

"No," Michaela murmured again, her fingers tightening their hold on his shirt. She, too, stared toward the glow, her eyes wide, her breath coming in ragged gasps. "No." She pushed away from him suddenly and gained her feet.

"Michaela," Roderick barked. "Come back!"

But she was already stumbling toward the middle of the road, directly into the path of the looming, advancing glow, the disembodied, hellish roar. A trumpet blast echoed, like the screams of a hundred tortured souls.

"Lie down, Roderick," Michaela called back loudly but calmly. "Do . . . do not look at them! Mayhap they will pass you by."

Roderick knew she was giving him the old instructions from the legend, but he would not leave her standing so small and alone in the middle of the road, her shoulders squared, her chin lifted.

"They'll not pass *you* by!" Roderick shouted. He struggled to roll to his hip, to get his leg beneath him. "Michaela, help me up!"

"No!" The glow touched her face now, stretched out endlessly into the depths of the forest at their backs, reaching long tendrils through the trees and into the sea mist. She flinched as her face brightened, as if she could feel the light. Roderick could see her beautiful profile from where he was crumpled uselessly at the side of the road—her eyes appeared blackened, sunken. Her fear hollowed her cheeks. "Whatever you do, my love, stay down!"

But Roderick could not obey her. He began dragging himself to the nearest tree. Perhaps once there, he could pull himself aright, thieve a branch to—

An icy hand gripped the back of his neck with skeletal fingers, pushing his head into the deep, wet leaves beneath him. A voice full of frost and death hissed in his ear.

"Mayhap we should heed Miss Fortune, my lord."

Roderick turned his head with a hoarse cry, and Harliss, her thin, gray hair plastered to her skull, smiled a corpse grin at him. Her dagger point dug into the flesh beneath his chin.

"'Tis the Hunt, you know. A dangerous lot. We shall be very still, very quiet, you and I. After they've killed her, I shall deal with you myself, at last, you ungrateful, wretched, spoiled boy. And then . . . and then I shall go home. Magnus is surely wondering where I've been."

Her bony forearm was across the back of his neck, the length of her tall, spindly body covering his. Roderick tried to throw her off, but it was of no use. He was too weak from his battle with the sea.

Mayhap only yesterday, Roderick would have damned himself for his weakness. For being overpowered by Harliss, helpless to move, to fight, to even stand. But now, his mind only worked, trying to devise a way to protect Michaela.

Not only from the gray harpy that clung to him, but from the band of riders now materializing out of the glow, out of a storm cloud, out of the blood of a thousand centuries.

"Michaela," he choked, surprised at the weak whisper that came from his throat.

"Shh," Harliss hissed into his ear, and then rubbed her frozen, leathery face against his cheek. "It will all be over soon. . . ."

Michaela felt the dissolution of her knees, saw the black peppering of dots before her eyes and tried to blink them away.

She could not faint. She *would* not.

But the sight approaching her—a hundred riders on horses that looked to be the size of dragons, some even snorting black smoke with tosses of their giant, reptilian heads and black, glossy, sightless eyes, their hooves running six feet off the ground; hounds as big as calves, shaggy and coal black, their eyes red and glowing, their teeth shining alabaster sparks as they gnashed and snarled their torturous cries, circling and swooping around the band with great leaps and bounds, over, under, around.

The leader headed the damned party on a silvery steed made of nightmares. His rich, brown hair was impossibly long, hanging over one shoulder to fall to his waist. His arms—thick as branches from the oldest trees—were bare beneath his mail shirt, which sparkled like sunlight on water. In his hand he brandished a broadsword that looked to be as tall as Michaela herself, and his shield, like the wheel of a cart, hung at his side.

Yes, the leader was terrifying, but his party . . . Michaela felt her reality whirling into madness as her head tipped back on her neck and she looked upon the rider's companions.

They were . . . *monsters*. Some gray with rotten and bloated flesh, a noose around the neck of one, a gaping wound erasing the side of a skull of another. Some were black, burnt, as if they had just stepped from their own funeral pyres, their eyes startlingly white and shot with blood, their lips and ears melted away. One had horns sprouted just above his ears, and his eyes looked to be gouged out. One had the scales of a fish over his entire head and face, and a forked, black tongue that flicked the air in anticipation. Creatures missing limbs, men with their torsos ripped wide, their innards looped over their arms like the train of a gown. Michaela saw one man-beast, small, hairless and leathery brown, sitting on the pommel of another monster's saddle, eating what appeared to be a human hand. He caught Michaela's eye and raised his head to smile at her hungrily with tiny, bloodied, pointed teeth.

Surely Michaela looked upon Hell's honored guests, for each was a greater horror than the next. All except for the leader, and the man who rode behind him, a golden rope leashing him to the leader by his neck. This man looked almost human, save for his alabaster skin, his white-blond hair, his eyes that held no color, only black. He sat on his steed stark naked, and every inch of him was pearly white, ripped muscle. He stared at Michaela as if she was a small brown mouse, and he was a cat crouched in the tall grass, biding his time, waiting to pounce on her, his mouth around her neck and . . .

The leader's booming voice shook Michaela from her trance and he jerked viciously on the golden tether. As the rope tightened then slacked, she saw the deep scorched ring gouged around the pet's neck. "She is not for you, Alder."

The white-skinned man rocked in his saddle and sent the leader a growl, but to Michaela, he gave a sensuous smile with his full lips, the only spot of color on his person.

And then she saw that his eyeteeth extended in dagger points—fangs—as white as his hair and skin.

Michaela cried out and stumbled backward. She wanted to look toward Roderick, to assure herself of his safety, but she dared not take her eyes from the hideous band before her.

"You are not Agatha Fortune," the leader accused, his voice cracking like the splitting of a great tree. "And yet . . . you are."

"I am her daughter," Michaela choked. "Michaela."

"Michaela?" His eyebrows rose and a slight smile played about his lips. "Michaela. Michaela Fortune. You have something that belongs to me, yes?"

Michaela shook her head jerkily. "No. No, I have naught. I only ask that you leave . . . leave me in peace. Do me no harm."

"Ahh," the giant rider admonished. "You have a possession of mine. A thing I left in your mother's care, a promise for your father's life. It is here—I feel it. A part of me." His hand went to his chest over his mail, and although Michaela knew she should not have been able to see a void so small, so minute, her eyes clearly picked out the circle of black in his shirt.

A circle, where one piece of mail was missing.

Michaela shook her head madly again. "I don't have it. I . . . I lost it."

"You *lost* it?" the leader taunted. "That is too bad. I told your mother that I would return for my possession, and that recovering it would ensure Walter Fortune's black life, as well as hers and your own. If you no longer have it . . . "

"My father is a good man!" Michaela cried. "Not the man he once was!"

"It matters not," the leader reasoned. "A bargain is a bargain. Perhaps you haven't lost it after all, yes? Perhaps you . . . gave it away?" To Michaela's horror, the man's blazing eyes went to the darkened tree line, where Roderick lay.

She turned her head, and saw Roderick at the base of a dead, rotted tree, Harliss sprawled atop him, her blade at his throat. As the leader turned his attention to the wood, the glow of the band spread over the ground, illuminating Roderick and his captor.

"What have we here?" the leader said mildly. "Perhaps Michaela Fortune hopes to trade your life for her father's, soldier. She gave you my link, did she not?"

And Michaela could not stop her soft, helpless weeping.

For several moments, Roderick had fooled himself into thinking he had fallen unconscious from his injuries. That what he was experiencing at the wood's edge—Harliss atop him, his life blood throbbing against the jagged edge of her blade, the hellacious group of fiends standing judgment before Michaela in the road—was nothing more than an insane nightmare. But when the leader turned eyes to him, when Roderick, too, flinched from feeling the band's glow slide over his skin, he knew he was horribly awake.

"I have your link, Devil," Roderick called out as loudly as his awkward position would allow. "Around my very neck. Come and get it!"

The demon laughed as if highly amused by the challenge, then his eyes narrowed, his head tilted. "I know you," he said contemplatively. "I have seen your face before."

Before Roderick could answer, Harliss screeched, "You stay away! Stay away! He is mine! When he is dead you may take him back to Hell with you! In the name of . . . in the name of God, do I command thee!"

The riders in the band howled and screamed, the hounds bayed, the dragon horses reared and pawed at the air.

The leader's attention was only for the gray old woman now. He held up one palm slightly toward her, his brow furrowed as if in concentration. Then his hand snapped closed in a fist.

"Harlis-s-s," the leader hissed. "You dare call upon the name of God to defend thee?"

"How do you know me?" Harliss choked. "You know me not!"

The leader gave a brief chuckle. Then he cracked the leash in his hand like a whip, and the tether loosened and rose up from around the snowy-skinned man's neck and head.

"Alder," the leader said smoothly, and raised the now-coiled leash to indicate Harliss. "That one, you may take."

The naked man gave a guttural snarl and leapt into the air from his saddle. He bounded over the road and into the fringe of trees on all fours, his skin glowing, his muscles rippling, and he pounced upon Harliss, tumbling her away into the blackness like a cat with a ball of twine.

Roderick heard Harliss scream, but the sound ended in

an abrupt, watery rip. Then he heard drinking, slurping, chewing, echoing through the forest.

Roderick struggled to a seat against the crumbling tree trunk, and then pushed with all his might to stand. Michaela dashed from the road to his side, shrugging under his left arm to support him. Roderick gripped her shoulder tightly, pressed a quick, almost defiant kiss to the crown of her head, while never taking his eyes from the demonic party.

The Hunt leader watched them both with something akin to amusement, but his words were for Roderick alone. "Give me my link, soldier."

Roderick reached into his tunic and snapped the chain with one swift pull. Swinging up the ends to pool in his palm atop the glowing, throbbing metal link, he held it tight in his fist for a moment, thinking.

"You will do us no harm if I return it to you? You will leave us?"

The leader's eyes flamed and he only held out a palm.

"Give it to him, Roderick," Michaela whispered urgently. "It belongs to him."

Roderick tossed it through the air and the leader caught it with an easy swipe of his fist. The chain slithered away to the ground and dissolved into the mud, and the giant, glowing man placed the link in his shirt gently, delicately. Bright gold light burst from it for an instant, causing Roderick and Michaela to throw up arms to shield their faces, but then the dumb metal faded into the obscurity of the thousands of links surrounding it.

The leader then looked at Roderick as if he could see into his very soul. "Yea, I have seen you. You, who fought with your men, who watched them fall, who sacrificed"— the leader looked down at Roderick's half leg—"your own flesh so that others might live."

"How?" Roderick demanded weakly. "No man such as you was in my company; you are no Saracen that I faced. Never have I seen your loathsome countenance before, nor do I know your name."

"I ride in *every* company of war," the leader said in a quiet deadly voice. "And I have seen *your* face; I know *your* name. *Roderick of Cherbon.* Son of Magnus."

Roderick's throat seemed to close on itself and he knew a gut-melting fear for Michaela's and his life. What kind of demon was this, who rode with the monsters he collected through war? Who hunted people on dark, quiet roads? Who set the evilest of beasts to feed upon humans?

But the leader addressed Roderick no more, turning his attention—to Roderick's great dread—to Michaela. His hand dipped into the neck slit of his chain shirt and in a moment he produced a small object, glowing gold through the cracks of his massive grip. He tossed it to Michaela and she caught it with both hands. Roderick looked down into her cupped palms and saw a tiny, perfect golden chest, no bigger than the very center of her palm.

"For my faithful Agatha," the leader intoned. "Repayment for her bravery and steadfastness. She is your father's only gift—his wife, and his life."

Then the leader's hand returned to his chest, and he plucked the metal ring from his shirt once more and held it up as if to look through it. It glowed gold again, like a small sun, and was now smooth and perfectly circular. After a moment, he tossed this, too, to Michaela. It was a wide, shining band now—as if made to fit the finger of a lady.

"For you, my daughter." He smiled. "And when you don it this time, do not take it off."

"Thank you," Michaela whispered faintly.

Then the leader at last turned his blazing eyes back to

Roderick. From deep within a bloody pouch tied to his saddle, he retrieved a dark, crumpled object. "You are missing some article of your dress, soldier," he said mildly, and then tossed down the piece to Roderick. "I believe you already wear its mate?"

Roderick looked at the soft material in his hand—tallish, more a boot than a shoe, really. Rich brown leather, perhaps deerskin, worn nearly to the thinness of cloth. The sole was long and wide, the ties rough and thick. Roderick's stomach clenched as he realized this was the left boot to pair the one he still wore on his right foot.

Roderick did not miss the implied slight this otherworldly man had dealt him. But dare he tempt the demon's wrath by refusing it?

The leader sat his horse expectantly for several moments, until—as if he had read Roderick's mind—he said in a low, deadly voice, "Put it on, friend, lest I take offense."

Roderick swallowed what was left of his pride and allowed Michaela to wordlessly help him to the soggy forest floor. He shook open the boot and pulled it over his stump, lacing up the long, worn leather as best he could. While he struggled with the ties, the leader looked around the black forest, seemed to listen with a frown.

"Alder!" he bellowed, and Roderick's mind went to the glowing white, fanged creature-man who stole away with Harliss, the source of those awful screams.

"Alder, I command thee!" the leader shouted again, his cries shaking the very ground. Then he let out a wild, evil-sounding howl, tossing his head and his long hair. *"Find him!"* he roared to the macabre band behind him.

Roderick and Michaela ducked together as the Hunt swarmed around them, over them, into the black forest.

The leader's horse pranced impatiently—*growled.* Roderick had never heard a horse growl like that in his life, and never would again.

"I have a killer to hunt," the leader announced. "Get up. Go home. Forget. Live. You have earned your life and your peace. If you should see Alder, or mayhap a white wolf stalking the wood at night, I beg you, seek your shelter and pray to God that he does not smell your blood."

Michaela helped Roderick to stand once more and face the looming shade—all that was left of the hellish Hunt. Michaela would not be able to support his weight for very long, he knew, but he would try as best he could to get them both away from this foul creature—and the perhaps even deadlier Alder, roaming the Cherbon wood somewhere at their vulnerable backs.

Roderick made a short bow to the seated giant. "My thanks, fellow soldier, for the gift." It was an insulting present, yes, but both he and Michaela were as yet alive. It was enough. Roderick took one stiff hop toward Cherbon, jerking on Michaela's shoulders awkwardly.

But she would not move, her eyes pinned to the ethereal leader. "Who are you?" she asked in a frightened, desperate voice. "I must know."

The rider stared at Michaela, and his terrifying mount pranced. From the wood behind them, screeches and howls burst from the monsters who rode with him, as if they had heard Michaela's simple query and dreaded the rider's answer.

"I am Justice," he said to Michaela, and then looked to Roderick once more, a light of kinship in his eyes. A battle fever that Roderick had once known well. "I am War and Vengeance. I am Faith." His eyes found Michaela's again. "I am your guardian."

"But," Michaela pressed, and Roderick wanted to beg her to hold her tongue. "What is your name?"

Roderick wanted to beg her because he knew. Even before the horse's blissful scream, before the massive, gray wings unfolded behind the rider's back and spread to a horrific, thunderous, twelve-foot span.

"I am Michael," the leader said, his whisper deafening in the stormy gale his announcement has sparked. Then, with a mighty flap of his angelic wings, Michael and his mount rose up from the road in a blast of wind and rain, sweeping over Roderick and Michaela and away into the wood, taking the glow of his presence, of his terrible, certain judgment, with him.

In an instant, Michael, his Wild Hunt, and the violent storm that accompanied them were gone.

Michaela fell against Roderick's chest, her sobs quiet and full of relief and understanding.

"It's all right now," Roderick choked out over Michaela's head, holding her tighter than he ever had, kissing her crown, lifting her higher against him. "It's all right, my love. It's over, it's over."

After a moment, Michaela raised her beautiful face to look into Roderick's eyes, and he was startled to see worry and confusion there.

"What is it?" he asked.

She eased out of his arms, her eyes never leaving his, and took two slow steps backward from Roderick.

They stared at each other for a long, long time, it seemed to Roderick. Both of them too afraid to speak, to look away. And then they both looked down.

Roderick stood firmly on the ground, in his own heavy, black boot, and one old, brown leather shoe.

Epilogue

Six months later
Cherbon Castle

It was a lovely feast, even *with* the pointing and whispering. Michaela was not once pushed out of line when she joined in a dance. And that wretched young woman who had once stuck out a slippered foot and caused her to fall, now sat at Michaela's side, along with Elizabeth Tornfield. Juliette and her stepdaughter were fast friends now, and their company was easy, genuine, and most welcomed by Michaela.

Michaela had not once made a fool of herself. But she thought that the evening was yet young, and the idea made her smile to herself.

Michaela caught a glimpse of her parents across the hall—her own hall, this time. As always, they were tied together at the arms, still wearing identical expressions of bliss. The only changes were the newly made, rich clothing they wore, and the little dark-haired boy clinging to Agatha's skirts. Her parents lived at Cherbon now, Lord

Walter and his wife giving up their home as too much for them to manage. The small Fortune hold was now absorbed into Tornfield, and Michaela's parents were having the time of their lives in their new role as grandparents to Leo.

Although they lived at Cherbon, wore rich clothing, and planned on doing a bit of traveling, their expenses were not footed by Cherbon. No, indeed—they were quite independent, thanks to the little golden chest given to Michaela on Yule's Eve, the precious little box that had revealed itself to be more of a repayment than any of them could have ever imagined.

When Agatha had opened it for the first time, a single coin was nestled in a slit of cushioned velvet. Michaela's mother had given a soft cry of surprise, removed the coin, and snapped the lid shut, setting the trunk aside. She had been quite pleased.

"One coin, eh?" Walter Fortune had said ruefully, but then smiled at his wife's pleasure as he himself picked up the trunk. "Well, mayhap this piece is worth something. 'Tis finely made." He had flipped open the lid with his thumb and his eyebrows raised as he pulled out another coin. He handed it to his wife. "You overlooked this one, my lady."

Agatha had taken it with a sweet, confused frown. "I'm quite certain there was only—" She had stopped, taken the trunk, closed and opened the lid once more.

She withdrew another single coin.

And so it was to be, no matter how many times the trunk was opened and closed, whenever a coin was removed, another took its place. An endless amount of money, to do with what they needed and what they wished.

Even so, it had taken them three straight days of raising

and lowering the little golden lid before they could pay the whole of their accumulated debts.

Agatha had never asked Michaela where she'd gotten the trunk, or why it had been given to her, and Michaela had not volunteered the information. There was no need.

Elizabeth Tornfield touched Michaela's arm, drawing her out of her happy reverie.

"Lady Michaela," she said, and then pointed to where the musicians were clustered in a corner of the crowded hall. Gone was the insecure, speechless young girl, replaced by this striking, poised young woman. Michaela was so proud of her, and looked forward to seeing her grow fully into the lady she was fast becoming.

Roderick and Alan Tornfield were regarding Michaela with similar mischievous grins, and beckoned to her with their hands.

Elizabeth giggled. "I believe your talents are in demand."

Michaela smiled again as she watched Alan Tornfield give her husband a "wait one moment" sign and then cross the hall to stand before her. Alan was so mindful now, of what he thought of as Roderick's physical limitations.

"You simply must, Michaela," he said, and held out a hand to her, his blondness warm and soothing. The Tornfields were good friends of theirs now—family.

Across the hall, Michaela heard Leo cry happily, "Mama sing! Grandmamma, my mama *sing!*"

That was one summons Michaela could not refuse. She took Alan's hand and rose with a smile as anticipatory applause rang out through the hall.

Roderick hooked his walking stick over his elbow and brought his hands together with the rest of the guests as his wife made her way through the smiling crowd toward him. The cane was beautiful, carved ivory—a belated wedding gift from Sir Hugh Gilbert. Roderick's friend had sent it with word that he had found employ with a distinguished old lord who was a close advisor to King Henry, and they resided in London. Hugh seemed happy from his note, although he had not asked that Roderick call on him if ever he was in the city.

Perhaps one day, though . . .

Michaela was nearly to him now, and Leo joined her with his typical mad dash across the floor, tackling her legs and swinging about her skirts. Michaela swayed, hooted, and the crowd held their breath in anticipation of a tumble, but their applause grew when she righted herself and the boy with a smile.

She was so perfect. For him and Leo. For Cherbon.

Roderick could walk. He could not explain it, and in truth, he did not want to know the how of it. No other mortal save Michaela knew the truth about what had happened on the forest road that Yule's Eve six months ago, knew that Roderick could walk anywhere he chose now, with only a slightly noticeable limp. He could mount, he could spar— he had no need of the cane, really, only used it for the sake of their friends, and because it was a gift from Hugh.

As far as everyone else was concerned, Lord Roderick Cherbon was missing his leg from below his knee, down, and the soft, brown boot was a very expensive, very finely made prosthesis. He was not shamed by it—indeed, he now told everyone who asked that he had lost his leg at Heraclea. He was grateful that he had survived to return home and rule his demesne, raise his family—perhaps a growing family, if his suspicions were correct. He was a man—and a better man, for what he had lost.

What was truly beneath the brown boot—his own foot, or something frighteningly foreign—Roderick would never know. The boot was part of him now, as surely as his skin. And that was enough for him.

Michaela and Leo were almost upon him—his wife and his son—and her scent brought to mind the bunches of fresh spring flowers that were always present about the keep now—inside and out. At the graves on the knoll—even Magnus's—and perpetually filling the small chapel around the stone statue of the Archangel Michael, whose carved chain shirt bore a mysterious chipped mark over the heart.

Michaela held out her hands to Roderick, and the wide, smooth gold of her wedding band gleamed in the candlelight. He took them in his own and squeezed, his heart feeling whole and alive and healed. Michaela leaned up and kissed his scarred cheek.

"I sing this for you," she whispered in his ear.

Leo was attempting to scramble up Roderick's leg for a better view, and so he scooped the boy onto his forearm, letting him hold the cane.

"Hoo's stick?" Leo asked.

Roderick nodded. "That's right."

Leo kissed the handgrip and held it to his chest as he and his father gave their full attention over to the dazzling woman, named for an angel of war, who sang to them now.

And in the short time that the mesmerizing melody took flight from her tongue and floated on the air, bringing a heavy, grateful wetness to Roderick's eyes, everyone gathered in the hall seemed to realize they were seeing before them no Miss Fortune whatsoever, but a tiny glimpse of Heaven.

Perhaps the Cherbon Devil realized it most of all.

Author's Note

Dear Friends,

The battle at which Roderick was injured is my own creation, although many of the details are based on historical accounts of several different battles which indeed took place at or near Heraclea in 1101.

As for the paranormal aspect of this book, the story of the Wild Hunt is actually an ancient legend told throughout Europe. There are countless versions, and I incorporated bits and pieces from several—as well a healthy dose of my own twisted imagination—in the telling of this tale. The legends themselves are fascinating reading, if you're into that sort of thing.

Anecdotally, I would like to mention that as I wrote this story, I couldn't help but pronounce Michaela's name "Michael-ah," as opposed to the modern (and perhaps *correct*) pronunciation more similar to "Mick-aye-lah." Hence, Leo's "Mike-lah." I did so because, the name being the feminine version of Michael, I feel Agatha Fortune would have wanted the origin of her daughter's name to be absolutely clear to anyone who heard it. Of course, as you read, you pronounced it in your own mind however you felt appropriate, and that is always correct.

Some of you might have recognized Alder, the intriguing vampire escaped from the Hunt. The story of what happens to him after fleeing the Cherbon wood can be read in the novella, "The Vampire Hunter," as part of the HIGHLAND BEAST anthology, in stores now. For those of you who've already read "The Vampire Hunter," thank you, and I hope you enjoyed the wider glimpse into the beginning of Alder's search for Beatrix—and his own redemption—in this book. As always, you can visit www.HeatherGrothaus.com for the latest news on upcoming releases.

I hope you've enjoyed Michaela and Roderick's love story. Thank you for your continued support and encouragement. You are in my thoughts with each word of every book I write.

With love,
Heather